#1 *NEW YORK TIMES* BESTSELLING AUTHOR

MIKE EVANS

a Novel

TEN BOOM

BETSIE, PROMISE *of* GOD

TIMEWORTHY
BOOKS

P.O. BOX 30000, PHOENIX, AZ 85046

Ten Boom: Betsie, Promise of God

Copyright 2013 by Time Worthy Books
P. O. Box 30000
Phoenix, AZ 85046

Design: Lookout Design, Inc.

Hardcover: 978-0-935199-92-5
Paperback: 978-0-935199-93-2
  Canada: 978-0-935199-94-9

This book is dedicated to
my four beautiful granddaughters:

Ashley, Isabelle, Elizabeth, and Brooke.

I love you more than words
can express...Papa

CHAPTER 1

AUTUMN SUNLIGHT cast a glare down the street as we walked home from school. Willem, my brother, led the way with Nollie, our younger sister, close behind. Vincent and I came behind them. He was by far the tallest boy in our class and, with his blond hair and blue eyes, and I thought, obviously the most handsome.

Our route home took us up the alley at the back of the school building and out to Barteljorisstraat, one of the oldest streets in Haarlem, an ancient Dutch city and the place we called home. Directly opposite the alley was Grote Markt, a paved city square around St. Bavo's Cathedral, where farmers from the countryside came to sell their produce. From there we turned right, past the police station and the telegraph station, which had only recently been expanded to include the telephone station. The year was 1897. It seems such a long time ago.

We came that way—my sister, brother, and I—every day, but not always with Vincent, at least not in the earlier years. His aunt lived farther down the street past our house and sometimes in the afternoon he went to stay with her, though I never knew why he didn't simply go home. The house where his parents lived was six blocks in the opposite direction, and walking all the way to his aunt's house meant he had at least twice as far for the return trip. And I was certain he went home before coming to school the next day because I checked the clothes he was wearing to make sure. I liked Vincent and, with the increasing frequency of his walks home with us, it never occurred to me he might have come with us for any other reason than me.

As we came near the house I saw the shop sign hanging from the bracket by the second-floor windows. Father was a watchmaker. He worked from a shop on the first floor of our house, a place we affectionately dubbed the "Beje," in honor of the street where we lived. My grandfather bought it long before I was born.

When we reached the door to the shop Willem pushed it open and turned to go inside. Vincent called after him, "Time for a game of cricket?" I could tell by the sound of his voice that what he was really saying was, "Not yet. Don't go inside yet."

Willem glanced at me and I nodded my head ever so slightly. I didn't want the walk to end, either. "Sure," Willem replied. "I'll get the ball and meet you in the alley." Then he looked at me and said in the teasing way brothers sometimes do, "Betsie, are you coming inside?" He knew what I wanted, so I just shook my head and looked away.

Cricket was all the rage back then and the whole of the Netherlands was excited by it, even the queen, who attended a match when we played the team from England. I enjoyed it, though mostly watching from the side. Running and playing were difficult for me, as I easily became short-winded. And our equipment wasn't the best. The ball Willem went to fetch was nothing more than twine wrapped tightly around a small clump of paper. Willem made it himself and covered it with glue. Our bat was a board that Papa cut down on one end to form a handle. It didn't look much like the bats shown in the newspaper but it was better than nothing. Willem and the kids from the next street wore it smooth playing with it.

When Willem headed inside, Nollie followed after him, leaving me alone on the street with Vincent. We weren't really alone, though—Papa was at his desk in the shop. I could see him through the window bent over a watch, tools in both hands, carefully placing each piece inside the casing. He held a pipe in his mouth which he puffed while he worked and the smoke from it encircled his head. His eyes were focused on the watch, but I knew he saw me and so I made sure Vincent kept a respectable distance between us. He glanced over at me with a nervous smile. "Did you understand today's math lesson?"

"Yes," I did my best to sound confident for the both of us. "It wasn't that hard."

"I never get math the first time."

"Perhaps I can help you."

His face brightened. "Yes," he smiled. "Perhaps so." Then his face clouded over and he dropped his head. "But I—"

The alley door on the far side of the shop opened and in a moment Willem peered around the corner. "Ready?"

"Sure," Vincent nodded as he turned in that direction. I wanted him to finish his sentence, but he was on his way before I could speak so I followed him into the alley that ran alongside our house. Willem met us there and brought a trash barrel, then set it in place for the batter's wicket. We used a discarded doormat for the opposite one and batted into the alley. That way, we had less chance of hitting someone as they passed by on the street, and we had less chance of losing the ball.

"You're up first," Willem said, pointing to Vincent.

"We need a few more players."

Willem tipped back his head and called up to the window above, "Nollie!" In a moment she appeared with Corrie, our youngest sister, at her side. Willem waved his hand for her to come down. She disappeared from the window.

"She won't be able to do it by herself," Vincent commented. "Shall I get one of the kids from the other street?"

"I'll play on her side," I offered without a second thought.

Willem gave me a questioning look. "You sure?"

"Of course I'm sure," I answered in an offhanded way. "Why shouldn't I?"

"It's just that you've never—"

"I'll be all right," I said curtly, hoping he'd catch my meaning and not make a big deal of it. Thankfully he said nothing more, and I hurried down the alley to get into position.

Willem stepped around the trash barrel and paced off the distance to his bowler's spot. When he'd gone a sufficient distance, he marked the place with the heel of his shoe, making a line in the dust, then kicked the doormat into position farther down the way.

By the time Nollie arrived from the house, I was halfway to the opposite street and out of breath. She stopped partway to me and motioned with her hand. "Come up. You're too far." I'd never played cricket before, or any other game for that matter, and hadn't a clue where to stand, but that day, with the sun shining and Vincent smiling at me, I wanted to be out there, to participate with him in a game he seemed to love so much.

With the bat firmly in his grip, Vincent stepped in front of the trash barrel and took an imposing stance. I was sure he'd knock the ball into the street behind me. Willem gripped the ball in his right hand, did the quirky running windup we saw the professionals use, and let loose a pitch. Vincent brought the bat around in an underhanded swing that sent the ball sailing over Nollie's head. I ran to catch it but it hit the ground before I got to it. Laughing all the way, I scooped it up and did my best to throw it in. The ball, of course, sailed far to the left of Willem and he had to run after it. Vincent scored three runs because of it. Willem scowled at me, but I was happy.

After three more swings at bat, Vincent and Willem swapped places. Willem wasn't as good at the bat as Vincent but he connected on the third pitch. The ball went wide to the right, bouncing off the wall of the building next door. I ran to retrieve it but Nollie got there first and threw the ball in to Vincent. I'd wanted to do that, but it was just as well. My breaths were coming in short gasps then anyway and my arms felt weak and limp.

Then, as I backed my way down the alley to my position, the ground beneath my feet pitched up on one side. Off to the left, the Beje started to spin around and around, passing in front of me again and again, faster and faster. I shut my eyes tightly to make it stop but I could feel my body swaying from side to side. Waves of nausea swept over me. I heard Nollie call out to me and the sound of the bat hitting the alley floor, but that was all I remembered.

Sometime later, I felt a cool, damp cloth on my forehead and I heard Papa's voice. "I think she's coming around," he said in a low and quiet tone. Then I opened my eyes to find I was lying in the bed in my room. Mama, Papa, and Aunt Anna hovered over me. I could smell the scent of Papa's pipe tobacco and a hint of peppermint that he always carried in his pocket. Willem and Vincent stood near the foot of my bed with Nollie and Corrie leaning against them. The back of my head throbbed with pain and I felt sick to my stomach, but I remember thinking how much I would have liked to be leaning against

Vincent's shoulder.

"She got too excited," Aunt Anna offered.

Willem spoke up. "It's the third time this week."

"We saw her at school," Nollie added.

"No," Mama replied softly, still stroking my forehead with the damp cloth. "It's the fourth." She smiled. "I think you had a spell in your room the day before yesterday, didn't you?"

"Yes," I replied weakly. I had no idea she knew about that, but I could never lie to her and deny it.

"We should get the doctor," Papa said.

"I agree," Mama added, then turned in Willem's direction. "Go down the street for Dr. Brunel. Vincent, you go with him."

"Yes, ma'am," Vincent replied.

When they were gone she looked back at me. "We'll get to the bottom of this. Don't you worry. Just lie still until the doctor comes."

Thirty minutes later, Dr. Brunel arrived. Willem was with him but Vincent was nowhere in sight. I wanted to ask what happened to him but Dr. Brunel took over and shooed everyone but Papa and Mama into the hallway. Then he leaned over me and began his examination. He lifted each eyelid and gave me a careful, discerning look. He gently pulled down my dress from the shoulder and tapped against my chest with his finger. With due deference to propriety he slipped a hand beneath the sheet and pressed against my abdomen, then again he looked in my eyes.

"You've had this problem for some time?"

"Yes," I whispered.

"When did it first start?"

"A few months ago."

"Year before last," Mama corrected. I glanced in her direction and she looked at me with an arch of her eyebrow. "I notice more than you think." I smiled at her, and the look on her face softened.

Dr. Brunel lifted my eyebrows and gazed down at me for a third time. Then he stood and folded his hands behind his back. "I'd like to see her in my office tomorrow."

"After school?"

"No." He shook his head. "She should see me in the morning. I don't think she'll be going to school for a few days."

Mama's face turned serious. Papa, always unflappable, rested a hand on Dr. Brunel's shoulder. "This is something more than a little girl's excitement getting the best of her?"

"Yes," Dr. Brunel glanced back at me. "If I remember correctly, you're already fourteen years old, aren't you?"

"Yes," I replied.

He looked over at Papa. "She's not so little anymore."

Brunel turned toward the door and Mama followed him into the hall. As they moved toward the steps I heard her ask, "How serious is this?" But they were too far away for me to hear his reply.

For the next hour or so I lay in bed, staring up at the ceiling, wondering if something terrible was wrong with me. I'd been surprised that Willem noticed the fainting spells from school, and even more surprised by what Mama knew, but none of them understood the whole story. Over the past three years I'd fainted many times and, unlike today in the alley, for no apparent reason.

In a little while Aunt Anna came to my room carrying supper on a tray—beef stew with a slice of bread and a cup of hot coffee. She was Mama's sister and since the death of her husband she'd lived with us. Mama was often sick with a horrible cough—a condition Papa and many of their friends referred to as the consumption. I even heard Dr. Brunel use that term a few times. The more correct name was tuberculosis. At the time, no one realized just how contagious the disease was but at Dr. Brunel's suggestion, on those days when the coughing was worst Mama stayed in her room. She didn't feel like doing anything else anyway. While she was in bed, Aunt Anna ran the house.

She set the tray on a table beside the bed and helped me sit up. Then she moved the tray to my lap and positioned it so it wouldn't slide onto the floor. "Do you need me to help you eat?"

"No," I said with a smile. "I'll be fine."

As I ate from the bowl of stew, Willem appeared in the doorway and grinned. "You gave us a scare."

"What happened to Vincent?"

"He walked with me up to Dr. Brunel's office, then said he had to get home."

"Home? Not his aunt's house?"

"I think that is his home."

Corrie appeared beside him, interrupting our conversation. "You didn't read to me," she said in a plaintive voice. Not yet old enough for school, she and I spent most afternoons seated by the window where I read to her. She could read for herself but enjoyed listening and I relished the time we had together.

"I know. But I'm not well and the doctor says I should stay in bed."

"You could read to me from there."

"Yes. I suppose I could."

Book in hand she came toward the bed as Willem drifted away. A thousand thoughts ran through my mind—about Vincent, his home life, and why he'd led me to believe something different about where he lived—but the moment for discussing that was lost. I spent the remainder of the evening reading to Corrie.

CHAPTER 2

THE FOLLOWING MORNING, after Nollie and Willem left for school, Papa and Mama walked with me up the street to Dr. Brunel's office. Corrie, not yet old enough for school, stayed behind with Aunt Anna. Mama had spent most of the previous day in bed with the cough and didn't look too well that morning but she insisted on accompanying us. I was nervous about the visit and I think that was the reason she refused to let me go with only Papa. She assured me she would stay with me the entire time.

Dr. Brunel's office was located above the Grand Café on the corner past the police station, facing Grote Markt. To reach it, we passed by the building that housed the school. Windows from the second floor opened above the sidewalk and as we walked past I heard the younger children reciting their lessons. My class met in a room on the opposite side, and although it was out of earshot the thought of it was enough to stir images of Vincent in my mind where I could see him seated at his desk a few rows over from my own, hunched over his book and tablet, diligently working the lesson. The thought of it put a smile on my face, but as we drew near the corner I saw the sign for the doctor's office and my face turned serious again.

Dr. Brunel was waiting for us when we reached his office. He ushered Papa to a chair near the desk, then took me with Mama through a door that led into an examination room. A table stood to one side with a screen around it. "You can change over there," he gestured toward it. I had no clue what he meant and glanced at Mama with a questioning look. She smiled and came toward me. "Here, I'll help you."

A white gown lay on the table and she held it up for me to see. "Put this on," she said. I hesitated at the thought of changing clothes, but she insisted and having her to help made things better. In a few minutes I was dressed in the robe and Dr. Brunel joined us. His nurse, Irene Drebbel, stood nearby.

With a gentle touch, he once again pressed along my abdomen, tapping in places around my stomach. Then he listened in those same places with a stethoscope. Finally, he moved to my neck and pressed his fingers against the flesh beneath my jawline. As he did, he stared down at me and tilted his head from side to side, as if watching the reflection in my eyes. When he finished, he stepped back from the table and took a seat on a chair in the corner.

For a long time he just sat there, staring in my direction. Not really looking at me but as if his mind was lost in thought. Then Mama placed her hands on her hips and said, "Well, what is it?"

"I did some reading last night," Brunel began. "And I can't be sure without blood tests, but I think she may have anemia."

"Anemia?"

"Oh, not enough vitamins?" Mama asked.

"Yes." Brunel's face looked grim. "If I'm right, this is pernicious anemia."

"What does that mean?"

Dr. Brunel cleared his throat and glanced in my direction. "Perhaps we should talk about this outside."

"No," Mama replied, with a look of realization that Brunel wanted to talk about me without me being present. "We should talk about it here."

"Casper should hear."

"Then we will talk about it together." She gestured toward me. "All of us."

"Very well." Dr. Brunel looked over at me. "Get dressed and we'll join your father." Then he stood and turned toward the door.

When he was gone from the room, Mama helped me out of the gown and into my clothes. By then I was worried. "What's wrong?"

"Don't let it bother you," she replied. "The doctor will tell us in a few minutes and whatever is wrong we will find a way. God will make a way."

"But what is anemia?"

"I'm not sure."

"Why was he so—"

"Hush now," she admonished in a stern but quiet voice. With a tug or two, she pulled my clothes into place and ran her hand down the side to smooth a wrinkle. "There, you look very nice." Then she took my hand in hers and we started toward the door. As she did, I could feel the tension in her fingers, and in spite of what she'd said I knew she was worried.

We came from the examination room to find Dr. Brunel seated at his desk. Papa was in a chair across from him. They stood as we entered the room.

"Here we are," Mama said with a smile. Papa helped Mama and me to a seat beside him and when we were in place, she looked over at Dr. Brunel. "Now, whatever you have to say, say it to all of us. Betsie is not a young girl anymore. You said so yourself last evening. Whatever is wrong, it's wrong with *her* body. She has a right to know what it is."

"As you wish," Dr. Brunel settled into the chair behind the desk. He rested his hands in his lap and laced his fingers together. "Anemia," he began slowly, "is a condition in which your body lacks vitamins. Normally, that is a matter of diet and can be cured simply by altering the food you eat or by taking supplements each day." His eyes focused on me. Mama reached over and rested her hand on mine as he continued. "But your condition is different. If I'm correct, your anemic condition isn't caused by lack of vitamins in your diet. It's caused by an inability of your body to absorb them."

"If you're correct?" Papa asked.

"Yes," Brunel nodded.

"How will we know if you are correct?"

"There are tests that can confirm the diagnosis."

"What kind of tests?" Mama asked.

"Rather simple ones from a blood sample. But you should know …" Dr. Brunel looked away. "This condition does not respond to treatment with supplements."

"What are you saying?" Mama asked. "Say whatever it is."

"This condition," Dr. Brunel sighed, "is…pernicious."

"And what does that mean?" Mama's forehead was wrinkled in a frown and I could tell by the sound of her voice that she was getting frustrated.

"Pernicious," she said insistently. "What does it mean? Don't hide behind the words. Just say what it is."

"Fatal," the doctor said flatly. "The condition is fatal."

The words hit me hard but I gave no immediate reaction. I knew fatal meant deadly, but I didn't feel that bad—just tired and I got out of breath very easily—and besides that, as the words hit my ears a sense of confidence welled up inside me. I was as certain as a fourteen-year-old could be that this was not the end. I could not have said it that way back then, but that's how I felt. God had more for me to do than die from a lack of vitamins in my blood. Mama, on the other hand, didn't take it so well. She sagged against the back of the chair as if all the energy had suddenly drained from her body. "Is there nothing that can be done?" she lamented. "You mentioned tests. What about that?"

Dr. Brunel scooted forward in his chair. "There is a doctor at the hospital in Amsterdam. His name is Johan Tromp. He's doing research in this area. Rather than spend time with me, guessing at what might be wrong, I suggest you see him." He took a small tablet from the far side of the desk and scribbled down the name. "Here," he handed the note to Papa. "If you tell me when you're going over there, I'll send him a telegram and notify him to expect you."

"Okay," Papa nodded.

"We'll go tomorrow," Mama interjected, the life suddenly returning to her voice.

Papa looked surprised. "She has already missed one day of school this week," he said with a gesture in my direction.

"And she'll likely miss many more," Mama retorted. "But if the condition is fatal, we should get to it with urgency."

Papa smiled the way he always did when he knew Mama was right. "Yes, we should indeed." He looked over at Dr. Brunel. "Tell Dr. Tromp we'll be there tomorrow."

The doctor acknowledged Papa with a nod and looked over at Mama. "Are you feeling well enough for a trip?"

"It's only to Amsterdam," Mama retorted.

❦ ❦ ❦

The next day, while Willem and Nollie went off to school, and Corrie remained at home under the watchful eye of Aunt Anna, I followed Mama and Papa in the opposite direction to catch the trolley. We took it uptown to the train station and rode to Amsterdam. On most occasions a train ride was a treat, and I was glad to see the countryside beyond Haarlem, but that day all I could think of was Vincent and the two days I'd been absent from school.

Half an hour later we arrived at the station in Amsterdam. I'd been to the city before and never once thought of it as imposing. In fact, I found its size and congestion energizing, but that morning as we left the train, I wondered if Papa knew where the hospital was located and which trolley to take to get us there. I was about to ask when he stepped confidently to the curb and hailed one of the horse-drawn carriages that waited out front. Mama, normally even more frugal than he, never said a word of protest. She just held out her hand and waited for him to help her up to the seat. That's when I knew Papa was worried about me, too.

The ride through the city was pleasant. With the clip-clop of the horse's hooves on the pavement and the jingle of his harness it seemed as though we were on a holiday rather than a quest for medical attention. I gazed out at the people as we passed and wondered where they were going. They looked so earnest and serious as they made their way along the sidewalk. *Business*, I thought. *They are all business.*

After a pleasant ride through the city, we arrived at the main entrance to the hospital. A stately brick structure, it looked larger than anything I'd ever seen. Papa helped us from the carriage and led the way up the steps to the front hallway. A nurse pointed us toward the south wing. There we found a ward reserved solely for Dr. Tromp's patients, but he was nowhere in sight. One of the nurses guided us to an examination room.

Like with Dr. Brunel, I was instructed to change to a gown for the examination. I shed my clothes and put it on much easier than before, but I was nervous about what would happen next and wanted to ask Mama about it. But before I could speak, Dr. Tromp entered the room. Unlike before, he asked Mama to leave the room and examined me alone. I was uneasy about that, but she assured me she would be just beyond the door and that I would be fine. The examination didn't take long.

When he was finished, a nurse drew a blood sample from my arm, which she repeatedly explained was necessary for tests to diagnose my condition. I think she said that because I was young and she thought I wouldn't understand. As the nurse left the room, Dr. Tromp appeared again but only to tell us that the tests would take a day or two and that they would contact us when the results were ready. After Dr. Brunel's suggestion that I might not have long to live, and then the tension of traveling to a large city, our experience at the hospital provided less than the conclusive answer for which we'd hoped. We rode home to Haarlem relieved that this much of the experience was over but tense about what lay ahead.

Two days later, a telegram arrived telling us the test results were ready in Amsterdam. Mama and Papa traveled with me back to the hospital where Dr. Tromp confirmed what Dr. Brunel had suspected: I was anemic.

"But it's not simply a vitamin deficiency," he explained. "She has a condition that prohibits her body from absorbing vitamins. She could take vitamin supplements, and that might help other aspects of her health, but it won't change her basic condition."

"How long can she live?"

"Most patients with pernicious anemia only live a few years beyond diagnosis." Tears came to Mama's eyes. Dr. Tromp quickly added, "But we are making progress on that. Some of our patients are now doing quite well." He glanced in my direction. "Would you be interested in that program?"

"And would that be expensive?" Mama asked before I could respond.

"Not at all," Tromp replied. "The queen has generously endowed our research with a grant from the crown. Treatment would be free, in exchange for participation in our research, of course."

"And what would that involve?" Papa asked.

"We use experimental treatments. None of it is toxic but most of it has never been tried before. And there would be more blood tests like the one you had a few days ago, to follow the treatment results."

"This is all new to us," Papa replied. "And it seems to be happening quite rapidly."

Mama looked across at him. "It is happening quickly, Casper, but I don't think we have any alternative." That was the first and only time I ever heard her refer to him by his first name, and that's also when the seriousness of the moment finally caught up with me.

"I'm scared," I squeezed Mama's hand.

"I know," she said softly. She put her arm around my shoulder and drew me to her side. "But I think the doctor can help you and I am certain in my heart that it will be all right." She looked down at me with a kind smile. "Aren't you certain of it?"

"I was yesterday."

"Then hold on to that hope and live from it today."

"Of course," Dr. Tromp spoke up, "she would have to be available each day for the tests and treatments."

"Each day?" Papa asked.

"Yes. The treatments and tests must be administered under tight control and at specific times, and all of it documented precisely."

A cloud came over Mama's face. "The trip each day would be a bit difficult."

"I have a cousin who lives here," Papa suggested.

Mama had a skeptical expression. "But would they help?"

"We can ask."

From the hospital we traveled across town to visit Father's cousin, Gerrit van der Pol, and his wife, Margriet. They lived in Amsterdam's Jewish quarter where Gerrit had a jewelry shop that, like Papa's watch shop, occupied part of the first floor of their home. I remembered seeing them only once before, at Grandfather's funeral, but they seemed to know me from the moment we arrived. Margriet led us through the house to a table in the kitchen. Not long after we arrived Gerrit came from the jewelry shop and joined us at the table while we all drank a cup of coffee. Afterward, I sat quietly listening while Papa and Mama told them about my condition and explained the situation with the daily treatments and tests at the hospital. Before they could ask, Gerrit interrupted. "That is too much travel each day. It will be expensive and not a good situation for Betsie. She should stay with us. Margriet will see that she gets to the hospital each day."

"Yes," Margriet added enthusiastically. "I would be happy to help." She looked in my direction. "And we have a room upstairs that is perfect for you."

She reached across the table for my hand. "Come. I will show it to you." When I hesitated to follow, Mama urged me on with a nod. She wanted me to be comfortable in these new surroundings, but I could see sadness in her eyes and I knew she did not want us to be apart.

After a tour of the house, we ate lunch and then returned home in the middle of the afternoon. I spent the remainder of the day with Aunt Anna, packing my clothes. Mama helped us a little but her cough got the best of her and she retreated to her room. Nollie came in and out of the room with things to loan me, and Corrie kept us company with her constant chatter. I could tell by how fast she was talking that she didn't understand what was happening or why I was leaving. After she repeated the same questions for the third time, I figured out that she just wanted to talk her way through it. So I ignored the questions and talked to her, repeating again every detail of the two trips we'd already made, descriptions of the hospital and the ward, and of Gerrit and Margriet's house. That seemed to satisfy her and by the time I'd run out of things to say, we were done and the trunk was full.

The next morning, after the others said good-bye and left for school, Papa called a wagon for my luggage. While he and the driver loaded it, Mama came from her room and I said good-bye to her in the hallway. I assumed she would return to bed but instead she followed me downstairs. She did her best to be brave and was calm and composed right up to the moment I turned away to step onto the wagon. As I put my foot on the metal step to swing onto the seat, she grabbed me with both arms, squeezed me close, and sobbed. I burst into tears and Papa turned away. We stood there for what seemed like a long time until finally she leaned away and brushed my hair with her hand. "You go now and get well quickly so you can come right back."

"Yes, ma'am. I'll do just that."

Then Papa helped me up to the seat, climbed up after me, and we rode together to the station for the trip back to Amsterdam.

CHAPTER 3

PAPA RODE WITH ME on the train all the way to Amsterdam, then hailed a carriage to take us from the station to Gerrit and Margriet's house. We arrived with the trunk strapped on back. Gerrit and a neighbor carried it inside and lugged it up the stairs to my room, which overlooked the street from the second floor. Gerrit invited Papa to stay for lunch but he was intent on returning to the shop before noon. "My watches are waiting," he said with a smile. I knew what he really meant. We had to say good-bye. Staying for lunch would only draw out the inevitable and make it that much worse. I walked outside with him, expecting he would take a carriage back to the station, but when I learned he was riding the trolley, I hooked my arm in his and accompanied him to the corner. As the ding of the trolley bell drew near, tears filled my eyes.

"There, now," he soothed. "Don't worry about a thing. The doctor will help you get well and this will all be over soon. Before you know it you'll be back in your own bed at home."

I smiled through the tears. "I'll be home before you know it."

Then the trolley came to a stop beside us and he stepped onboard. We waved to each other, me at the corner, him leaning out the doorway, until the trolley rounded the next corner and disappeared from sight.

Back at the house, I had lunch with Margriet and Gerrit, then spent the afternoon unpacking the trunk and putting my things away. Margriet helped, and talking with her helped me get over the loneliness I felt at saying good-bye to Papa.

Early the next morning we were on the trolley, headed toward the hospital. We arrived before eight and I spent the day with examinations and tests. The following day, we were there early once more, and the daily schedule repeated throughout the remainder of the week. That Friday, Dr. Tromp gave me a concoction made from liver extract and liquid vitamins. Like everything else on the ward, it was a new and experimental treatment. It also tasted horrible, but I held my nose and gulped it down as fast as possible.

Over the next several weeks I grew stronger. I no longer tired so easily and my breathing was better. Then one afternoon as I sat waiting for the lab nurse to draw yet another sample of blood, I overheard the ward nurses talking from the far side of the room.

"She's so young."

"But not that young. My sister is only three years older and she's already married and pregnant."

"Too bad for Betsie."

"Do you think anyone has told her?"

"I don't know, but I'm not. It's not my place."

"No, it's not. But she should be told."

"I'm sure Dr. Tromp will discuss it with her sooner or later."

I felt my heart sink and for the rest of the day all I could think about was whether I could have children. But Papa always said the truth would set us free, so rather than keeping those worries to myself, I talked to Dr. Tromp the next day as he made his rounds through the ward.

"Tell me something," I began, trying to sound confident.

"What would you like to know?"

"The other day someone suggested that I might not be able to bear children because of this disease. Is that true?"

"Well, first of all," he explained, "it isn't a disease. It's a condition. So far as anyone can tell, it isn't caused by something from outside the body. It just happens."

He was giving me the usual adult response—avoiding the most difficult part in hopes the question would go away. I wanted an answer. "But what about babies?" I asked.

A troubled frown appeared on his forehead. "Aren't you too young to be worried about this?"

"I'm fourteen. Lots of girls are married and pregnant by fifteen."

"I doubt that will be you," he said with an amused smile.

"Why?"

"You seem too smart for something like that." He stepped away from the table. "But since you asked, I'll tell you." He backed into the corner and took a seat on a stool. "Even if we can successfully treat the condition, child-bearing would be too difficult for your body and it would expose you to too many risks. Not the delivery, but the stress on your body of bearing a child. Of carrying a pregnancy to term."

"So I can never have children?"

"It's not that you *can't* have them. It's that you *shouldn't*. Your body, so far as I can tell, is perfectly capable of conceiving a child and there is nothing else about you that would prevent you from carrying that child to term, other than this condition."

"So, I could have children, but I shouldn't have them."

"Yes," he nodded. "I think you should consider your life from the perspective of making it the least complicated possible, and the least stressful. That would allow you to manage your condition the best."

Even at my young age, the suggestion that I avoid complicating circumstances didn't ring true with me. I understood what he meant, about not having children, but the rest of it was out of step with our family history and with the manner in which Papa and Mama lived out their faith in God. In spite of appearances to the contrary, they were complex people. Our lives were a tangled web of relationships with the people around us. At the time, of course, I wasn't really thinking of it in such an analytical way. I just didn't like the notion of simplifying my life. But the notion of not having children was a different matter. That was a physical issue, a medical issue, and it struck me to the core. I wrestled with what that meant and how it would affect me not just right then in my fourteen-year-old world but in the future, as well. That led me to thoughts of Vincent, and very quickly fantasies of a life with him played in my head.

Shortly before noon we returned to the house. As I came through the doorway, Gerrit called to me from the shop. "There's a letter for you." I hurried to his desk to find an envelope lying near the corner. Notes from home were always a joy and I was eager to hear the latest news from Nollie, Willem, and Corrie. I picked up the envelope and scanned the handwriting expecting the familiar script of Mama or Nollie, but to my surprise this one was written in a different hand. The letters were straight and lean, but inconsistent in form. Then I saw the return address in the corner and knew this note was from Vincent. At once my heart soared as memories rushed to replace the fantasies I'd indulged since talking to Dr. Tromp, and then, just as quickly, my emotions plunged as I remembered that conversation. All of that happened in an instant as I retrieved the letter from the desk. I thanked Gerrit for it, clutched it against my chest, and hurried upstairs to my room.

With the door closed, I lay across the bed and carefully pried open the flap of the envelope, being mindful not to tear it. I slid the letter out and gently unfolded it along the crisp, straight creases.

"Dear Betsie," it began, "I hope this letter finds you well and rapidly growing stronger. School today was particularly empty without you." My heart fluttered and tears filled my eyes. He continued with news of our classmates, their struggles with the lessons, and his latest observations of Willem and Nollie. Reading it made me homesick for them and opened my eyes to just how deeply I cared for Vincent. It sounds silly now, a young girl taking her first infatuation so seriously, but that's how I thought about it. Vincent had been my friend since we first started to school but as the years went by our friendship grew deeper, into the kind of affection a girl has for a boy—a particular boy—and I was certain that sentiment would only continue to deepen. And if my relationship with him did not culminate in marriage it would most certainly awaken the joy of finding someone else, and that would end in marriage. And that brought me around, again and again, to the issue of children.

Since my earliest memories I had dreamed of bearing children, rearing a family, watching them grow from infants to toddlers through adolescence to adulthood. Facing their fears with them and reveling in their joys together as we built a life as rich and rewarding as the one I knew at home with

Mama and Papa. Only now I knew that could never happen. So, I reasoned, if I could not bear children, then I should never marry. A man would want children and in spite of knowing my condition he would pressure me, however tactfully or subtly, to give them to him and eventually, against my better judgment, I would relent. And the result would be tragic for everyone. So I resolved that day, with Vincent's letter in my hand, my heart aching for him as only a fourteen-year-old heart could ache, and with tears streaming down my cheeks, that I would never marry. Not Vincent. Not anyone.

That all made sense to me as I lay on the bed in my room with the letter in my hand, but as the afternoon wore one, my resolve waned. I sat by the window staring down at the street below or off in the middle distance, doing my best to fill my mind with thoughts of scripture Papa made us memorize, or recounting things that Nollie and Corrie had said. But the more I tried to think of something else, the more my mind became preoccupied with thoughts of Vincent. Images of him at school and the times he walked home with us kept crowding my mind. The sound of his voice, the look in his eyes when he smiled, the way his forehead wrinkled when he was lost in thought.

Finally, I heard Margriet call to me from the kitchen. I turned away from the window and walked downstairs to find a cup and saucer sitting on the table. "Thought you might like some tea," she said. Then she poured from a teapot and brought a cup for herself. We sat together awhile, sipping tea in silence. Then she set her cup aside and looked over at me. "So, tell me what's on your mind."

"Not much," I tried to avoid her interest.

"You didn't say a word on the trolley ride home, and you've been sitting in your room all afternoon. That isn't like you." She paused to take another sip from her cup, then said, "Tell me what's bothering you."

"I talked to Dr. Tromp today," I said with a heavy sigh.

She looked curious. "What about?"

"I overheard some of the nurses talking about what a shame it was that my condition would prevent me from having children." Tears unexpectedly filled my eyes. I wiped them and took a deep breath. "So I asked him about it."

She reached across the table and took my hand. "Aren't you just a little young for that topic?"

"Maybe," I shrugged. "But I know girls who are fifteen and have their first child already."

She smiled at me. "That doesn't sound like you, though, does it?"

"That's what Dr. Tromp said." I gave her a smile and drew my hand free to wipe my eyes.

She took up her cup again. "What else did the doctor say?"

"He said that there was no reason why I couldn't do it. Physically there was no reason I couldn't have children." I toyed with the teacup while I talked. "But that the stress would be too great."

Now Margriet looked angry. "I don't think I like the notion of you talking to him about this. Not at all. Certainly not alone. Where was I when this conversation took place?"

"In the waiting area."

"I should have been there. He should have sent for me."

"Perhaps."

"Perhaps is right," she said in an imperious tone. "I think I'll say something to him about it when we're down there tomorrow."

"No," I implored. "Please don't. It was just a conversation."

"Yes." She held her chin at a haughty angle. "A conversation that has upset you rather greatly."

"No," I insisted once more. "I asked him to tell me the truth, and he told me. Papa says we never have to fear the truth. That the truth will always set us free. I just wanted Dr. Tromp to tell me the truth. If you talk to him about this, he won't speak openly to me, and if he starts holding things back because he thinks you'll get angry, then I may never get well."

She took another sip of tea while she thought about it, then nodded her head gently. "Okay," she whispered. "Okay." Then in her full voice, "I won't say anything this time. But in the future, maybe you should remember to include me on these conversations from the beginning."

"Yes ma'am."

"Where did you leave it with him?"

"He told me, and then he left," I explained. "That's about all there was to the conversation."

"But what do you think about it?"

"About my condition? I think he's right. Having children would be hard on my body. I can sense that just from…myself."

She must have sensed my quandary because she arched a single eyebrow and gave an amused grin. "But?"

"But?" I asked, perplexed.

"But what's the rest of it?"

My shoulders sagged and I lowered my head. "Vincent," I sighed.

Once again, she reached across the table and rested her hand on mine. "Listen, you don't have to apologize for how you feel. Who is Vincent?"

"A boy in my class."

"A special boy."

"Yes. But don't tell anyone."

"I won't. Does he know he's special to you?"

"I think so."

"Well," she said with a satisfied look, "he's a blessed man to have caught your eye. He must be special indeed."

"And I would hate to disappoint him, but I think I must."

"Dissappoint him? About what?"

"About children."

"Oh," she laughed, then quickly tried to recover when she realized I was serious. "Perhaps you should let that work itself out. You have plenty of time to decide about that."

But I *was* serious, very serious. Mama said I had been that way all my life, always planning and deciding, figuring things out in great detail well in advance. That's the way I liked it. To see as far ahead as possible so that I had as much time as possible to plan and prepare. When I was much younger I overheard a teacher describe me as obsessive. Aunt Anna called it precocious. To me, it was just the way I was. This thing with Vincent was an issue I would one day have to face. To my way of thinking, it was better to face it now and move on rather than leave it lingering always in the background, casting a shadow over everything else. The thought of it wasn't going to leave my mind until I dealt with it, so I might as well deal with it now.

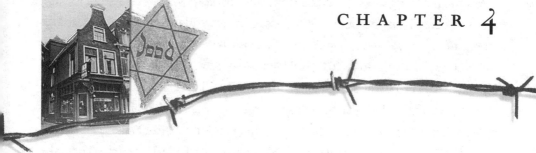

CHAPTER 4

EVERY DAY I SPENT with Gerrit and Margriet began just as it did at home with Papa and Mama. We gathered at the table for breakfast, almost always bread with jam, after which Gerrit read a selection from the Bible, usually a chapter from the book we read the previous day. Then we prayed. If we were all together at noon, and when we gathered at night for supper, we followed the same routine.

Part of the morning prayer time each day was devoted to praying for the peace of Jerusalem and blessing for the Jews, a practice begun by my grandfather, Gerrit's uncle. Long before any of us were born, Grandfather's pastor came to see him at the shop in the home in Haarlem where we now lived. In their conversation that day they learned that both had felt prompted by the Holy Spirit to "pray for the peace of Jerusalem" and they resolved that morning to do so every day. Since then, at Grandfather's house and at the homes of almost all his descendants in each succeeding generation, Ten Booms of every shape and size prayed each day for the peace of Jerusalem and for blessing on the Jews. At our home in Haarlem those prayers had been offered continuously each morning after breakfast since 1844.

As my treatments with Dr. Tromp continued, and as I grew stronger, visits to the hospital became shorter. After a month or two, he sent me home with the vitamin and liver extract in a bottle. His nurse gave us instructions about how and when to administer it and a journal for Margriet to make notes

MIKE EVANS

of each dosage. After that, morning trips to the hospital were reduced to just three days each week and then only to allow the nurse to draw blood for the tests that monitored my condition. That left more time free with Margriet.

One morning as we returned from the hospital, we passed a shop located a few blocks from the house. We passed it every day and I had wanted to stop, but there was never time. Now that our trips to the hospital were much quicker, we had time to go inside. When I suggested it to Margriet, she readily agreed. "This is a great shop," she grinned. "You'll love it."

As we entered the shop a man came from the back of the room and approached us with a smile. "Margriet, this is your cousin Betsie?"

"Yes, this is Betsie ten Boom. She's visiting us from Haarlem." Then she turned to me. "Betsie, this is Tomer Berman."

Berman grasped my hand in his. "I am so glad to finally meet you," he beamed. "Welcome to our shop." He gestured with a sweep of his arm. "We have beautiful dresses on the racks along the wall. Lovely lace on the shelves in back. And in between, anything you can imagine."

Margriet wandered to the left. I moved to the right, past a table covered with hats, and thought of Corrie. Even at a young age she loved hats. Mama and Aunt Anna insisted she wear a bonnet like other girls her age, but Corrie had an eye for the hats on the shelf in my room, and when we were in there together I took them down for her to try. Seeing them now in the store and thinking of her brought back many memories, and for the first time since I left home I was not overwhelmed with sadness. I lingered there a moment, then moved on across the store. As I drew near the first dress rack, Mr. Berman came to my side. "If you see something you like I can make you a terrific price."

"Okay," I nodded, but I had only a few coins in my purse. There was no way I could afford even the cheapest of the clothes he had to sell.

"Margriet tells me your father and Gerrit are cousins," he continued.

"Yes," I nodded. "Gerrit's father and my grandfather were brothers."

"I did not know those men," he smiled, "but your father is the watchmaker, Casper ten Boom."

The sound of my father's name caught me off-guard and my eyes opened wide. "How do you know him?"

30

"I do not know him personally. But everyone knows about Casper ten Boom. My brother is neighbors with Gideon Prins. You know Gideon?"

"Rabbi Prins?"

"Yes," Berman nodded eagerly. "You know him?"

"He comes to the shop almost every week to visit with Papa."

"Gideon grew up near us," Berman added. "I see him when I go to Haarlem to visit my brother."

We made the rounds past all the racks. It was a nice store but I think Margriet had no more money to spend than I. So after we made our way around the shop, we said good-bye and started up the sidewalk toward Margriet's house. As we walked, she glanced over at me. "What did you think?"

"Nice store."

"Yes. And he knew who your father was."

"You told him?"

"I told him you were coming and gave him your name. He asked about your father on his own."

"I did not know Papa's reputation reached this far."

"Well, now you see, you aren't so far from home after all."

"No. I suppose not. He knows Rabbi Prins, too."

"Yes. Rabbi Prins visits our neighborhood often."

"You know him?"

"Certainly."

"Rabbi Prins is one of Papa's best friends," I continued, glad for the chance to talk about the familiar things of home. "They visit almost every week." I looked up at her. "And sometimes they even pray together."

She had an amused smile. "You say that as if I should be shocked."

"Well, sometimes it seems a little strange to me. But most of the time it just seems right."

"Yes," she nodded. "It does."

"Do you have Jewish friends you pray with?"

"I do."

"Sometimes," I added, "I think Papa is better friends with the Jews than with the Christians. And Rabbi Prins is more a pastor than the priests at St. Bavo's."

"I don't doubt it," Margriet laughed. "But since you are so much at home here now, I have another friend you should meet."

My forehead wrinkled in a frown. "Another of Papa's friends?"

"No," she shook her head. "Another of *my* friends. Her name is Ann Selinger. She lives five blocks from here." Then a questioning look came over her. "Can you do that? Can you walk that far?"

"Yes," I said confidently. "I am much stronger than when I first came here."

"I know, but we'll have to climb several flights of stairs. Do you think you can do that, too?"

"I can," I nodded.

"Okay." She sounded less than convinced. "If you think you're up to it."

I touched her hand. "I'll be fine, Margriet."

"She is sick and I have been taking food to her."

"You sound like Mama. She's always taking food to the neighbors. Sometimes all we have is bread and coffee but she takes soup to our friends."

"Good, then," she said with a laugh. "Since you are experienced at this, you can help me prepare the food."

Back at the house, Margriet and I worked together in the kitchen, cutting meat and vegetables for soup, then baking bread while the soup pot simmered on the stove. When everything was ready, we poured the soup into a serving bowl, wrapped the bowl in a clean towel, and set it in a large picnic basket. We took the bread from the oven, covered it with a separate cloth, and tucked it beside the warm soup bowl. Then, with Margriet leading the way, we started on the five-block walk from the house to Ann's apartment.

At first I had no trouble keeping up, but the farther we went the more tired I became. My strength lasted longer than before but even so, by the time we reached the apartment building I wondered if I could make it up the stairs. Margriet must have wondered too because she glanced back at me with a worried look. "I can take this up to her on my own if you need to wait here."

"No," I said insistently, gesturing with my hand for her to continue. "I'll be fine."

An amused grin spread across her face. "We used to see your father often, when we were younger. This is how I remember him."

"How?"

"Just like you," she said playfully.

I held the door open as Margriet entered with the basket, then I followed her down the front hall to the stairway and started up behind her. With each step up the stairs my legs grew heavier and heavier, but I made it to the second floor and we paused there so I could catch my breath. "This is good exercise," I said.

Margriet wasn't convinced. "Exercise isn't your problem."

"No, but I am much stronger than I was before. Last year I could not have made it to the corner past your house, much less this far."

After a moment to rest, we continued up the next flight. I was glad when Margriet paused at the landing and turned down the hall. She paused at the third door and rapped on it with her knuckle. We waited patiently while someone inside unlocked it.

When the door opened at last, a frail, thin woman appeared. She had large, sad eyes that seemed to sink into their sockets. Beneath them her cheeks were hollow, and the paper-thin skin along her jaw pulled tight against the bone. By the slump of her shoulders I knew she was too tired to stand, but when she saw Margriet a smile came to her face. Her eyes brightened and color returned to her cheeks.

"Margriet!" she exclaimed. "I was hoping to see you." She stepped aside to let us pass, then closed the door behind us.

Margriet walked to the kitchen table and set the basket there. Ann, still standing near the door, looked at me with a curious smile. "So you're the cousin from Haarlem."

"Yes," I nodded. "I am Betsie."

"You look just the way Margriet described you," she replied, then her eyes fell on the basket and she brushed past me toward the table.

A row of cabinets lined the wall to the left above a counter with a small sink. Margriet opened a door near the far end and reached inside for a soup bowl. In a drawer beneath the counter she found a spoon and ladle. While Ann took a seat at the table, Margriet set the bowl and spoon before her, opened the basket, and lifted the lid on the serving bowl. Using the ladle, she dipped soup from it and filled the smaller soup bowl. Then we both took a seat and watched while Ann ate. It didn't take long.

As she scooped the last spoonful from the bottom of the bowl, Ann looked up at me. "Betsie, your cousin Margriet has kept me alive. Twice I was near death's door and twice she appeared in the nick of time with a basket of food."

"You're not going to die," Margriet said with chuckle. "You're just hungry."

"And sick," Ann added quickly.

"And that won't last forever, either."

Ann smiled at me. "Are you as optimistic as she is?"

"I'm trying," I answered.

"Good." Ann reached out her hand and rested it on Margriet's arm. "Because the world needs more people like my friend Margriet." She looked across at me again. "You be a friend like that to someone, too, you hear?"

"Yes ma'am," I nodded. "I will."

After Ann had a second bowl, she and Margriet began talking about people in the neighborhood. I knew little of the things they discussed but sat quietly listening to their conversation. As they talked, I glanced around the apartment. It was sparsely furnished with a single chair by the front window. Next to it was a table with a lamp, but there was no sofa. In fact, there was nothing else in the room at all, not even pictures on the walls. Then I noticed the lamp on the table by the chair had no oil. A glance toward the ceiling told me the apartment wasn't wired for electricity, either. Sunlight through the windows might have provided enough for Ann to see during most of the day, but as the afternoon grew late and the sunlight faded, the room would become dark. A damp chill hung in the air and I remembered Margriet had not lit the stove to warm the soup.

Conversation between them lagged and Margriet ladled the last of the soup into the soup bowl and set the bread on a plate. It was still wrapped in cloth, just as it was when we packed it from the house. Then a few minutes later we returned the serving bowl to the basket and started toward the door.

When we were downstairs on the street I asked Margriet about what I'd seen. "No," she replied. "Ann does not have gas or electricity."

"That apartment would get rather cold at night."

"That's part of the reason she is sick."

"Does she have water?"

"Yes. Though I'm not sure why or how."

"Doesn't she have relatives who could give her a better place to live?"

"I suppose, but I don't know who or where they are."

"We have Mama's sister living with us. And there was a time when we had *all* her sisters."

"I think Ann prefers being on her own, even if her conditions are less than the best."

"The Jews seem to be always struggling."

"That's part of their history."

"What do you mean?"

"Since the Middle Ages they have been the object of hatred. Sometimes by workers who see competition for their job as a threat. I think that's how they wound up confined to this neighborhood."

"You mean they can't live anywhere else?"

"Perhaps in Amsterdam, but not in other places."

"I don't understand how people could treat them like that."

"I think they are just afraid." She paused a moment, as if in thought, then she said, "Or they might just be mean."

We laughed together, then I added, "All I know is Papa says we should pray for peace in Jerusalem and for blessing on the Jews, and that's what we do."

"And that's a good way to look at it."

CHAPTER 5

AS SPRING NEARED, Margriet and I rode the trolley to the hospital just as we had throughout my stay. This time, however, Dr. Tromp was waiting for me when I arrived on the ward. Normally, I saw only the nurses but he was there himself and led me to an examination room. With a nurse standing nearby, he examined me as thoroughly as the first day I arrived. When he was finished, he took a seat on a stool in the corner. From my place on the examination table I glanced over at him and saw a faint smile on his face.

"Betsie," he said, folding his arms across his chest, "we have learned much from you, and what we've learned has led to a dramatic improvement in your condition, and in the condition of many others."

"I do feel better." I wasn't sure if I should respond but found myself compelled to say something. "I'm not as tired as I was when I first came here. And I can do most of my daily routine without getting out of breath."

"Yes," he nodded. "I am sure you can." He crossed his legs and leaned back. "I think we have learned all we can from you, and I think we have done all we can for you."

His words struck me in an odd way, arousing hope that I might be well and, at the same time, suggesting that I might yet be doomed to the short life Dr. Brunel had suggested. I chose to be hopeful. "Am I cured?"

"There is no cure." He shook his head, "But I do think you can manage your condition now."

"For how long?"

"For as long as you wish."

A smile spread over my face. "I'm not going to die."

"No," he said with another shake of his head. "You're not going to die." A grin turned up the corners of his mouth and pushed his cheeks higher, squeezing the corners of his eyes. "How would you like to go home to your parents?"

I bolted to a sitting position on the examination table. "I would like that very much!" I exclaimed.

"Good." He stood as if to leave. "I will send Dr. Brunel a telegram with instructions on how to continue your treatment." Then he reached into his pocket and took out a small bottle. "This is the liver extract and vitamin mixture you have been taking," he handed the bottle to me. "When I telegraph Dr. Brunel I will give him the formula. He can continue making it for you."

I held the bottle tightly in my grip and looked over at him. "Thank you so much."

"You are quite welcome." There was an awkward moment as if he had more to say, but instead he turned toward the door. Then, at the last possible moment as he was about to disappear down the hall, he paused and looked back at me. "You asked me once about children."

"Yes."

He stepped back inside the doorway. "It was cruel of me to speak to you so bluntly."

His comment puzzled me and I hardly knew what to make of it, so I asked the first question that came to my mind; a question I'd heard Papa ask many times before. "Was it the truth?"

Dr. Tromp had a quizzical look. "Was what the truth?"

"What you told me about children—was it the truth?"

"Yes," he said slowly. "What I told you was the truth. As long as you continue to take the extract formula, you can manage your daily life—even a vigorous one—but pregnancy would likely be too much for your body."

"Then why should you feel bad about telling me?"

"Many young girls dream of having a family." His eyes darted away. "I did not like taking that dream from you."

"But you gave me my life," I said, trying to relive the sense of guilt he obviously felt.

"No, God gave you that." He had a thin, tight smile. "I'm just helping you make the most of it." And with that, he turned away and disappeared down the hall.

From the examination room I hurried down the hall to find Margriet and tell her the news. We laughed and giggled all the way back to her house, but it was a bittersweet moment for both of us. Over the months I'd stayed with her and Gerrit, she and I had grown much closer than mere cousins, and the thought that we might not see each other again left us both feeling sad. Still, this was the point of my coming to Amsterdam—to get well and return home—and now that moment had arrived.

For the remainder of the morning, we worked in my room packing my clothes and other items into the trunk. After lunch, Gerrit and a workman from his shop carried it down to the first floor. Then he sent a message to Papa and Mama telling them the news and arranged for a wagon to take us to the train station.

In the middle of the afternoon, I said a tearful good-bye to Margriet, climbed onto the wagon with Gerrit and the driver, and started to the station. Gerrit purchased a ticket for me and deposited the trunk with the station clerk, then escorted me to the platform. We waited there in awkward silence, him with his hands folded behind his back, me with my eyes fixed on the tracks, scanning the horizon for any sign of the approaching train.

Before long, a column of smoke appeared in the distance, rising from between the buildings. Then the locomotive emerged, rounding a curve in the track. It slowed to a crawl as it approached the station and took forever to reach the platform where we stood, but at last, it came to a stop with a door to the last car just a few feet away. Gerrit slipped his arm around my shoulders for a hug, then gestured with his free hand toward the coach steps. "Let us know when you get home," he said quietly. I agreed to send them a message and boarded the train.

The conductor helped me to my seat and I settled into place next to the window. Already my mind was preoccupied with thoughts of home but I glanced out the window for one last look at Amsterdam. Then I remembered

Gerrit and scanned the platform to catch his eye and give him a wave. But he was nowhere to be seen.

A few minutes later a bell rang, then the train began to move and we rolled slowly away from the station. Before long, we were in the open countryside and the train picked up speed. Houses and farms zipped past in a blur. The railcar rocked gently from side to side in time with the clack of the wheels against the rails.

❋ ❋ ❋

Papa was waiting at the station when the train arrived. I saw him on the platform as we approached and hurried from my seat to stand at the door. The train seemed to take forever to stop moving but as it did I jumped to the platform and ran into Papa's arms. He squeezed me tightly and I buried my face in the fabric of his jacket, filling my nostrils with the familiar scent of pipe tobacco and peppermint.

We took a wagon from the station to carry us and the trunk. I chattered the whole way about Amsterdam, the hospital, Dr. Tromp, and a thousand other things I don't remember now. It seemed as though I had been gone for years. I had much to say and felt compelled to say it all right then. When I paused to take a breath, Papa broke into the conversation. "Listen," he said quietly, "your mother isn't well today. She's in bed. So when we get there you must be quiet."

"Yes, Papa," I replied. "I will do my best."

"Perhaps it would go better if you greeted Nollie and Corrie outside, on the street."

I was puzzled by his request. "On the street?"

"Yes," he nodded. "If you meet them out there, you girls can do your squealing and shouting before you get inside. That way it will be quieter for your mother."

"Oh," I replied with a grin. "That's a good idea." I thought it was ingenious and gallant, but it would all go for naught.

A few minutes later, the wagon turned the corner onto our street, and a few blocks up ahead the Beje came into sight. My heart skipped a beat at the sight of it. I was home! At last. As the wagon came to a stop outside the shop entrance, the door flew open and out came Nollie and Corrie, followed closely by Mama and Aunt Anna. So much for Papa's plan to keep things quiet.

Before my foot hit the pavement, they grabbed me and hugged me. Nollie squealed and Aunt Anna burst out laughing. Mama's face was pale and I could see she didn't feel well, but even so she wrapped both arms around me and squeezed me closer than I'd ever been squeezed before. I wasn't sure she would ever let me go, but then Willem appeared. He looked a foot taller than the last time I'd seen him, and just when I thought Mama would give me a break from the hugging, Willem grabbed me and gave me a squeeze. "Good to see you," he said. I looked up at him, sure that I saw tears in his eyes. "Good to see you, too," I replied.

After a few minutes outside on the sidewalk, Mama turned toward the door. She opened it and gestured with her free hand. We all knew what that meant and in a dutiful procession, Nollie, Corrie, and I started inside. Nollie led the way past Mama and up the stairs, with Corrie and me right behind. As we did so, Corrie took my hand in hers and gripped it tightly. I wanted to complain but the moment I opened my mouth to speak I remembered the time she kept repeating questions months earlier when I was packing to leave for Amsterdam. The tight grip now meant the same thing. She wanted to say something, or do something, that let me know she was glad to see me. Squeezing my hand tight enough to stop the blood flow was all she could think to do. So I took a deep breath and bore the pain in silence.

Upstairs in the kitchen, Mama and Aunt Anna went to work slicing a freshly baked cake and pouring cups of coffee for everyone. They rarely let a joyous occasion pass without baking something. My arrival was only the most recent excuse to send Nollie to the store for a pound of sugar. We ate cake and drank coffee until it was all gone, and in between bites I recounted as many of my experiences in Amsterdam as I could remember—except for the part about whether I could bear children. That, I kept inside in that secret place where I put my thoughts and prayers that were too personal to mention.

The following day, Dr. Brunel came to the Beje to check on me. As before, he gave me a thorough examination. Aunt Anna stood watch while he did. Mama was too sick to get out of bed. "I received a telegram from Dr. Tromp about the liver extract. You have some of it still?"

"Yes. He gave me a bottle before I left."

"Good. It will take a day or two to obtain all the ingredients and several hours to mix it properly, but once we get the hang of it I can prepare it for you every month."

"Thank you for sending me to him."

He smiled. "You're quite welcome. You'll need to take the extract every day. The vitamins will help but only if you continue to take the extract."

"I will."

"Even if you feel fine and think you don't need it any longer."

"Yes sir. I'll take it."

"Otherwise," Dr. Brunel continued, "your body won't be able to use the vitamins."

"I understand."

"As long as you take it, you should live a normal life."

Just then, Mama appeared in the doorway. "I'm a little concerned about how active she should be."

"Moderate activity isn't a problem—walking to school, the park, that sort of thing. But you should take precautions to avoid getting ill. Avoid crowds in the winter, keep warm, don't get wet and chilled. Usual precautions. Illness would be very stressful for your body." He looked back at Mama. "How are you feeling today?"

"Not so good right now. I was much better yesterday, but now I'm feeling rather faint."

"As I told you, this will take some time to pass."

The following Monday, Vincent came home with Willem and Nollie. We talked about friends and classmates and all the gossip I'd missed. When we tired of that, he suggested we turn to the day's lesson in mathematics. Having been away for so long, I assumed I would have to repeat the year. Trying to catch up with the class now seemed futile, but schoolwork was always fun for me and for almost two hours we worked problems from the textbook. All the time my mind kept running back to the conversation I'd had with Dr. Tromp about children and my inner need to tell Vincent.

In a while the afternoon light began to fade. Vincent gathered his books and prepared to leave. With a final good-bye to Mama and Aunt Anna, I led him downstairs to the street. As we reached the first floor I turned to face him and was about to speak when he smiled at me and said, "I've been reading about your condition and ..."

"Where did you find something to read about it?"

"My mother wa—" He caught himself as if he'd made a mistake and for an instant his eyes darted away, then he quickly recovered and continued. "My mother is friends with a doctor on the other side of town. He has some medical books and journals that have articles about your condition. There's even an article in one of them about Dr. Tromp's research. He's a rather famous doctor, you know."

"No," I said with a shake of my head. "I didn't know that." And it was true, I really didn't know, but right then I didn't care. I needed to tell Vincent about my decision regarding babies and marriage and at the same time I wanted with all my heart to run, to sing, to take a walk—anything except the thing I felt compelled to do.

"I didn't understand much that I read," he rambled on, "but they all say that you should avoid getting sick. You can have a normal life if you continue to take the medicine Dr. Tromp compounded and avoid the kinds of things that put too much of a strain on your body."

At last, there was my opening in the conversation. "Yes, well, about all that, I—"

He cut me off before I could get started, "It'll be dark before long and I have a ways to go to get home. I need to ..." He glanced nervously up the steps as if checking. "It's just that...well...it's been a long time since I've seen you and I don't know what you're thinking, but—"

All at once he leaned over and kissed me on the cheek. I think it surprised him as much as it did me and we stood there staring at each other, his cheeks looking as red as mine felt, neither of us knowing what to do next. After a moment, he smiled and in the sweetest voice said, "I'm glad you're home." Then he opened the door, stepped outside, and was gone.

❖ ❖ ❖

Because of Dr. Brunel's advice, Mama kept me home from school for the remainder of the year. She made arrangements with my teachers to supply homework, and even though I'd missed almost the entire school year they agreed that, if my grades proved sufficient during the final months, I could advance with my class. To do that, I needed to catch up on the work I missed and spent most days seated at the dining table working through our textbooks. Most days I did two lessons for each subject. I made good progress the first week, but what I missed were the comments in class that helped clarify the topics. Willem was a grade behind me, so he wasn't much help. I did the best I could but after two or three weeks my pace slowed.

At the same time, I continued to wrestle with what to tell Vincent. By then I was fifteen and time seemed to be hurtling us toward a future I wasn't sure we were ready to face. I wanted to tell him everything but I was afraid he would think I was being too forward. We'd never even discussed whether we had a relationship, much less what our future might be like. If I said something to him now it would only look like I was infatuated with him because he kissed me on the cheek.

I was seated at the dining room table trying to complete a lesson in history when Mama appeared at the doorway and rescued me from my thoughts. "Want some coffee?"

"Sure." Coffee with Mama meant time alone with her, seated at the kitchen table, where we often talked for hours. I could never pass up a chance for that, so I laid aside my textbook and followed after her.

Instead of sitting in the kitchen, though, she handed me a cup and said, "Come on. Let's go up on the roof."

Haarlem was an old city. People had lived there for centuries. As a result, it was crowded with buildings crammed together side by side, covering every inch of available space. Squeezed so closely beside each other, there was no space for a lawn, and most people had to be satisfied with a few flowers in flower boxes that hung beneath the windows. But when Grandfather owned our house, he purchased the house behind us. It faced the opposite direction, toward the next street over. The two structures stood back to back with a narrow alley in between. Later he joined them together, filling in the alley. That part of the house was now the staircase and it went all the way to the top where a door led onto the roof. Up there, above the buildings, there was plenty of sunshine, and that's where Mama kept her garden.

Coffee cup in hand, I followed her up to the rooftop where we wound our way past pots of flowers and containers of vegetable plants, most of them just beginning to leaf out in the warm spring air. She took a seat on a wooden chair Papa made just for her. I sat beside her on one we brought up from the kitchen.

"I haven't seen Vincent around. I don't think I've seen him since the day you returned."

"No. He hasn't been back around."

"Something happen between you two? You used to be good friends."

"We *are* good friends."

"Then why isn't he coming around?"

I took a sip of coffee, trying to think of a way to avoid telling her. Then I just gave up and told her about overhearing the nurses on the ward talking about me, my conversation with Dr. Tromp about bearing children, and talking to Margriet. Hearing myself talk about it now, I wasn't so sure it was the right thing to do and before I was through I was wishing I'd never said anything. I sounded officious and like I was stuck on myself.

From the faint smile on her face, Mama must have been thinking the same thing. When I finished telling her, she looked over at me in a way only Mama could do and said, "Aren't you being a little hasty? You are, after all, only fifteen."

"I'll be sixteen before school ends next year. Lots of women have children by that age."

"I suppose they do, but that's not you."

"Margriet said the same thing when I told her."

A smile came to Mama's face. "And Margriet was right."

"But if I can't have children, why marry at all?"

"Having children is a wonderful blessing, but there are other ways of finding fulfillment in life."

"Yes, but a husband would want children, wouldn't he?"

"Most would."

"And if he asked and kept asking, I would give in and try to give him what he wanted. And the result would be disastrous for everyone."

"Maybe."

"That's what Dr. Tromp said."

"He said it would be too difficult for your body. Isn't that what he said?"

"Yes."

"But he was talking about something that wouldn't happen for another five years, at least. He can't predict the future."

"What do you mean?"

"I mean he's a doctor, not a prophet. He doesn't know what your future holds."

"I still think it's better to avoid the issue altogether and live my life as a single woman."

We sat there for a while, both of us staring off into space, neither of us looking at each other, but I could tell she wasn't satisfied with my decision or my attitude. She wasn't interested in pushing me to marry—I understood that well enough. What she didn't like was the way my self-important answer about the future closed the door on possibilities. That was something she wouldn't allow for herself and insisted that we avoid. "The future belongs to God," she used to say. "Better to leave the future in His hands."

After a while, she pushed herself up from the chair and moved to one of the pots that sat nearby. She pinched off a leaf near the base of a plant and, without turning to face me, said, "I guess you better get back to your schoolwork."

"Yes, ma'am," I replied. "I suppose I should."

For the rest of the day and for six days each week throughout the remainder of the term, I focused my energy on completing the year's lessons. Working sometimes until after supper, I completed the required assignments, and Mama administered the final examinations. We submitted them one week before the end of the spring term and waited for a response.

On the last day of class before the summer, Willem brought home a note from our teacher telling me that I would be advanced with my class for the fall term. I was glad because that year was our final year of secondary education. But before all that, there was the summer.

CHAPTER 6

BEGINNING THE WEEK after the school term ended, Mama found ways to get me out of the house. It was an abrupt departure from her resolve to protect me from contracting an illness, but she insisted it was not a change of mind. "That was my attitude in the winter," she argued. "This is summer. The weather is warm and sunny. You should be outside." She took her own advice, too, and we went on walks to the grocer, the flower shops around Grote Markt, and the park. I argued with her about it because I was fifteen years old, but in my heart I did not mind being outside. Quite to the contrary, as the summer wore on I used her advice as an excuse to spend every possible minute out of doors, though I avoided the games children often played in the street and limited myself to more sedate activities like wandering from shop to shop, staring through the display windows at the items inside. As far as I can remember, that day when I fainted while playing cricket with Willem and Vincent was the last time I played any physical game of any sort, but I enjoyed the summer immensely.

When I wasn't roaming the shops or strolling through the park, I busied myself helping to care for Corrie. In spite of her young age she had a delicate touch and we learned needlepoint together from Aunt Anna. Once we'd gotten the hang of that, Mama taught us knitting. She also put us to work tending her many rooftop flowers and vegetables.

Early one morning, Corrie and I were on the roof watering the plants when I found a bag of unused tulip bulbs. "I wonder if we can plant these?" I asked.

Corrie had a quick answer. "Mama says you're supposed to plant them before spring."

"*Before* spring?" I asked in a condescending tone.

"While it's still cold," Corrie replied.

"Does that make sense to you?" Sometimes when she was right she looked really cute, and other times she really got on my nerves. This was one of those irritable moments and I spoke to her in a demeaning manner.

Before Corrie could respond, Mama emerged from the open stairway door. "That's right, Corrie," she said with a smile. Then she turned to me with a stern expression. "You should listen to her."

"I do," I said lamely.

"No, you just hear the words, but you don't listen to what she's saying."

"So, we can't plant these?" I asked, gesturing with the bag of tulip bulbs and trying to avoid an argument.

"Not now," she replied, shaking her head. "It's too late in the year."

"But summer is just beginning."

"Yes. And it won't be here long." She pointed to the sack I was holding in my hand. "You have to plant those bulbs while it is still cool. In between winter and the first days of spring. That way they have the longest time to grow."

"Between winter and spring?"

"Yes." She bent over one of the flowers and pinched off a sucker near the base of the stem. "There's a lot you don't know about plants."

Again I ignored the temptation to argue and I held the bag of bulbs for her to see. "What can we do with them?"

"We can keep them until next spring. Put them in a dark, dry place and they won't grow. I suggest the corner of a cabinet in the kitchen."

"How do *you* know so much about plants?" There was a sharp edge to my voice and I was afraid I had said too much. I knew Mama was aggravated with me for the way I responded to Corrie about the tulip bulbs, and that, in turn, aggravated me. She'd only caught the end of the conversation, ignoring all that I had done with Corrie since school ended, but the part she heard set her nerves on edge and she was doing little to control *her* disposition. I was tired of trying to control *mine*, too, but I didn't want to be mean about it. She was my mama. So I waited, but the expected rebuke never came. Mama kept her head down, with one hand resting on her thigh while the other combed through the leaves of the plants. "I listen to them," she said after a while.

My irritable mood quickly gave way to curiosity. "You listen to them?"

"Not actually listen," she explained. "Plants don't speak in an audible voice. But they do speak through color, leaf, and stem. I pay attention."

"Wasn't one of our ancestors a good gardener?"

"Your father's grandfather," she replied dryly. "He's the one who grew strawberries in winter for one of the royal families." She glanced back at me. "Is that what you're talking about?"

"Yes, ma'am," I replied.

Mama stood up straight and looked me in the eye. "Be kind to Corrie," she said with her voice barely above a whisper. "She's watching your every step." Her eyes darted back to the plants and she continued in a normal tone. "Your great-grandfather grew those strawberries on an estate not too far from here. They say his brother could grow things the same way. But that was your father's relatives." She smiled at me. "Not from my side of the family."

"Did you know him?"

"Who?"

"My great-grandfather. Papa's grandfather."

"No." She shook her head, slowly drawing out the sound of the word for emphasis. "He was dead while your father was still a boy. I knew your grandfather, but everyone from the generation before him was dead by the time I came along."

"I remember Grandfather." It was true. I had a few faint memories of him, and the thought of it put a smile on my face.

Mama had a skeptical frown. "You were very young when he died. Barely able to walk."

"I know. But I remember going with him to see his father's grave. He was holding me in his arms. There was a headstone right below me and I was looking down at it. He said, 'This is where they put my papa.'"

Mama arched an eyebrow as her skeptical look turned to a knowing smile. "I never knew you remembered that." She rubbed the elbow of her left arm. "We were out there for his brother's funeral. I was standing just a few feet away. He wanted to hold you but I was afraid he'd drop you, so I kept close."

"Someone had put tulips by the headstone."

"They were growing there. Your grandfather planted them the year his father died. They came up every year after that."

"Even now?"

"I suppose," Mama nodded. "I haven't been out there in a long time, but they were blooming when I was there last."

"I think tulips are a sign from God," I added proudly.

"And a lot of people around here would agree with you," Mama chuckled. "But you sound like your father when you say that."

"He likes tulips, too."

"Tulips," she sighed. "All the ten Booms are tulip crazy."

I was still holding the bag of bulbs. "Do you think I could plant some of these in the window boxes? They are all empty. We should put them to good use."

"I tried growing tulips in those boxes years ago," Mama replied, "when we first moved here. The tulips came up and grew nice stems and leaves, but they couldn't get enough sunlight to bloom. And that was planting them early. This is late."

"Still," I replied, "I want to try anyway."

"Suit yourself," Mama shrugged.

With Corrie's help, I took the bag of bulbs to the front side of the house—the side facing the street. We dug in the boxes to loosen the soil, then buried the bulbs in a row, spacing them a few inches apart. Corrie brought a watering can. "Well, if they don't bloom," she said as she dampened the soil, "at least they'll make pretty green plants."

"That's right," I agreed, trying to take to heart Mama's earlier suggestion. "They are living things and they'll bring life to everyone who sees them."

"You sound like the preacher," Corrie giggled.

She was right and I laughed. Papa had little regard for the priests at St. Bavo's. We only went there because he felt it was where God wanted us to go, in spite of the things they said from the pulpit on Sundays. They sounded as pompous as I did just then, talking about the tulips. I looked over at Corrie and burst into laughter.

Summer went by fast that year, and just like Mama said, the tulips sprouted, grew into beautiful stems and leaves, but failed to bloom. Still, Corrie and I enjoyed them from the window of our bedroom and while we did, I read to her.

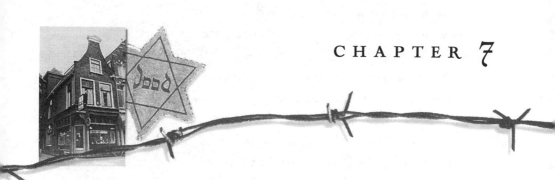

CHAPTER 7

ALL TOO SOON, summer came to an end and school opened for my final year. I greeted it with mixed emotions. On the one hand I had reached an important point in my life that gave me a sense of accomplishment. At the same time, many of the students in my class would move on to other pursuits and I likely would never see them again.

No one had seen Vincent in months and I wondered what had become of him. Over the several years we had known him, we had never seen him as frequently in the summer as we did during the school year, but we'd never before had a summer when we didn't see him at all. A few days before the term began, several girls from our class stopped by to see if I would be returning. During our conversation someone said she had heard Vincent wouldn't be attending class, but I didn't think that was true. He might have gone the summer without seeing me but he wouldn't have left school or town for good without saying good-bye. And sure enough, when I arrived for the first day of class he was waiting with that big, wide, inviting smile of his, seated across from me in our classroom.

For the first few months, Mama allowed me to attend school every day. I rose early to prepare, then walked the short distance from our house with Willem, Nollie, and Corrie, who was entering her first year of primary school. I enjoyed the few minutes we had together each morning, just the four of us without any adults around. Private moments like that were in short supply at our house. In the afternoon Vincent or one of our other friends would sometimes join us for the walk home and even stay at the house for a while to visit, but in the morning it was just us. I liked that.

As winter approached, however, Mama once again worried that I would contract some unspecified illness. The year was 1900, and it marked the dawn of the twentieth century in Europe, a region beset with any number of diseases. Tuberculosis was always a threat, though we had plenty of exposure to that in our own home, and influenza posed a perennial risk to everyone, particularly the elderly and people like me who had a chronic debilitating condition. Throughout October, Mama made my risk of sickness a topic of conversation every morning at breakfast. I assumed it was her way of wrestling with the issue, but as the month came to a close she could stand it no more. Beginning in November, she kept me at home and I did my lessons from the dining table.

After my first week of absence, Vincent came to the house to check on me. We sat upstairs at the dining table and talked about the lectures that I'd missed in class. Discussing them with him was helpful but once again the angst about my feelings for him and the prospect of a life lived on less than normal terms became an issue. He continued to come by, returning almost every day, and each visit followed the same routine. We studied upstairs for an hour or two, often over cake and coffee supplied by Aunt Anna, and then he would let himself out. I said good-bye from the top of the stairs, with Mama or Aunt Anna always in sight. I did not want a repeat of the time when he kissed me and I did my best to offer him no indication to the contrary.

As the days passed, however, I sensed Vincent was growing frustrated with this arrangement. One day in December, as we were reviewing a history lesson, he glanced up from the book and looked me squarely in the eye. "Something changed last year," he said.

The comment came with no prompting from me and left me puzzled. "What are you talking about?"

"One minute we were playing cricket in the alley, laughing and having fun. Then you fainted and went off to Amsterdam. When you came back you acted as if you didn't know me. What happened?"

"I didn't act as if I didn't know you," I protested.

"Yes, you did. I tried to talk to you after you got back, but you hardly had a word to say."

I leaned closer and lowered my voice to a whisper. "Are you forgetting the kiss you gave me?"

"That's just it," he said in a voice too loud for my comfort. "One day you—"

"Shhh," I interrupted with my finger to my lips. "Everyone will hear you."

"I don't care if they hear me."

"Well, I do."

He took a deep breath and began again, this time in a softer voice. "That's just it. One day we're walking home from school together, playing, laughing, getting along just fine. If I'd kissed you then, you would be strolling up the street on my arm right now. Instead, you act as if we're meeting to discuss the lessons because it's part of an assignment."

"I didn't ask you to come by," I said coldly. "You chose to do that on your own."

"I don't care about that." He dismissed my response with a wave of his hand. "I want to know what happened that things changed between us."

Mama was in bed with one of her coughing spells, but Aunt Anna was in the kitchen, just across the hall from where we sat. She already knew everything that happened in the house, but I didn't want her listening to us while I explained things to Vincent. I stared at him a moment, thinking about what to do, and then I remembered the rooftop. In an instant, I grabbed his hand and stood. I gave his hand a tug, "Come with me."

With Vincent's hand firmly in my grasp, I led the way from the dining room to the stairway and up to the roof. It was cold outside and snow was piled in the corners, but I ignored it. I turned to face him when we were by the chairs, "You want to know what happened? This is what happened." I let go of his hand and folded my arms across my chest. "I have a condition. A medical condition known as pernicious anemia."

"I know that, but—"

"Hush," I snapped with a quick wave of my hand. "I'm not finished."

An amused grin turned up the corners of his mouth and he leaned against the back of Mama's wooden chair. "Go ahead and finish."

"While I was in Amsterdam, being treated by Dr. Tromp, I learned that…
bearing children …" It was difficult for me to say those words. In our house, in
those days, husbands and wives rarely discussed the topic, much less teenagers, and certainly not a girl with a boy. Vincent's mouth dropped open and I felt
my cheeks blush, but I ignored it and forced myself to continue. He wanted to
know and I was determined to tell him. "Dr. Tromp says that bearing children
would put a strain on my body. So much so that he warned me not to do it."

"Are you crazy?" Vincent threw his hands in the air in a gesture of frustration. "We shouldn't be talking about this. Somebody might hear us."

"No, we shouldn't be talking about it," I agreed, "but you asked what happened and I'm telling you."

"I didn't ask about this."

"You wanted an answer and I'm giving it to you." I took a deep breath
and plunged ahead. "So, since I can't have children, I decided that I shouldn't
marry, either."

"But I'm not asking you to marry me." His voice was an octave higher
than normal and his face was twisted in an expression of incredulity. "What
are you talking about?"

"Whatever you felt for me, it was strong enough to kiss me."

"Yeah, but I didn't mean all this. And I didn't mean to offend you."

"I wasn't offended. I was flattered. And that's just it. If this keeps going,
where will it end? And if it can't end in marriage, why let it go any further?"

The expression on his face softened. "Who says it can't end in marriage?"

"I do. That's what I'm telling you. I've made that decision. I'm not getting
married."

"I'm not sure why we're having this conversation," he sighed. "Should you
be worrying about this now?"

"If I don't worry about it now, I won't be able to control what happens
later."

"I don't know," he shrugged. "Aren't we too young to be worrying about
children? I like you. I kissed you on the cheek because I like you. Shouldn't
we just enjoy the moment?"

"That's what everyone says. But a man would want children, and I can't
have children. If I get married, I'll resist for a while but then I'll relent and

then bad things will happen. And if that's so, there's no point in marrying. What I'm trying to tell you is there's no future in our relationship beyond friendship. Not another kiss. Not a hug. Not a romantic stroll at sunset."

"Just friendship?"

"Just friendship," I nodded.

"Well, at least we have that." He pushed away from the chair and reached for my hand. "Come on."

"What are you doing?"

"Come on," he repeated. "It's too cold for you to be out here, and we aren't finished with the history lesson we were working on."

I pulled away. "That's it?"

"That's what?"

"That's all you have to say?"

"No," he grinned. "I would kiss you again, right now, but you've already said we can't do that, so let's go finish the lesson instead." We stood there a moment, staring at each other, and then we both burst out laughing. And right then I wondered if I'd made a mistake, because suddenly I wanted to kiss him more than anything I'd ever wanted, and not just on the cheek.

❖ ❖ ❖

That spring, I graduated from secondary school with my class. Our teachers held a ceremony to honor the occasion, followed by a reception. Parents supplied the cake and coffee. Vincent's aunt attended but his mother was absent, and when I realized she wasn't there I became curious. Surely any parent would be proud of a child attaining an education and reaching such a mark in life. And so I decided to find out why she wasn't at the reception. Vincent was standing to one side with several boys from our class, all of them sipping coffee. As I approached, the others drifted away, leaving the two of us alone. As usual, Vincent greeted me with a smile.

"So," he said, "this is it. The end of the beginning, I suppose."

"You actually read the literature assignments," I replied playfully. His remark about *the end of the beginning* was an allusion to a quote from Seneca, an ancient Roman philosopher whose writings we briefly studied in class.

"Yes, and don't you think it odd that with all the studying we did together this year we never once discussed literature?"

"Not really."

"Oh? And why not?"

"Literature is subjective. How you view a book could be very different from my own view, and both of us would still be right. I thought about it, but then I realized if we tried to study it together all we would do is argue."

"I suppose." He was amused by my comment, but at the same time there was a sense of awkwardness about him that I had rarely seen. Normally, he was the most confident boy in the class, but that day he seemed ill at ease and terribly out of place.

"So," I began, with a glance around the room. "Which one is your mother?"

His eyes opened wide in a startled expression. "Excuse me?"

"Which one?" I gestured to the adults gathered on the opposite side of the room. "Which one is your mother?"

"Uh ..." He looked away. "She's not here."

And suddenly I was embarrassed for asking. "Sorry," I said meekly. "I thought she'd be here." I touched his arm. "I didn't mean to—"

"No," he said, still not looking at me. "It's okay. She's not been here for a long time." He raised his head and looked me in the eye. "And you're the first person I've admitted that to."

"Where is she?"

"She left a few years ago."

"A few years ago?"

"Yes," he nodded. "After my father died, she drifted from job to job and from man to man. Then finally she found someone she liked and moved with him to Germany. I think she's living in Berlin now."

"You don't keep in contact with her?"

"No." He shook his head. "And she doesn't keep in touch with me, either. My aunt is more a mother to me than my real mother ever was."

"All this time, you've been living with your aunt? Not just visiting her occasionally after school?"

He sighed. "I should have told you before now, but I guess I wondered if you would still like me if you knew."

"Why would that affect how I felt about you?"

"I don't know," he shrugged. "I suppose it shouldn't, but sometimes things affect people in ways you didn't expect." Our eyes met and he had a knowing look. "And after you returned from Amsterdam and we talked on the roof, all I had was your friendship. I didn't want to lose that, too."

Tears filled my eyes as he spoke. I reached up to wipe them with my finger, when a classmate joined us. He seemed not to notice my distress, and Vincent deftly turned him aside while I recovered. But I don't think I ever recovered from that moment. When we were alone again I took the conversation in a different direction.

"Will you be staying in town this summer?"

"Yes, but only for the summer. I'm going to the university at Leiden in the fall."

"Oh!" I exclaimed. This was the first I'd heard of it. "I didn't realize you were doing that."

"I want to study engineering."

"You'll be good at it."

"Thanks to your help with math," he grinned.

"You're good with math," I countered. "You just needed a little... encouragement."

"You're a good encourager." He took a sip of coffee. "I was wondering, though, if we might write each other while I'm away at school. Nothing serious," he added quickly. "Just to stay in touch."

"Okay," I nodded. "Just to stay in touch."

❖ ❖ ❖

At home after supper that evening, Mama and I were doing the dishes. She washed. I dried and put them away. "I saw you talking to Vincent this afternoon," she mused as she handed me a plate.

I had no idea where she was going with that comment, so I tried to divert her attention. "Did you enjoy the reception?"

"It was nice. But I noticed when you were talking to him that you seemed on the verge of tears."

My shoulders sagged. "It was awful, Mama."

"What was awful?"

"I asked about his mother—if she was there and which one she was."

"And she wasn't there." Mama said it as a matter of fact.

My mouth dropped open. "You knew?"

"Yes," she nodded. "I thought you did, too."

"No. He said she went to Germany with her boyfriend."

"I think they are married now."

"Why didn't I know this?"

"There was no reason to tell you."

"So, you knew Vincent was living with his aunt all this time?"

"Yes," Mama nodded. "You would have known it, too, if you had been paying attention."

"I thought I was."

"Not everything is communicated with words. Sometimes the most important things are said by what is not said."

"He told me he is going to the university at Leiden. Did you know that?"

"I heard he wanted to."

"Where did you hear that?"

"From his aunt."

"He wants to write."

"He's your friend," she said with a smile. "Why shouldn't he?"

I leaned against the counter. "Do you think I made the right decision?"

"About what?"

"About ...you know...not getting married and all that."

"That is not for me to say. Are you having second thoughts about him?"

"I don't know," I sighed.

"You are always so serious."

"You say that as if it is a bad thing."

"It's not bad, but sometimes I think you do too much."

"I just don't want to make a mistake."

"I understand. That is a good thing. But being careful isn't always the answer."

"So, how do I know if I made the right decision?"

"If you pray and ask, God will show you."

I had been praying, but it seemed I never received an answer. Still, I took Mama's suggestion as a prompting to try again. So that evening before going to bed, I prayed and asked God to show me if I had made the correct decision about my future.

The next morning, I awakened to a bright, sunny day. I threw back the covers, walked to the window, and pushed back the curtains. Across the street, the sun was just rising over the buildings and I watched it a moment as it rose higher and higher.

As I turned away, my eyes caught a glimpse of something red. I looked again and saw the tulips blooming in the window box outside my window. The bulbs Corrie and I had planted the year before, the ones that grew but never bloomed, remained in the box all winter. They came up again in the spring but I put them out of mind, knowing they wouldn't have any flowers. But now here they were, blooming and beautiful, contrary to prior experience and everything Mama told me about gardening.

A smile spread across my face, and I stood there staring at the tulips for a long time. Those blooms were a sign, I was certain. An answer from God to my prayer the night before. Confidence welled up inside me. I felt alive and free. However troubling it might be now, I had made the correct decision regarding Vincent and whether or not to marry. My path to the future was set. Now it was time to move forward into whatever was next.

CHAPTER 8

THAT SUMMER I went to work for Papa in the watch shop. When I was younger, he did everything himself—waited on customers, ordered parts, performed repairs, and kept the books. Business was steady and provided us with plenty to eat and clothes to wear, but often we lived from week to week, sometimes day to day, and on occasion from watch repair to watch repair. By the time I had started secondary school, things had improved and he hired an apprentice named Louis, who had recently moved to town from Belgium. Louis helped with repairs and occasionally waited on customers or wrapped packages for delivery, but Papa still kept up with parts orders, looked after watch and clock inventory, and maintained the ledger of income and expenses— sort of. Together, they did an excellent job with repairs and were adequate in obtaining parts and wrapping packages, but in keeping track of bills, invoices, and receipts from sales they were sorely lacking. That became my job.

At first I found Papa's ledger confusing. There were entries for parts that had been ordered but no corresponding record of payment for them, repairs ordered by customers but no indication the work had ever been billed, and entries for sales but no indication of our cost. To make matters worse, I knew nothing about bookkeeping. Before my first day in the shop, I'd never even seen a ledger, much less recorded the entries in one. Still, it was mostly numbers, I reasoned, and I was good with math, so I dove into the task and did my best to keep things straight.

In between maintaining the ledger, I ordered parts, paid the bills, and wrapped packages for delivery. Those tasks were pleasant and I especially enjoyed preparing the packages for shipment, but by far my favorite duty was waiting on customers. Papa often said that working on a watch wasn't a job, it was a privilege, and that was exactly how I felt about the customers. Helping them choose a watch to purchase, or explaining a needed repair wasn't a duty, it was a joy.

One of my first customers was Joseph Meijer, a Jewish fabric merchant. His shop was located across Haarlem from us, but he made the trek to bring his watch to Papa for servicing. My first day in the shop he brought a pocket watch for cleaning. With him that day was his daughter, Hannah. She was about my height and looked to be about my age, but she was much slimmer, and that first day I saw her, she looked haggard and tired. Papa introduced us and while he and Joseph talked, Hannah and I visited. She was polite but seemed preoccupied, and I found it difficult to engage her in conversation. When they were gone, I asked Papa about it.

"I think it's a matter best left alone for now," he replied.

"Do you know what's bothering her?"

He didn't look up at me as he spoke but kept his eyes focused on the work at his desk. "You should let Joseph deal with it."

A few minutes went by while I thought about it and then I muttered in a voice just loud enough for him to hear, "Aren't we supposed to pray for the peace of Jerusalem?"

"Betsie," he said slowly, drawing out the sound of each syllable in a tone that said he knew I was up to something. "Better to leave it with them."

"Well, aren't we supposed to pray for the peace of Jerusalem?" I insisted.

Papa continued to work. "Why are you asking me this? We pray for the peace of Jerusalem every morning. You know the answer to your own question."

"Yes," I acknowledged. "We pray for Jerusalem every day. And that prayer includes a blessing for Jews everywhere, right?"

"Yes."

"Including individual Jews we might know or meet," I continued.

"Whatever's going on with Joseph Meijer and his daughter is none of your concern. Except for the watch they left for repair."

I couldn't drop it. "Are we not instruments of the blessing we seek?"

This time Papa arched an eyebrow and shot a look in my direction that said he'd had enough. "Yes," he said curtly. "We are often God's agent for the blessing we seek for others."

"Then how can I ignore what I saw and sensed about her? Should I look the other way just because the issue is troubling? Can I at least ask her about it the next time she comes in?"

"You are planning to see her again?"

"Yes," I nodded. "I think I will see her again. I think God brought her across my path for a reason and she'll be back."

"Oh?" Papa had an amused expression on his face. "And how do you think that will happen?"

I smiled. "Someone has to return to pick up the watch."

"Ha!" Papa laughed. "I suppose they will."

A few days later, Papa's friend Rabbi Prins stopped by for his weekly visit. Papa put aside his tools, took down a Bible from the shelf behind him, and the two of them picked up their most recent theological debate, returning to the place where they'd left off during his last visit. When Mama heard them talking she sent down coffee and cake, and for more than an hour they argued and jousted with each other over passages of scripture from the Old Testament. As their discussion neared an end, Papa looked over at Prins and said, "Answer a question for me."

"That is what I have been doing since I walked in the door," Prins chuckled. "I have been trying to help you see the truth."

"I'm serious," Papa added. "I need you to answer a question."

"Certainly, Casper," Prins replied, his face turning serious. "Whatever you wish to know, ask me and I will tell you. So far as I am able."

Papa leaned forward and propped his elbows on the desktop. "Jews still follow the practice of arranged marriages, right?"

"Yes," Prins nodded. "Many of us do, even to this day."

"Where does that practice come from?"

"From the *Torah*. Surely you know this."

"Where in the *Torah*?"

"Abraham sent his servant to find a wife for Isaac. That's the first we have of it, though I'm certain it was not the first time a marriage was arranged, but it was the beginning of the practice for us. We've been following that custom ever since. It is part of our tradition."

Papa had a curious smile. "Still today?"

"Yes," Prins nodded. "At least among the faithful. We have some who do not follow the law, but it is still the orthodox expectation."

Papa glanced over at me and kept going. "How does that work? Do you tell them who they are to marry?"

"Sometimes I do, but most of the time the father and mother arrange the marriage. It's not as harsh as it sounds. Usually, as a child approaches marriageable age the parents determine who among the young people might make a good match for their child. Then they tell their child, 'This one would be acceptable.' Or, 'That one would be good for you.' Then they let the children take it from there. But it is not supposed to be coercive and it is never to be done before the child reaches the age of consent."

"They don't force them to marry?"

"No." Prins shook his head insistently. "That is not allowed, according to the law. There have been many forced marriages, but it is not the law. But I—" Suddenly Rabbi Prins' eyes opened wide and he jerked his head around to look in my direction. "You are arranging a marriage for Betsie?"

Papa leaned back from his desk in a defensive posture. "No, no, no. It's just, the issue came up the other day, and I wanted to make certain we understood the tradition."

"Oh." Prins relaxed. "Well, that's the tradition. Parents of a daughter begin to look for a husband as she comes of age. Same for the parents of a young man. The parents know the families and children of the community—their reputations and qualifications—and they decide whom among the eligible young people they think would work best for their child. The most compatible. But they don't force the couple to marry. At least, not many do."

Louis spoke up. "Nobody tells us who to marry. Not anyone's business."

"We Jews have many traditions that appear strange to the rest of the world," Rabbi Prins explained patiently. "But we respect our traditions just the same."

"A little too much to expect someone to go along with that today." Louis was bent over the worktable, repairing a watch. He spoke without looking up and did not see Papa's eyes. If he had, he would not have made that last comment. I wondered what would happen next, but Rabbi Prins seemed to welcome the challenge of explaining himself and he responded before Papa could speak up.

"On the contrary," Prins countered with ease, "what young man, as he comes of age, could possibly approach this decision with a realistic view of marriage? He knows nothing of what is required to build a lasting relationship, nurture a family, and endure the challenges of life. All he can think of is how beautiful some particular young woman might be, how desirable she might appear, and the conjugal rights he will attain with marriage." Prins glanced at me. "I do not mean to be impolite. I'm just saying, young men—and young women for that matter—are ill equipped to make such a life-changing decision solely on their own. They need help. Our traditions regarding marriage give them that help."

Rabbi Prins' explanation of the Jewish marriage tradition was not without merit, I just didn't like it. I think it made sense to Louis, too, because he had nothing else to say. He focused on the repair work at his desk, and I focused on the ledger. Papa and Rabbi Prins continued to talk awhile about other things until half an hour later, the cake and coffee consumed, he left.

When he was gone, I glanced in Papa's direction with a questioning frown. "Why did you bring up the marriage question? Are you thinking I should get married?"

"No," he said with a wave of his hand. "It had nothing to do with you."

"Then why did you bring it up?"

"I thought it would help you with Hannah Meijer, to understand their traditions—if you see her again."

"Why would that help me with—" My eyes opened wide with a look of realization. "You think that's what was bothering her?"

"I am certain of it." Papa picked up a small screwdriver and focused on the watch that lay on his desk. He spoke while he worked. "Her father and mother arranged her marriage long ago."

"How do you know that?"

"Joseph told me about it."

"When?" I laid aside the pencil I'd been holding in my hand and focused my attention on Papa. "When did he tell you? The other day when they were in here?"

"No," he answered, glancing up at me. "He told me back then. When it was arranged."

"When? How long ago?"

"When she was a young girl," Papa replied.

"A young girl. Before she was accountable?"

"Yes. Long before that."

"Rabbi Prins said it wasn't supposed to happen that way."

"I know," he sighed.

I moved my hands to my hips. "So now she wants out, is that it?"

"Based on what he said the other day, I'd say so."

"Based on what he *said*?" I repeated. "He talked to you about this?"

"Yes."

"Why didn't you tell me then?"

Papa laid aside the tools and looked over at me. "Betsie, in spite of the way they handled it, this is a matter for them to decide. It is none of our business."

"Then what should I say to her if she returns?"

"You should pray about that."

"I will. But I'm not going to ignore her."

Papa picked up the tools again. "I wouldn't expect you to do that."

❖ ❖ ❖

A few days later, Joseph Meijer returned to the shop to collect the watch. As I expected, Hannah came with him. In spite of Papa's warning, I was determined to learn the truth about her situation. As Joseph moved toward Papa's desk, I glanced over at Hannah. "Would you care to join me for tea?"

"Sure," Hannah replied.

I gestured for her to follow me up the stairs. "The kitchen is up here."

Mama, I already knew, was on the rooftop with Corrie tending to the plants. Willem and Nollie were with Aunt Anna at the market, which meant Hannah and I could sit at the kitchen table and talk without interruption. I lit the stove and put the kettle on to boil, then took a seat with Hannah at the table while we waited.

"Having a good summer so far?" I asked, trying to start the conversation.

"I don't know," she shrugged. "I suppose so."

"That doesn't sound like a ringing endorsement." I smiled at her. "Something wrong?" It was a little forward of me to ask a direct question, but I didn't have much time. Joseph was only there to collect the watch. Even with Papa's fondness for conversation, their business together wouldn't take long.

"I'm sorry." Hannah gave a polite smile. "I don't mean to be a poor guest."

"No. It's okay," I said, hoping I hadn't offended her. "I wasn't trying to pry. Just making conversation." I caught her eye. "But you look like you might need to talk."

"I don't think I should."

Water in the kettle on the stove started to boil. Steam passing through the spout interrupted us with a whistling sound. I rose from the table to tend to it. "Do you live near here?" I asked as I stepped to the stove. I already knew they did not, but I wanted to keep her talking.

"We live on the opposite side of town."

I placed tea in the teapot and poured the hot water over it. "Papa said he knew you when you were a little girl."

"Yes," she nodded. "I've known your father for as long as I can remember."

"I can't believe we never met. Are you still in school?"

"I have one more year of secondary classes." She dropped her gaze to the floor and lowered her voice. "But I'm not sure I'll get to finish it."

I placed the lid on the teapot, placed the kettle on the cool side of the stove, and took a seat across from her. "Why not?"

She looked up at me a moment, then glanced away. "I shouldn't have said anything," she mumbled.

I reached across the table and touched her hand. "It's okay. I think you need to say whatever's on your mind." She looked up, and as our eyes met I gave a pleasant smile. "I think you want to tell me."

"I want to tell someone." Tears came to her eyes. "I am…to be married… in a few weeks."

Papa was right. That *was* the problem. Tears streamed down Hannah's cheeks, but I forced myself to remain calm so I could keep her talking. "To whom? Who are you supposed to marry?"

"Tobias Franken," she whispered. "Do you know him?"

"No," I replied. And now that she'd opened up to me, I was at a loss of what to say next, so I asked the next obvious question. "Who is he?"

"His father is an art dealer in Amsterdam."

"So, he is someone you know?" It sounded like a dumb question—I mean, she'd just told me his name—but the whole idea of an arranged marriage was absurd to me.

"Yes." Hannah apparently did not notice the irony of my question. "We've known each other all of our lives." Then she caught herself. "Well… all of *my* life."

"Will he finish school?"

"He's not in my class." Her eyes grew dark. "He's older than I am."

I leaned back in my chair. "How much older?"

"Ten years," she whispered.

This was precisely the thing that bothered me most—an older man taking a younger woman for his wife, forcing her to submit to him, consigning her to a life of misery. I couldn't imagine Papa allowing something like that to happen to one of his children, much less arranging it. "Does your father know how you feel?"

"Yes," she nodded. "But he insists there is nothing he can do."

"What does he mean there's nothing he can do?"

"Tobias' father is a powerful man in Amsterdam. President of the synagogue. Very wealthy. And besides, there was an agreement."

"You agreed to this?"

"No. Not me. I did not agree to anything. But our parents *did*."

"I thought parents selected possible men for you, but you had the final choice."

"I was never given a choice." She wiped her eyes with her fingertips. "The marriage was arranged before I was six years old."

"By your parents." I already knew this and said it by way of indictment more than anything else. The thought of her parents doing this to her really made me angry.

"And my grandparents," Hannah added, pausing to take a deep breath. "My grandfather and Tobias' grandfather were best friends." She gave me a wan smile. "It is the way things have always been done." Then she lowered her head once more. "But I can't do it."

"Then what will you do?"

"I don't know, but I—"

"Hannah," Joseph called from the first floor, "I'm ready to go."

She stood. "I am sorry. I must leave now." Then she turned from the table and started toward the stairs. My heart ached at the thought of what was about to happen to her. And after all she'd told me, I couldn't just let her walk away. I had to do something—anything—to help her.

As she stepped from the table, I came behind her quickly and touched her hand. She turned back to face me, and I said in a low voice, "I will help you. Whatever I can do, I will help you." In the instant I said those words, a light flickered through her eyes, and I knew that she meant what she said—she had no intention of following through on her father's commitment for her to marry Tobias. I only hoped I meant what *I* had said.

"Thank you," she mouthed in response. Then she turned away once more and hurried downstairs.

Hannah was a few steps ahead of me as we moved down the stairs. When we reached the bottom, I moved behind her and held the door open while she and Joseph left the shop. After they were gone, I returned to my desk near the display cases. Papa picked up his loupe, placed it against his eye, and bent over the watch that lay on his desk. "You spoke with her?" he asked while he worked.

"She won't go through with it."

"She has no choice. You heard what Rabbi Prins said. It is their custom."

"Just because it's a tradition doesn't make it right." The anger I'd felt upstairs flared again inside me—anger at Joseph Meijer for dooming his daughter to a life of misery just because he was too afraid to stand up for her and repudiate a decision that should never have been made, anger at the grandparents for their arrogance in attempting to orchestrate the lives of an entire generation solely for their own aggrandizement, and angry at a system that held such a low view of women.

For a moment I was so angry I could hardly move a muscle. I just stood there, staring down at a page of the ledger, the words and numbers a blur of meaningless black marks on a white page. Then I heard the stairway door open in the kitchen. Mama was down from the rooftop. She would know what to do. She always knew what to do. Quietly, I once more laid down my pencil, closed the ledger book, and ran upstairs.

Mama was standing near the stove when I reached the top of the steps. "You didn't pour the tea," she observed. "Would you like some now?"

I flopped down on a chair at the table. "Is it still hot?"

"Oh yes." She poured two cups from the teapot and brought the sugar bowl to the table. I stirred some into my tea, took a sip, and explained what had just transpired with Hannah. Mama brought a cup for herself and took a seat beside me. "You should listen to your father," she said softly. "He knows about these things."

"He knows about the way things have been done in the past," I groused, "but those things are changing."

"Perhaps not as much as you think."

"Women vote now," I argued. "They hold jobs and do things men once did. Nothing is the way it was when he was young."

"But we are not talking about the government or employment." Mama paused long enough to take a sip of tea and swallow. "We are talking about the relationship between a father and a daughter."

I glanced over at her. "You know I respect Father."

"Yes, but I meant the relationship between Joseph and Hannah."

My eyes opened wide at the mention of their names. "You know them, too?"

"Of course I know them. I was there the day Hannah was born. Sat up with them the night her grandfather died. We've known them a long time."

"I didn't know that."

"There are many things you do not yet know and all of them must be learned." She reached across the table and rested her hand on my forearm. "I admire your zeal, Betsie, but you must temper it with understanding. Listen to your father. He is only trying to help you."

CHAPTER 9

A FEW DAYS LATER, Hannah appeared at the shop unannounced. She glanced in Papa's direction as she came through the doorway but quickly looked over at me. "Can we talk?"

"Certainly." I closed the ledger and ushered her out to the sidewalk where Papa and Louis couldn't hear us. "What's the matter?" I asked when we were alone.

"After I saw you the other day, I tried to talk to Father again but he wouldn't listen. He insists there is nothing he can do and that I have no choice but to marry Tobias." She was on the verge of tears.

"Are you going to do that?"

"No!" She shook her head vigorously from side to side. "I can't. I just can't do it."

She was crying by then, and it occurred to me that she might be in physical danger. So I asked, "Has he hurt you?"

"Who?" She looked up at me with a puzzled expression. "Father?"

"No. Tobias."

"No," Hannah looked stricken. "He hasn't touched me. Not even so much as to hold my hand or kiss my cheek." She looked me in the eye. "And I will not let that happen. I'll run away and live in the woods before I allow that man to put his hands on me."

I searched my mind for the proper response, but all I could think of was her father and how angry he would be if he knew she and I were talking. "Does your father know you are here?"

"No one does. They would be livid if they knew I was talking to anyone about this. Especially to someone who is not a Jew." She wiped her eyes with her hands and looked at me once more. "What can I do?"

"What do you *want* to do?"

"I don't know," she answered, the frustration mounting in her voice. "Can you help me?"

She was trapped in an impossible situation, but now I realized I was, too. Hannah was trapped by the promise of her father and grandfather, and I by my own offer to help her a few days earlier. "Yes," I answered confidently, though I was anything but certain of what to do next. "I told you I would help you before, and I will." My mind raced to keep up with my mouth as I continued to speak. "You can spend the night with us tonight while we try to figure this out." Then I took hold of her hand and led her back inside the shop.

Papa glanced up at me as we entered, and I could tell by the expression on his face that he was concerned. But before he could say anything, I announced, "Papa, I have invited Hannah to spend the night with us."

Papa stared at us a moment, then calmly said, "Perhaps Hannah should ask her father first."

Hannah shook her head. "I do not want to do that," she whispered.

"We'll send Willem instead," I improvised. It sounded good when I said it and I turned toward the stairs without looking in Papa's direction, all the while hoping he didn't stop me. To my relief, he remained silent as I hurried up to the second floor, but with each step doubt rushed in. What was I doing? This was none of my concern. I barely knew these people. Why did I care what happened to Hannah? I pushed those thoughts aside and did my best to remember where Willem was right then. Was he in his room, or did Aunt Anna send him to the market already? I couldn't remember.

When I reached the kitchen, I came face-to-face with Mama. "What are you doing?" she asked in a tone even more serious than the look she gave me.

"I invited Hannah to spend the night. Papa thinks we should ask her father first. Have you seen Willem?"

She stood with her hands on her hips. "Why do you need Willem?"

"To send him to see Hannah's father and tell him she's spending the night over here."

"You mean to ask if she can spend the night," Mama corrected.

"Yes, we need to ask him if she can. Is Willem still here, or did he go to the market?"

Instead of answering my question, Mama took me by the arm and led me to the far side of the room. "I do not like this," she said in a low but stern voice. "I don't think this is such a good idea, getting involved in something that is obviously family business. Someone *else's* family business."

"But, Mama," I explained, "she's desperate. If we don't help her, she'll run away. She'll be out there on the street alone."

The look on Mama's face turned from anger to worry. "Run away? What are you talking about?"

I raised an eyebrow. "That's how serious she is about this. She's not going to marry Tobias. She'll leave home before she does that."

Mama looked over at me. "Have they thrown her out? Did she come here because they threw her out of the house?"

"No. She says they don't even know she's here. She came over here on her own. But she's serious about not going through with the marriage. I think she has decided to leave."

"Well," Mama sighed and her face relaxed. "I still don't like being in the middle of this."

"I know, Mama. I know. But she came to me. She sought me out. I don't think I should turn her away. Would you?"

"No," she admitted reluctantly, "I wouldn't. But we will see what her father says. Willem is upstairs in his room. Tell him to go find Joseph and ask if it's okay. We'll let that be the choice. If he doesn't object, she can stay. But if he wants her at home, she must leave. She can't stay here."

"Yes, ma'am," I nodded. "If he says no, she'll have to go home."

From the kitchen I climbed the staircase to the third floor where I found Willem in his room, lying across the bed. I told him our predicament and asked him to take a note to Joseph Meijer.

"That's all the way on the other side of town," he complained. "Mama will never let me go that far alone."

"She sent me to find you and tell you to go."

He pushed himself up from the bed. "All right," he groaned, "but this is going to cost you."

"How much?"

A mischievous look came over his face. "Dishes for a week."

"Okay," I nodded. "I do the dishes." Corrie would help me without even being asked. It was no big deal. I just needed him to get moving.

"Every meal," he continued. "Whenever it's my turn, you take it. When someone asks me to help, you respond."

I smiled. "Agreed—for a week."

He slipped on his shoes and held out his hand. I gave him a blank stare, and he scowled at me. "The note? You were going to give me a note to deliver."

"Oh," I gasped. In my excitement about getting him to go I had forgotten to write the note. I took a piece of paper from his desk and scribbled a message to Joseph, then folded it with even, crisp creases, and handed it to Willem. He took it from me and stepped toward the door. As he was about to disappear into the hallway he paused and looked back at me. "This is about Hannah, the girl who was over here the other day?"

"Yes," I replied. "You saw her?"

"We saw her as she was leaving. Aunt Anna and I were coming back from the market. She's about your age?"

"No," I replied, more than a little amused at his obvious interest. "She's exactly your age. But she's not available right now." That was too much to say and I felt as if I'd betrayed her confidence, even if only in a small way. To cover for it I shooed him with a wave of my hand. "Get going. We need you back before supper."

He looked at me with a grin that spread from ear to ear. "Don't forget the dishes," he quipped, then he moved past the door and out of sight.

"Give that note to Joseph Meijer," I called. "No one else."

"Just make certain you keep up your end of the bargain," he shouted.

By then, the sound of his footsteps on the staircase told me he'd reached the kitchen. I sat on the bed and listened a moment longer as he continued down to the first floor, rattled open the shop door, and stepped outside.

When I was certain he was gone, I rose from the bed and made my way downstairs. Hannah was waiting by my desk. She looked over at me as I arrived and gave me a curious look. "That was your brother who just left?"

"Yes." From the look on her face I knew she was as interested in him as he was in her, and because he was my brother I gave her a hint of encouragement. "He's about your age."

"I thought so."

"He asked about you."

"He did?"

Papa was seated at his desk and just then he cleared his throat, a sign to tell me I should change the subject. "Yes. He did," I answered Hannah, then moved quickly on. "You know, we never actually had that tea I offered you the other day. Care for some now?"

"That would be lovely," she replied. I started back up the stairs and she followed. As she did, she returned again to Willem. "What was your end of the bargain?"

I glanced back at her over my shoulder. "My end of the bargain?"

"Yes. Your brother said something about it as he was leaving."

"Oh. That," I said in a dismissive tone. "Don't worry about that. It was nothing."

"It looked like it was something to him."

"He doesn't like to wash the dishes," I explained. "We take turns each day doing them, and he never likes it when it's his turn. I told him I would wash in his place for the next week if he would take a note to your father."

Hannah's countenance looked troubled. "I am sorry to trouble you. I shouldn't have even come to—"

I said, cutting her off before she could finish the sentence. "Nonsense! You aren't troubling me at all. And besides," I grinned, "I enjoy doing the dishes."

❖ ❖ ❖

Shortly before supper, Willem returned and reported that everything was set with Hannah's father. "He wasn't glad, but he said it was okay." I glanced at Mama and she nodded her approval. A few minutes later, Papa came from the shop and we all sat down to eat around the kitchen table.

Later that evening, after the dishes were washed and put away, Willem and I took turns at the piano. Corrie turned the pages for us and the five of us—Hannah, Willem, Nollie, Corrie, and I—sang at the top of our voices until the neighbors complained about the noise. After that, we played cards at the kitchen table until Papa sent us all to bed. Hannah and I shared the bed in my room. I lent her a gown for the night and she slid down beneath the cover as low as Corrie did when she slept with me. As we lay there, Hannah began to talk.

"I'm not mad at Father for what he did. I know why he did it."

"Why was that?"

"His father and Isaac Franken's father were both lace merchants. They competed against each other for business, so Father and Isaac did, too. Not in business, but in…everything else. Only, Isaac always came out on top. Father, it seems, was never quite his equal."

"You realized this, even as a young child?"

"No, my mother told me."

"How does she feel about the marriage? What's her opinion?"

"She's against it, but she's a woman. Her voice hasn't much sway with the men, other than Father. In public she makes certain to give the appearance that Father is in charge, but at home, out of sight, she is the one who sets the pace."

"I think it must be that way in every home."

"Your mother is that way?"

"Yes," I nodded, "but you'd never know it by watching them together."

Hannah glanced over at me. "We must learn that trait."

"Yes," I nodded. "We must."

She lay there, staring up at the ceiling a moment before continuing. "So, Father and Isaac competed against each other in everything. School, business, even the women they married, always trying to come out ahead of each other. My grandfather liked it that way, the two of them jousting back and forth, but Father hated the constant struggle. Then one night, when I was still a young girl, Grandfather said to Father, 'Joseph, I'm going to help you out. I'm going to give Hannah to Tobias as a wife.' At first, Father objected. 'But that means Isaac wins everything.' 'No,' Grandfather replied, 'it only looks like he wins. But in reality, you win. Isaac is destined to be a rich man. You are not. His children will inherit his wealth, and when you are old, they will use Isaac's money to take care of you.' Grandfather thought that was funny, Isaac devoting his entire life to beating Father, only to spend his fortune caring for Father—at least in one sense—when Father was old." She let out a long, loud sigh. "But I do not think it is humorous at all. In fact, it was rather painful for me and for Father." She looked over at me again. "And that's how it happened. True story."

"So, he did it…on a whim?"

"No," she said with a shake of her head. "He had it all planned out. Apparently the result of much thought on his part. But not a single thought about what I might one day want, or what Father wanted."

"So, why doesn't your father tell Isaac Franken it's off?"

"Because …" Her voice broke. She swallowed hard and tried again. "Father owes Isaac Franken a lot of money. And if he makes Isaac mad, Isaac can take the house we live in, and Father's business, and everything else he and Mother own." She closed her eyes and pulled the cover beneath her chin. Tears rolled down her cheeks and she wiped them on the sheet. "But I have decided to help Father out of his dilemma," she continued quietly. "I am going to make the choice for him. When they go to the wedding ceremony, I won't be there. Isaac Franken can get as mad as he likes but he'll have no reason to be mad at Father. It won't be Father's idea. It will be mine. And by then I will be far away."

That didn't sound like a workable solution to her problem, but I didn't argue with her. Getting her to see that Isaac Franken could think it was her father's trick did nothing to move us toward the answer she needed. So I asked the next logical question. "Where will you go?"

"I don't know." Her eyes opened and she cut them in my direction. "Have you any suggestions?"

"Yes."

Her eyes opened wider and she turned on her side to face me. "Where do you suggest?"

"I have cousins who might be able to help."

"Where do they live?"

"That's just it," I grimaced. "They live in Amsterdam."

"Oh," she groaned. "Tobias lives in Amsterdam."

"I know. My cousins live in the Jewish quarter. Does Tobias live there?"

"Oh my, no," she said with mock disdain and a playful roll of her eyes. "He only goes to the quarter when it is absolutely necessary. The Frankens live on the eastern edge of the city. All the way on the opposite side from here." Then a questioning look came over her. "Are your cousins Jewish?"

"No. But they know almost everyone in Amsterdam who is. And almost everyone there knows them."

"You think they can help me?"

"I think if anyone can, they can."

"Father will not listen to them, and Isaac Franken won't, either. He does business with anyone, but he thinks non-Jews are genuinely untouchable."

"I'll give you their address tomorrow." In spite of what Hannah said, I was certain this was the right thing to do. "If you go there, tell them I sent you and ask if you can spend the night. They will let you stay with them, and if you tell them your problem, they will do their best to help you."

We talked for a while longer, but it was late and conversation lagged. After a few minutes I noticed Hannah's eyes were closed and her breathing took the easy rhythm of sleep. I lay there a little longer, just to make certain. Before long, I heard the clock on the shelf downstairs by the shop window strike the hour. It was eleven o'clock, and even with all that ringing, Hannah didn't budge, so I was convinced she really was asleep.

Carefully, I rolled aside the cover, crawled from the bed, and opened the top drawer of my dresser. A pouch lay in the back corner. I lifted it out and tugged on the golden drawstrings that held it closed. With my fingers, I reached inside the sack and took out twenty guilders. I'd collected the money from gifts I received over the past year and from the salary Papa paid me for working in the shop. It wasn't much but it was enough to purchase train fare to almost any city in the country with a little left over for a bite to eat along the way. I'd come by it through considerable effort and the thought of giving it away raised a moment of doubt in my mind, but I pushed against that doubt. Hannah needed the money far more than I did, and besides, I would have more next week when Papa paid me.

I placed the money on the dresser top and found a piece of paper from a bookshelf by the door. Standing near the window, in the light from the moon and the glow of a streetlamp on the corner, I scribbled down Gerrit and Margriet's address, then put the paper on the dresser with the guilders and returned to bed.

CHAPTER 10

WHEN I AWAKENED the next morning, Hannah's side of the bed was empty. I pressed my palm against the sheets and found they were cold. Wherever Hannah was now, she'd been gone from my room for quite some time. Slowly I turned back the cover, swung my legs over the side of the bed, and shoved my feet into my slippers. A robe lay across a chair near the dresser and I snagged it, then slipped my arms into it while still seated on the bed. Finally, I pushed myself up to a standing position and rubbed my fingers over my eyes. "We stayed up too late," I said to myself.

As I started toward the door, my eyes fell on the dresser and I saw the money and note were missing. Downstairs in the kitchen, Mama confirmed what I already knew. "She left this morning. Your father saw her leave as he came down to put on the coffee."

I took a seat at the table, propped my elbow on the tabletop, and rested my chin in my hand. "Think she'll go back home?"

"I don't know," Mama replied.

Aunt Anna passed by my chair. "You look tired. How late did you stay up?"

"I heard the clock strike eleven."

"No wonder you're moving slow this morning."

Mama spoke up again. "What were you two talking about that kept you up so late?"

"Tobias, the marriage, and how much she doesn't want to go through with it."

"Do *you* think she's going back home?"

"I don't—"

Just then, Corrie appeared in the doorway. "Your friend Hannah left already," she blurted out. "I saw her out my bedroom window."

With my eyes barely open I smiled at her. "Did you tell her good-bye?"

"I waved to her," Corrie offered. "But she was already outside by the time I came from the bed." She moved to the stove and reached for the coffeepot. Aunt Anna stopped her with a word of caution and handed her a potholder. "Use this instead of your bare hand."

"Oh, right," Corrie said sheepishly. "I keep forgetting."

"You won't do it twice," Mama chided. She glance in my direction but thankfully never returned to the conversation Corrie interrupted. And I didn't wait around for her to remember it again, either. I rose from the table and returned to my room to dress.

❖ ❖ ❖

Later that morning, Joseph Meijer came to the shop looking for Hannah. I was at my desk working with the ledger when he arrived. Papa glanced up as he entered. "Joseph," he said in a friendly voice. "Three times now in the space of two weeks."

"I just came to collect Hannah," Joseph replied in a businesslike manner. "No time to visit today."

"She isn't here," I replied.

"Where is she?" he asked with a puzzled look.

"I don't know. She spent the night," I explained, "but left before I awoke."

Joseph looked away for a moment and ran his hand over his forehead. "I know she was upset," he sighed. "I assume you know why."

"Yes, sir."

"Any idea where she went?"

When I hesitated, Papa spoke up. "Betsie," he said in a parental tone, "there's no point in hiding the matter."

"Mr. Meijer," I began as I pushed back my chair and stood, "could I ask you something?"

His puzzled look turned to one of irritation. "What?" he said with a sour tone.

"If you know she's upset, and you know why, then why make her go through with it?"

"I'm afraid it is not that easy," he answered in a curt manner.

"It can't be that difficult, either," I countered.

He took a deep breath and let it escape, as if pausing a moment to muster his patience. Then he said, "The man to whom she is promised for marriage is the son of an important leader in the synagogue in Amsterdam." He glanced in Papa's direction. "Isaac Franken. He's an art merchant and a dealer in rare coins and books. You know him?"

"No," Papa replied. "I don't. But I don't know as many people in Amsterdam as I once did."

"He is very wealthy," Joseph continued. "Well respected and held in esteem by almost everyone."

"And his son?" I interjected. "What is his reputation?"

Joseph dropped his gaze to the floor. "A boy of privilege in a man's body." He said it without affectation, but I could see the anger in his eyes.

"And Hannah doesn't like him," I continued.

"No," Joseph agreed.

"Then," I shrugged, "what is the problem with not marrying him?"

"It would not be a good idea to disappoint the father."

My eyes opened wider. "And I know why," I said softly.

Joseph's eyes suddenly came alive and he glared at me. "She shouldn't have told you that."

"I don't think you'll be able to avoid that issue, do you?"

"What do you mean?"

"Whether you stop the wedding, or Hannah fails to appear, the result will be the same. She and Tobias will not be married."

"That's my problem," he said with a sharp tone. "Do you know where she is?"

I took a deep breath. If I refused to answer, Papa would demand it and if I persisted in my refusal, a scene would follow. But if I told Joseph what he wanted to know, he might go looking for Hannah and that would be a problem, too, and not just for Hannah but for Gerrit and Margriet. At the same time, Hannah needed her father to rescue her and in order for him to do that, he had to know where she was. All of that presented a dilemma for me and I rolled it around in my mind as we stood there staring at each other.

Thinking about what to say took longer than I expected and when I didn't speak up promptly, Papa rose from the chair behind his desk and came to my side. Gently, he slipped his arm around my shoulder and pulled me close. "I think you should tell him," he said calmly. "But if you don't, I'll stand behind you."

The kindness in his voice caught me off-guard. I knew he loved me and that he only wanted the best for me, but right then I was overwhelmed by his display. Tears came to my eyes and I swallowed hard, trying to retain my composure. At last, in a soft voice I said, "I think she went to Amsterdam."

A frown wrinkled Joseph's brow. "To Amsterdam?" He looked worried. "You mean she took the train?"

"I don't know for certain. But that would be my guess."

"She didn't have any money of her own. How would she pay the fare?"

I gave him a knowing look and saw an angry scowl come over his face, but Papa spoke up. "Joseph, they are just two girls trying to make their way through a dangerous and uncertain world."

"I know," Joseph sighed. "It's just, Tobias lives in Amsterdam and I don't want her to see him right now without me present." He looked down at me. "Was she going to his house?"

"No," I replied. "I don't think so."

"Then where?"

I moved away from Papa's grasp, leaned over my desk, and scribbled the address for Gerrit and Margriet on a scrap of paper. With the note held firmly in my hand, I faced him and said, "I'll give you this address if you promise not to make her marry him."

"She is my daughter." Joseph squared his shoulders and thrust out his chin in an oddly defiant manner. "She must obey me."

"She is your daughter," I replied in as tender a voice as I could manage.

"You must love and defend her."

At those words, a sense of sadness came over him and the corners of his eyes drooped. "A refusal to marry Tobias would ruin me," he lamented. "It would ruin the entire family."

"It might bring you to that end," I conceded, still with my eyes focused on his. "But if the situation is ruined, I think you know what caused it and it wasn't Hannah."

Joseph's shoulders slumped, and for a moment I was sorry I'd said anything at all. Then, just as quickly, I remembered Hannah and the look in her eyes the first day I met her. She deserved more of a life than she was about to get with Tobias, and it was a life she didn't have to take. One made necessary only because Joseph refused to take responsibility for his own decisions. Part of me wanted to reassure him, to extend a sympathetic nod and let him off the hook, but the other part of me wouldn't budge. So I stood my ground and waited for a response. He could promise not to force the marriage and get the address, or he could refuse and find Hannah on his own.

After a moment he nodded his head. "All right, I'll agree. She doesn't have to marry Tobias. I won't make her."

"Good." I thrust the paper toward him.

He took it, scanned it quickly, and reached for the door. As he was about to step out, he tipped his hat to me and said, "I hope she always has a friend like you."

❀ ❀ ❀

A few days later, Isaac Franken appeared at the shop. He had an arrogant, condescending way about him, not as a man born to privilege but one much harder—of one who had fought his way up, endured, and never met a challenge he couldn't overcome. By force of will and with great effort, he'd reached a level of success that insulated him from many of life's economic undulations. Yet having attained that level of comfort it turned on him and made him harsh toward others. It was as if he'd deserved that lifestyle all along and only been deprived of it earlier by the schemes of others too cheap or afraid or unwilling to take it for themselves. I don't know how I knew this or whether I really ever *knew* it. I just felt it. He was arrogant and at the same time brusque in a defensive way. His clothes were perfectly tailored, each hair on his head was combed neatly in place, his shoes were shined to a brilliant luster, but just the way he walked set my teeth on edge. Even before he spoke a word, I did not care for him.

Tobias trailed after him, always a few steps behind. Shorter and not nearly as dignified, he reminded me of a puppy that cowered behind its master. Like his father, he wore clothes made to impress, but he carried himself in a sloppy, less intentional manner and certainly not as one who commanded respect. Rather, the kind who couldn't tell you what he wanted in life, and whatever he had, whatever life he led, it was just always there for the living, and so he lived it as it came to him—not in a carefree manner, either, but as the scraps of someone else's life that somehow fell onto his plate.

With a quick turn of his head, Isaac glanced around the shop, his eyes surveying the display cases and shelves on the wall behind Papa as he introduced himself, but he wasted little effort on polite conversation. Instead, after he and Papa shook hands, he got straight to the point of his visit. "I understand Hannah Meijer is residing in your home."

"No," Papa replied. "She is not here."

"I was told she was."

"You were told in error."

"I must warn you," Isaac continued. "Finding her is a matter of gravest concern to me. I have many friends in influential places and they will all tell you I won't stop until I find what I'm looking for."

"I'm sure Hannah's safety is of much concern to you, but I assure you, she isn't here."

Isaac gave Papa one of those tight, condescending smiles. "Her safety is of concern to me, but that's not why I'm here and I'm sure you know it. Mr. Ten Boom, you are known in Amsterdam as a man of honor and someone sympathetic to the Jewish cause. As one knowledgeable in our ways, and a friend of Joseph Meijer, I am sure you know the nature of my business with young Hannah."

"Actually, I believe it's your son's business. Not yours."

"It was a promise to me," Isaac retorted. His face was red and his jaw tense.

"It was a marriage promise," Papa replied coolly.

"Yes!" Isaac roared. "A marriage promise. A sacred commitment!"

"But it was not a promise that Hannah made," I said, diving into the conversation.

At the sound of my voice, Isaac snapped his head around and glared at me. "Young lady," he fumed with eyes bright as flames, "must I remind you that women are to be seen and not heard? You should keep to your work and remain silent until I request a response from you."

Papa bolted upright from his chair at the desk, but I responded before he could speak. "The promise you're looking to enforce was a promise made by Hannah's grandfather to your father. It wasn't a promise from Hannah. She didn't agree. So not only was it not her promise, it was contrary to your own tradition."

Isaac looked over at Papa. "Who is this urchin?" he demanded.

"She is my daughter," Papa said calmly.

"And you allow her to speak to me this way?"

"It's not him you're angry with," I kept going, "and it's not me for speaking out of turn. It's that promise that makes you angry."

"You are not only rude, you're insolent. But since you brought it up, how would a promise of a bride for my son make me angry—except that you people are standing in the way of that promise's fulfillment?!"

"You're angry because you know I'm right. The promise of Hannah's grandfather cannot possibly bind her with an obligation to your son, or to anyone else, for that matter. And it was an attempted commitment that stands in direct contradiction to your own sacred tradition, a tradition that requires her consent, which is why marriage commitments cannot be made before one reaches the age of accountability. And so this promise will fail—it must fail—and there isn't anything you can do to prevent it except shout at a young girl and a watchmaker. Because for the first time in your life you will fail to get the best of Joseph Meijer."

"This is utter nonsense and an outrage."

"No, sir," I retorted. "The outrage is in your behavior."

"My behavior?"

"Yes. Your behavior. Attempting to coerce that young girl into a life of slavery." I pointed to Tobias. "A life she would spend waiting on your son, hand and foot. A life she would spend at his beck and call, any time of the day or night."

"The life you describe is the life of any woman who marries. Even a Protestant woman such as yourself."

"Perhaps it is, but at least for us it is a life we choose. Not one to which we are shackled against our will by the decision of a prior generation and enforced by the coercion of the present."

Isaac looked back at Papa. "She can't talk to me this way. No woman may speak to me in this manner and certainly not a mere girl. I protest this indignity."

"Protest all you like," Papa replied. "Your father made that promise, and that promise died with him five years ago when he pitched headlong from a wagon." He looked Isaac in the eye. "Yes," he nodded, "I know a few things about you, too. And I know your reputation, one of bullying others into doing as you demand. It isn't going to work here."

Franken's face turned red and his eyes narrowed. "How dare you speak of my father in this manner."

"And how dare you barge in here and accost us like indentured servants."

"This is a Jewish matter, between our families, to be settled by our traditions and customs."

I spoke up once more. "No. It isn't. This isn't about your traditions. It's about a sum of money Joseph Meijer owes you—one he cannot repay—and your attempt to use it against him to enforce the promise of a dead man. And all to get your son a wife so he can give you a grandson."

Isaac was taken aback by the unexpected revelation of his private affairs. "A sum of money?" he gasped. "What are you—"

At last Tobias interrupted. "Father, what is she talking about? This is the first I've heard of money."

"Stay out of this," Isaac snapped at him.

"But if it—"

"I assure you," he said tersely, "it has nothing to do with that."

"Joseph Meijer thinks it does," I added, hoping to keep Tobias engaged in the argument. "That's why he won't say anything to you about voiding the marriage."

Isaac looked at us both, first at Papa, then at me, and with a snide voice said, "You two only think you know what you're talking about. But I assure you, you don't. Now give me the girl, or tell me where I can find her, and we'll be on our way."

"She isn't here," I said.

"Then tell me where she is."

"I can't," I replied, shaking my head.

"Perhaps I should call the police and file charges. Then they will search this place from top to bottom, and who knows what they will find."

"On what charge?" Papa asked.

"Oh, believe me," Isaac said with a sarcastic tone. "I can find a charge that will suffice to turn this hovel inside out."

"Insult us all you like," I said defiantly. "But I'm not telling you where she is."

Isaac turned to Papa, but he pointed at me. "She will ruin you if you let this continue, Casper. I promise, she will ruin you."

Papa stepped toward the door, then turned, "Mr. Franken, you can get any order you like and return with any policeman you like." He reached the door and opened it. "The station is just up the street. But for now, get out of my shop." Then he opened the door even wider and gestured with a sweep of his free hand. "I think it's time for you and your son to be gone."

Isaac stared at Papa a moment, as if he was unsure what to do, then reluctantly motioned for Tobias to follow and together they stepped out to the sidewalk. When he was outside the shop, Isaac glanced back at Papa one last time. "You will regret this decision."

"I doubt it," Papa replied and pushed the door shut.

Father and I watched through the window as Isaac and Tobias started down the street in the opposite direction from the police station. While we watched, I heard footsteps from behind us and turned to see Mama at the bottom of the staircase. "I have never seen a more arrogant man in my life," she gasped. "Who on earth was that?"

Papa smiled at her. "You were listening?"

"Yes, I was listening. I couldn't avoid listening. He was speaking so loud, the neighbors probably heard." She glanced at me. "Who was he?"

"Isaac Franken."

"Such arrogance," she said with a tone of disbelief. "Such utter arrogance." Then she looked over at me. "You were right about this. All along you were right. Hannah has no business marrying into that family."

A satisfied grin spread over my face and I felt my cheeks turn warm. Inside I felt full and rich and lovely. Sometimes Mama could say the nicest things.

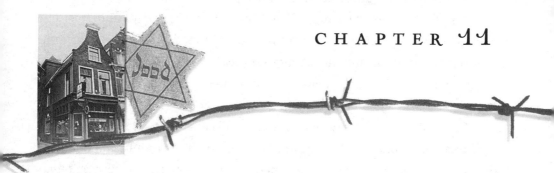

CHAPTER 11

FOR THE REMAINDER of the summer, life followed a typical and much calmer pattern. Our day began each morning with our family gathered for breakfast around the dining table. Afterward, Papa read from the Bible and we prayed, always including a request for the peace of Jerusalem and blessing on the Jews. Then I followed Papa downstairs to the shop while Mama, Aunt Anna, Corrie, and Nollie tended to the house. Willem helped them with some of the tasks and ran errands to the market for the merchants in Grote Markt, but for the most part he was left to himself, which usually meant reading a book in his room or playing sports in the alley with kids from the street behind the house. In the fall, that routine changed as Willem, Nollie, and Corrie returned to school, but for the next several years we followed that basic pattern—awaken, breakfast, devotions, and the tasks of the day.

The shop was open on Saturdays, but Sundays were a day of worship and rest. We attended services at St. Bavo's Cathedral, about a block from our house. Papa thought the ministers who served there were far too theologically liberal and, left to his own devices, would have attended church somewhere else, but he felt compelled by the Holy Spirit to attend St. Bavo's. So every Sunday morning we put on our finest clothes and walked up the street to sit in what Papa called "the great stone edifice." During the warmer months—spring, summer, and early fall—I attended those services, but as winter approached I stayed home to avoid exposure to illnesses that typically emerged during our coldest weather. Dr. Tromp had been correct in his assessment of my condition. With regular doses of the liver extract formula he created, I was able to maintain a normal but careful lifestyle.

As the years passed, Corrie grew from a little girl always underfoot to a young lady on the verge of blossoming into adulthood. About that same time she began spending time in the afternoon with a friend from class named Emma Schouten. The Schoutens lived about four blocks from us in an apartment above Mr. Schouten's butcher shop.

Every afternoon, Corrie and Emma would come to the house for a snack, and then they would sit at the dining table or up on the rooftop amid Mama's flowers and talk, mostly about the romance novels they were reading. Emma's mother loved romance novels, and that's how Emma got interested in them. She, in turn, convinced Corrie to read one, and after that, Corrie had her head in one of those cheap paperback books all the time. I once tried reading one of them just to see what it was like, but I only made it through three paragraphs before tossing the book aside. The writing was trite, the characterization thin, and the premise nonexistent—the sole point being a cheap and tawdry appeal to one's otherwise restrained and inhibited interests. When Corrie wasn't reading, she was daydreaming about a life that reflected events and values in those stories. In short, she was a typical impulsive, self-absorbed teenager.

Late one afternoon I found her in her room, stretched across the bed, reading yet another of Emma's novels. Being an older sister and quite certain I knew how to order the lives of those around me, I confronted her on the matter.

"You spend a lot of time reading those books."

"They're fun. And besides, it helps me."

"Helps you with what?"

"Well," she explained, "this one's written in German. So reading it helps me learn that language." Papa insisted we all learn at least one other language besides our native Dutch. I learned English, as had Mama. Corrie took German lessons from a woman who lived three blocks over who taught her in a conversational style, not by a textbook. It was great for conversation but not much help with reading, and if the romance novels forced her to perfect her language skills, that much was a good thing. So I switched tactics.

"How much time do you spend reading the Bible?"

"Enough," Corrie replied, turning away to focus on the novel. "Papa reads to us morning, noon, and night." The tone of her voice made me bristle, but I forced myself to keep quiet. I stood there trying to think of what to say next, but she was absorbed in the book, so I found an excuse to leave the room.

By then, Nollie was in her final year of secondary school. Willem was attending the university in Leiden, where he was studying for a career as a clergyman. One weekend in November he came home for a visit and brought a friend named Karel. They were both first-year students, which meant Karel was five or six years older than Corrie. Later in life, an age difference of that amount might mean very little—plenty of men marry women four or five years younger than themselves. But when one is fourteen and the other nineteen or twenty it's a disparity not only of age but of temperament and interest, a disparity too great to ignore. It's also a difference an adult would notice immediately, but a fourteen-year-old of the opposite sex might not readily perceive. Corrie perceived it not at all and spent the weekend following him from room to room, staring up at him with her big brown eyes as if lost in some romance-novel trance. When she wasn't tagging along with Willem and Karel, she was in the kitchen with Mama talking about him. I heard them from my desk downstairs in the shop, and after supper, when Willem and Karel were studying, she came to my room and talked about him until bedtime.

But if Corrie was self-absorbed, Karel was self-centered. At that age, Corrie's world view was defined only by her own interests. She was not uncaring or malicious, she was simply and totally preoccupied with the world as she and Emma wanted it to be and as they found it in those romance novels. Karel, on the other hand, was manipulative, duplicitous, and attuned only to the personal advantage he could gain from the situations he encountered. This attitude appeared in the way he served himself first at the table, reaching for a bowl without passing it to others, insisting on the softest pillow at night, and appropriating the most comfortable chair. On Saturday afternoon we sat in the parlor playing the piano and singing, and all the chairs were taken. When I entered the room, he remained seated, refusing to offer his place to me. But when Mama arrived, he was ever so solicitous of her. She was, after all, the one who cooked and cleaned for him while he was our guest.

These were little things, of course, and easily dismissed or explained, but they bothered me and because of them I came to have a low opinion of him, even in those first few days he was with us. In the beginning I thought it had more to do with me being irritated by the disruption a guest brought to our daily routine, but the more I observed the more convinced I became that I was right—he was conniving, manipulative, and sneaky. I never liked people who were sneaky.

Late that Sunday afternoon, Willem and Karel boarded the train for the return trip to Leiden. They were gone and I was glad of it. Seeing Willem was always a treat, but I had endured all the Karel manners from him and all the Karel talk from Corrie that I could stand. I was looking forward to a few hours of peace and quiet at the house. But no sooner were they gone than Corrie launched into another long-winded account of the virtues of Karel. And not just for one afternoon, but for the next two months all we heard from her was talk about Karel. I tried, as gently as I could, to raise the age difference, the attitude issues, and her obsessive fixation on him, but she paid no attention to my hints or suggestions. Finally I did as I had always done with her, I just listened and let her talk until she'd talked herself out. Only now she wasn't a little girl anymore, and those sessions took much longer.

One morning, after enduring yet another breakfast dominated by Corrie's recollections of Karel's weekend visit, Mama called me aside. "Wait with me," she said, and I stood with her by the counter while the others went downstairs. When they were gone she said, "Let's have some coffee."

It seemed like an odd request. "We just had breakfast."

"I know, but we'll get some coffee and take it up to the roof."

It was early December and already there was snow on the ground. I gave her a questioning look. "Isn't it cold up there?"

"We'll be fine. I was up there earlier and dusted off the chairs." Aunt Anna was at the stove and she turned to us with two cups already poured. "Ah," Mama smiled, "thank you, Anna." Then she opened the door to the stairs. "Come on," she gestured with a nod of her head. "We can spend a few minutes together before you go down to the shop."

On the roof Mama took a seat in the wooden chair and I sat on the old one from the kitchen. I could tell by the marks in the snow that she'd placed them side by side. I took a seat next to her and placed both hands around my coffee cup to keep them warm. The air was indeed cold up there. Steam rose from the coffee, and ice crunched beneath my feet, but from all I could tell, Mama didn't mind. She settled into place and took a sip of coffee as casually as if we had all morning to spend. After a moment I asked, "What's this all about, Mama?"

"I've been listening to you in your conversations with Corrie."

"Well," I said slowly, "we haven't had much of a conversation lately. Mostly it's her chattering incessantly about Karel, and me listening."

"That's what I want to talk to you about." She paused to take another sip of coffee, then continued. "I know that you have chosen not to marry and I understand why. But that was your decision based on your own reasoning about your medical condition and the circumstance that poses for you. I don't fault you for it at all. But Corrie does not live with the things you do. She is free to choose her own way and that might not be the same as the way you've chosen for yourself." Mama glanced over at me. "In fact, I doubt very much that her life will be anything like yours."

I wasn't at all comfortable with the tone of her voice but she was Mama and I knew better than to give my emotions free rein in addressing her. "What does that mean?" I asked.

"It means she's not a little girl anymore. She's fourteen now, with only two more years of school to complete. If she wants to marry and move away—if they all marry and move away—and you are left here alone with your father and me and Anna, then that's how it will be. And if the thought of living like that makes you uncomfortable, then perhaps you should reconsider your decision about how to live your life and whether or not to marry. But you can't expect Corrie to stick around this house the rest of her life, just to keep you company."

"Is that what you think this is with her? Is that why you think I'm suspicious of Karel?"

"I don't know what it is or why you're suspicious, but the thought did occur to me. And it also occurred to me that you might not be aware of your motives."

Sometimes Mama could be so infuriating. "I am certainly not trying to keep her from marrying." Anger flared inside me but I stuffed it down. "I just don't like him."

"You've made that quite clear."

"And I'm afraid she sees this as a scene from one of those romance novels she's always reading." Of that much I was certain, but I hadn't much insight into my own emotions about the matter.

"She does spend a lot of time with them," Mama conceded, "but this is a matter for her to decide."

"She's only fourteen years old," I snipped.

"Yes, and I would remind you, at that same age you were telling me that was plenty old enough to make the decisions you made about your future."

She had a point, but I wasn't ready to concede it. "That was different," I sighed.

"Not much."

We both paused and lifted our cups to take a sip when the stairway door opened and Nollie appeared. "Let me guess," she said, not at all startled to see us, "you're talking about Karel."

"No," I corrected with a snide tone, "we were talking about Corrie."

"Okay," Nollie regrouped, "about Corrie *and* Karel."

"You two should be careful about gossiping." Mama looked up at Nollie. "I thought you were in school."

"I forgot an assignment, and Mr. Van der Beck let me come home to get it."

"So you found it, I suppose?"

"Yes."

"Then what brings you up here?"

Mama was in a mood and Nollie knew it. She glanced at me with a look that said so, then smiled back at Mama. "Aunt Anna said you were here," she said quickly. "I'm glad you two are discussing the situation with Corrie. All she ever talks about is Karel this and Karel that. It's driving us all crazy. Does she not realize how much older he is than she?"

I nodded in agreement. "I've tried to tell her about that, but she won't listen to me."

"I mean," Nollie continued, "he's an alright guy, I suppose. I'm not interested in him, but he seems okay to me. It's just that Corrie won't stop talking about him."

Mama lifted her cup for a sip of coffee and peered over the rim at Nollie.

"Make sure you stay uninterested in him."

"Mama," Nollie retorted, "why do you say such a thing?"

"Because you have to respect Corrie's feelings. Both of you. She has shown you her affections for the man, and whether you think they are genuine or merely the infatuation of a schoolgirl, you must respect her enough to give him and her a wide berth."

I was astounded at what she said and looked over at her. "Mama, you can't possibly mean that you would approve of a relationship between them."

"Of course not. I haven't lost my mind yet. A mother could not possibly allow a fourteen-year-old to get involved with a man five years her senior." Mama pushed herself up from the chair. "I simply require peace in my own household. The last thing we need around here is for the three of you to get jealous of one another." She gestured with a wave of her hand. "Come on, both of you. Time for us to get busy."

CHAPTER 12

MAMA WAS RIGHT, of course. I still wrestled with my decision not to marry, and seeing Corrie fawning over Karel brought my personal angst to light in a painful way. I wanted nothing to do with him emotionally, but the notion that Corrie was free to pursue a man's company and affection, and I was not, left me feeling irritable. And, as only an older sister could do, I channeled that frustration into a sense of superiority, as if anyone serious about life would have made the same choices I made. It was all very condescending, although I didn't see it that way at the time, nor did Corrie.

Looking back now from my current perspective I can see that for most of my life up to that moment I was afraid of intimacy in almost all its forms—emotional and intellectual as well as physical and, perhaps, even spiritual. But back then my understanding was clouded by one simple fact: More often than not, I was correct in my assessment of others. I might have gone overboard in trying to orchestrate the circumstances and events in the lives of family and friends, and I might have communicated my opinion in a less than temperate manner, but my perception of the truth about their circumstances was usually right. I was right about Hannah and her desire not to follow through with a marriage arranged by her grandparents and ratified by her parents, and I was right about Karel's attitude. I was also right about many aspects of Papa's business—the condition of the ledger and his on-again, off-again billing practices, just to name a few—but he was reluctant to admit it at first.

Then one morning not long after Mama talked to me on the rooftop about Corrie and Karel, a large delivery truck arrived on our street and rumbled to a stop in front of a vacant building directly opposite us. The building was located next door to a furrier, Benjamin Weil, and had last been occupied by a cobbler's shop, but it had stood empty for most of the year. With the truck parked out front, workmen spent most of the morning busily moving back and forth between the empty storefront and the truck as they unloaded boxes and furniture, then everything inside.

As the morning passed, I kept an eye on them through our display window while I worked at my desk but I wondered who might be moving in there. It was clear to me they were taking the furniture at least to the apartment upstairs on the second and third floors. The shop on the first floor wasn't large enough for everything they unloaded, which meant that whoever was moving in was planning to live there, too. I tried not to say anything about it—Papa didn't like it when we paid too much attention to our neighbors. He thought of it as snooping. Nollie and I thought of it as a heightened sense of concern about the interests of others. So I kept my thoughts to myself and did my best to contain my curiosity about what might be happening at the shop across the street.

Shortly before lunchtime the workmen finished emptying the truck. They slammed the doors shut, latched them, and drove away. At last, as the truck disappeared up the street, I could restrain myself no longer. "Who do you suppose is moving into that old cobbler's shop?" I asked to no one in particular.

"I'm sure we'll find out soon enough," Papa replied casually.

Louis looked over at him. "How so?"

"Benjamin Weil," Papa chuckled. "He'll find out all about what's going on and he'll be over to tell us before long. Weil has never been good at keeping a secret."

Sure enough, in the middle of the afternoon Weil came to the shop, beaming with a sense of pride one often gets from knowing something others do not. "You saw the truck?" he asked, knowing full well that we did.

"Yes," Papa replied. "They spent most of the morning unloading it."

"They're opening a shop over there." Weil was bursting to tell someone what he knew and his words came in rapid fire. "Meyer and Gretel Kan. Came here from Rotterdam." The smile on Weil's face became an irrepressible grin. "And you know the other part?"

"Tell us," Papa said, though Weil needed no encouragement.

"He's a watchmaker," Weil laughed, "just like you. Can you imagine?" He slapped his leg. "A watchmaker moves his family here from Rotterdam to open a watchmaker's shop, and he puts it right across the street from the best watchmaker in town."

"Ah," Papa nodded in mock approval. "A colleague. What brought him here to Haarlem?"

"I don't know," Weil shrugged. "Family, I suppose. He has a cousin who lives a few blocks over."

"Interesting," Papa nodded once more.

The look on Weil's face turned sober. "I hear Kan is good."

"Where did you hear that?"

"Lenny, the cousin who lives a few blocks away, told me. And his neighbor's brother lives in Rotterdam, too, and knows Kan. Said he's a good watchmaker and a shrewd businessman." Weil's sober expression turned to a look of concern, as if this new shop might pose a threat to Papa's business.

Papa seemed not to mind at all. "Shrewd?" he asked, just to keep the conversation going.

"That's what he said."

"Maybe that's why he left Rotterdam," Papa suggested as he leaned back in his chair.

Weil looked puzzled. "What do you mean?"

"Sometimes shrewd translates into something worse." I'd never seen Papa play someone quite like this and I enjoyed every word of it.

"Ah," Weil nodded. "I see your point. I don't know, but I'll find out." That's what Papa wanted—more information.

"And," I added, hoping to encourage Weil to say even more, "putting your business near another of the same type isn't a bad idea. People are already coming to that neighborhood for your competitor's products anyway, might as well let him do your advertising for you."

Weil had a troubled expression. "Hmm, I never thought of that." We'd heard a rumor earlier in the year that a new furrier was coming to town and might be locating on our street. With the shop empty next to Weil, I had speculated that the new furrier might locate there, but Weil refused to consider the possibility, dismissing it as a ridiculous suggestion from one who knew nothing about business. I hadn't argued with him at the time but endured his disdain in silence. Now, with a new watch shop located opposite ours, his earlier argument evaporated and I didn't appear so much like a young girl in a man's world.

Weil and Papa talked a few minutes more and then Weil wandered back across the street. As I watched him through the window, Papa came from his desk and stood there gazing across at the newly occupied shop. With a glance over his shoulder in my direction he asked, "You think they really did that?"

"Did what?"

"Opened their shop across the street from ours to take away our customers."

"Yes," I replied. "I think they did."

Papa stared out the window a moment longer, then returned to his chair behind the desk, picked up his loupe, and fitted it against his eye. "I suppose we'll find out soon enough."

At first nothing much happened with Kan's new shop. He opened for business about a week after moving in, and I noticed a few people stopping to gaze through his display window, but no one seemed in a rush to shop there. Our business, meanwhile, remained unchanged. We sold a few watches each week but received most of our income from repairs and cleanings. Two weeks later, though, that all changed when traffic into Kan's shop increased noticeably.

Neither Papa nor Louis said anything about it, but I couldn't keep quiet. "What do you suppose he's doing in there that attracts so many people to his shop? It's a watch shop, after all, not the meat market or the grocer."

"We have all the work we can handle right here behind our own door." Papa cautioned, "Just keep to your own tasks and let them do theirs."

I didn't care for his tone of voice but it was true—for once he and Louis had a backlog of work waiting to be performed. Still, the sight of all those people at our competitor's store instead of ours bothered me. "You think we ought to go over and see?" I asked.

"I think people are curious about someone new in town," Papa replied without looking up from the watch he was adjusting. "That's all. Just curious." He cut his eyes in my direction. "You are, and they are, as well."

"We haven't sold a new watch all week," I continued, ignoring his last comment.

"It'll settle down in a few days."

But it didn't and I watched through the window as more and more people streamed into Kan's shop and our own work declined. Papa and Louis caught up on the cleanings and repairs, which meant they had time during the day with nothing to do. At first, Papa spent the extra time reading the Bible but after a few days he added a midmorning walk on which I accompanied him through the neighborhood. During one of those walks I asked again about going over to see Kan's shop to find out what he was doing that attracted so many people.

"You should stick to bookkeeping," Papa replied, repeating his earlier suggestion that I mind my own affairs. "Don't make any more of it than it is. God knows we are here. He will send business when we need it. That is enough."

After a week or two, repair and cleaning picked up again and Papa felt vindicated in his view of how to conduct business, but new watch sales remained slow and I was worried. Clock sales dwindled to little or nothing. Finally curiosity got the better of me and I sent Louis across the street to visit Kan's shop. I think Papa was curious, too, because he didn't object. When Louis returned, he told us the news.

"They have a selection of watches at least as large as ours, and about the same age, but his are all mass produced."

"Mass produced to look just like our handmade watches?"

"Yes," Louis nodded. "But he sells them at prices below ours."

"For inferior quality," Papa added.

"Yes," Louis nodded. "But I don't think the customers can tell the difference."

"They will in a year or two," Papa replied.

"We could sell ours at cost and point out the better quality."

"But we could never match his price," Papa argued. "We would always be higher."

"We could show people he is a fraud," Louis added.

"No," Papa snapped. "I will not attack a man simply to gain a sale."

"We could try a different supplier," I suggested.

"We've been using the same suppliers since I took over the shop," Papa replied curtly. "It would be an insult to them for us to take our business elsewhere."

I glanced up at Louis. "So he's deliberately setting his price below ours?"

"He sends people in here to check our prices, then he sets his price just a little lower." It didn't take long for word to get around that you could buy watches like the ones we offer for less just by walking across the street from our shop.

"But they aren't the same watches," Papa observed.

"That is something we can point out without attacking Kan." I didn't wait for Papa to reply but looked over at Louis. "Any idea how many cleanings he gets?"

"None," Louis said flatly.

His answer astounded me. European watchmakers were traditionally just that—watchmakers. They made watches. In days gone by, they acquired the pieces, fitted them into the cases, and assembled them from scratch. Many had their own designs for critical parts and they all had a unique touch for adjusting the settings. That kind of craftsmanship produced an exquisite product but it was also expensive. Sales of new watches were infrequent and once purchased, owners were reticent to dispose of them, which meant watchmakers spent more of their time repairing and maintaining older watches than they did selling new ones. Mass production of cheaper watches was changing that practice, but no watchmaker in Haarlem sold only mass-produced pieces without also engaging in the repair side of the business.

"None?" I asked.

"I heard someone ask about it and he said he wasn't equipped for it right now."

The next day, Herman Slurring, one of Papa's friends and a loyal customer, was in the shop browsing through the display cases. Slurring inherited ownership of a thriving steel mill from his father and had money enough to shop without regard for price. As a result, he had an extensive collection of watches and clocks. When he visited our shop, he insisted on seeing only our best watches, which made waiting on him especially joyful.

While I was assisting Slurring that day, Weil arrived to pick up a watch he'd left for repair. Papa came from his desk to get it for him. "I saw your apprentice go into Kan's shop," Weil said, with a glance in Louis' direction. "You were checking him out?"

"We were curious," I replied, speaking up before Louis or Papa could answer. "I sent him."

Weil had a wide grin. "Kan brags about sending people over to check your prices, then setting his just a little lower. He does it on purpose. Says you never even notice." He glanced back at Papa and his voice took a serious tone. "Kan wants all of your business, Casper."

"Others have tried," Papa chuckled. "But they're gone and we're still here. And we'll still be here long after Mr. Kan is gone, too."

"He's selling an inferior product at a premium price," I added. Papa shot me a disapproving look but I ignored him and kept talking. "His watches look like ours but they aren't handmade."

Weil's eyes opened wide. "He's selling mass-produced watches at a price comparable to your prices for handmade watches?"

"Exactly," I nodded.

"And hoping no one can tell the difference," Weil sighed.

"Or, that no one cares," I responded.

When Weil was gone, Papa put down his tools and looked over at me. "Betsie, I thought we weren't going to do that."

"Do what?"

"Attack Mr. Kan."

"I wasn't attacking him. I was merely pointing out the difference between our product and his."

"Well, I don't like it."

"Papa, most of our customers are our friends. They have a right to know the facts about the products they purchase. We have an obligation to advise them properly."

Papa turned his attention back to the watch on his desk. "Telling Weil is like announcing it to the world," he muttered.

"Which is only the reverse of how you use him," I countered.

"What does that mean?"

"It means you use him to gather information from the neighborhood without having to inquire directly yourself. I'm just doing that in the other direction."

While we talked, Herman Slurring looked through the display case by the window. Normally, discussions like that were reserved for times when no one else was around, but Slurring wasn't merely a customer. In spite of their differences in wealth and social standing, he and Papa were the closest of friends. Slurring had dined with us often and spent many Sunday afternoons in the parlor with Papa discussing theology, the news, and the nature of their respective businesses. He turned to Papa with a smile. "I admire your confidence."

"I'm not worried about Kan."

"I didn't mean that," Slurring laughed. "I meant your confidence in arguing with Betsie." He looked over at me and gestured with the watch he was holding in his hand. "Kan's strategy only works if people don't care about the quality. What does that tell you about your customers?"

"Some shop for price. Others shop for quality. And it's always been that way."

"Exactly. People who know quality and aren't opposed to paying for it will never leave you for an inferior product, so long as they know it is inferior."

"And we have a strength he doesn't have."

"What is that?"

"Right now he doesn't do repair work."

"So he's not a competitor in the repair business."

"No. And if he continues to sell a cheap product, we'll actually gain repair work from repairing the watches he sells."

Slurring looked over at Papa with a grin. "Betsie has a good mind for business. You should be careful I don't steal her away to work for me."

After that, Papa stopped questioning my ideas about how to run the shop and started listening to me.

CHAPTER 13

WHEN FALL ARRIVED, Corrie began her final year of secondary school. She was fifteen years old. Nollie was still living at home but studying to be a teacher. Not long after the new school year began, a letter arrived from Willem, who was still at the university. It was addressed to Nollie. She read it to us at the supper table.

"'The university music department is having a special event the second weekend in October. Several of our student choirs are preforming along with a choir from London. I thought you might like to come for a visit. You would enjoy the concert, get to meet some new people, and have a taste of university life.'" There was more to the letter, but she paused and glanced around the table. "Sounds like fun. What do you think?"

"Perhaps that would be a good thing," Mama said.

Almost immediately, Corrie piped up. "Do you think I could go, too?"

Without so much as a glance in anyone's direction, Papa said, "Only if your sister agrees."

Nollie gave Mama a knowing look. Mama shrugged, and Nollie said, "Well, okay. It might be good not to travel up there by myself."

For the next three weeks, Corrie chattered about Karel at every possible moment. She wondered aloud if he would remember her. Fretted constantly about what she should wear for the trip, worried about how many outfits she should take and what she would need for the various events. Aunt Anna must have sensed my growing frustration because without being asked she took over the packing process, helping Corrie determine what to take. I heard them at night in Corrie's room and from the sound of their laughter Aunt Anna enjoyed the task as much as anyone possibly could.

When the day finally arrived for the trip, Papa hired a cart to carry Nollie, Corrie, and their luggage to the train station. He and Louis helped the driver load everything and when it was time for them to leave he gave Nollie and Corrie a few guilders to spend. Money was often tight for us, but Papa never allowed us to embark on a trip, no matter how short or long, without money in our pocket.

After they were gone, Mama walked upstairs and I returned to my desk in the shop. Later that evening, though, I found myself in the kitchen talking about Corrie and her obsession with a university student as old as her brother. Once I got started, I couldn't stop and I chattered about Corrie as much as Corrie chattered about Karel, recounting for Mama and Aunt Anna yet one more time all my concerns about him.

"I am certain she will see him. He and Willem are good friends. They spend a lot of time together. It would be impossible for her not to see him."

For the first time, Aunt Anna spoke up on the topic. "And that's a problem? Her seeing him is a problem?"

"It will just start the Karel talk all over again."

"Seems to me she's had a pretty good go of it already, without seeing him."

"Yes," I nodded. "My point exactly. She was insufferable before the trip, she'll be even worse when she gets home."

"I thought he was a nice boy," Aunt Anna continued. "Very polite when he visited us."

"Yes, but that's just it," I protested. "He seems nice enough until you look closer."

Aunt Anna gave Mama a roll of her eye but said nothing more about it, and we all worked in silence for a while.

"Well, Betsie," Mama said finally, "I trust your intuition and your ability to hear from God but I also trust Corrie, though I admit she's a little impulsive at times."

"And totally obsessed with this."

"I know," Mama continued, "but whatever you do, be careful. These are real lives—hers and his—and you don't want to make a mistake."

❖ ❖ ❖

Corrie and Nollie returned home late Sunday evening. Papa collected them from the train station and hired a wagon to bring their luggage. They arrived at the house with much to tell, though Corrie occupied most of the conversation with talk of Karel. Apparently, he remembered her and, from what I could tell, they spent a good deal of time together. After they were settled from the trip, I caught up with Nollie in her room, hoping for a better accounting of the weekend from her perspective.

"It's true," Nollie acknowledged. "He remembered her and from the way he acted I'd say he is interested." I folded my arms across my chest. She put up her hands in a defensive gesture. "I know that's not what you wanted to hear, but I think Karel really likes her. They spent a lot of time together."

"Alone?"

"Not too much alone. We did almost everything with him and Willem. The four of us, and one or two others sometimes. But Karel and Corrie were obviously a pair. He looked after her and escorted her wherever we went."

"But not alone?"

Nollie's eyes darted away. "A walk or two, I think."

I knew what that meant. "How many times?"

"I don't know." She turned away and arranged things on the desk near her bed. "We weren't there that long. Just a couple of days. Why all the questions?"

"I'm just concerned."

"Concerned?" She shot a glance in my direction. "About Karel?"

"Just concerned," I replied, avoiding her gaze. "How was the trip otherwise?"

"It was good." She moved away from the desk and sat on the bed. "Great concert. And a beautiful campus."

"Wish you had gone there instead of normal school?"

"No." Nollie had a curious little smile. "I like things where I am just fine."

"What does that mean?"

"Oh, nothing," she replied.

I knew better but decided not to make an issue of it and turned to leave. "There is one other thing," Nollie added as I reached the door. I turned back to face her. "On the train home, Corrie was writing a letter to Karel."

"She has his address?"

"Yes," Nollie replied. "And I think he agreed to write to her, as well."

I just shook my head in disbelief and walked away.

❖ ❖ ❖

Late that winter, we learned that Dr. Brunel was retiring from his practice of medicine. I was concerned about what that might mean for my health and how I would obtain the liver extract formula that had kept me alive. He assured me that a new doctor, Jan van Veen, was coming to take over his practice and that they had already discussed my case.

A week after his arrival in town, Dr. Van Veen came to the house to check on Mama and me. His sister, Tine, came with him and during the visit we learned that she worked as his nurse. She was a beautiful young woman, about Willem's age, and contrary to my reaction to Corrie and Karel, I was struck by the notion that she and Willem needed to meet each other. I was also mindful that if she was working as Dr. Van Veen's nurse, then Irene Drebbel must have been dismissed.

Early that spring, Willem came home from school for a weekend visit. While he was there, Dr. Van Veen made one of his regular house calls to check on Mama. As before, Tine came with him. I introduced her to Willem, and the two began seeing each other socially. The ensuing courtship brought Willem home every other week. On each visit, Corrie peppered him with questions about Karel.

During one of those visits, I found a few minutes alone with him and asked about Karel. "I'm worried about Corrie. She's at least five years younger than he, and the distance and—"

"She seems quite taken with him. Are you aware she writes to him almost every day?"

"I know. And he writes to her."

"I had no idea Karel was corresponding with her. He made it sound like she was the only one doing the writing."

"And I had no idea she was writing him every day. But it makes sense. He's about all she ever talks about around here."

"I can imagine."

Willem had a knowing look on his face that left me thinking he knew more than he was saying. "What is it?" I asked. "What are you not saying?"

"It's just …" He had a pained expression on his face, which sent my curiosity soaring. I had to bite my lip to keep from pressing him harder to give me an answer. "It's just that … This is awkward to say. But …Karel isn't like us."

I had a puzzled frown. "What do you mean?"

"He's studying for the ministry, but he has a very different approach from the one I have taken."

"What does that mean?"

"He doesn't really see the ministry as service to God. More like …"

"What Father calls the 'liberal' view?" I asked, finishing his sentence.

"Somewhat," Willem chuckled. "I think he actually believes, which is more than I can say for some, but more than that, he sees the ministry as a profession, not a calling. A way up and out, not a means of service to God or others."

The corners of my mouth turned up in a look of disdain. "It's a job."

"Yes," Willem nodded. "Exactly. A job. A path of upward social mobility. An avenue toward some ideal of respectability."

"And how does Corrie fit into that?"

"That's just it," Willem grimaced. "His view of marriage, of women he's seen socially, is much like his approach to the ministry. It's not really something he feels from the heart—I sense no passion about the institution of marriage or the notion of being with someone for life. Not with Corrie or any of the other girls he's seen since we arrived on campus. I think for him marriage is rather another means of improving his and his family's lot in life."

"His family?" The frown on my forehead deepened. "What do they have to do with his choice of a spouse?"

"It's been their sole aim since the day he was born."

"His selection of a spouse?" I found the notion of their meddling in his choice quite preposterous, though that was exactly what I'd been doing with Corrie.

"Yes," Willem acknowledged. "They intend for him to *marry well*, economically speaking, and I don't think Corrie—or our family, for that matter—meets that expectation."

We talked a little longer, then it was time for him to meet Tine. When he was gone, I went up to Mama's room to check on her. She was in bed recovering from another coughing spell. I sat on a chair next to her, intending to stay only a few moments, when she took my hand in hers. "I overheard you talking to Willem."

"You heard us?"

"My door was open."

"Oh. Sorry."

"No. Don't be. You were right in your intuition about Karel."

"Oh, Mama," I sighed. "What shall we do?"

"I don't know, but whatever it is, we must do it carefully and prayerfully. We can't let Corrie make a mistake in this, but we can't protect her completely, either."

"This is a difficult thing to make sense of."

"I know. But that's because it's a matter of the heart, not the head. You can't make rational sense of love and romance."

"It's all those romance novels she reads."

"She's still reading them?"

"Oh my, yes," I said in a flabbergasted tone. "Now more than ever. I think it's her way of escaping. She reads those books and sees herself in them with Karel. It makes no sense to me for her to do such a thing but I try not to talk to her about it."

"That's what I'm talking about. You see things from an intellectual perspective. As a matter of the head. For Corrie, this is a matter of the heart."

"Did you know she is writing to him?"

"Yes," Mama nodded. "I saw her writing to him just the other day."

"Willem says she writes Karel every day."

"And she's received almost as many letters from Karel."

"You know about that?"

"Your father sorts the mail each morning. He gives them to me."

"He doesn't want me to see them?"

"He knows how you feel about Karel."

"She's my sister."

"Yes. And those letters are for her. Not you."

"So, what are you saying?"

"I'm saying, Corrie is old enough now that she'll have to sort this out for herself."

"She's not thinking about sorting anything."

"I know. But whatever she's doing, we'll have to let her do it. And if that means she gets hurt in the process, we'll have to be the ones who are big enough to let her try, and fail, and still be there for her in the end."

I didn't like that advice. My natural inclination is to fix whatever is broken. Still, her comments rang true within my spirit and I decided right then that I would say nothing else about the matter and let the relationship run its course. That would prove to be more difficult than I first imagined.

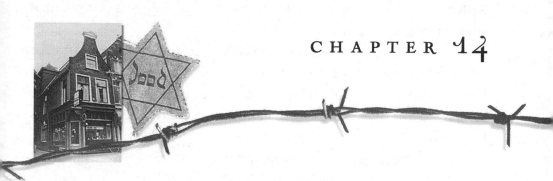

CHAPTER 14

WHILE LOVE AND ROMANCE dominated our household, tensions rose across Europe as political pressure increased from many groups demanding reform of the monarchies that ruled most European nations. Women demanded the right to vote and enjoy the same social freedoms afforded men. Though less militant, those favoring democracy in many places sought to minimize the power of the monarchy by strengthening the legislature and adding a prime minister to serve as head of government. Communists and Socialists wanted to end monarchical government altogether. Every edition of the newspaper brought reports of protests in the streets of all the major cities. Constitutional monarchy became the watchword of the day. For those of us who loved the queen and trusted her to do the best for all, anarchy seemed ready to overwhelm us.

In response to growing unrest, monarchs throughout the continent began spending more and more on national defense. This was particularly so for those who felt threatened by the widespread push for change. Our own Queen Wilhelmina, though not opposed to change, was no different from the others in that respect and increased spending, too. With extra money in the economy, business at the Ten Boom watch shop was good.

As other groups agitated for change, Jews became more vocal and active in the drive for better living conditions. Long the objects of oppressive policy, they wanted an end to many of the social restrictions placed upon them. Some were calling for the creation of a Jewish political state in Palestine and the reestablishment of the nation of Israel as a political entity. Rallies were held in various cities around Europe. One was planned that summer for Amsterdam.

A few days before the rally was to take place, Rabbi Prins came by the shop with Chaim Wolffsohn, a professor from Manchester University in England and current leader of the Zionist Organization, the largest of the several groups leading the call for a new Israel. He and Papa became friends immediately.

"Rabbi Prins has told me of your interest in Israel," Wolffsohn said heartily. "And of the Jews here in Haarlem."

"God's chosen people are still His chosen people," Papa replied.

"That is not a concept many of your fellow Christians are willing to embrace."

"Sadly," Papa nodded, "you are correct."

I understand you and your family pray every day for the peace of Jerusalem." Wolffsohn had a questioning look. "Is that true?"

"Yes," Papa nodded again. "We have done so for almost a hundred years."

"But not Casper personally for that long," Prins laughed.

"Oh no," Papa said with a chuckle. "I am getting old, but not that old. It began with my grandfather and then my father, and we have continued that prayer in a line of intercession that reaches all the way to my children. Every morning we pray for the peace of Jerusalem and for God's blessing on the Jews."

"I was wondering," Wolffsohn said, "could you tell me why you do this?"

"We're told to. It's right there in the Psalms. 'Pray for the peace of Jerusalem! May they prosper who love you.' David exhorted his people to do that, and we are doing it still."

"We are glad for the support, but we need more good men like you to help us. Non-Jews who will speak up and act on Israel's behalf."

"There are some here who are sympathetic to the Jewish cause," Prins added, "though I think some support us because they think if we had a state in Palestine we would all leave here and go there and they'd be rid of us."

"Tell me something." Papa leaned back in his chair. "If you had this new state, how many people do you think would actually go there to live as full-time residents?"

Wolffson sighed. "That is difficult to say. We were driven from our land by the Romans almost two thousand years ago. Since then, we have wandered the world without a home. Some settled in Spain, others in the area that is now Poland, yet though we've been in Europe almost as long as anyone, still we are treated like outcasts. I do not know how many of our people would actually move there immediately, but I think that number would grow as they saw it as a place where they could worship and live in freedom, without the prejudices and hatred we endure now."

"I agree," Papa nodded. "And I think God agrees with you, too."

Their visit lasted almost an hour, and when Prins and Wolffsohn were gone, Papa and I went for our morning walk. He had work to do at the shop—interest in Kan's watch business had ebbed, helped along by news that his prices did not match the quality he offered—but the morning walk that we'd added to our routine to fill up the slack time back then had become part of our normal routine. It was an enjoyable break from the sometimes tedious work of watch repair and gave Papa a chance to see people who didn't normally come to the shop.

As we made our way over the four-block route that encompassed our neighborhood, we came upon Rolfe Ameling, a policeman who patrolled the streets near our house. He paused as we drew near and waited for us to reach him. I could tell by the look on his face that he wanted us to stop. Papa tipped his hat as if to pass him by, but Rolfe spoke up. "Mr. Ten Boom, I understand you had a visitor this morning."

"We have many visitors," Papa replied with a smile. "That's the point of having a shop."

"Rabbi Prins came by to see you."

"As he does every week. Is that a problem?"

"No. Rabbi Prins is a fine fellow, but we've had some questions about the man who was with him this morning."

"Wolffsohn?"

"Yes."

"What kind of questions?"

"Some people are saying he's here to organize the Jews for a revolt."

The normal blue of Papa's eyes turned to hazel, and I knew he was upset. "Anyone who would say that," he replied, "hasn't taken the time to talk to him."

"That's probably true," Rolfe chuckled. "Do you know why he's in town?"

"He's trying to organize support for the creation of a Jewish state. They're having a rally in Amsterdam next week." Then he looked Rolfe in the eye. "Just who exactly have you been talking to?"

"I'm not sure I can say."

"So," Papa said with a hint of indignation, "you can stop me on the sidewalk and ask me questions that besmirch the name of a man you never met, and do so at the insistence of someone else, but you can't tell me who it is that's making these accusations?"

Rolfe glanced around, checking to see if anyone was watching, then leaned closer and said in a low voice, "Irene Drebbel."

"Dr. Brunel's former nurse?" I asked.

"I'm afraid so," Rolfe replied.

"She's just angry because she wasn't hired by Dr. Van Veen when he took over Dr. Brunel's practice."

"That's probably true," Rolfe nodded, "but she found out about your visitors and came straightway to the station. Spent an hour talking to the desk officer. So," he shrugged, "I have to talk to you."

"Well, you've done your talking," Papa said with a dismissive gesture.

"I'm sorry, Mr. Ten Boom," Rolfe continued. "I'm just trying to do my job."

"Look," Papa said with a hint of frustration, "I've known Rabbi Prins longer than you've been alive. His character is above reproach."

Rolfe nodded. "I would concur but—"

"And," Papa said without giving Rolfe a chance to continue, "I didn't spend much more than an hour with this Wolffsohn fellow but I'd say he's straight, too. As for the revolution, perhaps you should inquire as to whether

Mrs. Drebbel has taken to strong drink." Then Papa tipped his hat and with a curt, "Good day to you, officer," he led me up the street.

When we were a safe distance away I turned to him, my mouth agape and my eyes wide. "Papa, I've never heard you talk like that about anyone."

"Mrs. Drebbel was always a busybody," he growled.

"But you suggested she was given to strong drink."

"Maybe someone should look into it," he said with a mischievous smile. "You never know what they might find."

"But you don't know that for a fact, do you?"

"Rather like suggesting to Weil that Kan sells second-rate watches at first-rate prices?"

"Oh, Papa," I giggled. "That was different."

"Not so much as you think."

I wanted to know more about Mrs. Drebbel but I knew better than to press the issue right then.

The rally in Amsterdam was held as planned, but without Papa's presence. Although it was widely publicized it was not as well attended as organizers had hoped, primarily because events surrounding other issues overshadowed it. Political tension, already running high, reached a fever pitch over emerging Serbian nationalism. Within weeks we received reports that Franz Ferdinand, Archduke of Austria, had been killed by a Serbian gunman as part of an ill-fated attempt to pry Slav provinces from the Austrian-Hungarian Empire. Papa was certain that would be enough to push everyone into war. "They all have mutual defense treaties," he worried. "Supposedly it would keep them from being able to fight, but I think the opposite is true. They will be compelled to fight." His words proved prophetic.

In July, the Austrian-Hungarian army invaded Serbia. Soon all of Europe was plunged into war with Great Britain and France leading the Allies into battle against the Central Powers of Germany, Austria-Hungary, the Ottoman Empire, and Bulgaria. Everyone assumed the Netherlands would join the war on the side of the Central Powers, but Queen Wilhelmina declared our neutrality. We were relieved, as it meant there would be no conscription of soldiers, which in turn meant Willem wouldn't have to face the dilemma of whether, as a minister of the Gospel and a candidate for ordination in the church, he should serve or declare himself a conscientious objector.

As one of their first acts of war, the Allies established a blockade to prevent supplies from reaching Germany. In spite of the Netherlands' neutrality and the protest of the queen, our ports were included in that blockade. Ships attempting to travel to or from our coastal cities were seized. The flow of goods into the country shrank dramatically and before long, shops in Haarlem experienced shortages. Many of the everyday items we had come to expect were difficult to obtain, and the economy took a turn for the worse. Business at our shop slowed even more than when Kan came to town.

In spite of the war and the hardships it brought, Willem and Tine continued to see each other on a regular basis, with Willem coming home two or three times each month. That winter, to no one's surprise, he proposed and she accepted. The wedding was set for May. Corrie, of course, was swept up in the romance of the moment.

With the war raging, fabric and sewing notions were in short supply, but Famke Janssen, who owned a millinery shop down the street from us, had connections to fabric merchants in Austria and they were able to get a bolt of silk. She had known Willem since he was a baby and offered the fabric to us at cost. Even so, it was still expensive but we scraped together enough money to pay for it and thought of it as a gesture of support for Willem and Tine. With the material, Aunt Anna and I made dresses for us all and a handkerchief for Papa to tuck into the pocket of his suit jacket.

While we worked on the dresses and gathered ideas for the wedding service, Corrie chattered, slipping seamlessly between talk of the wedding and of Karel, occasionally blurring the distinction between the two. More than once I was certain she'd lost track of just whose wedding we were planning. Several times I wanted to suggest that she find a different subject for conversation, but each time I tried to speak, Mama cut me off with a look that said I should keep quiet. And on those occasions when I was not looking for her signal, Aunt Anna pressed her foot against mine in a not-so-gentle manner, followed by a shake of her head.

On the morning of the wedding, I helped Corrie dress and prepare her hair. She was even more excited than before; she could hardly sit still, and all the while she talked of Karel.

"Do you know for certain Karel is coming?" I asked in the hope of somehow breaking the verbal stream long enough to make her think.

"His last letter said he was."

"When did that arrive?"

"Two weeks ago."

"You've been writing to him every day?"

"Yes."

"And he writes you every day?" I knew the answer but I didn't want to admit it.

"No," she replied. "Usually about every two weeks. I know," she added hastily. "I write more often, but he's busy with school."

"So you haven't heard from him in two weeks?"

"No. But I can't imagine that he would miss the wedding. He's one of Willem's friends."

She continued to talk about him, though at a somewhat slower pace than before, telling me what Karel had said in his letters, the things they had in common, all the wonderful character qualities he possessed. Once or twice she slipped in comments about what she wanted for her own wedding, and I was certain she had convinced herself that she and Karel would soon be married.

In the afternoon, Willem and Tine were married at St. Bavo's Cathedral. Mama, Aunt Anna, Corrie, and I appeared in our silk dresses, and though they were all cut from the same fabric, we looked quite fashionable. As Corrie expected, Karel attended the wedding and, from what I could see, was impressed by the way she had rather obviously blossomed into an attractive and eligible young woman.

After the service, we all walked together down to the house where Karel visited with us until late that evening. When it was time for him to leave, Corrie walked with him downstairs while Mama, exhausted and coughing, went to bed. Aunt Anna and I straightened up the dining room, then turned to the dirty dishes in kitchen.

"Karel seemed quite the charming guest," she said, baiting me for the familiar topic.

"Yes," I replied while I decided whether to take the bait. "He was quite the gentleman."

"Are you still worried about him?"

"No," I said, shaking my head.

"Betsie." Aunt Anna cut her eyes at me. "Tell the truth."

"Okay," I sighed, giving in to one more round of Corrie and Karel. "I'm not worried about him. I'm worried about Corrie."

"Why?"

"She is just so...infatuated with him she's not even thinking about this in rational terms."

"And that is wrong?"

"I know. I know. It's a matter of the heart, not the head. But I just think she's looking right past the obvious and seeing what she wants to see."

"The obvious?"

"He's almost finished with college. She just finished with secondary school. He's five years older than she. And—"

"She's a beautiful young girl," Aunt Anna said, interrupting me. "He's a handsome man. She's supposed to be infatuated with him."

"Yes, but there is something about Karel that I don't like."

"You've made that more than abundantly clear."

"I just want what's best for Corrie and I don't want to see her hurt."

"Listen," Aunt Anna said, resting her hand on my shoulder. "I agree. Not everything about him adds up, but I think we must let Corrie deal with that part. We must respect her feelings and give her some space."

"I'm just afraid she will end up terribly hurt. She still thinks of this as a page from a romance novel."

"Yes," Aunt Anna nodded. "She may end up with a broken heart. But she can recover from that. If we intervene, she'll be hurt by us, and I'm not certain she would get over that so easily."

Just then I heard the door close downstairs and Corrie's footsteps coming slowly up the stairs behind me. I glanced over my shoulder as she appeared in the doorway, and from the smile on her face I knew what happened as they said good-bye.

CHAPTER 15

IN JUNE, Willem graduated from the university. A month later he was ordained and assigned to a church at Lisse, halfway between Haarlem and Leiden. It took a few weeks for him and Tine to get moved and settled, but we made plans to travel there to hear his first sermon. First sermons were a big event in the Dutch Reformed Church. People came from everywhere to hear him. We all traveled by train to attend and arrived several days early.

Willem and Tine lived in a large three-story house located across the street from church, and with just the two of them to occupy it they had plenty of room for guests, so we stayed with them. Arriving early gave us plenty of time to get settled and catch up on the latest family news. While we visited, Mama, Aunt Anna, and I helped Tine unpack the remaining boxes from their move and arrange the house to receive the many guests we expected would stop by on Sunday afternoon after Willem's sermon. Papa spent the extra time touring the town, meeting other watchmakers and shopkeepers.

Corrie was supposed to help us clean and decorate, but the day after we arrived, Karel came to call. He and Corrie went for a walk and were gone most of the afternoon. I wanted to protest—we were all working hard to help get the house ready—but Mama stopped me. For the duration of our visit, Corrie and Karel spent every afternoon together, walking, talking, and whiling away the time.

At night, after everyone else had gone to bed, Corrie kept me up until well past midnight talking nonstop about where she and Karel had gone and the things they talked about—for the most part, dreams for the future and how that might unfold. I kept quiet and listened, but the more I heard the more troubled I became. If Corrie's version of their time together was accurate, their relationship had grown far more serious than I first imagined.

That Sunday, Willem delivered a brilliant sermon and afterward the congregation held a reception to celebrate his entry into the ministry. Corrie was there and very much with Karel, hanging on his arm, smiling while he talked, laughing at all his jokes. I watched from across the room while standing near several of Willem's former classmates from the university. With little effort, I overheard them talking about Karel, laughing over memories of life when they were in school. Then their banter took a more serious turn.

"Who is that?" one of them asked with a gesture toward Corrie.

"She is Willem's sister," someone replied.

"Lovely girl," another commented.

"Yes," the first one acknowledged, "but poor thing. Look at her. She's obviously been ensnared by the Karel charm."

"Too bad," the second replied, "he'll never stay with her."

"Mother won't allow it," another chimed in.

"Ah yes," the first one said with a mocking tone, "dearest Mother. Can't disappoint her."

After a while, people drifted away and before long the crowd had thinned considerably. I walked with Tine over to the house and we prepared a light lunch for Papa, Mama, and the others. They arrived within the hour and we ate in the dining room. A little later, Mama went upstairs to rest and Papa dozed on the sofa in the front parlor. Then Karel came by for Corrie and they went for yet another walk, which left only a few of us at the house. I found Willem alone on the back porch, propped against the railing, staring out at the flowers that grew in the yard.

"Great sermon," I said.

"Thanks," he replied without looking. "I was a little nervous."

"No one could tell."

He glanced over at me. "Could you?"

"Once or twice," I shrugged, "but only because I've seen you speaking in Mr. Van der Beck's class."

A smile pushed up his cheeks. "That was a long time ago."

"Yes, it was."

He stood and turned to face me. "Corrie seems to be spending a lot of time with Karel."

"Yes," I nodded. "She is indeed. Is he enjoying it as much as she?"

"Difficult to say."

"Oh? How so?"

"He has always been the kind to say one thing and do another. After Corrie visited the campus that weekend, she started writing to him. I saw him one day with one of her letters, and he said rather derisively, 'Another missive from your little sister.' But I noticed he read them all. And kept them, too, by the way."

"He kept them?"

"Yes. Had them in a box beneath his bed."

"I was standing with some of your friends this afternoon at the reception."

"I saw that. They wanted me to join them but I refused. Last thing I need is for them to tell my parishioners old college stories before anyone has a chance to know me themselves." He had a playful smile. "Whatever they said about me, I assure you it wasn't even half true."

"Actually, they were rather cute about it."

"Must have been on their best behavior. Some of them haven't seen the inside of a church since confirmation."

"They did have telling remarks about Karel, though."

"What did they say?"

For the next few minutes I recounted their conversation. Willem listened with a pained expression. "That's what I was referring to before," he said when I was through. "That day we talked about this at home. That's what I meant. He is intent on marrying someone at the top of the social order. Royalty would barely meet his family's standard," he scoffed.

The back door opened and Tine appeared. "Is this a private conversation or can anyone join?" she asked with a smile.

Willem slipped his arm around her waist. "We were just talking about Corrie and Karel."

"Oh," Tine said, rolling her eyes. "You mean Karel and his *mother*."

I raised an eyebrow. "You know about this?"

"Everyone who knows Karel knows about his devotion to his mother," Tine replied. "No man has ever been so desperate for approval."

"Like I said before," Willem continued, "Karel's an only child. His mother and father have big plans for him. Ministry is just one step toward fulfillment of those plans. Marriage is another. They have been planning this since the day he was born. His one overriding goal in life is to *marry well*."

"And," Tine nodded in agreement, "I'm afraid Corrie will never fit into that picture."

"She would be an excellent wife," I said defensively.

"No doubt about it," Tine replied. "But she's not from the correct class of society. At least not for Karel's mother."

"And it's not just Corrie," Willem added, "but all of us. It's the entire family. *We* don't fit into the life she has in mind for him."

"Well," I said with a resolute sigh, "I think we have to talk to Corrie about this."

"But not today," Willem replied. "I don't want to talk about it now. It's too late and she will have just come in from seeing him. That would be cruel."

"Then tomorrow." I was determined to face this down once and for all. "We can talk to her in the morning."

The next morning after breakfast, I found Corrie alone in the front parlor. Willem joined us and the three of us stood near the window looking out on the lawn and the street beyond. Willem glanced in her direction. "Are you and Karel going for a walk today?"

"Yes," she replied. "I think so. He's not going home for a few days yet."

"We need to talk about him."

"Oh? What about?"

"Are you under the impression that things are getting serious between you two?"

"Well, I suppose." She glanced away nervously. Her cheeks turned pink. "You could say that." Willem cleared his throat and glanced down at the floor. "What?" Corrie asked, her eyes suddenly wide with wonder. "Is something wrong?"

"Well...I don't know." Willem was struggling for the right way to say what we'd all been discussing. I wanted to step in and rescue them both, but I refrained. If this was going to work, it had to come from him. "It's just that...perhaps we should have a seat," he said, gesturing toward the sofa.

"No," Corrie snapped, her eyes ablaze with anger. "If you have something to say, say it. Don't treat me like I'm still a little girl. Treat me like a woman."

"Very well," Willem sighed. He stood there a moment as if frozen in place, unable to speak, then he blurted out, "Look, this isn't easy for me to say, but I've known Karel since we first came to the university. You're not the first girl he's shown an interest in."

"I would have expected that," she said in an exasperated tone. "Why are you telling me this?"

Willem raised his hand in a calming gesture. "Listen and I'll explain." He paused to take a breath before continuing. "One thing he's said consistently about every girl he's ever been with is that his mother would never approve. I asked him on any number of occasions about what that meant and it was always the same answer. He's an only child. His mother and father have certain notions about what it means to graduate from the university, become a minister, that sort of thing. They see it as a way for him, and for them, to step up in life."

"So, what are you saying?"

"They expect him to marry well."

"So you're saying I'm not good enough." Corrie's voice was loud and her eyes were filled with tears. "That he wouldn't be marrying well if he married me? What a horrible thing to say to your sister." Tears streamed down her cheeks. "What a horrible thing to say to anyone."

"It's not about you," Willem continued. "It's about us. All of us. They expect him to marry into a family of considerable social and economic standing."

"They want wealth and position," I added.

"Yes," Willem continued. "Wealth and position. And they see marriage as a way to get it."

Corrie glared at me. "I can't believe you would do this to me."

"I'm only trying to—"

"I've told you things I have never told anyone," she said through clenched teeth. "And now you're just using it against me because you're jealous."

"Jealous?" I roared. "I'm not jealous."

"Yes, you are." Corrie leaned forward, angrily jabbing with her finger as she talked. "You see me having a relationship with someone that you know you'll never have, and it makes you mad."

I sat back on the sofa and folded my arms. "I'm not jealous of you," I scoffed. "I'm perfectly satisfied with who I am."

"Well, if you want to remain unmarried the rest of your life, that's your business," she shouted as she jumped up from the sofa. "But don't take it out on me." And with that she rushed from the room and stormed up the stairs.

Around midmorning, Karel and Corrie left for their walk. They were gone most of the day and continued to see each other until the middle of the week when we boarded the train for home. During the ride back to Haarlem, she kept to herself, avoiding eye contact with me and speaking only with Mama and Papa.

When we arrived at home, Mama called me to her room. She was already in bed when I arrived. "I told you to be careful," she said as I came through the doorway.

"You saw how they were acting while we were at Willem and Tine's."

"Yes," Mama retorted, "and you saw how she was acting on the way home. Your father was not happy and neither am I."

"Well, I'm afraid it was unavoidable."

She shot a look in my direction. "What do you mean by that?"

For the next few minutes I recounted what I had heard at the reception, my conversation with Willem on the back porch, and our attempt to talk to her in the parlor.

"I understand all of that," she replied, "and I appreciate your concern for your sister, but there are limits to what you can say and do. She's not your property or your child."

"I know that," I said, affronted by the suggestion once again that I was motivated by anything less than love for my sister. "I'm not merely trying to spoil her fun."

"Well, just the same, you have said your piece and you must say no more. You'll just have to let it run its course now."

CHAPTER 16

LATER THAT SUMMER, Nollie completed school to become a teacher. A small ceremony marked her graduation. Mama was too ill to attend, but the rest of us went to commemorate the occasion and celebrate a great achievement in her life. When the event was over, I walked with Nollie and Corrie down to the exit. As we made our way in that direction, I saw Vincent standing alone near the front door. He smiled at me as we approached and I felt my heart rate quicken. "Betsie," he grinned. "I was hoping I would see you here today."

Something inside me jumped at the sound of his voice. "I didn't know you were here," I exclaimed. "All this time, you were in Nollie's class?"

He shook his head. "No, I'm just here for my cousin. We're about all the family either of us has left."

That was a puzzling comment, so I asked, "How is your aunt?"

He glanced away, and the joy left his voice. "She died a few months ago." The smile vanished from his face, too. "She'd been sick most of the year. It was tough on her. On all of us, actually."

Once again, I blundered my way into details of his life that I should have known—first about his mother when we talked at our graduation and now about his aunt. "I'm sorry," I lamented. "My life has been limited to Papa's shop and the customers we see there. I had not heard the news about your aunt." I really hadn't heard, and I felt bad because of it.

"Not many did," he responded, looking up at me. "She was confined to the house for the year and before that she'd kept to herself anyway, especially after I graduated from school."

"Still," I fretted, "I should have known."

"It's okay."

By then, Corrie and Nollie had walked outside. I could see them through a window in the door. Papa passed me, and I glanced in his direction. "Go ahead," I suggested. "I'll catch up later." He tossed a wave in my direction as he pushed open the door. When he was with the others, I turned back to Vincent. "What are you doing now? Still at the university?"

"No, I have a job across town."

"Oh." That was another surprise. "I didn't realize you were living here now."

"Yes," he nodded sheepishly. "Still right here."

"So, what kind of job do you have?"

Once again he looked away and let his gaze drop to the floor. "I read meters for the city electrical service," he said quietly.

From the tone of his voice I could tell he wasn't proud of it. "Numbers," I replied, trying to think of something positive to say. "You were always good with numbers."

"And I get plenty of exercise," he chuckled, "walking from place to place to read the meters."

"I'm sure you do."

"It's not the career I wanted but it gives me a way to make some money and, if everything works out, maybe I can attend the university next year."

"What was the career you wanted?" We were bouncing from topic to topic but I couldn't think of anything else to say and, as strange as it seemed to me, I wanted him to keep talking.

"Engineering, I suppose."

"Was that really it?"

"No." He had a pleasant smile. "I wanted to be a mathematician."

Just then the president of the school approached us. "Time to go. We need to turn out the lights."

Vincent placed his hand against the small of my back and gestured toward the door. "Come on. I'll walk you home."

A tingle ran up my spine as he touched me and without hesitation I walked with him toward the door. "You don't have to do that. I can find my own way." I really could find my way safely home, but in my heart I was hoping he would insist on accompanying me. The sound of his voice was like music, the look he gave when he smiled made me melt, and my mind raced. How could I have ever been so foolish to turn him away? How could I possibly live a happy life, with gladness and joy and fulfillment, if he wasn't in it? On and on my mind ran, like the schoolgirl who walked home with him to play cricket in the alley, and much like I imagined Corrie must have with Karel. All the while, pangs of guilt stabbed at my conscience. I'd had nothing but good intentions when I spoke to her of him, but now I was more certain than ever that much of it had been driven by my own unsettled attitude toward my decision never to marry. Such a hasty decision straight from the mind of a foolish, self-important child, engrossed only in her myopic vision of right and wrong, certainty and purpose, and all of it so narrow and self-serving.

I wanted to hit myself. Where did I get these ideas? What changed? One minute I was a calm, rational woman attending my sister's graduation, thinking of invoices I needed to send and bills that needed to be paid, and the next minute I'd turned to mush. Before, I wanted nothing to do with Vincent or any other man. Now, with all my heart, I wanted him to—

"You shouldn't walk alone." Vincent's voice cut through the confusion in my mind, separating confidence from doubt, clarity from disorder, and saying the very thing I wanted him to say. "I'll go with you."

Then I thought of what he'd said earlier about why he was standing by the door. "What about your cousin? Weren't you waiting for him?"

"No," Vincent said, to my everlasting relief. "He left just before you came along."

I was suspicious about whether that was the truth and in my mind I imagined him lingering by the door waiting for a chance to see me, hoping I would pass by, just as I did, but there was nothing more to say than, "Well, then, let us be off."

From the school, Vincent and I made our way slowly back toward the house. He was in no hurry and neither was I. My heart no longer raced at the sight of him, but I wanted the evening to go on forever, so I kept asking questions and he kept talking.

At last we arrived at the shop and came to a stop outside the display window. I moved near the door and leaned against the doorframe, hoping he would kiss me. He continued to talk a few minutes longer and then said, as casually as ever, "It's been nice talking to you. I hope to see you again."

"Yes, that would be nice. Do you live around here?"

"No. But it's not that far and I'll be home before long. Maybe hitch a ride on a delivery truck." Then he turned away and started up the street. I wanted to run after him, wrap my arms around his neck, and kiss him as he had never been kissed before—in a way that would make him want to stay as much as I wanted it. But I just stood there and watched until he reached the corner a block away. As he would have made the turn and slipped from my sight, he glanced back over his shoulder, raised his hand high, and gave me a wave. Tears came to my eyes at the sight of it and I was as full as the night, long ago, when he kissed me on the cheek.

◆ ◆ ◆

Through the summer, Corrie and Karel continued to write, and she continued to talk about him at every opportunity, only now I didn't object. My eyes were opened and now I knew how she felt.

Day after day I returned in my mind to that afternoon when we were walking home with Vincent, and I was with him. The giddiness of being liked by someone special. The hint of things to come. The tingling down deep as every cell of my body came alive to the wonderful possibilities that life had to offer. Now I remembered all that afresh and anew, as if feeling it for the first time, and I kept silent when Corrie talked and looked away when she checked the mail. I knew there was only an occasional letter from Karel, in contrast to the ones she sent daily, but now, instead of needling her about it or arching an accusing eyebrow, I helped her cover for his lack of correspondence, agreeing with her that he was busy finishing school, busy with his position as an assistant rector, and preoccupied with the details of a new job.

And late at night Corrie came to my room to talk, only now I was not a hindrance to the discussion but the facilitator, and together we plunged like sisters into a world straight from the pages of those novels she read, a place where love and romance prevailed and where marriage was no longer a dream. And it was in those conversations I learned that Corrie expected a proposal almost any day. Perhaps by Christmas she would be engaged, followed by a midsummer wedding. Only now I hoped with all my heart that dream would come true.

As I had wanted, Vincent returned, and through the remainder of the summer he called on me almost every night. Nollie was busy looking for work as a teacher, and Corrie spent the evenings in her room, writing to Karel, which meant Vincent and I had the parlor to ourselves. When we tired of it we went for a walk in the cool of the evening, when all the shops were closed and the city grew quiet and still. As we strolled along the empty streets, I hung on his arm and soaked up every word that fell from his lips.

Eventually summer ebbed, and one night in August, as we strolled the streets of Haarlem, I learned that Vincent's dream of returning to the university wasn't merely a dream. Through hard work and a frugal lifestyle, he'd saved enough money to cover the first semester's expense. "Perhaps," he said with characteristic optimism, "I can do well enough to get a scholarship for the rest."

"I shall join you in praying that it is so."

When we arrived at the house, I bid him good night and turned to go inside. All at once he took me by the arm and gently turned me toward him. Only this time he did not kiss me on the cheek as he had so long ago. This time he placed his lips softly against mine, and I welcomed them there.

Not long after that, Vincent left for school and the evenings became unbearable. I spent most of the time lying on the bed reading one of Corrie's novels and thinking how much like her I'd become. At first I thought I was doing a great job hiding my moodiness, then Mama knocked on my bedroom door. Before I could answer she let herself in and took a seat in a chair between the bed and the window.

She smiled. "You've had quite a summer."

"Yes, ma'am," I agreed. "Rather different from what I had expected."

"Did you enjoy your time with Vincent?"

"Yes," I nodded. "I did."

She asked wryly, "How do you feel about that?"

"As I said, I enjoyed his company." I wasn't sure what she was asking.

"No," she corrected. "I meant, how do you like the fact that you enjoyed it?"

"Oh." Questions about my private life always left me flustered. "Well... that's a little different."

"I suspect so," and she gave a little flitter of a laugh when she said it.

"Rather a departure from what I was telling Corrie just a few months ago."

"Yes, I've thought of that. And I think that's how God works. If we can't see what He wants us to see any other way, then He leads us into an experience that opens our eyes."

"My eyes are open," I assured her.

"I realize that." She paused a moment and looked away, as if searching for just the right thing to say. Then she looked back at me and in the kindest voice imaginable said, "You know, I don't think you should feel bound by a decision you made years ago."

This time I knew precisely what she meant. "I'm still a person with pernicious anemia," I reminded her.

"Yes, only now it's not quite as pernicious as it once was. And not nearly as scary."

"I still don't think I should bear children."

"Perhaps not," she said in a conciliatory tone, "but that is only one side of the matter. Marriage brings on many things that cannot be obtained by any other means. Love, commitment, fulfillment, completion—you can't find those to the same degree anywhere else."

"But it would be a marriage without children."

"Marriage without children doesn't have to be sad or contentious."

When she was gone, I tossed aside the book I'd been reading and lay on the bed thinking about what she'd said. That promise I'd made to myself to never marry was the promise of a young girl. It was based on the best information available at the time but it was a promise for that day and that moment. Since then, time had moved on and my circumstances were different. Back then, no one knew for certain if medical treatments would forestall the long-term effects of my condition. After years of medical care my body had proved that was no longer an issue. So lying there in the still of the evening, I resolved that I would no longer be bound by that promise. I would take each day as it came and wait to see what the future might hold.

◆ ◆ ◆

Fall continued its downward slide into winter, and as December approached, Corrie was certain St. Nicholas' Eve, a traditional Dutch holiday in early December, was the time when Karel would propose. His letters, though more irregular now than ever and somewhat cryptic, spoke of the details one must consider in whether to marry—a couple's intellectual compatibility, their desire for children, and whether they hailed from complimentary social ranks. That last criterion struck me as telling, but I pushed aside my concern and joined Corrie in believing this would be the moment for which she'd longed all her life.

"He would want to spend Christmas with his family," she reasoned. "Everyone wants to be home for that holiday. But St. Nicholas' Eve is different. Being away from home is much more acceptable then and he could come here for the entire week. That would be perfect. He could talk to Papa, give me a ring, and we would be all set."

Just to make sure, early in the month Corrie wrote to Karel and extended an invitation for him to celebrate the holiday at our home. He replied almost immediately, which was rather unlike him, and agreed to stop by a few days early, though not for the holiday itself and not for an overnight visit. He had something he wanted to say and it needed to be said in person. As you might expect, Corrie looked past the nuance of the letter, focused solely on the fact that he wanted to tell her something, and was swept into a state of euphoria. I thought something was amiss and, for the first time in months, was genuinely worried that she would be terribly hurt, but I ignored the warning signs and joined her in the bliss of the moment.

Nollie worked as a teacher, which kept her away all day, and Mama was confined to her bedroom most of the time. I helped as much as time allowed but with Christmas not far off, business in the shop had picked up and we were actually on the verge of turning a profit for the year, which with the war dragging on and no end in sight, we had not expected. Tending to customers and keeping the ledger straight took most of my attention. As a result, most of the preparation for Karel's visit fell to Corrie and Aunt Anna. For the next three weeks they worked to put the house in perfect order, cleaning, sorting, stacking, and arranging. So much so that Papa complained it was hard to relax in the parlor with all the furniture in an unfamiliar location.

At last, after everything in the house had been arranged, rearranged, and moved once more, the week of celebration arrived. On Monday, Corrie was in a frenetic state, running to the window at every sound, staring out for hours at the street below, hoping for a glimpse of him. When nighttime came and he still wasn't there, she languished near despair, imagining that the worst had happened. I assured her there was nothing to worry about, though inside I was more worried than ever and tried to distract her by insisting that we play the piano. With Nollie and Papa helping, we spent the evening singing and laughing.

The following day, about the middle of the afternoon, the shop door opened and I looked up from my desk to see Karel standing just a few meters away. He had a smile on his face but it didn't seem at all pleasant, and when I'd had time to recover I saw why. Trailing behind him, but holding a tight grip on his hand, was a willowy wisp of a woman. She was about his height, though much younger, with long blond hair and large round eyes. Although pretty, she was by no means gorgeous, with delicate features and prominent cheekbones. But as my eyes fell on her hand, my heart, already wounded and shaken, sank. For there on her finger was a diamond ring, and I could not believe it.

From upstairs came the hurried thud of footsteps, and I knew Corrie had heard his voice. A moment later the sound reached the top of the steps and the thud turned to patter as she came lightly toward the first floor. "Karel!" she exclaimed. "You made it!" Then the pace of her footsteps slowed as she saw the woman who clung so tightly to Karel's hand. I turned to watch as Corrie reached the bottom of the stairs, came to an abrupt stop, then took a halting step toward them.

Karel glanced at the woman beside him and, with a broad smile, said, "This is Willem's little sister. Isn't she just like I described?"

By the look in her eyes, I knew those words plunged like knives deep into Corrie's heart. *Little sister.* Is that really how he felt about her? I'd read some of his letters, and one might have concluded from them that he was being less than forthright, but no one would have believed that he only saw her as someone's *little sister.* I wanted to slap him right there but before I could say or do anything, he continued.

"Corrie," he said, looking her squarely and unflinchingly in the eye, "this is Isabelle Campert." He gestured with a nod to the woman. "She is my fiancée. We are to be married in June. That is what I wanted to tell you when I wrote you before. I just didn't think it proper to tell you in a letter. A friend such as you deserves to hear it in person."

Friend. I shuttered at the sound of that word and felt it rip into Corrie's soul. Her eyes filled with tears and a soft gasp escaped her throat. In an instant, I sprang from my chair and moved between them. Corrie was on the verge of losing control, and I wasn't about to let that happen. Not right there in front of Karel—the dishonest, vapid little man and his oh-so-proper, newly announced little—

I caught myself and forced a smile. "Isabelle," I cooed. "What a lovely name."

"Thank you," she replied.

I extended my hand to her. "Let me take your coat." She slipped it from her shoulders and draped it over my arm. "Karel," I said with a nod. "If you'd let us know you were coming by, I would have dusted the shelves."

"Oh, no need to make a fuss. We can't stay long."

"Nonsense. You can come upstairs for coffee and cake. Aunt Anna baked last night, and I hear her putting the coffee on now."

By then, Corrie had retreated to the kitchen. I turned toward the stairway to lead them up and gave Papa a look to say he should follow. For once, he understood what I meant and came without delay.

When we reached the second floor, Papa took Karel by the elbow and guided him into the parlor. "Tell me something. I hear there's a chance this war may end soon. What do you hear?" I ushered Isabelle to a chair near the piano and pulled another beside her so we could talk. A few minutes later, Aunt Anna served coffee and cake. Mama came from her bedroom intending only to greet our visitors and return to bed, but stayed to talk when she saw what had happened. Corrie remained in the kitchen, her back turned to us, her face hidden from view.

Karel and Isabelle stayed almost an hour, talking and chatting as if we were old friends and that everything was right with the world. It was so surreal. Like a scene from an inverted version of Corrie's novels. When it was time for them to go, I walked with them downstairs. Behind me, I heard Corrie's footsteps as she rushed in the opposite direction toward her room.

When we reached the door to the street, Karel paused and looked up toward the second floor. "I had hoped to speak with Corrie before we left."

"I think she's occupied right now," I replied. "Perhaps another time."

"Yes." He had a perplexed look on his face, and his mind seemed to be somewhere else. "Perhaps another time," he mumbled. Then they said their good-byes and the two of them stepped out to the sidewalk. No sooner had they crossed the threshold than I closed the door behind them.

For a moment I just stood there, trying to make sense of what had occurred. Was he really that stupid? Did he not know the impression he'd given Corrie about their future? Or was he simply calloused and uncaring?

I would have stood there longer, but the clatter of dishes in the kitchen caught my ear and I moved upstairs to help Aunt Anna.

"I can't believe he—"

"Hush," Aunt Anna snapped, cutting me off. "I don't want to talk about it now."

"But he—"

"Hush!" she shouted and I was caught off-guard. She'd never shouted about anything. "I don't want to talk about that worthless rag of a man right now."

So we worked in silence and when we were finished I made my way to Mama's room. I would have preferred the rooftop but it was too cold to go up there, and she wasn't well enough to get beyond her room. She was propped on a pillow when I entered.

"Poor Corrie," she said, reaching up to dab the corners of her eyes. "She must be so embarrassed."

"Perhaps I should check on her," I offered.

"No," Mama replied, lifting her hand from beneath the cover to wag a finger at me. "Your father will handle it."

"You've spoken to him about this already?"

"I don't have to. He knows what to do without being told."

"Well, there's certainly no need for her to be ashamed or embarrassed." I was talking to myself as much as to Mama. "I know she is, but she didn't do this, even if she misunderstood what he was really like."

"Caring for someone is a risk, no matter who the person is or what kind of relationship it might be, but even after this I think it is a risk well worth taking."

"Yes. You're right." I sighed and shook my head. "But I can't believe how cruel and insensitive he was."

"But you must always remember—God loves him as much as He loves Corrie. And as much as He loves you."

"That's difficult to fathom."

"I know, but you can't let bitterness find a place in your heart. You must forgive him and move on."

"I know, but what about Corrie? How is she going to forgive him?"

"Perhaps," Mama suggested, "it would help if we thought about the situation from Karel's perspective. Family pressure. A mother insistent on having more and seeing him as the one to give it to her. Years of expectations drilled into him. Perhaps this was the best he could do."

I didn't want to think of it that way. And I didn't want to forgive him. Karel was wrong and he should pay for it. But I knew Mama was right, so sitting there in her room we prayed for him and said aloud the only words that ever set anyone's spirit free. "I forgive you."

CHAPTER 17

THAT WINTER our lives continued to change. The war in Europe drew to a close and business at the shop picked up. Karel disappeared from our conversations, but the memory of what happened lingered. My initial assessment of him had been correct, but my response to their relationship—poorly framed and badly flawed—had served only to drive Corrie and me apart. With a rekindled relationship of my own with Vincent, my eyes were opened to my mistake, and after the injury from Karel's unthinkable behavior, Corrie and I were closer than ever. We'd been sisters before—companions by birth and blood. What we endured together made us companions of the heart.

In the following months, winter grew colder and with it my relationship with Vincent cooled, as well. He was away at the university and though it wasn't that far by distance, his visits were limited to holidays. I saw him on St. Nicholas' Day and again at Christmas and even though he had only been in school a single semester, I could tell that he was not the same. He no longer looked at me in the longing, infatuated way he did before. When he talked he spoke not of life and love and happiness, but of issues, historic forces sweeping the continent, the gathering storm on the political horizon, and a hundred other ideas he'd heard at school. I listened, but the infrequency of his visits and lack of correspondence let me know that whatever relationship we might have had before was now coming to an end.

At first, old regrets returned and I pummeled myself mentally and emotionally for having turned him away so forcefully when we were younger. Later, as I thought of him and how our relationship had ended, and how things ended with Corrie and Karel, I became certain that Corrie and I would live in the Beje together to the end. Vincent had been my opportunity to marry, and that opportunity had passed. After Corrie's experience with Karel, I was all but certain the moment had passed for her, too.

I was thinking about that one day while alone in the shop. Louis was off on an errand, and Papa was visiting Rabbi Prins at the Rabbi's home, so the shop was empty except for me. With a few minutes alone, I was beating myself up inside, wondering if I'd heard from God years before when I'd made that decision not to marry, and wondering if I'd heard Him now when trying to discern the future path of my relationship with Vincent. In the midst of that, the shop door opened and Papa appeared. He held a single tulip stem with a lovely red bloom on top.

"Where did you find that?" I asked in amazement. Blooming tulips were a treat anytime, but this was the dead of winter.

"Rabbi Prins," Papa smiled triumphantly. "He loves them as much as you and grows them in the winter. When I was over there today I saw them inside, near the window, and asked him to send one to you." He laid the tulip on my desk. "Rabbi Prins was glad to do it." I gently lifted the flower from the desk and started upstairs to place it in a vase.

Tulips, I've always said, are a sign from God. Rabbi Prins might have sent it, and Papa might have delivered it, but God put the desire to grow them in Prins' heart for just such a day as this when He could give one to me.

In spite of the changes in our personal lives, our daily activities fell into a familiar routine. We rose early, ate breakfast together as a family, listened while Papa read from the Bible, and prayed. Afterward, Nollie left for her job as a schoolteacher, Papa and I went downstairs to the shop, and Corrie worked upstairs with Mama and Aunt Anna. It was an easy, comfortable pattern, one we'd lived all our lives in one form or another, and we followed it without question until the day Corrie rushed into the shop.

"Come quick," she cried in a panic. "Something's wrong with Mama."

I leapt from my seat at the desk and started toward the staircase. Papa, moving quicker than I'd ever seen before, came behind me. We arrived at the top of the steps to find Mama lying on her back on the kitchen floor. Aunt Anna knelt beside her, wiping her forehead with a damp cloth. Mama's lips moved and I heard her make a sound, but no one could understand what she was saying.

"Quick," I said to Corrie. "Get Dr. Van Veen." Without a moment's hesitation, she rushed down the steps, threw open the door, and charged out.

Papa glanced over at me. "Do you think we should move her to her bed?"

"No," Aunt Anna replied, shaking her head slowly from side to side. "We should leave her right here until the doctor arrives."

That seemed right to me and I said so, but Papa just stood there looking as helpless as we all felt. After a moment he gave a heavy sigh. "Yes," he said in a voice so low I could barely hear it. "I suppose you're right." He brought a chair from the dining table and sat beside Mama. I took a seat on the floor.

In a few minutes, the door downstairs opened. Footsteps thundered up the stairs toward us, then Corrie appeared with Dr. Van Veen in tow. He paused when he saw Mama, and something in the way he looked at her made me think he already knew what was wrong. With deliberate, unrushed effort, he set his black bag on the floor, removed his coat, and knelt beside her.

Gently, he felt her neck and a little way down her chest. He took a stethoscope from his bag and listened to her heart, checked the pulse in her wrist, then with the scope listened to the veins in her neck. After a moment, he leaned forward with his head directly over hers and lifted the eyelid from her right eye. He did the same with the left then sank back on his haunches and looked up at Papa. "I think," he said quietly, "she's had a stroke." Aunt Anna let out a gasp and tears filled her eyes. "From what I can tell," Dr. Van Veen continued, "she probably has a ruptured blood vessel over here." He turned back to Mama and pointed to a place above her left temple. "We should move her to her bed and get her as comfortable as possible."

Corrie and Aunt Anna moved to a place on either side of her and slipped their hands beneath her thighs and legs. Papa and Louis lifted her torso. Dr. Van Veen held her neck and head. With coordinated movement, they lifted her from the floor, carried her to her room, and placed her on the bed. Papa ran his fingers through her hair to brush it away from her face. Then Aunt Anna stepped forward and shooed us out. "Leave," she ordered. "I will arrange everything and you can come back to see her then." When we hesitated, she waved her hands at us with an angry look. "Go. I will tell you when you can come in. She is my sister. I will take care of her now."

Papa caught my eyes. "We should do as she says," and he started toward the doorway. I followed him out to the hall, and the others came with us. We gathered in the kitchen to talk.

"What can we do?" I asked.

"I'm afraid there isn't much anyone can do," Dr. Van Veen replied, "except keep her comfortable and see how she responds."

"That's it?"

"Yes," he nodded. "That's it." He'd left his black bag on the kitchen floor when we picked up Mama to carry her. The doctor stooped over and retrieved it. "I'll check on her this evening," he said as he moved toward the stairs. "If anything happens before then, come get me. I'll be in the office."

Shortly after he left, Aunt Anna opened the door to Mama's room and the four of us—Papa, Corrie, Aunt Anna, and I—quietly stood by her bed. She lay there, eyes staring up at the ceiling, her chest rising and falling with each breath, but there was no sign of Mama in her eyes. No fire of purpose or light of character. Tears trickled down my cheeks and when I reached up to wipe them away, I saw Corrie and Nollie were crying, too. Aunt Anna, stoic and strong, stood on the far side near Mama's head, her hand just inches from the pillow. "I will not weep," she said stubbornly. "I will not give the enemy of my soul the satisfaction of it."

We took turns sitting with her. Corrie went first, followed by Aunt Anna, then me. Not long after I took over, Nollie arrived from her teaching job. I heard Papa talking to her in the parlor, telling her what happened. From the sound of sobbing that filtered through the wall, I assumed she wasn't taking the news well, but when she came to the room she was composed.

Late in the afternoon Mama closed her eyes, and her jaw went slack. I assumed she was sleeping, but when I pointed this out to Aunt Anna she was concerned. "I do not like this," she grumbled. "Look, her head is over to one side and her foot is pointed in the same direction." Indeed, her feet were beneath the covers but even so, they were obviously pointing in the direction Aunt Anna noted.

Around dusk, Dr. Van Veen called on her. After examining her again, he confirmed she was in a coma. "Her vital signs are good, but her brain has suffered a serious injury. She could remain like this for quite some time. Or," he sighed, "she might never come out of it."

After supper, Nollie sat with Mama until it was time for bed, then Aunt Anna took over and remained with her for the night. For the next two months Aunt Anna, Corrie, Nollie, and I took turns sitting with her, but with Nollie teaching and me in the shop with Papa, Corrie and Aunt Anna did most of the work.

Then one day, not long before spring, Corrie called for me, and I ran upstairs to find Mama propped on her pillow, trying to talk. Mama had come back as one returning from the dead. We were glad to have her with us, but she was never quite the same. With great and prolonged effort she was eventually able to get out of bed and sit by her own strength at the dining table. Dr. Van Veen thought of it as a miracle and we all agreed.

CHAPTER 18

CORRIE AND AUNT ANNA continued to work with Mama, and she regained much of her physical strength. After a few months she could walk with assistance and sit at the table, but try as we might, none of us could get her to say more than a few words—most often only *yes, no,* and *Corrie.* She sat with us for each meal and in the evenings she joined us in the parlor while we played the piano and sang, but her interaction with us was limited to those few words, a shake or nod of her head, and a smile.

At the same time, Nollie's teaching job kept her busy during the day but at night she was home with us. As we talked at mealtime and in the parlor afterward, I noticed that her conversation became increasingly laced with comments about Flip van Woerden, one of her fellow teachers. I had heard this kind of chatter before from Corrie and knew what it meant.

Nollie and Corrie were very different. Corrie was impulsive, gregarious, and unassimilated. Nollie was disciplined, orderly, and intentional. When they were younger, Corrie spent the afternoons in the street behind the Beje with the neighborhood children, and no matter what game they played, she was the natural leader. Nollie spent her afternoons doing homework or reading a book. Corrie had a tough time with school and was glad simply to graduate. Nollie graduated at the top of her class. Romance came to them at different ages, too. Corrie had been all of fourteen years old when she became infatuated with Karel. Nollie was older, settled, and far more mature when she began seeing Flip.

Yet in spite of that, and despite Mama's admonition that love and romance were matters of the heart and not the head, I thought an intentional, thoughtful discussion of the matter was necessary, if for no other reason than to keep the relationship on course. And I was certain Nollie's introduction of the topic into family conversation was an appeal from her for our involvement, not so much in deciding for her but in helping her discover whether and how Flip might fit into our family. She liked him and I think she wanted to know if we would like him, too.

Under normal circumstances I would have discussed this with Mama before doing anything, and several times I went to her room to raise the matter with her. She had always given me great insight into the issues our family faced and how things in my own life affected the way I perceived others. Those conversations weren't always pleasant, but they had become an integral part of my maturing attempts to understand what God was saying to me and what He was doing in my life. But with Mama unable to speak I realized those discussions were no longer possible, which brought me to the conclusion that I was moving to a new phase of my life. One that forced me to rely on my own ability to hear from God and find within myself the courage to act on what I heard Him say, without the comfort of Mama's opinion.

Left to my own discernment, I found only two options for addressing the situation between Nollie and Flip; either keep quiet or talk to her. There was no comfortable middle ground, no room for equivocation. Looking back now it seems like I worried over nothing, and sometimes I wonder why the thought of talking to her caused me such trouble, but back then I was deeply concerned. I'd made a mess of my relationship with Corrie, which took time and personal pain to repair. Nollie and I were much closer in age and my relationship with her was very different from the one I had with Corrie, but even so, there was risk in stepping into the issues of her life and I wanted to be careful.

As winter faded into spring I had the sense that Nollie's relationship with Flip was growing more serious every day. So, with time and events moving rapidly forward, I braced myself and walked to her bedroom, determined to talk and, at all costs, avoid the mistakes I'd made with Corrie. She was seated at her desk when I entered.

"So," I began, feeling awkward and out of place but intent on getting to the point, "you and Flip are seeing a lot of each other."

She turned in the chair to face me. "Yes, we are."

I took a seat on the edge of her bed. "You like him."

"Very much," she nodded. "And I think you would, too."

Her openness was refreshing and so I pressed the issue. "Well, if this relationship is developing like I think it is, Flip needs to meet us."

"Yes," Nollie laughed. "I suppose he does."

My eyes darted away. "I'm just trying to help," I sighed.

"I know," Nollie grinned. "Do you really think Papa will like him?"

"There's one way to find out."

"I know." The smile vanished from her face. "But with Mama and everything, I wasn't sure I could have him over."

A puzzled frown creased my brow. "You're worried about what he will think of her?"

"No," she replied quickly. "Not at all. It's just that she takes a lot of Corrie's and Aunt Anna's time, and having Flip over would be a lot of extra bother for everyone. I'm not here during the day to help."

"I don't think they would mind."

"I just didn't want to add any more work to what everyone's already doing."

"That won't be a problem. When can you bring him for dinner?"

"I don't know." Then she lowered her voice and looked over at me. "Do you think he will like us?"

I touched her knee. "If he likes you, we won't matter."

"I hope so."

"There's only one way to find out." I rose from the bed and stood. "Let's have him for dinner."

"We should discuss that with Aunt Anna."

"Yes," I nodded, feeling relieved that we weren't arguing. "She's in her room. Let's go up to see her now."

The following Friday, Flip arrived at the shop door just as we were taking supper from the oven. Papa was impressed by his punctuality. Everyone else was impressed that he brought flowers for Mama. We ate and talked at the table, then moved to the parlor, where we gathered around the piano to play and sing. Flip joined in as if he'd always been among us.

Later that evening after he was gone, Nollie came to the kitchen, where I was washing dishes. "That went well," I said.

"Yes. It did. What did you think of him?"

"Nice man."

"Nice?" she laughed. "Is that all you have to say?"

"Well," I added playfully, "I would say, if you don't want him I'll take him, but that wouldn't go over so well."

Nollie picked up a towel and began drying a plate. "Are you worried about us?"

I shot a glance in her direction. "About you and Flip?"

"He's very different from Karel, you know."

"Yes, he is," I agreed, "And no, I'm not worried."

"Good," she grinned.

We worked in silence awhile, then I asked without looking up, "Does Flip need to talk to Papa?"

"Maybe," she grinned.

❋ ❋ ❋

Several months later Flip came to the shop. He arrived about midmorning, which was an odd time considering his job as a schoolteacher, and visited with us while Papa and Louis continued to work. I could tell he was nervous and did my best to keep the conversation lively and engaging.

Sometime before noon, I suggested that instead of taking his daily walk with me, Papa should allow Flip to accompany him. Papa agreed and the two of them left for a stroll through the neighborhood. They were gone much longer than normal but when they returned Flip seemed more at ease and genuinely relieved. I was pretty sure I knew why.

That afternoon Nollie did not come home, and as suppertime approached, Corrie and Aunt Anna grew concerned that she still hadn't appeared. "The food is ready and the table is set," Corrie fretted. "Should we wait a little longer?"

"No," Papa replied. "I'm certain she'll be okay."

"I don't like it," Aunt Anna said with a scowl. "She should be here by now. I'm afraid something has happened to her."

"Nothing has happened," Papa soothed as he took his place at the table. Mama was seated across from him and he gave her a knowing look. She grinned at him in response.

Two hours later, we were in the parlor playing the piano and singing when the door downstairs opened. It banged shut and then we heard the sound of footsteps on the stairway. A moment later, Nollie appeared in the parlor doorway with Flip standing with her. When they told us they were engaged, no one was surprised.

As with Willem and Tine, the wedding was held at St. Bavo's Cathedral in the spring. Mama attended the service and, with everyone in the family helping, not many of the guests realized she had difficulty walking or talking. Midway through the litany we sang her favorite hymn, "Fairest Lord Jesus." I knew she loved it but wondered if she was sad about not being able to sing along, but as the organ finished the prelude and we began to sing the melody, Mama opened her mouth and sang every verse with gusto. I thought it was a sign from God that she would fully recover from the effects of the stroke.

Four weeks later, Aunt Anna entered Mama's room to prepare her for breakfast. However, after repeated attempts she was unable to awaken her. Corrie ran up the street for Dr. Van Veen and he came to the house immediately. He checked the pulse in her neck, then her wrist, and listened to her chest through the stethoscope. Finally he stood and looked over at Papa. "Mr. Ten Boom," he said sadly, "I am sorry to tell you she is gone."

Mama's funeral was held at St. Bavo's Cathedral, then we buried her in the cemetery near Papa's relatives, not far from the graves I had visited with Grandfather when I was a little girl. I suppose we all knew Mama would die one day. Everyone dies. She'd been sick off and on throughout most of her adult life and she'd had at least one stroke. We never talked about the possibility of her dying, but we all knew it would likely come sooner rather than later. Still, I'd heard her sing the hymn in St. Bavo's at Nollie's wedding and I was sure it was an indication that God had heard our prayers. That He would intervene and she would be well. I'd relied on that inner voice all my life, and on every occasion I had heard correctly. Now she was dead.

For the next several weeks, I stayed away from the shop. I didn't tell Papa I would be absent and didn't ask Corrie to cover for me or work out a plan to ensure that the details were covered. I just didn't show up.

Instead, each morning after breakfast I found a reason to linger in the kitchen while Papa went downstairs. When I was certain he'd reached the bottom of the steps, I poured myself a cup of coffee and took it up to the roof where I sat alone in the wooden chair—Mama's chair. Summer was just arriving in the Netherlands, and most mornings the air was pleasant, though by no means warm. As I sat there, surrounded by the flowers, sipping coffee, and watching the sky come alive to a new day, I searched my heart for an answer. I'd been so sure she'd be well, and now she was gone.

If the days were filled with long periods of contemplative silence and reflection, the nights were restless bouts of tossing and turning. Sleep came only in fits and starts, and when I did finally get to sleep my dreams were episodic—chaotic pieces of disconnected scenes rather than the seamless stories I normally experienced. Often I awoke feeling more tired than when I went to bed.

Papa let this go on for a few weeks without saying a word to me about it. Then one night he came to my room. "Betsie," he said in a soft voice, "this has gone on long enough."

Tears filled my eyes. I knew what he meant and the thought of it filled me with sadness. In a whisper I said, "I miss her."

"I know," he nodded. "And you've been holding on to her with a tight grip. It's time to let her go on to heaven."

"But there were so many things I wanted to ask her."

"I know." He took a seat on the bed and patted the spot beside him with his hand. "But those questions will have to wait." I took a seat beside him, then he placed his hand atop my head. "I'm going to pray for you now and you'll be released from your grief."

I heard him take a breath to speak, and at the last second I jerked my head from beneath his hand. "But I don't want her to go yet," I sobbed.

"Yes, you do," he replied and returned his hand gently to my head.

He was right. I'd been holding on to Mama ever since she died and traveled to the depths of grief. At first it had been sweet in an odd sort of way—to sip from Mama's presence long after the others had said their good-byes. On the roof, with a cup of coffee in the morning, I once again had her all to myself. But after a while, the sweetness of the moment turned sour as I realized she wasn't really there and was never coming back. I was ready to be rid of the grief and the thought life I'd built around it, only by then I was in its grip and couldn't shake free. Papa's visit to my room was a gift from God.

When he was finished praying for me I crawled into bed, rested my head on the pillow, and pulled the covers up to my neck. No sooner had I closed my eyes than I fell fast asleep.

While I was sleeping, I dreamed I was floating effortlessly through the sky, high above the ground. Below me was a huge house with gardens all around and flowerbeds that were filled with tulips of every size and color. Men and women tended the gardens and Corrie was with them. The dream went on for what seemed like a long time, me floating above, Corrie and the others quietly caring for the flowers. And when I awakened from that dream I felt refreshed, alive, and free.

After breakfast I decided to take one more day for myself and went shopping for Aunt Anna at the market. While I was there, browsing from one vegetable vendor to the next, I saw a copper teakettle among a junk dealer's wares. It was dented and there were pinholes in the bottom, making it useless for heating water, but it had a wonderful patina and I was smitten by it. Without a second thought or a moment's hesitation, I spent some of the food money to buy it and brought it home to the kitchen. Then I went up to the rooftop and clipped a tulip from among Mama's flowers. Back in the kitchen, I placed the tulip in a cup of water and set it inside the kettle with the bottom of the stem resting in the cup and the bloom sticking out through the top. Then I placed the kettle on the shelf to the right of the stove for everyone to see. The bloom, a bright red, looked majestic and regal in that old kettle. Just thinking of it now makes me smile.

When Corrie arrived for lunch she took one look at the kettle and shook her head. "Where did that thing come from?"

"I found it at the market."

A frown wrinkled her forehead. "The junk dealer?"

"Yes."

"Most of what he sells is useless," she scoffed as she took a seat at the table.

"I know."

"Probably has a hole in it."

"Yes," I nodded. "It does."

Corrie's head jerked up, her eyes sharp and focused right on me. "How did you pay for it?"

"I used part of the food money," I replied calmly.

"The food money?" she retorted in a loud voice. "For that worthless scrap?"

"Settle down, Corrie," Papa cautioned.

But Corrie would have none of it. "She sits on the roof all day," she shouted. "Spends the rest of her time wandering around town buying junk. Taking food from our table to buy trinkets from the junk man! And you tell me to calm down?"

"Look at how beautiful it is," I interjected, hoping to steer the argument back to a conversation.

Corrie just shook her head. "I can't believe you spent the food budget on a worthless piece of copper," she muttered.

"Well, I assure you," I added, "supper will be wonderful. And in the meantime, we'll have something beautiful to look at."

CHAPTER 19

AFTER PAPA PRAYED FOR ME, I went back to the shop and took over my old job. Corrie returned upstairs. But the following November, I became sick with influenza—really sick—and was confined to bed. Dr. Van Veen treated me, but my recovery was slow. Corrie went back downstairs to help in the shop. Although I'd spent much of the time after Mama's funeral grappling with her death and what it meant for me, I'd noticed that Corrie seemed frustrated over her work in the shop. Now, being forced to return to those duties, I sensed her frustration increasing once again, enough so that even though I was bedridden I knew she was struggling.

At first I thought she was upset because she would have rather been upstairs keeping house with Aunt Anna, but as I listened to her I learned that she didn't like the way the books had been kept. "I don't know how you do this," she said more than once. "The accounts are unorganized, bills seem to have gone unpaid, and there's no way to determine for certain who has paid us and who has not. I fixed most of this, but now it's in a mess again." I bit my tongue to keep from responding, but in my mind I was thinking, *She should have seen it when I first took it over.*

At first during that illness I simply lay in bed and slept but after a week or two my condition improved and I became bored. All day long I lay there reading, thinking, and staring into the distance without focusing on much of anything. Over time, however, I noticed dust along the top edge of the baseboards. The few times I went to the kitchen I saw pots and pans sitting in a jumble on a cabinet shelf, plates were at odd angles, drinking glasses haphazardly arranged in no certain way, and all of them demanding to be placed in order. But I resisted the urge to straighten them out and forced myself to return to bed.

As the illness lingered I thought of my anemic condition and how Dr. Tromp had cautioned me that an illness of this nature could be very difficult for my body. Even fatal. My thoughts turned to Mama. She was sick most of her life and young when she died. Too young. I didn't want to die and I didn't want to spend my life in bed. Slowly, fear crept into my mind. Not merely fear of anything but of something very specific—fear of dying.

Finally I could stand being in bed no longer. Instead of just lying there with my mind dragging me deeper and deeper into despair, I threw back the covers, slid out of bed, and quietly began doing some of the things I'd seen that needed to be done. With Aunt Anna's help, I rearranged dishes in the kitchen cabinet, sorted and straightened the pots and pans, swept the floors, and dusted. Then I turned to a door down the hall that I'd wanted to refinish.

Two days before Christmas I slipped out the back door and walked up the street to the market, where I purchased flowers to decorate the parlor. Corrie was waiting for me when I returned. The look on her face told me she was not amused.

"What are you doing?" she railed.

"No one thought to get flowers," I replied with a smile, "and Christmas is almost here." I placed the flowers in a vase with water and set them on the dining table, all the while hoping she would watch quietly and return downstairs.

"You're sick," she fumed. "You're supposed to be in bed. Dr. Van Veen said so. Rest. Plenty of fluids. Not running down the street to buy flowers or stripping the doors to refinish them."

"Look, I know you don't like working in the shop but—"

"No," she snapped, cutting me off before I could finish. "I love working in the shop. What I hate is housework. But what makes me angry is when my sister won't take care of herself."

"Corrie," I began, trying to calm her, "I'll be okay. I just had to—"

"I've lost a mother," she shouted. "I don't want to lose you, too."

I put my arm around her shoulder and drew her close to me. "You won't lose me," I whispered. "You won't lose me."

She wrapped her arms around my back and rested her head on my shoulder. "You'll never get well if you don't rest."

I let go of her. "Okay, I'll get back in bed. But I didn't know you liked the shop."

"I love the shop with the watches and all the parts and everything working in perfect order," she said as she walked with me to my bedroom. "I even love the ledger...at least I did until you got hold of it again."

"Ha!" I cackled with laughter as I slipped beneath the covers. "Do you realize what has happened?"

She gave me a questioning look. "What do you mean?"

"I've been down there working in the shop all this time and wishing I was up here cooking and cleaning and keeping house. And you were up here doing the housework and wishing you were downstairs."

"Yes," she chuckled. "I suppose you're right. I was just doing what had to be done. You were already in the shop. They didn't need one more person in there."

"And I was simply doing what needed to be done when I *went* to the shop. Mama and Aunt Anna did the housework, but they either didn't like the shop or couldn't make heads or tails of Papa's accounting."

"What accounting?" she asked with a derisive roll of her eyes. "It's a mess."

"And really," I added, "it was even worse when I took over."

"I know," Corrie nodded. "I saw what you did with it and I actually came to understand how you kept track of it. But all you have to do is line up—"

"Hold it," I said, interrupting her. "You know how to keep it straight and correct?"

"Yes. Of course. It's really very simple."

"Good," I grinned. "Then why don't you stay in the shop with Papa and I'll stay up here with Aunt Anna?"

"We'll do that," Corrie said, pulling the covers a little higher. "But right now you're going to rest."

◆ ◆ ◆

By Christmas I was well enough to work in the kitchen and we enjoyed a feast for our holiday meal. In the days that followed, the soup pot was never empty and the aroma of fresh coffee filled the air. Downstairs, the shop ran as smoothly as the clocks on the wall and as effortlessly as the watches in the case. Louis moved up from apprentice to assistant and took over all the cleaning jobs. Papa hired a woman named Toos to take over the ledger and wait on customers, and Corrie became Papa's apprentice. Two years later, she was the Netherlands' first licensed female watchmaker.

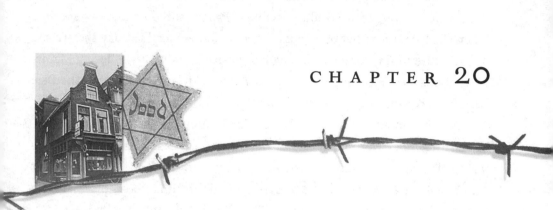

CHAPTER 20

FOR THE NEXT SEVERAL YEARS I worked upstairs with Aunt Anna. She taught me to cook in ways I'd never imagined and showed me things about housekeeping that saved time and effort. She also taught me needlepoint stitches that I didn't know existed. I still missed Mama and occasionally retreated to the rooftop to sit among her flowers each spring, but I was at peace with her absence and my life reached a settled routine.

Then one day, as the approaching fall brought us cool crisp mornings, Aunt Anna failed to appear for breakfast. I sent Corrie to check on her, but she found the bedroom door closed and assumed Aunt Anna was still dressing. That was unlike her and twice while I was setting the table I thought to check on her again, but I didn't.

When Papa came down to join us he insisted we look in on her, so I went to her room. The door was still closed but I tapped on it lightly and pushed it open. Aunt Anna, wearing a blue cotton dress that was her favorite, lay crossways on the bed with her arms spread wide, her face pointed toward the ceiling, and her eyes closed. Her feet were bare and I tickled the bottom of one, thinking she was dozing. She gave no response, so I shook it. "Aunt Anna," I said playfully. "Time to get up." There was still no response, so I stepped to the hallway and called for Papa. He took one look at her and sent Corrie for Dr. Van Veen. A few minutes later he confirmed what we already suspected. Aunt Anna was dead.

Willem conducted her funeral and we buried her near Mama. She'd lived with us for as long as we could remember. Papa assured us there was a time when she led a life of her own, but even he couldn't recall the day she arrived at our house to stay for good. Losing her wasn't as traumatic as losing Mama, but her absence left a gaping hole in our lives. After she was gone, the Beje became very quiet and very empty, but that didn't last for long.

About a month after Aunt Anna's death, a customer in the shop mentioned that Elka Nordheim, one of our neighbors, was sick. Elka had two young children, a girl named Estella and a boy named Daniel. I couldn't bear the thought that they might be hungry so I cooked up a meal, placed it in a picnic basket, and carried it to them. They lived about two blocks away.

When I arrived at Elka's apartment I found she was far sicker than we first thought. She was in bed under three blankets and shivering from a fever. Estella and Daniel sat on a sofa in the front room. I can still see them in my mind, their thin little bodies with dark circles around their eyes and an emotionless expression on their faces.

I set the basket on the kitchen table and checked on Elka, then returned to dish out the food. Elka was too sick to eat, but Estella and Daniel watched my every move as I prepared bowls of soup for them and set it on the table with hunks of bread and fresh butter. They slurped it up and I knew then that I'd been right: Those children were hungry and in need of attention.

While they ate, I returned to Elka's room and gently placed my palm against her forehead. She was hot to the touch. I tried to talk to her but she was shivering so hard she couldn't respond, so I busied myself straightening the room and listening as she labored to catch a breath.

After an hour or so I returned to the Beje. Corrie glanced up from her desk as I entered. "How was Elka?"

"Not good. I need you to find Dr. Van Veen and take him to her apartment."

"Now?"

"Yes. Now. She's sicker than we first thought."

"I can't go off on an errand like that," she protested. "I have too much work."

I lowered my voice and leaned over her. "Elka is sick and will likely die before morning. Her children are there with her. All by themselves. They need help and we're the ones to give it to her."

"The kids aren't in school?"

"No. And from the look of it, they hadn't eaten in a while."

"But you fed them."

"Yes. I fed them, but they need more help. Get Dr. Van Veen and go over there."

"They'll need someplace to stay," Papa added. "If she dies, the police will have to come and write a report. If no one's there to take the children, the police will put them in the orphans' home."

I looked over at Corrie. "Then you better be there to take them."

"We can't just take them."

"We won't just take them. We'll tell the police that's why we are there. To get the children so they don't have to go to the orphans' home. The police will understand."

"But how will we know when to go?" I gave her a knowing look. She stared at me a moment, then a look of realization came over her. "No," she said, shaking her head. "I'm not sitting over there waiting for her to die."

"You stay tonight. I'll come over in the morning."

She sat there in silence, elbows propped on the desktop, glaring up at me. I knew she didn't want to go, but I was certain Elka was not going to survive and we had to be ready to care for her children.

After a moment Papa cleared his throat. "Corrie," he said, "I think she's right."

Reluctantly, Corrie pushed back her chair from the desk and stood, then put on a sweater and started toward the door. As she left, I took Louis from the shop and went upstairs to prepare rooms for the children. When the furniture was arranged and everything was in place I returned to the kitchen and put on a pot of stew. Louis went back to the shop.

Late that night I was awakened to find Corrie standing over me. "Elka died," she said grimly. "I brought Estella and Daniel home with me."

"Where are they?"

"In the parlor."

I sat up and swung my feet over the side of the bed. "Any trouble with the police?"

Corrie took my robe from the chair by the door and held it for me. "No,

I told them what you said," she explained as I stood and slipped on the robe. "That I was there to get the children. They just nodded and told me to get them out of the apartment."

"What time is it?"

"After midnight."

"Are they sleeping?"

"I don't think so."

"Poor things are probably starving."

I tied the sash of the robe around my waist and followed Corrie down to the kitchen. The pot of stew I'd put on earlier was on a back burner. I felt it with my hand and found it was still warm. A ladle hung from a peg to the left and I used it to fill two bowls. Corrie placed them on the table, then added bread and glasses of milk. When it was ready, Estella and Daniel came in from the parlor, and while they ate I motioned for Corrie to follow me back to the kitchen. We stood together near the sink.

"Did Rolfe Ameling come by Elka's apartment?"

"Yes. He was one of the patrolmen."

"Did he say anything?"

"Not really. I think he knew why I was there. They want us to come down to the station later today."

"Dr. Van Veen came, too?"

"Yes. I sent a neighbor to find him and to tell the police. Do you think they'll cause trouble?"

"Not really. Not Rolfe, at least." I nodded toward the children. "Look at them. They ate that stew like they haven't eaten in a week."

"There wasn't much over there to eat. A lady across the hall brought a few sandwiches. That was about it."

"They're dirty, too."

"No telling when they last had a bath."

"We can take care of that right now," I replied.

Even though it was late when Estella and Daniel had eaten, we gave each of them a bath. They were quite dirty. Then I found some clothes for them to wear for the night and we put them to bed. They had little trouble getting to sleep.

With such a late night, I assumed the children would remain in bed until noon, but the next morning they were at breakfast with us. As we sat at the table, watching them eat, I smiled over at Corrie and Papa. "This is what we will do."

Corrie had a questioning look. "What we will do…about what?"

"With this empty house," I said, gesturing to the room around us. "We will make our house a home for those in need."

"That, my dear," Papa said with a smile, "is exactly what your mother would want."

Later that morning, Rolfe stopped by the shop and asked to see me. I assumed he was there to question us about Estella and Daniel and to tell us they were doing everything they could to find their relatives. Instead, after politely inquiring about their condition, he glanced down at the floor and said, "I hate to add to your troubles, but do you have room for one more?"

"Of course," I replied without hesitation. "We always have room for one more. Who is it?"

"I found a boy last night," he explained. "Says his name is Edmund Heenk. Looks to be about seven years old. He was sleeping in a doorway two blocks down the street. Apparently no place to call home."

"Where is he now?"

"He spent most of the night at the jail. We had no other place for him. Just waiting for a bed at the children's home."

Papa spoke up. "Bring him here."

"I'm not sure we can do that right now," Rolfe replied. "I was just asking in case we can't get him in the home."

"Nonsense," I blurted out. "Of course you can bring him. I'll go with you. We'll get him now." I opened the door and started outside. Rolfe hesitated, lingering near Corrie's desk. "Come on," I said insistently. "Let's get the boy."

He tipped his hat to Corrie and Papa and followed me out to the sidewalk. As we walked toward the station, I said, "In the future when you find children like this with nowhere to go, you should not take them to the police station but bring them to the shop. We will care for them."

"That's rather irregular."

"But having a child in a jail that houses adult criminals is even worse."

"I see your point."

"And as for this young boy, Edmund, you will make sure they have no place for him at the children's home, won't you?"

"I'm sorry, ma'am." He looked confused. "I'm not sure I understand."

"I don't think it would be good for him to get settled with us, then uproot him just to take him to the children's home." I smiled over at him. "I mean, by then he would already have a home with us, so what good would it do to move him?"

"Yes, ma'am," Rolfe nodded. "I see your point indeed."

Three nights later, Rolfe knocked on the shop door. I went down to answer it and found Rolfe there with a young boy. His name was Jans Leendert. And so the practice continued, and over the next several years we cared for a dozen children this way. Some of them were with us for only a brief stay before being placed with family members. Others grew up in the Beje and became a second family for us, attending the same school Corrie and I attended, praying with us each morning at breakfast and each evening after supper, laughing, arguing, and becoming wonderful young men and women.

GRADUALLY, THE FOSTER CHILDREN grew up and moved on with their lives. Estella and Daniel, our first, went to live with their uncle in Amsterdam. Edmund Heenk attended the university at Leiden and became a lawyer. He returned to Haarlem and opened an office near Grote Markt, just up the street from the Beje. Jans Leendert attended normal school and became a teacher at the same school where Nollie and Flip worked. We had assumed we would always have extra children in the house and had become accustomed to the sound of their presence. As the Beje emptied and no new children arrived to take their place, Corrie and I wondered what we would do to fill the void. We needn't have been concerned.

By the time the children were all gone, Nollie had two sons, Peter and Robert. Willem had a son, Kik, and a daughter we called Cocky. As the Beje emptied of foster children, our nieces and nephews refilled it, stopping by for a visit almost every day and often staying over for the weekend. Peter, who enjoyed music, came by each afternoon to practice on the piano upstairs under Corrie's watchful eye. She was the first to notice his musical talent and was determined to help him make the most of it.

With the house to keep by myself, I had plenty to keep me busy but in spite of that, Papa and I still went for a walk through the neighborhood each day about midmorning. It did us both good to get away for a few minutes. On one of those walks I glanced through the window of Rene Schouten's butcher shop and saw a group of men gathered around a shiny new radio that sat at the end of the counter. I tugged on Papa's arm to bring him to a stop and pointed. "Look. Rene has a new radio."

When radios first became popular, many of Papa's generation thought they were dangerous. Rene Schouten was one of them and adamantly declared he would never own one. "Don't want all those electrical waves coming into my shop," he once said. Then commercial broadcasting expanded and stations sprang up everywhere. Radio became not only popular but a vital source of information and an enjoyable form of entertainment. References to news items and shows from the broadcasts quickly found their way into everyday conversation.

Ownership of a radio also became a status symbol—an indication of one's level of sophistication, and a measure of success. Schouten was not a vain man but he knew the value of keeping up with the times as well as any good businessman. If his customers were interested in it, perhaps he should be, too. Without telling anyone, he purchased a radio and kept it at his house so he could listen in private, keep up with the latest news, and not have to endure the ribbing he'd get over his prior assurances he'd never own one. But listening exposed him to a number of shows broadcast from London and he became a fan of the BBC. At last, unwilling to miss even a single broadcast, he brought the radio to his shop so he could listen while he worked. As expected, no one let the moment pass without reminding him of what he'd said before.

The radio we saw that day was a new one, so we went inside the shop to see what they were listening to. We stood with the others for a while, listening to the news. Actually, Papa listened. I checked the prices of meat and thought about what to prepare for supper. When we left to resume our walk Papa said, "We should have one of those radios in the shop."

I was skeptical of whether we actually needed a radio, but Corrie agreed with Papa and at their insistence we started saving money to buy one. A few months later Corrie rode the trolley to a department store across town and made the purchase. She brought the radio to the shop and Papa sat it in the corner near his desk, where he plugged the power cord into a wall outlet. When he switched it on we all heard the sound of an announcer's voice broadcasting from a station in Vienna. Papa scooted his chair up close and for the next hour turned the dial first one way then the other, listening to find stations as far away as possible.

This went on for several days, with Papa's attention alternating between the work on his desk and the dials on the radio. Then one morning after breakfast I glanced in the parlor and saw the radio sitting on a table near the piano. As I stood there a moment, wondering how it came to be in that location, Papa came behind me and placed his hand on my shoulder. "It was in the way," he explained. "I needed the elbow room and it was too much of a temptation. Kept me away from my work." He moved to the staircase and glanced back at me with a smile. "Besides, we can all enjoy it up here." And that's what we did.

Several times each week we gathered around the radio and listened to a concert from some distant city, often with Peter seated on the floor, listening with rapt attention. And each evening after supper we listened to the news broadcast in English from the BBC. Papa said they were the most honest and accurate.

From those nightly reports we learned that changes were coming in Germany as Hitler and the Nazi Party solidified their hold on political power. His speeches regularly outlined Germany's problems with unemployment and a weakened economy, and laid responsibility for it at the feet of a vast Jewish conspiracy. Usually delivered in a belligerent rant, Hitler went on to blame the Jews for Germany's defeat in the Great War. We listened to him as he shouted and raved like a madman, but Corrie and I found him difficult to take seriously and dismissed him as crazy. Papa was deeply troubled. "I am worried about the Germans," he said one night after a particularly offensive address.

Corrie glanced at me with an amused look, then over at Papa. "You're concerned about the Germans?"

"Yes," he nodded. "Hitler is a charismatic leader and a brilliant orator. The German people could easily be swayed by the charm of his personality and the emotion of the moment."

"They can hear him as well as we can," Corrie countered. "Surely they can tell he's crazy."

"Except that they *did* vote him," I cautioned.

"They should be careful what they listen to and what they think," Papa continued, "lest evil overtake them and they actually do those things he's talking about. The Jews are still God's chosen people. He has not forgotten them nor has He forgotten His promise—those who bless them receive a blessing. Those who curse them receive a curse."

Corrie and I thought of Hitler as a German problem, perhaps not in the same way as Papa did, but we never considered him a threat to the Netherlands. We listened to Hitler's speeches at night and heard the news reports, but pushed aside the suggestion that Germany was preparing for war. Papa thought otherwise. He was certain the Germans would drag us all into a new round of conflict. Willem agreed and several times spoke of dark forces rising in Europe. Corrie and I let them talk but we thought they were worried over nothing.

In the spring of 1938, Germany invaded Austria. Most people knew this was coming and were not particularly upset. Many Austrians thought of themselves as Germans anyway and resented being arbitrarily excluded from their homeland by national borders that were re-drawn at the end of the Great War by the Allied Powers. They turned out in throngs to greet the advancing German troops and treated them like liberators instead of conquerors. Reporters on the radio and in the newspaper indicated many outside the region shared their opinion.

A broad consensus of Europeans saw the Treaty of Versailles, one of several agreements that concluded the most recent war, as unduly punitive against Germany and the source of Hitler's belligerent stance. Germany's invasion of Austria, so the common wisdom went, merely righted some of those historic errors. Papa was not convinced and thought it a big mistake to let Germany take control of its neighbors. "If they continue gobbling up their neighbors," he argued, "they will soon control us all and there will be no one left. All of Europe will be German."

With Austrian citizens welcoming the invaders, news of the conquest quickly faded. Reports focused instead on accounts of German benevolence and the gracious manner in which they treated Austrian citizens. We heard reports from Polish radio stations telling of Austrian residents who were forced from their homes and sent to camps, but the German response characterized those who were detained as criminals and political dissidents. There had been rumblings about this sort of thing from Germany in the years before the invasion, though no one confirmed the rumors and German officials denied any wrongdoing. We weren't overly concerned about it at the time.

Not long after the Germans took control of Austria, Samuel Levy came into the shop. He was accompanied by a man who he never introduced. I heard Samuel talking with Papa and came downstairs to say hello. He was a good customer and I remembered him fondly. While I greeted him, Papa tried to talk to the other man, but he was very reticent to speak, eventually growing so uncomfortable that he excused himself and stepped outside to the street.

When he was gone, Samuel explained. "He is my cousin who just arrived from Germany. He's a little nervous."

"Nervous?" Corrie asked. "About what?"

"He had to get out quickly," Samuel replied. Papa looked puzzled and Samuel glanced over at me. "You understand, right?"

"Not really," I shrugged.

"In Germany they are sending Jews to the camps," he said, as if telling us about something terrible.

Corrie was skeptical. "The camps?"

"Concentration camps."

"We've heard reports on the radio," I explained, "but we've been unsure exactly what was going on."

"I assure you," Samuel argued, "whatever you hear about this on the radio is all German propaganda."

"You mean they are intentionally trying to mislead us."

"Yes," Samuel said with a note of incredulity. "Of course. You don't send someone to a death camp and brag about it on the radio. Not to the world. You lie about it and if you can't lie, you put the best face on it. That's what they're doing."

Corrie looked concerned. "Death camps?"

"That is what the concentration camps are. Death camps. They either kill their prisoners outright, or they work them to death. Everyone knows these things. Have you not heard?"

"Tell us about it," Papa urged.

"The SS, their most powerful, evil troops, arrive in the night and force—"

"You know this for a fact?" Corrie interrupted.

"My own family members have experienced this. I have uncles in a camp at Dachau and cousins at Breitenau. I have heard these things firsthand."

"Go ahead," Papa urged. "You were telling us about the SS."

"They forced my uncles at gunpoint from their homes, herded them to the center of town, and gave them a choice—the camps, or leave the country. Either way, they would lose everything they owned. Some who were with them argued with the soldiers. They were shot on the spot. Others refused to make a choice. They were shot, too. When they were gone, Germans took over their houses, their businesses, their possessions. Whatever they like, they take."

"Why?" Corrie asked. "Why would they do such a thing?"

Samuel wiped his eyes with the back of his hand. "Because our people are Jews."

"Is it really all that bad?" I didn't think he would lie, but it was difficult to believe that someone—anyone—could be so inhumane. It was difficult to accept. "In the camps," I continued, "is it really as bad as all that?"

"Those who go to the camps write back that they are having a great time, but no one believes them and some have managed to let us know that conditions are terrible."

"Well, it must be okay for those left behind," Corrie added hopefully. "I mean, they can't gather up everyone. So, those who get left must be okay."

Samuel's gaze fell to the floor. "Synagogues burned," he muttered softly. "Shops destroyed. Old men humiliated on the street. Beards plucked out. Some of them set on fire." He looked up at us. "Much of it at the hands of youth while the adults stand by and laugh." A sense of desperation came over him. "I tell you these things because I think you want to understand. Because maybe you can help. Many have died. Others have simply vanished." He gestured toward the door. "My cousin is one of the blessed ones. He was able to get out."

When he was gone we talked about what he'd said. We'd known Samuel Levy for a long time and he'd been a good customer in the shop. But what he said sounded so surreal, so incredible, so utterly beyond the human context that we still wondered if it was true.

CHAPTER 22

THE SITUATION IN EUROPE took a dramatic turn in September 1939 when Germany invaded Poland. Reports on the radio from London and from a station in Krakow kept us abreast of the action. We listened to them at night and, in a departure from our normal routine, in the mornings at breakfast.

Germans, attacking from the west, drove quickly toward Warsaw. Two weeks later, the Russian army invaded Poland from the east. Near the end of the month, Great Britain declared war on Germany, but it did the Poles little immediate good. The fighting was over by October, with the Germans and Russians dividing control of the country.

In May of the following year, the British government of Neville Chamberlain collapsed. Chamberlain was replaced by Winston Churchill. With a vow to fight until he reached absolute victory, we knew that our hopes of a peaceful life had ended. Before long, British warplanes filled the sky over the Netherlands as they made their way to bomb German army positions.

As the conflict in Poland began, the Netherlands, holding fast to its historic position of neutrality, closed its borders to refugees. Yet in spite of that, Jews by the thousands fled Germany and poured into our country. In response, the government, with Queen Wilhelmina's support, constructed a refugee camp at Westerbork, in the northern part of the country. One morning, as we gathered for breakfast, Papa turned on the radio to news reports of squalid conditions in the camps. The description—people sleeping on the ground, no sanitation facilities, little food—left me appalled. "That must be horrible, living in a camp like that," I commented. It hardly described how I felt but I was compelled to say *something*.

"I'm sure it is," Papa replied in a distracted manner.

"Perhaps what we've heard about conditions in Germany is correct," Corrie added. "Otherwise, why would they leave?"

"It bothers me," I answered.

Corrie glanced at me. "What does?"

"Their condition," I explained. "The living conditions at the camp. Adults aren't the only ones living there, you know. I'm sure there are young children."

"The government won't let them starve," Papa replied.

"There's a difference between not starving and actually living," I quipped.

"Well," Corrie continued, "there's really nothing we can do about it. The problem is much too large for us to make a difference."

Her response only increased my sense of frustration on the topic. "But what does it say about us if we don't try?" I asked.

Papa looked over at me. "We can always pray."

"We've been praying," I replied with an edge. "Every day we pray for peace in Jerusalem and blessing on the Jews. But we have Jews right here in our country who need our help." The more I said the angrier I became. Angry at the Germans for causing trouble, angry that the Jews were forced to leave their homes, angry at my sister and father for their reluctance to act, and angry with myself for not doing something sooner. "It isn't enough anymore to pray for blessing on them and turn a blind eye to while they flee for their lives." I was ranting now but I didn't care. "We can't just pray and pat ourselves on the back about how spiritual we are."

Papa laid aside his fork and leaned back in his chair. "What are you suggesting?"

"We need to do something."

"But what?" he insisted. "What can we do that would change their condition?"

"It's not just about changing their condition," I argued. "It's about changing *our* condition. About changing our attitude. About becoming doers of the Word, not merely hearers. And maybe if we do something, others will join us and they'll be encouraged to do something, too."

"But what?"

"We could...gather clothes...blankets...food. I'm sure they could use almost anything we could give them."

"And how would we deliver it to them?" Corrie asked.

"I don't know. Surely someone would help us with that."

"Well," she sighed. "Okay...where do you suggest we begin?"

"We'll begin with our own things," the idea suddenly occurring to me without any previous thought. "We can rummage through our closets and dressers for clothes we no longer wear and don't need. Usable items, not the worn-out things. And then we'll ask our neighbors to help." I rose from my place at the table and started toward the hall. "Come on. We can begin now."

"But what about the shop?" Corrie protested.

"Papa can get started without you."

Our search through the dressers, closets, and the attic produced three boxes of clothes and shoes. Some of them had belonged to Mama, some to Aunt Anna. Parting with them brought back many memories, and several times we considered holding on to some of Mama's things, but we reminded ourselves that they were merely physical items—wood, hay, and stubble, as St. Paul put it. If we kept them stored away, they would one day deteriorate and be of no benefit to anyone. Passing them on to those in need put them to good use and in a small way helped preserve the memories we treasured.

With no other place to store the boxes, we placed them in the shop. As customers came by and saw them, they asked what we were doing. Corrie explained about our desire to help refugees at the camp and before long word spread through the neighborhood. Very quickly the shop filled with boxes and sacks of clothes, shoes, and bedding.

As we were running out of space to store the donations, Willem, now pastor of a church in Heemskerk, a village just north of Haarlem, stopped by one afternoon to pick up Kik and saw how the shop had filled. He came upstairs to see me and asked what we were doing. His eyes lit up when I told him, and he asked how we were going to transport the boxes to the camp. Pastoral ministry had proved very different from what Willem expected. Studying at the university opened his eyes to a wider world and the increasingly complex lifestyle that defined most Europeans. He wanted to address broader social issues that the narrow confines of a Sunday sermon could never accommodate. That moment, when he heard what we were doing and our attempts to help the refugees, I saw a spark of the old Willem, the person we'd known when we were younger and life seemed full of possibilities.

"I don't know," I replied. "We haven't figured that part out. Have any suggestions?"

"I think I can get a truck," he beamed.

"That would be great. Can you drive it?"

"Yes," he nodded. "Think we can simply load it and appear at the camp, without arranging it first?"

"I wouldn't know who to contact."

"Neither would I."

I grinned mischievously. "When can you get the truck?"

Early one morning a few days later, I heard a truck come to a stop outside the shop door. We'd just finished breakfast and I was clearing the table. When the door opened downstairs I heard Willem's voice and went to the top of the staircase to see what he was doing. He looked up at me with a wide grin, "I have the truck. Want to get rid of this stuff today?"

With Corrie, Toos, and Louis helping, we began moving the boxes from the shop to the truck. Two men came from a shop next door to assist and Weil sent over a third. Together, we loaded the donations in less than an hour. When we were finished, Louis went back to the shop and the others left. Papa, Corrie, Willem, and I stood near the curb while Willem closed the rear doors of the truck.

"You're going today?" I asked as he latched the doors in place.

"Yes, I'm leaving right now."

"I'll go with you," I said hastily.

"You think you—"

"No you're not," Corrie blurted out. "It's too far and who knows what you'll find when you get there."

"I have to go," I insisted.

"I don't think that is such a good idea," Papa added quietly. "Corrie's right. It's a long way."

"I need to go," I implored. "I want to see for myself what conditions are like and maybe I can talk to someone."

"Talk to someone?" Corrie looked puzzled. "About what?"

"About what the Germans are really like. About why they fled. About the things Samuel Levy told us."

"Well," Papa sighed. "If you feel that way about it."

"No," Corrie argued. "This is ridiculous. It's a long way up there. You can't do this."

I placed my hand on her shoulder. "I'll be all right. It's a ride in the cab of a truck."

Papa looked over at Willem. "Take care of her and don't let her get into trouble."

"I'll do my best."

Willem walked around to the opposite side of the truck. I stepped to the passenger door and reached to open it. Corrie was standing behind us, near the back of the truck, staring at me as if I were leaving for good. I smiled at her. "It's okay, Corrie. I'll be back." Then Papa took her by the arm and guided her toward the shop door.

Since the day Samuel Levy came to the shop, I'd been troubled by images his stories evoked in my mind—Jews attacked on the street, set on fire, shot on sight. The refugee camp wasn't in Germany, and it certainly was no concentration camp. Nevertheless, I had to see for myself what it was like. And I hoped against hope that someone would talk to me about what life was really like under the Nazis.

Westerbork was located all the way up near Groningen, not far from the German border, and almost as close to the North Sea. The drive to get there took most of the day. We arrived late in the afternoon. A shopkeeper in the town gave us directions to the camp, located in a rural area, and we made our way in that direction. It was pleasant country, with gently-rolling hills and woodlands, but as we rounded a curve in the road we saw ahead of us a most appalling sight.

The camp, almost two kilometers square and laid out over a hilltop, was ringed by a wire fence about four meters high. At each corner there were towers manned by armed guards. Soldiers on foot patrolled the perimeter. A stench enveloped us and, even from a distance, the smell was overwhelming.

Twice as we slowed to approach the entrance I had to swallow hard to keep from vomiting.

Large gates made with a wooden frame and the same wire mesh as the fence barred the entrance. More armed guards were stationed there and as we approached, one of them stepped out to stop us. Willem brought the truck to a stop and waited while the guard stepped to the driver's window, then he showed his identification card that indicated he was a minister in the church.

The guard, dressed in a Netherlands army uniform, glanced at the license and asked, "What is the nature of your business?"

"We have a truckload of clothes and other supplies that we wanted to deliver."

As they talked, other soldiers gathered around and the guard who'd stopped us nodded to them. In the mirror I saw them move to the back of the truck and open the doors. We waited while they climbed inside and I heard the sound of someone opening the boxes. They were talking excitedly, then a soldier emerged from behind us holding a leather jacket in his hand. I leaned near Willem to tell him, but he shook his head. "I saw it."

"He has a jacket," I said, jabbing the air with my finger for emphasis. "He took a jacket."

"Don't worry about it," he cautioned. "It's okay."

"But they stole it," I lamented. "Right here in plain sight."

"No," he said with an amused grin. "They didn't *steal* it. They took a sample for further examination."

That might be the way the game was played, but I didn't like it. In protest I folded my hands across my chest and slumped against the door on my side of the cab. A moment later the guard returned to the driver's window and asked, "Do you know where to go?"

"No," Willem replied calmly. "This is my first trip."

"Drive around the southern edge of the camp." The guard indicated with his hand which direction we should take. "About halfway down the fence you'll see a gravel road to the right. Follow it to the cafeteria tent. Someone will help you." Willem nodded and put the truck in gear. Soldiers who just minutes before had been rifling through the truck pushed the gates open and we started forward.

Beyond the fence were rows of what appeared to be hastily constructed wooden shacks with tin roofs and only one or two windows each. Between them, canvas tents were crammed into every available space. In the space between the wooden shacks and the fence, we found lean-tos constructed of shipping crates and packing material. Paths through the camp were muddy, and I saw people mired past their ankles in thick brown goo—and people were everywhere, oozing between the hovels like a human morass.

As we idled around the edge, I saw a little boy standing outside one of the tents. Not more than four years old, he was dressed in short pants. His bare feet were covered in mud to his knees, and he clutched a dirty blue blanket. Our eyes met and he looked at me with the hollow gaze of a hungry, lonely child. I wanted to grab him up right then, take him in my arms and whisk him away to the Beje, where he could be safe, warm, and clean. Tears filled my eyes as I realized that could never happen.

A little farther down the fence line we came to a narrow lane that led toward the center of the camp. The path had probably once been covered with gravel, but most of the rocks were now buried in mud. Willem turned the truck into the lane and we came to a tent near the center of the camp. Beneath it, there were wooden tables in rows with chairs haphazardly arranged around them. On the far side, just beyond the edge of the tent, steam billowed from a dozen enormous iron kettles suspended over an open fire.

"This must be the place." Willem turned the truck around in the center of the alley and backed it up to the tent. As the truck lurched to a stop, I opened the door and climbed from the cab. A woman came from among the kettles and stood near the front of the truck. She wore black military boots and the pants of a soldier's uniform with a wool sweater over a cotton blouse. Her hair was pulled behind her head and braided and she had smudges of dirt and grime on her cheeks.

"What's in the truck?" she asked.

"Clothes, shoes, blankets," I replied. "And a few food items."

"Good," she nodded. "We can use all of it." Before we could say anything more she disappeared behind the row of steaming kettles.

Willem unlatched the rear doors of the truck and swung them open, then climbed inside and handed me a small box. "Set this over there," he said, nodding to the tables beneath the tent. I turned to do as he said, wondering how we'd ever get the truck unloaded by ourselves, when the woman we'd seen before returned, surrounded by a dozen teenagers. Two of them climbed in back to help Willem, and the rest formed a line from the truck to the table. For the next thirty minutes they worked methodically through the boxes and sacks, passing them from the truck to one another down the line to the tables. While they worked, they talked, and the sound of their voices filled the air.

With the truck rapidly emptying, I glanced around to see if there was someone I could talk to, someone who could answer my questions. I scanned the tables and over to the kettles and saw no one, but to the right I saw a woman seated on the steps to a wooden shack that stood a few meters away. I made my way in that direction, but before I could reach her she saw me and quickly went inside. As I was turning away, an elderly man appeared at my side.

"You came with the truck?" he asked in a heavy German accent.

"Yes," I replied in German.

A smile brightened his face. "You bring us hope." Then just as quickly as it came, the smile vanished. "We have nothing."

"You left it all behind?"

"What they didn't take."

"The Germans?"

"Yes," he nodded. "The Nazis."

We took a seat at one of the tables beneath the tent and for the next thirty minutes he told me of the atrocities he and thousands of others had endured. As he talked I learned his name was Leonard Michelson. He'd been educated at Oxford and took a teaching position in Berlin, only to be ousted when the Nazis came to power. "They purged us all. Every Jew. Eliminated from the faculty. Only for a while did they let Jews pick up the garbage and clean the floors. Then they stopped even that."

"What did you do?"

"What could we do? At first I found odd jobs. There were still people who were sympathetic to our situation and who did not mind the risk of helping us. But gradually the Nazis became stricter, even sending people to the camps for helping us. No one wants to go to the camps."

"What do you know about the camps?"

"They work you harder than two men, feed you half as much as one would require, and if you complain or fail to do the work, they shoot you."

"Does that really happen?"

"That and things much worse."

"You saw this?"

"When those two men were shot in the German Embassy in Paris, the SS came to our village the next day. They said that ten of us would die for each of those men. So they walked down the street together, en masse, right there in the middle of the day. And as they went they grabbed whoever they saw. Took them to the center of town and shot them dead right there in front of us. Some of us went to claim the bodies but they beat us and told us to leave them. The bodies lay there for three weeks, rotting."

"And you saw this?"

"Yes," he fumed. "I saw this. Why do you keep asking me that?"

"Because I've heard stories, but never from someone who was actually there. Someone who actually saw it. And I want to know if these stories are true."

"One of the ones they shot that day was my brother. He was standing next to me when the soldiers came by. They took him but left me. I went to claim his body. They beat me." He turned his back to me and pulled up his shirt to reveal thick, ugly scars. "See what they did to me?"

"Y-yes." I choked back the tears.

He lowered his shirt and turned to face me. "One of them hit me with the butt of a rifle and knocked me to the ground. Then the others joined in, kicking me and stomping on me. Then someone brought a whip and they whipped me like an animal."

"I am so sorry," I sobbed. "I am so sorry."

He sat beside me and slipped his arm across my shoulder. "I can see you have a good heart," he said softly. "But if you want to know the truth, you must know it all. They use women for their pleasure, then they kill them in the most gruesome way you can imagine. Jewish women. Some of them mothers of the people you see around us. They use babies for target practice. Jewish babies tossed in the air and shot for sport. If they see someone—a

Jew—walking down the street, and they think of it, they shoot them with no regard or consequence to themselves. My neighbor, Oscar Herzfeld, was shot in the back of the head by a Nazi playing a game with his fellow soldier. They were up in the bell tower of a church, challenging each other to see who could shoot a Jew from the farthest distance. These things happened to us every day in Germany. That is why we are here."

CHAPTER 23

TRAVELING TO THE REFUGEE CAMP took a greater toll on me than I expected—both physically and emotionally. When we arrived back at the Beje, I was exhausted. Willem carried me up to my bedroom. I vaguely remember Corrie pulling the covers over me. For the next week I lay in bed, unable to do much else except think of the things I had seen and heard. As I did, I came to the conclusion that we could no longer ignore what was happening across the rest of Europe and even in the Netherlands. We'd given ourselves that luxury far too long. "I should have done something sooner," I thought to myself.

What I could have done, I don't know, but I'd seen firsthand how our efforts, weak though they may have been, motivated others to take up the cause, and that made the effort much more effective. I'd also heard firsthand of the atrocities visited upon the Jews by the Nazis and I could never forget that. The Nazis meant to eliminate the Jews, of that I was sure. Methodically, systematically, and in a way so subtle and disarming that many otherwise good, upstanding people would fail to oppose it. Someone—many, in fact— needed to tell the Dutch people what was really happening. I was sure one person who needed to do that was me.

As I lay in bed trying to recover and collect my thoughts about what to do next, Kik came to visit me. The trip, it seemed, was an eye-opening experience for Willem, too. Even as I lay in bed, he was organizing another trip to the camp, this time carrying much-needed food. "It's all he talks about now," Kik said. The way his eyes shone when he spoke I knew the work of helping the refugees resonated with him, too.

"I hope he doesn't forget he has to preach this Sunday," I said lamely. It was a wasted comment and from the moment it left my lips I wanted it back.

Kik raised his eyebrows. "He might have forgotten. I haven't seen him in the study all week. No telling what will happen on Sunday."

Later that week, Willem stopped by the house to check on me. I looked up at him from my pillow. "I hear you're going back to the refugee camp."

"Already been," he said proudly. "Went up yesterday, spent the night last night, on my way home now."

"Kik said you were taking food."

"You should have seen it." Willem was more excited than I'd seen him in a long time. "It was like a thousand Christmases rolled into one. Adrian had the kettles working and—"

"Adrian?" I felt my forehead wrinkle in a frown. "Who's Adrian?"

"The woman we met up there. With the boots and the army pants. That's her name."

"She never introduced herself."

"She didn't introduce herself to me, either. Someone else told me. But they started cooking and the smell was fantastic. People were lined up all the way to the front of the camp, waiting to eat."

"Did you have enough?"

"Food?"

"Yes."

"Oh yes," he nodded. "There was plenty to eat, but we'll have to go back in the next few days."

"What about the church?"

He had a puzzled look. "What about it?"

"Are they helping you?" It was another wasted comment but I couldn't seem to shed the big-sister role.

"I haven't really said anything to them," he replied. "But I'm going to talk to them this Sunday. They'll hear a sermon like they've never heard before."

"How are the children?"

"Kik and Cocky?"

I shook my head. "No, the ones we saw at the camp."

"Well, their bellies were full when I left," he grinned.

A sad smile spread over my face at the thought of that little boy I'd seen as we arrived. "I wish we could bring those children here. All of them. Fill the house to the roof with children. Keep them safe and warm. And clean."

Willem pulled a chair to my bedside and took a seat, then leaned close and lowered his voice. There was a twinkle in his eye and I knew something was up. "I think we may have a way of doing that…well…something like it," he said.

I frowned at him. "What are you talking about?"

"Some of us are putting together a plan to get the children out of the camps and send them to England."

"To England."

"Yes."

My eyes opened wide. "Can you do it?"

"I think so," he grinned. "We flew fifty children to London two days ago."

My mouth fell open. "To stay?"

"Yes," he nodded.

"Already? You sent them already?"

"That was the first trip, to test the system and see if it will work."

"Did it?"

"Smooth as glass."

"How about that," I sighed. "How long have you been working on this?"

"We started preparing for it last month."

"Last month?" I slapped him playfully on the arm. "Why didn't you tell me?"

"It was too risky. The refugees started showing up several months ago and we knew it was going to be a big problem, so we went to work on alternate plans, other than just leaving them in a refugee camp."

"That must be expensive. Flying them to London. Who's paying for it?"

"Some very wealthy people who don't like what they see happening. They're stepping up to do something about it, at least in some small way. I'm just helping."

"Well, it's not such a small thing to those children," I argued. "Or their parents."

"I hope it helps." He leaned back in the chair and his face turned serious. "But there are a lot of elderly in the camp, too."

"I know. I talked to one of them."

"He asked about you."

"What did you tell him?"

"I told him you were back here dreaming up more ways to help."

"No, you didn't."

"Yes, I did."

"Now he's going to expect me to come back."

"That's a tough place for people like him," Willem continued. "Tougher on the elderly than it is on the children. And there are more old people than young."

"Any way to get them out? The elderly. Take them someplace like you're doing with the children?"

"Nah, I don't think so. No one seems too interested in helping them." He looked over at me. "I thought I might do something for them."

"Like what?"

"Start a home for them."

It sounded like a very big project and I wasn't sure he could make it work, especially now that Europe was sliding into war. "What got you so interested in this?" I hoped to take the conversation in a different direction.

"You," he replied with a jab of his finger.

The answer caught me off-guard. "Me? What did I do?"

"Seeing what you did right here in the neighborhood. Gathering clothes and then going up there to deliver them." His eyes were full. "This is what I've been looking for. Doing something that affects people's lives. I don't think I was really made for pastoral ministry."

Perhaps he was correct but I knew Willem had responsibilities—a family and an obligation to his church. The thought of him turning his back on a career he'd planned and worked toward for so long left me not a little shaken. It also left me feeling very much alive and I decided there was no point in voicing the moderate approach—go slowly, take it one step at a time. We were well past that in our lives and besides, it sounded like he really wanted to do it. "So, where would you put this home?"

"At Heemskerk. Where we're living now," he explained. "There's a house just down the street from the church that would be perfect."

"How will *that* go over with your congregation?" It was an obvious question. I couldn't resist asking it and he needed to think about the church's reaction, if he hadn't already. "A houseful of elderly Jews," I continued, "living within sight of their church?"

"I know," he shrugged. "I've thought about it, but I don't much care anymore. Many of our members are already disgruntled over the time I've spent with the refugees." He looked me in the eye. "But there's just one catch to this great plan."

"What's that?"

"What if it doesn't work?" And for an instant I saw a look of fear flitter across his face.

I smiled at him. "How could it not succeed?"

"I'd have to house, feed, and clothe them. And we'd have to find a way to get medical care. These are elderly people. They're going to have medical problems. All of that could be expensive."

Once again the thought came to me about how risky this venture was, but I pushed aside the voices of gloom and doom and said bravely, "You'll take this one day at a time. Find the house. Find the people. Fill the rooms. And if they need medical care, God will provide it. He'll bring someone along to help."

"Do you really think so?"

"I don't think it," I replied. "I believe it." And that was the truth. If I'd gone by what I thought, I would have never offered the refugees the first article of clothing. Having done that and having seen what God could do with the effort of just two women and an elderly father, I was certain God would see Willem through to success. "If God is calling you, it won't fail," I assured him. "And if it does fail, He'll have something else for you to take its place."

The following week, Willem rented a house down the street from the church and equipped it with beds and linens, all of it donated by people he'd come to know through helping the refugees and the airlift of children to England. Much of the furnishings were used and from what I heard had seen better days, but it was adequate for the moment. Donors who were helping with the other projects provided enough money to get the home started, and by the end of the following month Willem was ready to transport elderly refugees from the camp. Then, just before he was to leave to pick up the first group, he was called for an interview with the bishop.

The bishop, it turned out, had learned of Willem's plans from several parishioners who objected to housing the refugees in town. "Think of the risk," they urged. "No one has tested or examined these people. We don't know what diseases they are carrying. And we don't know what will happen to them once they're here. They could become a terrible burden on the village and the crown." One church member had gone so far as to suggest, "They might be German spies."

The bishop thought their concerns were spurious but didn't want trouble in the parishes. "Not now," he insisted. "This isn't the time. They'll be fine where they are. You can do this later, after everyone calms down."

Willem would have nothing of it and resigned his position on the spot. The following day he drove to the refugee camp, gathered up as many of the elderly as would fit in his car, and brought them back to Heemskerk.

At first the house was just a house. He and Tine did most of the work, along with help from Kik and Cocky. Gradually, he added staff members to help, many of them Jewish, and even employed some of the refugees. After he'd had time to get things sorted out, Papa, Corrie, and I rode out to see what he was doing. Willem said nothing of the bishop or the protests from the churchmen. Tine told us all of that.

It was a remarkable operation. The house was spotless and the guests looked as healthy as could be expected. We stayed with them a few hours and as they were preparing for supper we took our leave. As I made my way down the front steps of the porch, an image flashed before my eyes. Only for an instant but sharp and clear just the same. In place of the small front yard that was actually there, I saw a lush green lawn with a driveway that extended down to large iron gates. On either side of the drive were flowerbeds filled with tulips, all of them in full bloom. People of every age, men and women, healthy and infirm, tended the flowers, and as I watched one of them raised himself up straight and turned toward me. He was smiling at me and then I realized it was the man I'd met at the refugee camp.

Just as quickly, the image disappeared and Corrie was at my side. "Are you okay?" she asked with a look of concern.

"Yes," I nodded. "Just needed to stop for a moment."

Willem joined us. "Let me help you." He took my arm in his to guide me down the steps.

When we reached the bottom I asked, "Do you remember the man I talked to that day when we went to the camp?"

"Yes," Willem replied, and I saw a hint of sadness in his eyes.

"Have you seen him again?"

"He was on my list of people to collect on our first trip, but when I arrived they told me he had died the day before." Tears trickled down his cheeks. "The day I was meeting with the bishop. I was supposed to be there that day. If the bishop hadn't called I would have made it."

"But if he died," I said, trying to comfort him, "don't you think he was likely ill already?"

"I know, but still, I would have been there."

"Did he know you were coming for him?"

"Yes, and he was happy to be coming here." Willem forced a smile. "He wanted to see you again and talk with you some more. I think he was worried that what he'd said had upset you."

"I think he told me the truth, though." I took Willem's hand in mine. "Don't you?"

"Yes," Willem nodded. "He did. He said as much. But he wanted to see you again. I think he had more to say."

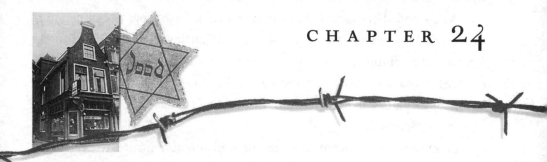

CHAPTER 24

A FEW MONTHS LATER, rumors circulated through Haarlem that the Germans were preparing to invade the Netherlands. Nothing in the newspaper or reports on the radio confirmed it, but talk around town suggested the German air force wanted to use our airfields to stage a defense against British bombers. Others suggested the Germans wanted to launch an attack on England.

Queen Wilhelmina assured us repeatedly that there would be no capitulation, but throughout the winter and early spring high-ranking officials made repeated trips to Berlin. They also made a point of insisting in every speech and at every public event that we had made our neutrality clear and had not violated its principles.

In May, the prime minister, Dirk Jan de Geer, returned to The Hague from yet another trip to Berlin. The night he returned he made a formal radio address to the nation and assured us that Germany would not attack. Once again he reiterated that he'd been conducting discussions with German representatives who assured him Dutch neutrality would be respected. We went to bed that night thinking there was hope. Within a few hours, however, a loud rumbling shook me awake and I lay in bed wondering what could possibly be happening, at first too afraid and bewildered to move. Through the curtains on the window I saw great flashes of light, some of them very close and more brilliant than any lightning I'd ever seen. The sound of it reverberated through the house so strongly it shook the pictures on the wall. After a few minutes curiosity got the better of me and I rose from my bed, crept to the window, and held back the curtain with my hand.

As I stood there gazing into the distance, a flash from the direction of the airfield illuminated the night sky and for an instant I could see in the foreground a column of smoke rising in the air. Another burst to my left took my eyes in that direction, followed by another to the right. Then I heard the sound of airplanes flying overhead and realized what was happening. We were being bombed.

Moments later, I heard footsteps behind me and turned to see Corrie coming from the hall. Her eyes were wide and her face had a look of panic. "What is happening?" Her voice was little more than a whisper but the fear in it was no less gripping than a terrified scream.

"The Germans," I said calmly, motioning her to my side. She stood next to me and I slipped my arm around her waist. "They appear to be bombing the airport."

"I thought they wanted to use the airport."

"That was the rumor, wasn't it?"

"Yes," Corrie nodded. "And, I might add, the rumors were far more accurate than the prime minister." She stood there with me a moment longer watching out the window, then rested her head on my shoulder. "Aren't you afraid?"

"I was when I awoke but I'm not now." I turned away from the window. "Come on. Let's have some tea."

There was no use standing there watching the destruction of our country, and we certainly weren't going to get back to sleep anytime soon. So we might as well have something warm to drink.

In the kitchen I put on the kettle and found some cookies in the cupboard. There was bread from breakfast the previous morning and I found jam to put on it. By the time I had that on the table the water in the kettle was hot and I poured it in the teapot with a few leaves of tea. We sat at the table, sipping and eating as the bombs exploded around us. Overhead we heard the drone of bombers and the whining sound of fighters as they fought through the night.

"This is not going as we expected," I said finally.

"No," Corrie replied with a shake of her head. "I suppose Hitler is no longer just a German problem."

"War is coming."

"War is here," Corrie noted.

"We must get ready. Our army is brave but it cannot hold out against the Germans, and I have a feeling this will end badly for us. Very badly for us all."

Corrie looked up from her teacup. "I heard you talking with Willem that day when we went to see their new home. You think the rumors about the way the Germans treat the Jews are true?"

"Yes. I know they are."

Corrie was concerned. "Will it be like that here?"

"I'm afraid so. And we will face the same dilemma that confronted the Germans."

"Which was ...?"

"Whether to do something about what we see or ignore it."

"I still don't know what we could possibly do to stop it."

"Nor do I. But we have to try."

We sat there awhile nibbling on the bread and sipping another cup of tea. Finally, Corrie said quietly, "I have this dream. I've had it several times the past few months."

"What about?"

"We're riding in the back of a wagon. You, me, Papa, Willem, others we know. Soldiers are guarding us and a crowd is gathered to watch as we ride in that wagon across the square at Grote Markt."

Hearing someone else's dream is never as compelling as having your own, but I tried to seem interested. "Is it a good dream?"

"No." Corrie shook her head. "It's a dreadful one."

While she was talking I was thinking of my own recurring dream and I wondered if I should tell her about it. She was my sister, after all, and she'd been brave enough to tell me hers. So after we'd sat there awhile longer, I said, "I've had a dream, too. And in that dream I am floating in the air above a very large house with a lawn and gardens filled with tulips. The flowers are in full bloom and you are there tending them with others, old and young, men and women."

"That sounds like a peaceful dream."

"Yes," I nodded. "It is, actually. But I've had it a number of times while I was sleeping and I saw it when we were leaving Willem's new house that day."

Corrie's eyes opened wider. "You saw it?"

"Yes," I nodded.

"Without being asleep."

"Yes."

She gave a musing nod and we fell silent again, both of us ruminating over what we'd heard from the other. A little while later, Corrie glanced around with a look of realization. "The bombing has stopped."

"Yes, it has," I answered, realizing it for the first time, as well. "And we should probably get back to bed." I pushed myself up from the chair and stood. "We can sleep a few more hours before dawn."

I heard the sound of Corrie's footsteps as she trudged up to her room on the next floor. I gathered the cups and plates from the table, but no sooner had I set them on the counter than once again I heard the sound of footsteps on the stairs, this time coming down. A moment later, Corrie appeared at the kitchen doorway. Her eyes were wide with fright and she held a jagged metal object, and blood trickled from her index finger. "There's a hole in the roof and this was lying on my pillow," she exclaimed, so excited she could hardly speak. "It was lying right where my head would have been. It's a piece of metal shrapnel from the bombing." Her lips trembled. "If I hadn't come downstairs…"

I pressed my finger to her lips. "Shhh. We're not going to speculate about that."

"But if I hadn't come down to your room and we hadn't—"

"There is safety in God's will," I said, interrupting her. "He has protected us to now and He will continue to protect us. But we must stay at the heart of His will, no matter what the circumstances may suggest to the contrary."

❖ ❖ ❖

Five days after the bombing started, with Rotterdam in Nazi hands and

Utrecht on the verge of capitulation, General Winkelman, commander of the Netherlands' armed forces, surrendered. Queen Wilhelmina, the prime minister, and most of the government fled to England just hours ahead of the advancing German army. We listened to reports of it on the radio. I felt like crying.

Within days of our surrender, German soldiers occupied Haarlem. Unlike the warm reception they received in Austria, few in the Netherlands welcomed their presence, but they had money to spend and didn't mind doing so. During the summer and into the fall our shop was more profitable than ever. We sold every watch and clock, even items that had been on the shelf for a long time, and though we could not readily restock we were glad for the business.

As fall approached, the Germans invited Queen Wilhelmina and other officials to return to The Hague and cooperate in governing the country. Prime Minister De Geer agreed with the proposal and wanted to return, but the queen refused and dismissed him. As a result, Arthur Seyss-Inquart, an Austrian Nazi, was named by Hitler to govern the country. A few weeks after that, the Germans imposed a curfew that required us to be off the streets by eight each evening. Shortly after that, they issued orders requiring everyone to obtain and carry an identity card.

And that is how the Germans operated. Slowly, methodically, one step at a time, no single individual step too objectionable, but each one moving us closer to their goal of absolute control over our lives. I bristled at the thought of having to carry a card, but there was little option other than to obey. Without the card, we couldn't conduct business of any type, not even to make purchases at the grocer or even from the vendors at Grote Markt. So, I went with Corrie and Papa to the Homeland Office to get the card. As we stood in line that day I saw Vincent seated at a desk behind the clerk's counter. He saw us but looked quickly away. I was appalled at the thought of him working with the Nazis.

Not long after that, a Food Office was established, supposedly to ensure an adequate food supply. Shortly after that, rationing began. Each adult was required to report to the Food Office to obtain a ration card, which allowed us to make purchases of specific restricted food items. Once again, we trekked to a government office and stood in line to register for a card. And once again I saw Vincent, this time as I made my way down the main corridor toward the registrar's office. He was seated at a desk in an office off the hall, only this one had a window and he was dressed as if he was in charge. I wanted to barge in there and scream at him, to bring him to his senses, but instead I continued down the hallway and lined up with everyone else. If he was stupid enough to believe the Germans, then he could meet his fate with them.

The line for the cards was long and everyone was irritable, so I did my best to keep quiet and wait patiently. All the while, though, I thought of Vincent, and the longer I stood there the madder I became. In a little while, one of the office assistants appeared at my side and instructed me to follow her. By then, my patience had worn thin. "I've been waiting over an hour," I protested. "If I get out of line, I'll lose my place."

"Follow me," she repeated, this time nudging me at the elbow.

A guard stood in the corner and when he heard us talking he started in our direction. Rather than face him I followed the woman back up the corridor. A moment later she led me to Vincent's office and gestured for me to enter. I paused at the doorway, wondering whether to go inside or simply leave. His eyes were focused on a file that lay on the desktop and when he didn't look up at me I decided to leave. But as I glanced back over my shoulder toward the hall, the woman who was with me gave a stern look and so, resigned to nothing but an exercise in the waste of time, I stepped into the office and took a seat.

Behind me I heard the click of footsteps as the woman disappeared up the hall. When she was a safe distance away, Vincent looked up at me and said, "I saw you last month at the Homeland Office. I wanted to—"

"What are you doing with these people?" I snapped, cutting him off. "Are you crazy? Have you become one of them?"

"No," he answered hastily. Then he lowered his voice and leaned forward. "I am not a Nazi, just a Dutch civil servant trying to make a living and keep alive."

"But you're obviously working for *them*," I continued. "Why did you do that? Why did you agree to work for the Nazis?"

"I didn't agree to work for *them*," he explained. "I took the job with the

Homeland Office because it was better than reading electrical meters. They liked the way I worked with numbers at Homeland, and when this office opened they put me in charge."

"What happened to the university and all the things you talked about?"

"I ran out of money after the first year and couldn't find a way to stay in school, other than to study for the ministry, and that wasn't my calling. I didn't want to just do it for the money to stay in school."

His comment made me think of Karel and the reasons he'd studied for the ministry, all of which I found reprehensible. Vincent's attitude was commendable, but I was still troubled seeing him working in that office. "Well," I sighed, doing my best to give him the benefit of the doubt, "we're all just doing the best we can."

A few minutes later a clerk appeared in the office doorway. Vincent caught her eye and nodded. She stepped near my chair and thrust a ration card toward me. "It's marked for renewal," she said, "but you have to retrieve them from the office."

"Each month," Vincent added. "You have to return to the office to pick up a new one each month."

"Do I have to stand in line?"

"Not that line," he answered, gesturing toward the far end of the hall. "And it'll move faster, too."

I stood and smiled over at him. "I suppose I should be going." I gestured with the card. "Thanks."

"Certainly," he replied, and before I was out the door, he turned his attention to the papers on his desk.

At home that evening while we ate supper I mentioned Vincent's situation to Papa and Corrie. We all agreed that if the country was to have a future, we had to find a way to survive, and with the Germans in control, survival would likely mean some form of cooperation.

"We've sold them every watch and clock in the shop," Papa added.

"Was that wrong?" Corrie asked.

"Well," Papa smiled, "we didn't refuse them."

"That wasn't so difficult and no one would have expected anything different from us," I suggested. "It also caused no one any harm. But we may face some tough decisions yet."

Corrie glanced over at me. "What do you mean?"

"Many of our customers are Jewish."

"Most of the best ones," Papa added.

Corrie still had a questioning look. "And how is that a bad thing?"

"What if the Germans treat them here the same way they do in Germany?" I asked. "What if they pluck the beards of the old men, beat them in the street, or turn them out of their shops? What will we do then?"

"We would lose most of our business," Corrie replied.

"We could lose more than that," Papa corrected. "Depending on how we answer Betsie's question."

Corrie looked across the table at him. "You mean, do we help them, or ignore them?"

"Precisely," Papa nodded.

"We have no choice but to help them," she added.

"No choice at all," I added.

It was not an easy decision, nor was it one we made that evening over supper. I don't know when Corrie decided, but I'd made that decision long before that evening and confirmed it to myself during the trip with Willem to the refugee camp. I do not regret it, and I would make the same decision a thousand times over, but no one should think that I came to it lightly or from a romantic sense of gallantry. None of us did.

For the remainder of the evening we sat in the parlor and listened to the radio. After the news reports from London, Papa switched to a Berlin station and we listened to the symphony. Normally, we would have gone to bed then but instead he tuned the radio back to a London station and we listened to recorded music.

The hour was well past my typical bedtime when I finally retired to my room. Though I was tired I could not fall immediately asleep. Instead, I lay there staring up at the ceiling, listening to the sounds of the night and imagining the horrors that might befall us. When I finally did get to sleep, I dreamed the dream again—of soaring high over a large house with lush grounds and flowerbeds filled with tulips. Men and women tended the gardens, and Corrie was with them.

Sometime before morning I awakened with a start to find my gown soaked through with sweat. Rather than risk a chill, I climbed from bed and made my way across the room to the dresser to change. As I slipped on a fresh gown, Corrie appeared at my bedroom doorway. "I heard you," she whispered. "Are you okay?"

Glancing at her I said, "I had the dream."

"Again?"

"One of many times. Why were you awake?"

"I've been lying in bed for three hours wondering what will happen to us."

"The discussion tonight disturbed you?" I asked as I crawled into bed.

She lifted the cover and got in beside me. "What will happen to us?"

"I don't know. But whatever it is, we shall face it together." I reached over and took her hand. "We shall face it together," I repeated softly. Then we both drifted off to sleep.

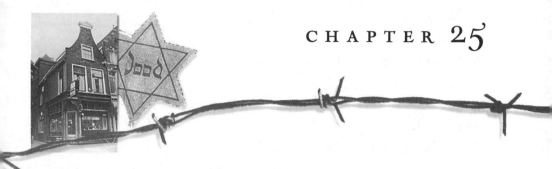

CHAPTER 25

AS THE NAZIS slowly tightened their grip on life in the Netherlands, newspapers gradually lost all objectivity. In place of real news and honest commentary, we received only pro-German articles. Like the radio reports we heard from Berlin, local papers reflected nothing but the predetermined Nazi Party line. They were, in short, merely a means of disseminating party propaganda. Most people recognized it for what it was straight away.

At the same time, the German army brought every aspect of the Dutch government under its control. Civil servants were expected to continue in their current jobs, and when we applied for the identity card, or the ration card, or had any other contact with agencies of the government we continued to deal with Dutch citizens. But always with a German army officer present and always under the watchful eyes of armed German soldiers stationed throughout each of the government buildings. Throughout the winter, that assertion of power slowly worked its way deeper and deeper into our lives.

In the spring, Seyss-Inquart, the Nazi puppet prime minister, approved an order making private ownership of radios illegal. Anyone who owned a radio was required to surrender it. Handbills announcing the policy were posted around town, and newspaper articles gave us the details about how we were to turn them over to the authorities. We also received written notice at the shop. Corrie brought the letter upstairs to show me.

"And it was delivered by a soldier?" I asked as I scanned the one-page letter.

"Yes," she nodded.

"A German soldier?"

"Yes," she nodded. "Why?"

"It seems different," I replied. "Being notified in person and by a soldier."

"I'm not sure what that means."

"So far," I explained, "we've dealt with civilian authorities. We've never had direct dealings with the German army."

"Is that worse than the policy itself?"

"Maybe," I sighed. "But we have a more serious issue."

"What's that?"

I looked her in the eye. "Whether to obey the order or not."

Since our initial radio purchase years before, we'd become quite fond of listening to broadcasts at night. Now, with the Germans controlling all other means of reliable news, the radio had become our lifeline to the outside world. In addition, several nights each week Queen Wilhelmina broadcast from exile in London. Her addresses were important sources of encouragement and information. None of us wanted to give that up. And, to make matters worse, we now had two radios, the older one in the parlor and a newer portable model in the shop.

"I suggest we surrender the one in the shop," Papa said as we discussed it that night. "It plays each day and people have seen it. If we don't surrender it, someone might question us about it and that would not be good."

We all agreed with his suggestion, so the following morning Corrie gathered up the portable radio, cradled it in her arms, and boarded the trolley for a ride across town to Vroom en Dreesman department store, the nearest authorized collection point. She was gone several hours and I was beginning to worry when I heard the shop door open downstairs.

"Any trouble?" Papa asked.

"No," Corrie replied. "But I had to lie."

"They asked if you had any others?"

"Yes," she nodded. "They seemed to insist we had more. As if they knew."

I heard the tone of her voice and came down the steps toward her. When

I reached the shop I looked over at Papa. "Do you think they know we have another?"

"No," Papa answered calmly. "They're just testing to see if we did. Wondering what kind of response they might receive."

Corrie was clearly worried. "You don't think someone has told them?"

"No," Papa replied once more. "Why would they?"

I wasn't so sure they didn't know. We'd heard rumors of informants—fellow citizens who betrayed others to the Nazis. My eyes met Corrie's. "Do you think they knew you were lying?"

She shook her head. "No. In fact, that was the worst part. It was easy to lie in a convincing manner." I knew what she meant.

Lying even a little put us in the unenviable position of acting just like our occupiers, but they gave us little practical option. If we were going to negotiate our way through the occupation, presumably to freedom on the other side, we had to know what was happening both in our own country and around the world. "What did the clerk at the store say?"

"I didn't deal with a clerk, except when I arrived," Corrie answered. "When I told them I was there to turn in a radio they pointed me toward a room in back. An army officer was there with three armed guards. It was rather unnerving at first." She managed a weak smile. "Then I lied and it seemed as though I was among friends."

A troubled frown wrinkled my brow. "You dealt with someone from the German army?"

"Yes," she nodded.

"No Dutch officials were present?"

"No," she said, shaking her head. "Just soldiers." She gave me a quizzical look. "You've asked me this before. What are you worrying about?"

"I think the army is asserting greater and greater control over everything."

"It was the army all along," Papa said without looking up from the work at his desk. "They were behind this from the beginning. Only appointed a prime minister to lull us into thinking otherwise." I didn't argue with him. I knew he was right.

In spite of Corrie's troublesome reaction to lying, we were glad to have the radio. When it wasn't in use, we hid it in a space beneath the rear steps. At night, we took it out and set it on the table in the parlor, then one of us played the piano to cover the sound while the others listened to the evening news.

❖ ❖ ❖

Like the radio, we'd also acquired a telephone years earlier, at first because of the novelty of it and in response to rising public popularity. Very quickly, however, it became an essential tool for our business. With it, orders could be placed to suppliers in distant cities, cutting in half the time previously required to obtain parts and new items. Our customers came to expect the speed that practice afforded. But not long after the prime minister's office issued the order about radios, the telephone stopped working. Two days later we received a notice, once again delivered by a German soldier, telling us that anyone who wished to place even a local call had to do so from a central operating office, access to which was strictly regulated.

Not to be outdone, Corrie and I decided to visit the office and attempt to phone our cousins in Amsterdam—Gerrit van der Pol and his wife, Margriet. If asked, we planned to say we were checking on their condition, but in reality we wanted to see how difficult placing a phone call might be. Two blocks from the phoning office we came to a line of people waiting to place a call, so we returned home. Any calling system that cumbersome would be monitored by the Germans and utterly useless for our purposes.

A few days later, Rabbi Prins came to the shop. Since the invasion, his visits had become less frequent and when he arrived that day Papa brought him upstairs. As they passed the kitchen doorway I noticed Prins was wearing a crudely cut yellow star that was stitched to the front of his jacket, between the lapel and the pocket. I wanted to ask about it but decided to wait.

Papa led him to the dining table and I brought cake and coffee. Instead of discussing theology, however, they talked about events that had transpired since the Germans arrived. I busied myself in the kitchen and listened.

"They have ordered us to form a Jewish Council," Prins said glumly.

"What for?" Papa asked.

"They say it is to give us rights of self-determination, but I do not believe them."

"Are you on that council?"

"A smaller one," Prins explained. "The central one is in Amsterdam, with smaller councils in the other major cities and committees in small towns. The ones that are not so big but have synagogues. We were all ordered to attend a meeting about it."

"I had not heard that."

"We are now required to register special with them, also."

"Didn't you get an identification card?" Papa asked.

"Yes, but this is different. This registration is only for Jews."

"When did this happen? I didn't hear about that, either."

"They didn't tell everyone. Only us. They are doing it now, still. The registration. They are still conducting it in Grote Markt."

"Why did they want you to register again?"

Prins answered with a wry smile. "I am not sure. It makes no sense to us. The Germans ask the same questions every time anyway. But when we registered this time they gave us this." I turned to see what he was talking about and saw him pluck the yellow star between his finger and thumb. "We must wear it on our clothes at all times."

"Why have I not heard of such an order?"

"Like I said, the policy was not officially announced to the public, but you will see the star. Jews must wear it in plain sight. On pain of imprisonment."

Over the next week, news of the yellow star spread and non-Jewish groups, led by the church, called for a countrywide general strike. The following Monday, trains and trolleys stopped running. The grocery store up the street closed for the day, and Papa closed the watch shop. That morning, he and I went for a walk and made our way up to Grote Markt. As we turned the corner by the cathedral I noticed that the square was completely empty of vendors.

In place of the farmers and their vegetables were tables set along the far side of the square, each of them manned by people who appeared to be Jewish. Lines of people stretched across the square and down an adjacent street, waiting to reach the tables. German officers were there also and wandered from table to table, watching, nodding, pointing with instructions to the men seated there.

"This is the registration," Papa explained finally.

I was puzzled. "The registration?"

"The one Rabbi Prins was talking about."

"It is still going on?" I thought it must have ended days before.

"They had many to register. And from the look of things, it is taking them quite a while to do it."

Papa stepped over to a man who was standing in line. "This is the registration?"

"Yes," the man nodded.

"For the star?"

"Yes," the man said, lowering his voice. "That is what I am told. We must be quiet or they will beat us."

Papa's eyes widened with alarm and he looked for a place to squeeze into line. "If that is so, then I will get a star for myself." The man we'd talked to tried to persuade him otherwise, but Papa insisted.

We stood in line for almost an hour until we reached the table. Papa stepped up, hat in hand, just as he had seen the others do.

"Name," the clerk droned without lifting his gaze from the preprinted form that lay before him.

"Casper ten Boom," Papa said loudly.

The clerk looked up, wide-eyed. "This is for registering Jews," he said quietly.

"If Jews must register and wear the star," Papa boomed, "then I will, too. We are all Jews."

The clerk leaned closer and lowered his voice. "Please, you must leave before there is trouble."

"I am Casper ten Boom and I demand my star," Papa said even louder.

An army officer stepped to the table. Stern and very serious he asked, "What is the trouble?" It was more of a demand than a question.

"My name is Casper ten Boom," Papa repeated bravely. "And I want my star."

"But you are not a Jew," the officer said arrogantly. "Only Jews must wear the star."

"If they must wear it, I must wear it. I am a Jew."

Just then Benjamin Weil appeared at Papa's side. He took Papa by the arm and whispered in his ear, "You are a fool for coming here like this, Casper. Do you want to get us all killed?" Without waiting for a reply he turned to the officer and, smiling, said, "Please forgive my friend. He is an old man and he sometimes gets confused. I will escort him home. There will be no trouble." And, with Weil holding Papa by one arm and I by the other, we hustled him away from the table.

"This is an outrage, Benjamin," Papa cried when we were safely out of the way. "An outrage!"

"I know," Weil agreed, "but you were about to get us killed."

Papa glanced around the square and, I think for the first time, noticed the armed soldiers that ringed the area. His eyes opened wide and he looked over at me. "They mean to do here what they have done elsewhere."

"Yes, Papa," I nodded. "I think they do."

When we reached the edge of the square, Weil let go of Papa's arm and turned away. Papa turned to call to him, but I tugged on his arm. "No, Papa. Let's go home."

He watched as Weil disappeared into the crowd, then straightened his jacket and we turned to leave. As we did, I saw Isaac Franken—the father of Tobias, the man Hannah was pledged to marry. He was standing beyond the tables with several older Jews who were mingling among the German officers. I pointed him out to Papa. "He saw us just now."

Papa looked in that direction and nodded. "Yes," he said slowly. "I see him."

"This can't be good."

"No. It can't. Those Germans are in a bad position."

"The Germans?" I frowned.

"They have touched the apple of God's eye. This will not turn out well for them."

When we returned home, Corrie could tell something was wrong. Rather than explain in the shop, I gestured for her to follow me upstairs. She did, and Papa joined us in the kitchen. When she heard about the scene he had made at the square, she was unnerved. "What were you thinking?"

Papa squared his shoulders. "I was thinking that if the Germans want to oppose the Jews, I want to be a Jew."

"Why?"

"Because I do not want anyone to think that I would ever harm God's chosen people. This is what we talked about before. We must decide now how we will react. If we wait until that moment, we will cower like everyone else."

"But you could have been shot right there," she worried, "and no one would have objected. Not even the Jews you were in line with. And all over a yellow star."

"It's not just a star," I said, injecting myself into the discussion. "This is the same thing the Nazis did in Germany and in Austria and in Poland. We've heard it before. They identify, divide, and vilify."

"You must decide now how you will react," Papa repeated. "If they shoot a Jew on the street today, there will be public outrage. But in a few months, no one will even notice. This is how they do it. One step at a time. I have made my choice. I am standing with the Jews even if they shoot me. If you wait until the day it happens, you will cower before the Germans like everyone else."

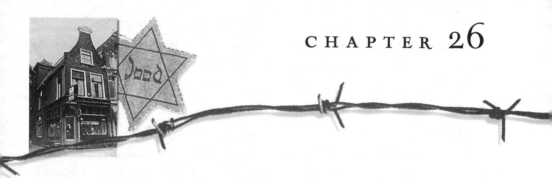

CHAPTER 26

THE NEXT DAY, shops in Haarlem reopened as usual. After break-fast, I walked uptown to Schouten's butcher shop. A notice in the newspa-per announced that pork was available. Meat was scarce and I wanted to get there before they sold out.

As I entered the shop I saw a German captain loitering near the door. He was not accompanied by any other soldiers, and I assumed he was there on his own. When on duty or official business, officers always traveled with three or four extra soldiers—for protection, I suppose. Often in the evening we saw them on the street alone or in the company of women Corrie and I assumed were prostitutes, though Papa chided us for our opinion. That morning, seeing an officer alone in the butcher shop, I concluded he was there in less than an official capacity. The way he leered at me as I came through the doorway told me I was correct.

Paying him no noticeable attention, I made my way to the counter, took a quick glance in the meat case, and tore the correct coupon from the rationing booklet. "Two pounds," I said when it was my turn.

"Betsie, I can only give you one," Schouten replied. I nodded and glanced over my shoulder toward the door, wishing he hadn't said my name.

A moment later, the officer appeared at my side. "Good morning, Betsie," he said with a smile. I nodded in response but said nothing. "I am Otto Bormann," he continued. "Captain Otto Bormann, at your service."

Schouten handed me a neatly wrapped package of meat and I turned away. Bormann followed me to the end of the counter. "Aren't you at least going to say good morning?"

I continued to ignore him and handed the store clerk my package. She calculated the charge, placed the package in a paper sack, and took my money. When she handed me the change, I picked up the sack and started toward the door. Bormann followed after me.

"It's a lovely day for a walk," he said as he came along behind me. But again I did not reply.

All the way back to the Beje, he lagged behind me, never quite touching me, never quite leaving me alone. People glanced at us as we passed, their eyes alert with interest, but they quickly looked away. We had learned early that it was better to go unnoticed if you didn't want trouble from the Germans, which was what I'd tried to do at the shop.

By the time I reached Papa's watch shop, I was thoroughly aggravated. Bormann was older than most of the soldiers we'd seen but he was certainly not as old as I. That he would follow me down the street was nothing more than harassment. He could not possibly be interested in me or I in him.

As I grabbed for the handle to open the door, Bormann's arm came around my side and opened it for me. Then he held it while I entered. Once again I refused to acknowledge even a polite gesture but went straight upstairs to the kitchen and prayed he would not cause trouble.

From the second floor I listened, hoping to hear the sound of the door as Bormann departed but instead I heard the shuffle of his feet as he looked around the shop. "You have a few watches left," he observed and I imagined him standing at the display case by the window where I knew three watches remained. "Most of your competitors have sold out their entire stock already."

"We received those three last week," Corrie replied, and I wondered why she would tell him that.

"You have connections for ordering more?"

"Limited connections," Papa said.

When it seemed Bormann would not leave soon I came down the steps to face him, hoping that if I confronted him he would see there was no use in pursuing me further. As I reached the first floor I expected to address him face-to-face, but he was standing with his back to me and spoke to Papa. "You were at the square yesterday, with the Jews. Causing trouble."

"I wasn't the one causing trouble," Papa answered.

"Oh?" Bormann arched an eyebrow playfully. "Then who was?"

"Your soldiers."

"My soldiers are disciplined young men. They would never harm a civilian."

"They would do whatever you told them to do."

"Yes," Bormann nodded. "That is correct. They would do what I told them to do." He glanced around the shop once again, still apparently unaware of my presence. "You like the Jews?" he asked after a moment.

"They are God's chosen people. I side with Him in their favor."

"God," Bormann scoffed. "You speak of him as if he actually exists."

"Oh, He exists, all right," Papa said with a smile. "And the Jews are His chosen means of redemption. When you touch them, you touch the—"

"Chosen people," Bormann chortled, cutting Papa off. "Chosen to torment us and to die a miserable death." Papa looked away, but I could tell from the tension in his jaw that he was not happy. Bormann turned to Corrie and pointed toward the case. "I'll take that one." She reached inside and carefully removed a watch. The casing was made of gold and the movement came from Switzerland. It was the finest watch we'd had in a long time. Bormann took it from her hand and bounced it on his palm, then looked over at me. "This is a good watch?"

"Far too good for you," I replied.

He shook his head and sighed. "One day you will learn that the Jews are our enemy. Yours and mine." His eyes met mine. "They will bring us only misery."

"If you bless them," I replied, "God will bless you."

The muscles in Bormann's neck flexed, and I could see the veins along his temple throb. He stood there a moment as if thinking of what to say or do, then shook his head once more and said with disgust, "Let me buy this watch and leave before I do something I might regret."

Quicker than I'd ever seen him move, Papa came from behind the desk and snatched the watch from Bormann's hand. "I will never sell you anything," he snapped. "Leave my property at once."

Bormann's eyes flashed with anger, but I could tell from the way the corners of his mouth turned up that he was more than a little amused by the notion of an elderly man standing up to a powerful German soldier. "I could shoot you now, old man," he chuckled, "and no one would ask why."

"You could shoot me now and lose your own soul," Papa retorted.

That response caught Bormann off-guard and in a slow, deliberate fashion he turned toward the door. As he opened it to step outside he glanced once more in Papa's direction and smirked. "An old man like you should be careful he does not make an enemy of a man like me."

◈ ◈ ◈

Not long after our encounter with Captain Bormann, Rabbi Prins returned. His already infrequent visits had become even more erratic since the occupation and we were all glad to see him. Accompanying him that day were a dozen young men, each of them carrying a tall stack of books. I could see them out the window as they stood outside the shop door while Prins came inside.

Corrie greeted him, but Prins brushed past her. I heard him as he made his way to Papa's desk and in a heavy whisper said, "I have a favor to ask of you, Casper. And it is a most serious matter."

Without a word, Papa scooted back his chair, rose from his seat at the desk, and started across the shop. Moments later he appeared at the bottom of the staircase with Prins right behind him. As he grasped the handrail and turned toward the first step, Papa noticed the young boys standing outside. He studied them a moment, then looked over at Prins. "They are with you?"

"That is my favor," Prins smiled.

"Tell them to come inside. They should not be seen out there."

Prins opened the door and directed the boys inside. They crammed into the shop and I heard Corrie showing them places to stack the books.

Before they were settled, Papa started up the steps toward the second floor and Prins followed.

When they reached the top of the stairs, Papa led the way into the parlor, where he took a seat near the piano. He crossed his legs and rested his hands in his lap while Prins took a seat next to him. When they were comfortable Papa smiled and asked, "How may I be of service to you?"

Prins cleared his throat and began. "You remember Samuel Levy came to see you some time ago?"

"Yes," Papa nodded. "And he brought his cousin with him."

"Samuel told you about the treatment his relatives received at the hands of the Nazis in Germany."

Papa looked puzzled. "You know about that conversation?"

"I talked to Samuel," Prins nodded. "He told me."

"What of it?"

"After the Nazis came to power, they sent all of Samuel's relatives to the camps. Every single family member known to him was sent away." Prins jabbed the air with his finger for emphasis. "Three of them are dead now. Two have disappeared."

"He told us something about it," Papa agreed. "But I didn't realize everyone had been sent away."

"All of them," Prins said emphatically. "And the same thing has happened to my family. All of my relatives were turned out of their homes where they had lived all their lives. Homes where their fathers and mothers had lived before them. And they were forced to leave everything behind when they were sent away. What the Germans found useful they took. The rest they burned. Books in particular."

"I have heard of book burnings in Berlin," Papa added.

Prins took Papa's hands in his. "They are coming for us here, too, Casper. And it won't be long now."

"Yes," Papa nodded. "I am afraid you are right."

"I have a lot of books, my friend." Prins had a worried look. "Beautiful books. Lovely books. Sacred books. They are a treasure to me and to others."

Papa's eyes opened wide in a look of realization. "Leave them with me."

"That is the favor I came to ask," Prins said, and I could hear the relief in his voice.

"You need not ask. It will be my pleasure to guard them for you." Papa stood and started toward the hall. "Tell them to bring the books up here. I have a place to put them."

With brief instructions from Prins, the young men made their way upstairs and followed Papa to the attic, where he stacked the books in a corner. When they were all in place he turned to Prins with a smile. "They will be here when the trouble passes."

I saw them there, two old friends standing by the attic door, staring at each other, wondering how many more days they had together. Prins had a sad smile and it seemed as if there was much more he wanted to say, but instead he said, "If I do not return, you will see that my books have a proper home?"

"I will," Papa replied.

❖ ❖ ❖

Later that week, a truck stopped in front of Kan's watch shop, just across the street from us, and a dozen German soldiers climbed out. Moving quickly, they rushed into the shop and, even though we were across the street and I was upstairs, the sound of screams and cries of anguish still reached us. We had talked about this moment earlier and I'd already decided what I would do. I hurried down the steps toward the door, but as I reached for the latch Papa called out to me, "Wait! We do not know what they will do."

"We cannot sit here and watch," I argued. "This is the very thing we have been discussing." I reached again to open the door, but Corrie grabbed me.

"Going out there now will only get you in trouble." She spoke in a firm voice, even and serious but not angry. "It won't help the Kans or anyone else."

"This is precisely why we decided this question already." I looked over at Papa. "Don't you remember?"

"Yes, but—"

"No." I snatched open the door. "You can't protect me from this." In my heart I was committed to acting, doing something—anything seemed better than nothing. But as I turned to leave the shop and start across the street, I saw two soldiers, one on either side, dragging Kan from his shop. They held him beneath his armpits, and his feet dangled in the air, barely touching the ground. With no regard for him at all, they threw him onto the back of the truck and one of them shouted, "Stay!" while another stood guard, rifle in hand, ready to shoot. Moments later they returned with Gretel, Kan's wife, and did the same to her. I watched, unable to move, my feet frozen in place, fear clutching my soul.

For the next twenty minutes soldiers moved in and out of the shop, tossing chairs and tables onto the truck. Gretel watched in horror, mouth agape, tears streaming down her cheeks, and she darted from piece to piece straightening them, stacking them, arranging them carefully in place. And all the while she cried out, "Why? Why? Why are they doing this to us?"

Finally, as the soldiers seemed to reach an end, Papa came to my side and took me by the elbow. "Come," he said gently. "It is not good for them to see you." Reluctantly I let him lead me back inside. I felt so ashamed at my inaction, and when the door was closed and I was safely inside, I took a seat on the steps at the bottom of the staircase, wrapped my arms around my waist in agony, and wept.

❀ ❀ ❀

A few days later a truck returned to Kan's old shop. Corrie and I watched from a window upstairs. Workmen climbed from the cab and a car came to a stop behind it. A tall, slender man stepped out from the rear door. He wore a German army uniform, and I recognized him immediately. "That is Captain Bormann."

"The soldier who followed you home from the meat market?"

"Yes," I nodded.

As we watched, a man and woman emerged from the opposite side of the car. Corrie pointed out the window. "That's Cornelius and Juliana Mussert." We knew them from St. Bavo's. He worked for the railroad. She was a seamstress. They lived on the east side of town. Vocally anti-Semitic and decidedly pro-Nazi, the Musserts had become active in the National Socialist Party when it was formed in 1931. Anger rose inside me as I watched them strutting along the sidewalk, smiling and admiring their new location, while workmen unloaded furniture and boxes from the truck. In my mind I saw images of the Kans in the back of a similar truck, frantically trying to hold on to their lives as the Germans shredded it before them.

CHAPTER 27

LATER THAT WEEK, Papa came upstairs and found me in the kitchen. "I know it's early," he said, "but I want to take our walk now." He had a worried look but I didn't ask any questions. I just slipped on a sweater and went with him out to the street in front of the shop.

Normally, we followed the same route every day, up the street to the left toward St. Bavo's, across Grote Markt to the next corner, then down to the cross street a block below the shop. This time, however, as we came from the shop he steered me to the right. "We need to go this way," he pointed, and I knew something was on his mind.

At the corner, two blocks down the street, he guided us to the right, and a little way in that direction we crossed to the opposite side. Near the center of the block we turned into a winding, narrow alley. I knew then we were on our way to Rabbi Prins' apartment.

Prins lived on the third floor of a building nestled deep in the heart of Haarlem's largest Jewish neighborhood. Constructed in the nineteenth century, it had been home to many of the city's elite. However, as time passed they moved to the suburbs. The building's large rooms and tall windows attracted artists who used the naturally lit spaces as both studio and residence. Later, the building was sold to investors from Amsterdam who divided the apartments in half, doubling the occupancy, which they rented to an influx of immigrants. Jews were but the most recent group to occupy it.

That morning we walked quickly down the alley to the front entrance of the building and made our way to the staircase. Four times we had to stop to rest as we trudged up the steps, once for me and three times for Papa, but he refused to quit and at last we reached the door to Prins' apartment. Papa rapped on it with his knuckle and waited. When nothing happened, he banged on it with his fist.

From behind us I heard the sound of a latch and then a door across the hall opened just enough for someone to see out. A moment later, it opened wider and a woman appeared. "You are Casper ten Boom?" she asked in a whisper.

"Yes," Papa replied. "Sorry to disturb you. I was looking for Rabbi Prins."

"He isn't here," she said, shaking her head.

"Do you know when he will be back?"

The woman glanced around warily. "They took him."

"Who took him?"

"The Germans. Came for him three days ago."

"Where did they take him?"

"We don't know," she said, backing away. "They just came for him and they took him." Then she shut the door and locked it, leaving me and Papa alone in the hall.

As we started downstairs, he said, "We were some of the last people to see Prins alive."

"Yes," I nodded. "I realized that while she was talking. Why do you suppose they took him? He isn't really a threat to anyone."

"Rabbi Prins speaks the truth, and that is always a threat to people like the Nazis." We reached the front door and stepped out to the alley. Papa paused for a moment and glanced around at the buildings. "The Germans are removing legitimate Jewish leadership." His words seemed to rise from deep inside, as if struggling to reach the surface of a mind immersed in thought. "People like Rabbi Prins...Samuel Levy...men who actually influence how people think are being replaced with men like Isaac Franken."

"I don't like the fact that he saw us the other day when we were at Grote Markt."

"Who? Franken?"

"Yes."

"I don't like it, either," Papa agreed. "Or Captain Bormann. Both of them are trouble." A cold shiver ran through my body at the mention of his name. Papa glanced over at me. "Are you all right?"

"Yes," I nodded. "I am fine." We walked a little farther in silence, then I picked up the conversation again. "With men like Rabbi Prins gone, the Jews will have no one to watch over them."

"Yes, they do," Papa corrected. "God himself is watching over them. They are His. He will not forget them, no matter how bad things look. He will not forget them. The Germans have placed themselves in a terrible position. They do not realize just how much danger they are in. I pity them most of all. They are trapped in evil's grasp."

This wasn't the first time he had told me that. I tried to understand what he saw in the soldiers and on many occasions tried to see it for myself, but I had trouble getting past the anger—both theirs and mine. "The soldiers seem so arrogant," I sighed.

Papa shook his head. "No, they are afraid."

"Afraid?" I gave him an amused grin. "Afraid of what?"

"That's just it," he insisted. "They don't know what they are afraid of. They are simply afraid. Fear has gripped their minds, their hearts, their souls. The lies they have been told—about the Jews taking their jobs, about the Jews stealing their money, about the Jews conspiring to destroy Germany—those lies have filled them with fear, and that fear has given birth to hatred, and hatred has blinded them to their true situation."

"We must help the Jews," I replied. "We can't let the soldiers come again to a Jewish shop like they did with Kan."

"And we must help the Germans," Papa insisted once again. "They are in danger of losing their souls."

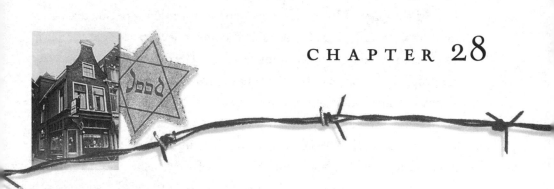

WE ARRIVED BACK at the Beje a little past noon. Noontime had passed and no one had eaten, so I hurried up to the kitchen and brought out leftover stew, a fresh loaf of bread, butter, and jam. Louis, Toos, and Corrie came from the shop and we sat down to eat while water for tea heated in the kettle on the stove.

Midway through our meal, the floor began to shake and a rumbling noise swept past the front of the house. Corrie and I rushed to a window in the parlor to see what was happening. When we looked down on the street below we saw a line of heavy trucks rolling past us. They lumbered up the street. They slowed near Grote Markt and turned right, disappearing from our line of sight, but straining against the edge of the window to see as far in that direction as possible I noticed a group of people gathered at the square.

At that point, Corrie and I were more interested in finding out where the trucks were going than we were in finishing lunch, so we left the dishes on the table and headed for the door. Corrie and Louis rushed ahead. I came with Papa at a slower pace. Toos remained at the shop.

When we reached Grote Markt we saw the trucks that had passed the house were parked side by side along the far edge of the square. The center of the square was filled with people, all of whom wore the yellow star on their clothing. Most of them clutched a small suitcase or a bag of what appeared to be their most treasured possessions—photographs, books, and one person was even holding a porcelain vase.

Around the edge of the square, townspeople formed a perimeter. Many of them were mere onlookers but some had come to jeer in anger at the Jews. Several shouted words of encouragement to the German soldiers who were herding people from the center of the square toward the trucks. The soldiers, who seemed to appreciate the crowd support, were shouting at the Jews to move faster and shoving them when they did not. I saw one soldier grab a small child by the back of his shirt and toss him into one of the trucks with the same mindless effort one would dispose of the trash. Another treated an elderly lady much the same. Suitcases and boxes littered the square with articles of clothing strewn about.

Papa held my arm as we stood there staring in disbelief at the scene unfolding before us. Tears ran down his face and he choked them back to say, "I knew that registration was wrong. And look," he pointed. "The Council is here, watching." To the left of the trucks were six men dressed in business suits. I recognized two of them as neighbors of Rabbi Prins. "They are responsible for this," Papa growled. "They sent their own people to the camps."

"But why?" Corrie lamented.

"To save their own lives, I'm sure," Papa snarled. "But the soldiers are in an even worse predicament. They cannot refuse to obey an order, and yet obeying that order means treating God's people like this. They will not get away with it."

Just then, two soldiers pushed past us. Between them was an older man about Papa's age and they were prodding him with the butt of their rifles, urging him to hurry. As they passed us, the old man stumbled and one of the soldiers reached down to help him up.

Suddenly, an officer raced toward them, red-faced, angry, and shouting at the top of his voice, "Get them in the trucks!" When he reached the soldier who was helping the old man, he shouted even louder, "Are you out of your mind? He's not your grandfather! He is the enemy!" As if to demonstrate the expected behavior, the officer kicked the old man in the leg, sending him tumbling to the ground. Then he stepped forward and kicked the man in the side repeatedly, emphasizing his words with each swing of his leg as he said,

"Get-these-stinking-Jews-on-the-trucks!"

The two soldiers joined in, kicking the old man as he struggled to his feet, but just as he was about to stand he fell again. The soldiers glanced over at the officer, who doubled over in laughter. The soldiers grinned and kicked the old man again.

Papa wiped his eyes and looked at us. "That is what I'm telling you. That soldier's first impulse was to do good, but he can't because if he does, the officer will discipline him. And the more evil they do, the more evil tightens its grip on them. Soon they won't even react with spontaneous kindness. Soon they will have no conscious awareness of good at all. And then they will be lost. Totally blind and totally lost."

All the while Papa talked, I wondered why *we* didn't do something. There were hundreds of people there and not more than fifty soldiers. We were not armed but they could not kill us all before we gained the upper hand. Perhaps we could not stop them from ultimately accomplishing their goal, but we could have prevented them from doing it that day. If we had acted on what I'm sure many of us were thinking, some of the Jews in the square would have been saved. Instead, we just watched, and the sight of it made me sick.

Before all the trucks were loaded, I gave Papa a tug and suggested we return home. He agreed and we started in that direction. Corrie and Louis followed.

When we arrived back at the Beje, we saw an army truck parked outside Weil's Furriers. Suddenly the door to Weil's shop flew open and he appeared followed immediately by two German soldiers who were hitting him with the butts of their rifles in much the same way we'd just seen others do at Grote Markt. Above them, another soldier appeared at an upstairs window, laughing and grinning as he threw Weil's clothes down to the street.

One of the soldiers on the street stuck out his foot and tripped Weil, sending him tumbling to the pavement. The others stepped forward quickly and kicked him once or twice. "You're lucky we didn't kill you," they shouted. "You filthy Jew! Stay out! This is no longer your shop."

With Weil lying in the street, the soldiers returned to the shop and brought out armfuls of furs, which they piled onto the truck. I'd been ashamed of myself for not helping Kan weeks before and sick over what we just allowed to happen in Grote Markt. Only minutes before, as I walked with Papa back to the house I had resolved in my mind that I would not stand by quietly again. So without hesitation I let go of Papa's arm, dashed into the street, and knelt at Weil's side. Corrie was with me and Louis joined us. Together we helped Weil stand.

"Come on," I said when he was on his feet. "Get your things. We can take them to the shop."

Frantically we grabbed up what we could carry in our arms and hurried Weil over to the Beje. When we were inside, Papa closed the door and locked it, then we continued up to the parlor and deposited Weil's belongings on the table. He was out of breath and blood oozed from a scrape on his forehead but he rushed to the window to look across at his shop. Corrie, Papa, and I joined him there and watched while the soldiers emptied the building.

"My wife is in Amsterdam," Weil said finally. "Visiting family. She's supposed to return in two days. I need to get word to her and tell her not to come back."

"With the phone service no longer working we'd have to stand in line to place a call," I replied. "Soldiers will listen to everything you say."

Weil looked over at me. "But I have to do something. I can't let her come back to this," he said, gesturing toward the shop across the street.

"What about Willem?" Corrie offered. "Think he could help?"

"He might," I nodded. He had developed connections to many people through his work with the home for the elderly. Someone might be able to assist Weil in reaching his wife.

"I could go find him and see," Corrie offered. Minutes later she was on her bicycle pedaling toward Willem's house north of town. It was quite a distance away, but we had no choice other than to try.

While she was gone, Weil and I sipped a cup of tea. He calmed down enough to take a few bites of bread but he wasn't interested in the stew, so I placed it in the pie safe, then cleared the luncheon dishes from the table. I was about to ask for his help at the sink when I heard the truck engine from across the street.

"Are they leaving?" I asked.

Weil walked to the window and looked out. "They're going." He started toward the stairway.

"What are you doing?" I shouted after him.

"I want to see if they left anything."

By then he was already downstairs at the door. I tossed aside my apron and hurried to catch up with him. If some of the soldiers were still in the house, or if they returned while he was there, they might shoot him on sight. I flew down the steps, jerked open the door, and dashed across the street. Papa was seated at his desk and Louis was at his workbench but I paid them no attention.

By the time I caught up with him, Weil was entering his shop. I expected him to stop and stare in sadness at the mess they'd made of his business and to hear him scream and shout. Instead, he charged up the steps to the second floor and hurried toward the back bedroom. By the way he moved I knew he wasn't merely looking around. He had something specific in mind.

Like the entire second floor, the back room was stripped bare. All the furniture was gone, as were the drapes and pictures from the wall. Weil seemed not to notice but rushed through the doorway to the far side of the room and knelt at the wall. He felt with his hands along the baseboard, then grasped it and gave it a tug. The board came free and a small cloth sack fell out from the wall. Weil held it in his hand and pulled open the drawstrings. A smile came to his face when he looked inside. "Her jewelry," he said, glancing back at me. "And some money." He shoved the sack into his pocket, replaced the baseboard, and stood. "I didn't think they would find it."

Just then, a car stopped on the street out front and I heard a door open. One glance out the window told me what I'd feared before. Two soldiers had returned. "We've got trouble," I said.

Weil looked puzzled. "What?"

"Germans." I started toward the door. "Where's the back staircase?"

"We don't have one," he said, following me up the hallway.

"Then come on. We'll have to hurry."

Walking on my tiptoes, I moved quietly down the stairs to the first floor. Weil was behind me and whispered, "There isn't a back door, either."

"You're kidding," I said in disbelief.

"No."

"Then what did you do with the garbage?" It sounds like a silly thing to say now, but at the moment it was the question that popped into my mind. Trash collection took place from the alley. If they didn't have a back door, they had to walk all the way around the block.

"We threw it out the window," he answered.

A window. Yes. We could get out that way. "Where's the window?" I asked. Weil pointed to the right and I went in that direction.

Behind me I heard the doorknob rattle and my heart skipped a beat. Then I heard a familiar voice and glanced over my shoulder to see Papa standing at the door, talking to the German officer. Something about trouble we'd had with soldiers in the neighborhood.

With Weil now in the lead, we doubled back behind the staircase and came to a window that looked out onto the alley. Sure enough, just beyond the building was a pile of garbage waiting to be collected. Weil pushed open the window and held my hand while I crawled out. Then he came after me and we raced down the alley to the right.

At the cross street we turned right again and came to the corner a block down from the Beje. We paused there hoping the soldiers were gone, but the car was still parked outside Weil's shop. So we continued on to the next corner and came up on the street behind our house. Papa was waiting by the staircase when we arrived through the back door.

"That was too close," he said with a worried shake of his head. "If that soldier had been looking where I was looking, you'd be in custody now."

"Thanks," I replied, trying not to make too much of the incident.

"You scared me," Papa continued.

"But I wasn't really scared at all," I quipped as we moved past him.

"Now I'm even more worried."

Our escapade had the opposite effect on Weil's nerves. He was calmer than ever and obviously relieved at finding his valuables. He was also hungry, and I led the way up to the kitchen for a bowl of stew.

In a few hours Corrie returned to say that Willem was not at home. "Only Tine and Kik were there," she reported. "But Kik has agreed to help. He's coming tonight."

"Tonight?" I asked. "What about the curfew?"

"He says it won't be a problem."

"It *will* be a problem if we get caught," Weil spoke up. "Perhaps this Kik is a Nazi sympathizer and wants me to wait here so he can turn me in."

"I assure you," Papa said, "none of my grandchildren would lift a hand against the Jews or assist anyone who did."

That evening, while we waited for Kik, we sat in the parlor and I played the piano. We knew better than to bring the radio from its hiding place and display it in front of Weil. Jew or not, he was human, and if pressed he might be forced to reveal its presence in our house. The less he knew the better for everyone.

About three songs into the evening activities the doorbell rang downstairs and Corrie went to answer it. I paused at the piano, listening to hear who it might be. Then Corrie exclaimed in a deliberately loud voice, "Captain Bormann, what brings you out so late?"

With just seconds to spare, I sprang from my seat at the piano and took Weil by the hand. Moving as quickly as I could without making noise, I led him to a storage nook behind the staircase. "Stay in here," I ordered in a whisper. "And don't come out. Someone will come get you when it's clear." Before he could respond, I closed the door and walked as calmly as possible back to the kitchen.

Corrie detained Bormann downstairs as long as she could, but finally he insisted on coming up to where we were. She was behind him, and as they approached she spoke up. "This is Captain Bormann. You remember him."

"Yes," I nodded, trying not to be too friendly lest, after the cold shoulder I gave him before, he now became suspicious.

"He's asking about—"

"I can ask my own questions," Bormann snapped.

"And what would those questions be?" I asked.

"I saw you in the street today with the furrier, Weil, and I was wondering what happened to him?" Bormann's voice took a rather effete tone and he seemed to be toying with us.

"What happened to whom? To Weil?"

"Yes. To Weil. We came to his shop, and then he was gone. Someone said he came over here."

"I don't know who would have said such a thing," I replied. It was true,

I didn't know who among our neighbors would have talked to the Germans, but it was a coy answer.

"Then you won't mind my having a look around." Bormann's tone was businesslike and serious.

I shook my head. "Not at all. Help yourself."

He wandered through the parlor and dining room, and every few steps paused and rapped on the interior walls with his knuckle. When he did, his head was turned sideways and there was a look of concentration on his face. "Checking to see if it's hollow," Papa said later when I asked him about it. "Looking for hiding places."

Bormann paused on the far side of the room and glanced around. "Perhaps the rumors we heard were just that," he said, flashing a smile in my direction. "Rumors." Then he tipped his hat, stepped out to the hallway, and started down the front steps.

I waited near the parlor doorway until I heard the sound of the front door closing, then stepped quickly to the window and looked out to see that he was really gone. In the shadows of the streetlight I saw him walking toward the corner down the street to the right.

From behind the staircase came a rattling noise, and Corrie turned at once. "No," she said with a frightened tone. I followed her around to the storage closet where Weil was just coming out. "No, no, no," Corrie said anxiously. "You must wait."

"But it's hot and stuffy in there," Weil protested.

"If he comes back and finds you he'll—"

The door downstairs rattled, interrupting Corrie in midsentence, and our eyes opened wide. Corrie gave Weil a push and closed the door in his face, then we started back toward the kitchen. As we turned the corner at the hallway, Captain Bormann appeared at the top of the steps. Papa, who was seated at the dining table, gave him a nod. "Good evening, once again."

Bormann did not reply but glanced around suspiciously, checking the hall. Still without saying a word, he turned away, retreated down the steps, and out to the sidewalk.

I cut my eyes at Corrie. "He is suspicious."

"Yes," she nodded. "I believe he is."

"And now I'm wondering if my meeting him at the butcher shop was an accident."

"You think they're watching us?"

"Yes," I nodded. "I do."

"But how?"

"Isaac Franken," Papa spoke up. "He is on the Council. We saw him at the square. He could have easily pointed Bormann toward us."

❖ ❖ ❖

Several hours later, Kik arrived to collect Weil. "Where will you take him?" I asked.

"You shouldn't ask too many questions," Kik replied playfully.

"What about his wife? Were you able to get word to her?"

"I'll send someone tomorrow for the details. We can contact her then."

"We can't get news to her sooner? We don't want her to return and find German soldiers in her apartment."

Kik shook his head. "Not tonight. I'll send someone in the morning."

"Who?"

"I'm not sure yet. Does it matter?"

"How will we know this person is from you?"

"Well," Kik grinned, "for one thing, he'll be a boy, dressed like a girl."

My mouth dropped open. "A boy dressed like a girl?"

"Conscription squads are patrolling the streets, looking for men able to work in German factories. They almost got Peter the other day on his way to school. Our house has been searched several times. Best way to avoid them is to not look like a boy."

"Boys go out dressed as girls?"

"No one wants to be taken to Germany," he grinned. "It's the best way to travel in the daytime."

"You've done this yourself?"

"You ask too many questions," he laughed. "But look closely. Some of them are rather convincing." Then he and Weil stepped from the Beje and disappeared into the darkness.

● ● ●

The next morning a woman appeared in the shop. She was wearing a dress and stockings and her hair was shoulder length, but when she spoke her voice had a husky tone. Corrie called upstairs for me and I came at once. She turned away as I approached and I was left to face the woman alone.

"You are Betsie?" she said with a husky man's voice.

For an instant I was speechless and Corrie burst into laughter. "You should have seen the look on your face," she cackled.

"I've come to see about a watch," he continued, trying to keep a straight face. "I was told to ask for Betsie."

"What's your name?" I asked.

"Hendrik," he replied. "Hendrik van Eyck."

I picked up a scrap of paper from Corrie's desk and took a pen from the holder, then scribbled down the information for Weil's wife. "We need to get a message to this person," I said as I handed him the paper. "That's her name and the address where she's staying in Amsterdam."

"What's the message?"

"Tell her not to return home."

"That's it?"

"The Germans have taken everything from her apartment and shop and her husband is in hiding. She should not come home."

"She'll probably want to get in touch with him."

"That's not possible. At least not for now." I let my eye scan his dress. "Nice outfit."

"No, it's not," Hendrik grinned. "But thank you for the compliment."

"Would you care for some soup?"

"No, ma'am. I must get moving." Then he opened the door, stepped outside, and was gone.

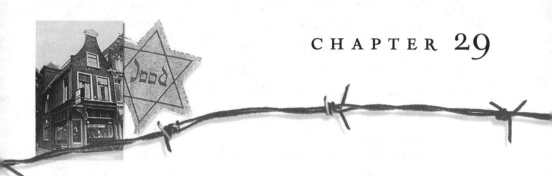

CHAPTER 29

FROM AN EARLY AGE, Nollie's son, Peter, had displayed a remarkable gift for music. While still in secondary school, Corrie and I taught him to play the piano and he learned the organ on his own. Later, he attended music school in Amsterdam, where he perfected his skills. While still in music school he applied for a position as organist at a church in Velsen, about halfway between Haarlem and Heemskerk, where Willem lived. Several other organists with far more experience had applied as well, but Peter got the job. He was not yet twenty years old. On his first Sunday, Papa, Corrie, and I took the train up to Velsen to attend the service.

Peter played flawlessly that day. I don't think I heard a single wrong note the entire morning. The congregation seemed inspired and they sang the hymns with spirit and determination, several times bringing me to the verge of tears. The priest, an amiable sort of fellow, delivered a wonderful sermon and then made a plea for repentance and invited the congregation to turn to Jesus in saving faith. After the final prayers and benediction, just as the congregation was turning to leave, Peter launched into a commanding version of "The Wilhelmus," our national anthem. Everyone froze in place.

After they invaded our country, the Germans made all expressions of Netherlands nationalism illegal. We were forbidden to display our flag or play "The Wilhelmus" in public. Peter's performance of it that morning, with all the stops out and at full volume no less, was an obvious and flagrant violation of German policy.

From the first note of the song, Papa was on his feet. Then someone across the way began to sing and soon the entire congregation joined in a rousing version, singing it with as much enthusiasm as they'd sung the hymns that morning. I knew it was against German edicts, but hearing all those people singing it with such devotion sent a thrill through my body. By the second line of the first verse, I was singing with all my heart.

Corrie didn't like it one bit and whispered her objections to me. "This is very dangerous and totally unnecessary. It is far better for us to do real acts of patriotism without attention to ourselves, rather than a thousand stunts like this." She stood silently, refusing to sing a word.

When we were through, everyone gave a round of applause and then we made our way from the pews. The priest, Johan Andriessen, was positioned at the door, greeting worshippers as they exited the building. As we drew near, he reached out to Papa and grasped his hand. "Thank you so much for coming today, Mr. Ten Boom. We are glad to have Peter at our church."

"And we are glad for him to be here," Papa replied, grinning proudly.

I was standing with them and added, "I hope his playing doesn't cause you any trouble."

Andriessen took my hand and said quietly, "These are trying times. We must all find the courage of our convictions." The look in his eye and the inflection in his voice gave his words unspoken meaning, and I was certain he knew beforehand what song Peter was going to play at the conclusion of the service.

On the way home, Corrie continued to talk about how reckless Peter had been with playing the song. "Something seemingly so small can easily become a very big problem."

"I can't imagine anyone being so sensitive to something so incidental as a song sung in church."

"The Germans aren't like us," she insisted. "They don't easily brush these things aside. And there are plenty of people who are looking for ways to ingratiate themselves. Did you notice the people who weren't singing?"

"No," I replied. "Not really. I was enjoying the song."

"They were watching and I'm sure they were making a mental list of everyone they saw who was singing."

"That would be a lot of people. I doubt they can remember all those names."

"I think we're going to find out."

"Seems rather petty, doesn't it, making such an effort over such a small thing?"

"They have much to hide," Corrie answered. "Appearance is everything to them."

The next day, Rolfe, the policeman who brought us some of our first foster children, came to the shop and escorted Corrie and me to the police station. He was polite and considerate in dealing with us, but he made it clear that refusing to go was not an option. We did as instructed and were questioned for almost an hour by a German army officer about the incident in church the previous day. We answered his questions but gave him as little information as possible.

As we walked back to the Beje, I glanced over at Corrie. "Maybe you were right."

"About what?"

"About Peter playing that song."

"I don't know," she sighed. "It's not much different than running into the street to help Benjamin Weil."

"I suppose not, but we seem unable to avoid calling attention to ourselves."

Two days later, Peter's sister Cocky came to the shop and told us Peter had been arrested. "They came to the house," she said, wiping tears from her eyes as she spoke. "Mama says they took him to a prison in Amsterdam." We were distraught, though not entirely surprised. Nollie and Flip went to find him. The rest of us prayed they would be successful.

That evening, Captain Bormann came by the house again. Corrie met him at the shop door downstairs and escorted him to the kitchen. Papa and I were seated at the dining table. Bormann dropped onto a chair across from us and told us of Peter's arrest. "You must be very proud of him," he added.

"Why do you say that?" I asked.

"You were in the street helping that Jewish furrier, in obvious contradiction to German intention, and now your nephew has incited an entire church full of people to a flagrant display of nationalism contrary to the expressed policy of the prime minister."

"It was the policy of the German government, not the Dutch people."

"Be that as it may," he said with a thin smile, "I am sure you are proud of him, though you know it put him in great danger. But I would remind you of something you must already know. Your family is not one that would wish to call attention to itself."

For a moment I could not tell if he was threatening us or trying to give us a warning. "What do you mean?" I asked.

"Your neighbors are talking. Your family has a reputation among them of being friendly with many Jews."

"The Jews are our neighbors and our customers," I said with a puzzled frown. "Why wouldn't we be friendly?"

"People are suggesting the three of you might be people to watch. That you are more than mere Christians trying to do good, but actually Jewish sympathizers."

"Is there a difference?"

"Cute," he chuckled. "If you were found to be helping them, it would mean the loss of your ration cards."

"Are you threatening me?"

"Not at all. I am merely explaining the situation so you know where you stand and what you are risking. If you were caught helping the Jews, there would be travel restrictions imposed on your entire family, and if your conduct was particularly egregious, you could go to prison."

Papa took a breath to speak, but I moved my foot beneath the table and stepped on his toes, pressing as hard as I could without making a face. He gasped with pain and while he was recovering, I continued, "We do not wish to cause trouble, Captain Bormann, but as you may no doubt expect, we must obey God in whatever we do."

"The Bible instructs believers to obey the law, does it not?"

"Yes," I responded, "but God is the ultimate law." The conversation was falling into the familiar pattern of Nazi doctrine versus Christian faith, a discussion I was unprepared to conduct. Papa was rubbing his foot and I said to him with a knowing look, "Are you still in pain?"

"Yes," Papa replied. "But I—"

"Do you need to lie down awhile?" I asked with a nod, trying to telegraph the response I wanted.

"Well, yes," he said weakly. "I suppose I do." So I excused myself and helped Papa from his chair. Corrie walked downstairs with Bormann to let him out. Meanwhile, Papa and I started up the stairs to the floor above. When we reached his bedroom door he said to me, "This is the test. These little things. They are the tests."

"Tests?" I asked with a puzzled frown. "What kind of tests?"

"If we turn our backs on the Jews in the little things—denying we care for them or denying that God is Lord of all—we will lose. We will be safe from the Germans, perhaps, but we will never reach the challenge of the big things and we will miss what God is really doing. We must always stand with the Jews. No matter how small an issue."

CHAPTER 30

NEWS OF OUR HELP for Benjamin Weil and accounts of the incident at Peter's church spread quickly. Two weeks after Peter was arrested, a woman appeared at the shop door just after curfew. Corrie was in her room, so I went down to answer the door and found Mrs. Kleermaker standing on the sidewalk. She and her husband operated a small dry goods store several blocks away. "May I come in?" she asked, glancing around warily.

I held the door open and gestured for her to enter. "What's wrong?" I asked when she was inside. From the look on her face and the tone of her voice I knew there was trouble.

"The Gestapo came to our store today and closed it. They said it wasn't ours anymore. I didn't know what to do, so I left."

"Where's your husband?"

"He was arrested the other day. When they loaded all those people on Grote Markt. He was one of the ones they took. He is gone. I don't think I'll ever hear from him or my son."

"Your son? Where is he?"

"He is in hiding."

"I am so sorry."

"Can you help me? They didn't arrest me this morning because I didn't go to my apartment. I was afraid they were waiting to take me there. I've heard you helped Benjamin. Can you help me?"

"Sure. Come upstairs with me." I took her by the arm and led her toward the staircase. "Let's see what we can do." I had no idea how to help her but I certainly wasn't turning her away, either.

On the second floor I guided her to the dining table and put on water for tea. Then I served her some bread and jam. Corrie came downstairs while we were still talking and I explained the situation. "We have four empty beds," Corrie said with a smile. "You are welcome to sleep in one of them." Mrs. Kleermaker looked genuinely relieved.

A few nights later, the same thing happened again—not long after curfew, the doorbell rang downstairs. This time Corrie was with me, and when we opened the door we found an elderly Jewish couple at the door. Corrie held the door and I helped them inside. They introduced themselves as Eduard and Carina Citroen. We didn't know them but they seemed genuine, so we let them inside. "We saw them making arrests on our street earlier today," the old man began.

"German soldiers were moving down the block from house to house," his wife added.

"We left before they got to our house," he explained. "We've been wandering the streets since."

She smiled at me, "We're afraid to go home and a friend of Gideon Prins said we should see you. Can you help?"

Of course we couldn't turn them away, but with three extra people in the house, I was worried about someone seeing them. It's not very difficult to hide one person, but three is a different matter. Even if there was space enough for everyone to sleep in their own bed, we were feeling crowded. I talked about this with Papa and Corrie, and all we could think of was Willem. Maybe he could help. So, once again, Corrie rode her bicycle to find him.

A few hours later she returned with a message. "He can help, but everyone must have ration cards in order to find places for them. No one will take them without the cards."

That evening at supper I asked Mrs. Kleermaker if she had a card, but she did not. Neither did the Citroens. "We were afraid to register," Eduard said. "We'd heard stories that they were arresting Jews who applied."

"My sister told us," Carina added, nodding her head for emphasis. "She lives near the office and knows about these things."

What they said wasn't true. It was only rumor but it had taken hold in the Jewish community, and no amount of explaining could dislodge it. Rather than try I just nodded my head along with her. But as I did, an image of Vincent flashed through my mind and I could see him seated at his desk in the office off the corridor at the Food Office. Every time I heard that rumor I thought of him and it made me bristle to think that people were saying something untrue about him. And just that quickly I realized he might be able to help. "I may know—" I caught myself. Better to keep Vincent's identity a secret, so I cleared my throat to cover. "I'll check tomorrow and see what I can do. If we can get cards for each of you, it will be much easier to place you with a family."

"You can't get us out of the country?" Eduard asked, his eyes alert as if he'd been expecting us to do that.

"We cannot. That's not what we do. But we *can* help you locate a safe place to live."

Early the next morning I took the trolley across town to Vincent's office. On the way, I thought about how to approach him and decided I had no choice but to be honest. That meant revealing to a government official that we'd been helping Jews and that we were harboring three in our home at that moment, which put both them and us at risk of going to prison, but there was no other viable option. I needed multiple ration cards for individuals who could never get past the front door of the building and who, if they did, would be arrested on the spot for even requesting a card. To get a favor like that, I had to trust him. I had to trust that the Vincent I saw in that office when we came to get our ration card was the same Vincent I knew when we were young. That Vincent, the one I walked home with after school, would never betray me to anyone. If that Vincent was still alive, I was safe. If the Vincent I once knew and loved had died with his appointment to the rationing job, then the Nazis would have succeeded, the free country we knew before would be lost, and I would likely be dead before morning. I chose to trust in the goodness of my friend's soul.

When I arrived at the building the guard waved me through the entrance and I made my way down the corridor toward the clerk's office. As before,

Vincent was seated at his desk in an office just off the corridor. His eyes opened wide when he saw me. "Betsie," he smiled, "what brings you out so early?"

I sat in a chair across from him. "We need to talk."

He rose from behind the desk and closed the office door. When he was back in his chair, he looked over at me and said, "So, talk."

"I need ration cards," I began. "And I need them for people who can't come to your office to get them."

"Okay," he said slowly. "Why can't they come in person?"

I arched an eyebrow, hoping he would understand. "They would be arrested."

The look on his face told me he knew exactly what I was talking about. "And how do you know these people?"

"They are my neighbors."

"Hasn't most of your neighborhood been cleared?"

A pang of fear stabbed me in the stomach. The language he used was the language of the Nazis. *Clearing* was their way of saying they'd removed all the Jews from an area. "Is that what you call it now?"

"It's what *they* call it. Where are these people living?"

"Three of them are living with me."

His eyes opened wide once more. "With you."

"Yes."

Vincent leaned forward and lowered his voice. "Do you realize how dangerous that is?" he whispered. "What if you get caught?"

"It is dangerous," I nodded, "but not so much for us. If we get caught, they will send us to prison. If they get caught, they will die."

He leaned back in his chair. "Still, I must advise that you stop this immediately." While he talked, he took a scrap of paper from his desk and scribbled something on it, then he turned the paper so I could see. In scrawled handwriting it read, *They may be listening.*

"We can help them, Vincent," I whispered in response. "We can find places for them to stay where they will be safe. But they must all have ration cards. No one will take them without the card. Can you help?"

He stared past me a moment, as if deep in thought, then came from the desk and sat beside me. With his lips near my ear, he said, "How many do you need?"

On the ride to see him I had thought of many things—what life would be like if we had married. Might we have been able to have children after all, would I have survived delivery, how was I going to ask him for the cards, and a thousand other things? I never once thought of how many cards I would need. I had assumed three, I think, but now I wasn't sure and the question caught me off-guard.

As he stared at me awaiting an answer, a large number came to my mind. It seemed like an impossible request and one that was sure to doom the entire venture to failure, but I could not escape the thought of it, so I took a deep breath and said, "One hundred."

Vincent never flinched. He just sat there a moment longer, thinking, then said, "That would be possible only if the office is robbed." I assumed he was just being polite and telling me "no" in a friendly way, when I saw the twinkle in his eye. "That happens more often than you would think," he continued, barely above a whisper. "Here, in this office, it would need to happen around noon, when I and the clerk are the only people here." A mischievous grin spread over his face. "And I think I know someone who might be willing to help."

❧ ❧ ❧

While we waited for news from Vincent about the ration cards, a steady stream of Jews appeared at the shop, looking for help. Corrie and I scrambled to find places for them but it was difficult juggling people from bed to bed. No one was turned away, but without ration cards it was next to impossible to locate people willing to take them, which meant that we often had seven or eight extra people at the house awaiting placement. Those first ones, in particular, were difficult to place because of their age.

Working without a phone made communication difficult, too. Corrie could only do so much on her bicycle, so I suggested we ask Kik for help. Corrie was apprehensive about contacting him. "I don't want to get him in trouble. He still lives at home and going there only draws the attention of the wrong people. Willem doesn't need that now."

"Well, we have to do something," I argued. "We can't keep going like this."

Reluctantly, Corrie pedaled off on her bicycle to find Kik. The trip took longer than expected because she had to dodge two German patrols, but she returned later with news that Hendrik would be available to us on a permanent basis.

The next day, Hendrik arrived at the shop dressed as a girl, as usual. To give him a reason for being there, we assigned him the job of sweeping the floor. When he was in the shop between assignments, he puttered around with a broom in his hand. Anyone who looked through the front window would hopefully see only a female, which we thought would not raise suspicions. When customers were present, we sent him upstairs. He was convincing as a female from a distance, but up close anyone who paid attention would see that he was a boy. Before long, though, Hendrik was too busy to sweep and he brought in a friend, Jan Berlage, to take over the broom.

◆ ◆ ◆

Later that month, Vincent came by the house. His face was bruised around both eyes and he had a cut on the right side, just above his cheek. "What happened?" I asked, startled at his appearance.

"The friend who helped us got a little carried away with the robbery part."

"Oh no," I gasped. "I feel terrible."

"Don't be." Vincent grinned with pride. "I was glad to do it." He reached into a leather pouch that hung from his shoulder and took out a stack of rationing cards. He waved them in the air. "One hundred. Just like you asked."

"You are an angel!" I exclaimed and before I knew it, I grasped him with both hands and kissed him on the lips.

His eyes opened wide in astonishment. "Wow! I should have brought you those cards sooner."

"Thank you," I continued, trying to ignore my impulsive gesture.

"You're welcome." An awkward moment passed between us, then Vincent moved on to explain, "The cards are couponed for reissue each month, which means they'll automatically be renewed. But that requires a new card."

"I'll need to pick them up?"

"Better let me deliver them," he offered. "If you come around too often, someone will get suspicious."

"Okay," I nodded. "We should come up with a plan to make sure that goes smoothly. You'll need a reason to be here. Other than the cards."

"There's always a watch repair."

"Yes. But that only works once. We need something better. Something that's an answer every time."

We thought for a moment, then a look came over him. "I know just the thing," he said. "I used to read electric meters. What if I come as the meter reader?"

"Excellent idea." And it really was. "Do you know where our meter is located?"

"Show me," he said.

I led him through the shop to the back of the building and pointed it out. He noted the location and glanced around as if searching for something. "Is this okay?" I asked.

"I'll need a place to put the cards. I can't leave them here in the open. They'll be discovered for sure."

The meter was fastened to the wall near the rear staircase. As I glanced around, I thought of how we'd hidden the radio beneath the steps above the second floor. If it worked for that, it would work for this. I pointed, "We could loosen the runner on the first step. You could put the cards in there."

"Good," he grinned. "That will work just fine."

❀ ❀ ❀

The following month when Vincent came to the house with the new cards he was dressed like a meter reader. He wore an official electrical service cap and carried a pad in one hand. Rolfe, the policeman, was there, asking Papa about an incident that had occurred on the street the night before. I panicked at the thought of them seeing each other, but Vincent never missed a beat. He walked through the house as if he'd been there before, checked the meter, and noted the reading. Then he lifted the runner on the bottom step of the staircase and deposited the cards inside the space below.

When he was finished, he came back through the shop the same way he entered and left without saying a word, just like the meter reader did each month. Rolfe never noticed a thing and when he was gone, Corrie came upstairs and told me all about it.

"That was close," I said. "Vincent should have kept going instead of coming inside when Rolfe was here."

"Maybe, but he had no way of knowing who was in the shop. We need a signal that lets our people know it's safe to enter."

Corrie glanced around the shop and pointed to an *Alpina Watch* sign that sat on a shelf behind Papa. She gestured toward the sign. "What if we use that? We could put it in the window if everything is clear, but if something is wrong, we take it out."

"Sign in the window, come on in. Sign missing, stay away?" I summarized.

"Yes," she nodded. "Exactly."

"Good," I smiled. "I think that will work. But we still have one more problem."

"What's that?"

"Some of the new cards need to go to people we've already placed."

"I don't think we can do that," Corrie shrugged. "We don't know where all of them are staying."

"Does Hendrik?"

"Yes," Corrie replied. "I think so. Maybe not all of them, but at least some."

"Then we should discuss it with him. We don't want the people we've already sent into hiding to lose their place because they no longer have a working ration card."

"Good point. We should ask him about it."

Hendrik was away on an errand but when he returned that afternoon I took him upstairs to the parlor and explained the situation with the cards. It seemed complicated to me, but he appeared unfazed.

"We'll take care of it."

"We?"

"Jan and I," he explained. "We know where some of them are located and how to reach most of the others."

That was the moment I realized we were part of a vast network, one much larger than I'd realized. Understanding the enormity of it left me both troubled and intrigued. If we were connected to a wide-ranging group, the possibility of being discovered and caught was much greater. At the same time, the potential to make a real difference was enormous.

CHAPTER 31

A LITTLE BEFORE NOON the following day, Hannah Meijer arrived at the shop. The fact that she arrived in the middle of the day was troubling—others came at night to avoid being seen—but she was a family friend and even if she wasn't we wouldn't have turned her away. Still, it was unusual for a Jew to be out in the open like that. Corrie brought her upstairs to the kitchen where I was preparing lunch. We sat in the parlor to talk.

When we were seated and alone I looked over at her and said, "I have to ask, did you marry Tobias?"

"No," she replied with a forced smile. "I did not."

"Good," I replied. "After you left that day, your father came here looking for you."

She nodded, "I know. I went to your cousin's house in Amsterdam as you suggested and they let me stay with them. He found me there."

"He was worried," I continued, trying to explain why I disclosed her location. "I didn't want to tell him where you were, but I didn't think I could really refuse. And I told him only after he promised not to make you marry."

"It's okay," she smiled. "Actually, I needed him to find me. And what you said helped him see that he could not solve his own problems by forcing me to marry Tobias."

"How *is* your father? Is he well?"

"No." Tears welled up in her eyes. "The soldiers took him just a few days ago. I am certain the Council selected him. They were asked to provide names of men who could be sent to Germany to work. He was on the list."

"How do you know that?"

"Tobias told me."

I arched an eyebrow. "You still see him?"

"Occasionally."

"His father is on the Council, isn't he?"

"Yes." A frown appeared on her forehead. "How do you know that?"

"We saw him here one day," I explained. "When the soldiers were loading the trucks in Grote Markt. He was with the officers watching the selection."

"Selection," she repeated. "I hate that word."

"As do I, but it has become the way of describing the process."

"They are *selecting* people to die." She had an angry scowl. "They see us as less than human."

"I know."

"Tobias' father is president of the Council in Amsterdam. They gave the list to the Germans. He is still angry that Father didn't make me marry Tobias. I am certain he had Father sent away out of spite." She cut her eyes at me. "He is angry at you, too."

News that he remembered me was unsettling, but I was not much worried. There was little I could do about it anyway. "The list of people angry with me is growing longer every day," I chuckled.

Hannah shifted positions in her chair. "I have heard that you help our people. Can you help me?"

"What do you need?"

"The Germans were clearing our neighborhood, going from house to house, rounding up those who managed to elude their earlier searches. I left Gerrit and Margriet because I didn't want them to get in trouble. I need a place to live."

"We can help with that. But first, we should eat lunch." I stood and gestured toward the kitchen. "Come help me. We can continue to talk while we work."

After lunch I took Hannah upstairs to the one remaining empty bed. She stowed her few belongings beneath it and I put her to work helping me keep house. She stayed with us for two days and then we sent her to live in the countryside.

A day or two after Hannah left, Cornelius Mussert came over from the apartment across the street where the Kans had lived. The sound of his voice drifted up the stairs and I heard him talking about a watch that needed to be cleaned. So I went down to see him. He was standing near Corrie's desk when I came from the staircase.

"Mr. Mussert. How are things on the railroad?"

The question seemed to make him uneasy and his eyes darted away. "Oh, you know. The trains are all running." He moved to the left, handed his watch to Papa, then glanced back at me. "I understand you had a young visitor the other day."

"Oh?"

"I saw her arrive...two days ago, but I have not seen her leave. She looked like someone I might know. Is she still here? I would like to say hello."

Corrie, still seated at her desk, fidgeted nervously with a pen. I ignored her and continued to talk. "I'm not sure who you are talking about. We have many people in and out of here."

"Yes," he said with a sarcastic tone. "I have seen them. Going and coming, and not just during business hours but at all times of the day."

He was right about that. We'd done little to hide the traffic in and out of the house. "You're watching our house?" I asked.

"I see everything that happens on our block," he said smugly.

"And I notice you have taken Kan's apartment," Papa said, injecting himself into the conversation. "But the clock shop remains closed. You are not a watchmaker?"

Mussert's look turned angry. "You know better," he snarled.

Papa removed the loupe from his eye and looked up. "Do you no longer work for the railroad?"

"For an old man," Mussert chirped, "you ask many questions."

"Yes," Papa chuckled. "I suppose I do. But one has to wonder how you are able to afford the apartment, and maintain your family, and remain at your window watching the street."

Mussert snatched back the watch from Papa's hand. "Never mind," he snapped. "But if you get arrested, don't blame me. Everyone on the street knows about your Jews." Then he stormed out the door and was gone.

I looked over at Corrie. "Everyone knows what we are doing."

"Yes," she sighed. "I think they do. But do you want to stop?"

"No," I smiled. "I don't."

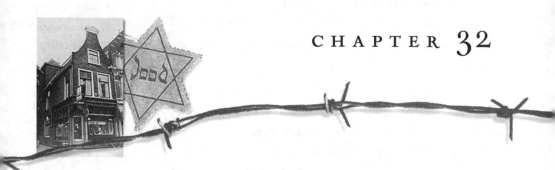

CHAPTER 32

AN HOUR AFTER SUPPER, the doorbell rang downstairs. Corrie went to answer it and found a woman carrying a picnic basket. "May I come inside?" she asked, glancing warily over her shoulder.

Corrie, suspicious of what the woman wanted, pointed to the basket. "What's in there?" She lifted the top to reveal a tiny baby lying inside, nestled beneath a soft cotton blanket. "Oh!" Corrie exclaimed and she opened the door wide to let them in.

When they reached the second floor, Corrie steered the woman into the parlor and called for me. I came just as the woman opened the basket and gathered the baby in her arms. We'd helped many people of every age and color, but this was our first infant. From somewhere deep inside, a strange maternal instinct welled up in me. Rising from a core at the depths of my being it seemed as though it would overwhelm me. I took a deep breath and forced myself to focus on the moment. "A baby," I exclaimed as I entered the room.

"Yes," the woman nodded. "A girl."

I drew near and looked at her with an admiring gaze, as adults often do. "Is she yours?"

The woman shook her head. "No, I'm a nurse at the hospital. She was born a few days ago."

"Then why have you brought her here?"

"Her mother is Jewish," she said, as if that should explain the situation.

I glanced away from the baby to look at the woman. "And the father?"

"We know nothing of the father."

"If the mother is Jewish, how was she able to give birth at the hospital?" We'd heard they had prohibited treatment of Jews in all Dutch medical facilities.

"Some of us care more for the lives of others than for Nazi rules," the woman replied. She pushed back the sleeve of her jacket and checked the watch on her wrist. "Can you help me?" Her voice took an impatient tone. "Can you find a place for her to live?"

"Where is the mother?" I asked calmly.

"The Germans took her. They wanted to get her before she gave birth but by the time they arrived we'd already delivered the baby. When they asked, we lied and said she had not yet had her baby. They took her immediately."

"Where is she?"

The nurse gave a knowing look. "I think you can imagine what happened to her." She tugged at the blanket to move it higher up the baby's chest. "I kept Rachel at the hospital as long as possible, but people were asking questions and I had to move her out."

"Who is Rachel?" Corrie asked. "The mother?"

"No." She bounced the baby gently in her arms. "This is Rachel." Then she looked over at me. "Can you help?"

"Yes," I replied finally. "Of course." Then I reached out to take the baby. She laid her gently in my arms I kissed her on the cheek. Feeling her close to me, so warm and cuddly, made me think of Vincent and for a moment I felt a twinge of anger at myself for putting him off way back then. But just as quickly I moved away from it and thought of all the things we needed to do now, to make certain Rachel had a life of her own.

The nurse never told us her own name, and we never asked. That night in the parlor was the only time I ever saw her. She watched us a moment being silly with Rachel and she seemed satisfied we could care for the child. Then without another word, she picked up the basket and started down the stairs. I listened for the door to open and heard her when she stepped outside.

After she was gone, Corrie said, "Now what do we do?"

"Well, I suppose we better figure out what to feed Rachel. We can't let her cry."

"No," Corrie agreed. "That would not be good."

"Who will take her?"

"I have no idea," Corrie replied. "We don't ..." She paused in midsentence, her eyes wide, as a broad smile spread across her face. "I think I know just the couple."

"Who?"

"Karel and Isabelle," she said with delight. "They'd be perfect."

It was a strange suggestion, coming from someone he'd so horribly jilted, but it did indeed appear to be the perfect solution. Karel was ordained and assigned to a church south of Haarlem. We knew from Willem, who still kept in touch with them, that Karel and Isabelle had been trying to have children but without success. Rachel seemed like the answer to their prayers.

In addition, they lived outside the city. Sparsely populated towns and villages on the outskirts were much less heavily patrolled. There'd be little likelihood anyone would notice Rachel. And, from what we'd heard, the house where Karel and Isabelle lived had plenty of rooms and lots of space. If they took her, perhaps we could later convince them to take others.

The following morning we sent a courier to Karel and asked him to come for a visit at his earliest convenience. A week later, he appeared at the shop. Corrie took him upstairs to the parlor, where they shared tea and cake. I remained in my room to give them a few minutes alone to talk. From what Corrie told me later, Karel seemed genuinely glad to see her, but he made no mention of the abrupt manner in which he'd broken off their relationship and offered no apology.

Half an hour later, I came down to join them. Karel stood to greet me as I entered the room and we said our hellos while standing. After which I brought a chair over from beside the piano, took a seat across from him, and got right to the point.

"We have a problem," I began. "We're hoping you can help us solve it."

He took a sip of tea. "Certainly, I'll do what I can. What's the matter?"

"From time to time we care for children who've been abandoned by their parents. We have a good relationship with the local police station and they work with us in finding homes for them."

He had a puzzled look. "I'm afraid I don't understand. You want *me* to find a home for one of these children?"

"Not exactly," I replied. "We have an infant living with us right now." He seemed startled by that, but I ignored him and kept going. "She's less than a month old."

"Oh my." Karel sank back in his chair.

I plowed ahead. "We were wondering if you and Isabella would like to take her as your own."

"As our own?"

"Yes," I nodded.

"You mean, raise one of these children—an infant—and pass it off as our own?" This wasn't going well. "I can't believe you're asking me this."

"Well," I said, determined to tell the rest, "there's one more thing."

"What more could you possibly ask of me?"

"The child is Jewish," I said flatly.

Karel's mouth dropped open and the cup began to shake in his hand. "Is this your idea of a joke?" he roared.

"Not at all."

"Oh, I know." He turned to Corrie with a cynical smile and pointed. "This is your way of getting back at me over all those fantasies you had about us."

"It has nothing to do with that," Corrie responded. "And they weren't fantasies. You practically proposed when we were at Willem's."

"Karel," I spoke up, trying to keep things under control. "This is not a joke. It's not revenge. We really have a Jewish infant and she really needs a home."

"You can't possibly have a Jewish infant," he retorted. "It's against the law." His voice went cold. "And if we took her into our home, we'd be breaking the law, too."

By then Corrie was angry. "You know what the Germans will do with her if they find her. Are you not a minister of the Gospel?"

"That has nothing to do with it," Karel snarled as he rose from his chair. "Caring for Jewish babies is not my responsibility. And I have no control over what the German army does."

I stood to face him. "But you could save this child's life."

"At the risk of my own?" Veins in his neck throbbed. "And the life of Isabelle? At the risk of losing all we've worked for?" He straightened his jacket. "I should think not! And besides, even if I agreed, Isabelle would never go for it. My mother and father would be devastated if they knew of the child's race. They're convinced the Jews brought all this...unpleasantness on themselves and on us as well by the way they live and act." He cocked his head at an imperious angle. "And I must say, I'm not totally convinced they're wrong." He handed me the teacup. "I have to go. I could be arrested simply for being here."

The sound of his footsteps echoed through the house as he made his way down the stairs and out the front door. In the quiet of that moment, with only the sound of the clocks ticking in the shop, I thought of his final comment—"*I could be arrested simply for being here.*"

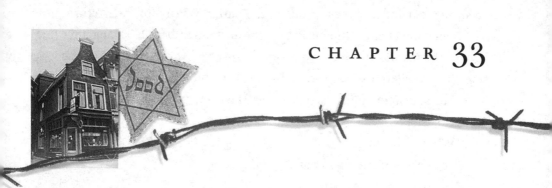

CHAPTER 33

TWO NIGHTS LATER, Kik came to the house after curfew. I met him at the door and took him to the parlor where Corrie was playing the piano. Papa was sitting in his favorite chair, reading the newspaper and complaining about the lack of news. Kik greeted them both, then said, "Aunt Corrie, you should come with me."

She turned from the piano to face him. "Where are we going?"

"It's better if you don't know."

"You mean I should trust you."

"Yes," he smiled. "You should trust me."

Kik was an honest young man and involved in almost everything we did to help resettle Jews and others in need of avoiding the Germans, but I was worried about them being out past the curfew hour. "You'll need a reason," I offered. "If someone asks."

Kik looked puzzled. "A reason?"

"A reason to be out. It's well past curfew. You should plan now what to say if you get stopped, so your stories will match."

"Okay," Corrie nodded. "I'll say we're on our way to see about my sister, who is ill."

"That's good," Kik agreed. "And I can say your sister is my mother, which is true. That way, I won't have to worry about looking guilty because I wouldn't be lying." The fact that he hadn't thought of this in advance only added to my concern about their outing, but Corrie seemed not to be worried at all. She followed him down the stairs and they went out through the rear door. Papa spent the remainder of the evening in the parlor waiting for their return.

Sometime after midnight, Papa went upstairs to bed. Not long after that, I heard the rear door open downstairs, followed by the sound of Corrie's footsteps. I was relieved she'd made it back safely and was waiting in the kitchen when she appeared on the second floor. "Have any trouble?"

"No," she replied. "Not at all."

"Where did you go?"

"To Herman Slurring's home."

"He took you to see Slurring?"

"Actually, it was a meeting with a number of people."

"What was it about?"

"No one said exactly. But I think they were part of the Dutch underground resistance. Everyone seemed to be involved in many different things—getting downed Allied pilots back to England, disrupting German activity wherever possible, providing extra sources of food for those who are in hiding. Which reminds me." She paused while she reached into her left coat pocket. "Slurring sent this for us." She handed me a small white packet. I opened it to find tea leaves. "Real tea," I gasped with my eyes opened wide. We'd been reusing the same tea for weeks and it was dreadful. The sight of fresh tea leaves made me forget how anxious I was feeling over the kinds of things her newfound friends were doing.

"And," Corrie grinned, "it will go well with this." She put her hand in the right coat pocket and brought out another small package and set it on the counter. "Real sugar."

My mouth fell open at the sight of it. We hadn't had real sugar in months. "Slurring gave you this?"

"Yes," she nodded. "And I can get more."

"Where does he get it?"

"I don't know," Corrie shrugged. "But he seemed to have plenty. He served cake and cookies and sweet rolls as if it wasn't a problem."

"Stop," I said playfully. "You're making me hungry." How Slurring was able to procure commodities of that nature was a mystery to me, but I was glad Corrie'd had an enjoyable evening. I put the sugar and tea on the shelf in the cupboard, then turned to her. "So, why did they want to see you?"

"I think just to put us in touch with a broader group of contacts. Most of them were familiar with what we've been doing but they all seemed to be like us—working with a network they built themselves. No one spoke about the details, but that was my sense."

"Meet anyone who can help us?"

"Yes, as a matter of fact. One of the men offered to build a secret room for us."

My forehead wrinkled in a frown. "A secret room?"

"A place to hide our visitors."

I was immediately suspicious. Many people made their living betraying their friends and family to the Germans. As the occupation grew longer, they became more devious in their means of luring others into a trap. I wasn't excited about allowing a stranger into our house and sharing with him intimate details of our work. "Why did he make that offer?"

"Why did he offer to help?"

"Yes."

"I think he's just sympathetic to the Jewish cause. They all are."

"But it sounds like they are into other things. Things that would expose us to terrible risk. Helping the Jews is one thing. Getting involved in the war effort would get us shot on the spot if we were discovered."

"You sound like Karel now," Corrie said with a smirk.

"I know, but with the Jews, we're just helping people who face dire circumstances. We aren't shooting at German soldiers or destroying their property. This group you met tonight, they're different."

"But a hiding place is a good idea and would be a big benefit for us and for the people staying at the house. We've developed a large network. At any given time we have a number of people here who are at risk. We are at risk just by having them here. If they get caught, we get caught. Having a hiding place could help alleviate some of that risk."

Papa appeared in the doorway, dressed in his pajamas and robe. "You both know Herman," he said without introduction. "He's been in the shop many times and a guest in our home often. If he says the fellow is reputable, I think we can trust him. What's the man's name?"

"Smitt," Corrie replied. She told me later that wasn't his real name, but we didn't bother explaining it to Papa.

"Well, anyway, I heard you two talking and wanted to say, I think we should do it." Then he turned around and started back to his room.

I looked over at Corrie. "If you think it's okay, then it's okay with me."

A few days later, Mr. Smitt arrived at the shop and I took him upstairs. He checked every room in the house and then I showed him the places we'd been hiding the valuables others brought to us for safekeeping. "Good use of space," Smitt said with a nod. "And a clever way of hiding the architectural defects. But it's the first place the Germans would look."

"The first place?" We thought the places were great for hiding things. "Is it that obvious?"

"Not to the untrained eye, but the Germans have searched many buildings many times. They would recognize these cubbyholes right away."

He seemed to know what he was talking about, so I asked, "If you built a secret room, where would you put it?"

Without a moment's hesitation he said, "In the bedroom you showed me on the third floor."

That was Corrie's room. "Why there?" I asked.

"It's located on the top floor. That gives your people the most time to get into the hidden room as the Germans search their way up." He gestured in that direction. "Take me to it again."

I took him upstairs to Corrie's room and watched as he glanced around. He nodded his head thoughtfully as he surveyed the space. "This will work just fine." He drew a measuring tape from the pocket of his jacket and measured a distance out from the existing wall. "We'll build a new wall right here," he added. "Set the bricks right where my foot is."

"Bricks?" I hadn't the faintest notion why he'd build it of anything other than wood.

"Wood rings hollow when struck," he explained. "One tap and they'd know it was a false wall."

Three days later, workmen arrived at the house. With the help of others from their network, they entered the shop under the guise of being our customers. Once inside they moved quickly upstairs where they unloaded bricks and dry mortar mix that they carried in small sacks beneath their coats. Over the next ten days the wall took shape and when they were finished, others came to plaster over the bricks. After the plaster dried, they painted the new wall to match the rest of the room and built a bookcase in one corner. The lower rear panel of it was the access door into the secret room.

When Mr. Smitt showed me the finished product, I was impressed. "Other than the smell of fresh paint, the wall looks as if it were always there."

"That's how we want it to look," he grinned. "Come on. You need to see inside the room." He knelt on the floor by the bookcase and placed his hand against the back panel two shelves from the bottom. "When you push here, the panel swings out of the way." He pressed his hand firmly against it, and the panel swung into the room, then he crawled inside. I followed after him and found the opening was just wide enough for us to fit through.

Once inside, I stood and looked around. "It's big enough for two people to lie on the floor," I noted. "But we often have more than that with us."

"You should consider limiting the number of people you keep here. I know it's difficult to turn someone away, but you'll be risking the safety of everyone if you don't."

"We've not been willing to turn anyone away."

"They can always alternate. Some can stand while others sit. I don't think five could sit together on the floor, but they might."

I was already feeling warm so I asked, "Won't it get stuffy in here?"

"The room's not airtight, so they won't suffocate, if that's what you mean. But, yes, it might get hot, but not so hot that anyone would die from it."

"We'll need a can for waste," I observed.

"And one for water," he added. "Hardtack would give them a little nourishment if they're in here for more than a day."

"And vitamins," I suggested.

"Vitamins would be great," he added.

"This will work well." I glanced around once more, admiring the handiwork, then dropped to my knees and crawled out to the bedroom. Smitt came out behind me and made sure the panel closed tightly. "If it isn't tight," he warned, "they'll see it right away."

"We can put some books on the shelves to help cover it."

"Yes. By all means. Use it and make it look real."

"You've done us a big favor," I said as we started toward the hall.

"Don't mention it. You're in good shape now. You just need a buzzer and you'll be all set."

I glanced back at him over my shoulder. "A buzzer?" I had no idea what he meant.

"A warning buzzer. Like your doorbell, only it makes a buzzing sound, so no one outside the house will hear it. To warn everyone when someone suspicious is approaching."

I was curious. "How does a buzzer work?"

"You'd hide little electrical button switches in places around the house—beneath the sill of a front window, under the top of a desk in the shop, other places like that. Someone sees a soldier coming, they press the button. Buzzer goes off. Visitors get in the room. The rest of you make the place look like only three people live here."

I was skeptical we could do all that. "We'd have enough time?"

"You will if you practice."

"I'll keep that in mind."

"Everyone who hides people has a buzzer," he added.

❖ ❖ ❖

In the coming weeks, the pace quickened even more with couriers coming and going by the hour. Our network grew to include eighty people actively involved in arranging places for Jews to live, then transporting them to the various locations. I was certain we were far too obvious, but people kept coming for help and in spite of what Smitt had suggested, we never turned down anyone.

Then one day Vincent came by with new ration cards and told us the telephone would be working again soon. "That would be great!" I exclaimed, and we checked it every day after his visit. When I picked it up on the fifth day an operator came on the line. We were thrilled. Having it meant we were back in touch with the world, at least in some small measure, even if most of our network had no access to a phone, but I was suspicious of it, too.

All phone calls still went through an operator's switchboard. Someone could easily overhear our conversation, or intentionally listen in. I raised my concerns with Vincent but he assured me that most of the telephone operators were on our side. Just to be sure, Corrie and I devised code language that referenced the watch business. It seemed an obvious choice. We operated a watch shop. Anyone calling our house ought to be calling about something related to a watch. Under our coded system, for instance, someone having problems with the face of a watch meant they had a person in need of assistance whose facial features were obviously and unavoidably Jewish—particularly difficult people to place because they had no hope of passing as non-Jews. Someone who needed to be hidden immediately was a watch in need of quick repair. Reference to two watches meant a husband and wife.

During that time, we also acquired a number of permanent residents at our home. Meyer Mossel was one of those whose appearance was too Jewish to avoid. At first we thought we could eventually find a home for him somewhere else, but the longer he stayed with us the more a part of our daily routine he became. After a while we stopped looking for someplace to send him and made him a permanent resident at the Beje.

Louis, the apprentice turned assistant, lived on the far side of town and traveled back and forth each day. One morning on the way to the shop he was confronted by German soldiers who were rounding up men to send to the factories as conscripted laborers. Louis managed to escape but it was a close call. After that, we told him not to go home. He stayed with us.

Edmund Heenk, the foster child who became a lawyer with an office up the street, faced the same problem. As did Jans Leendert, who was now a teacher. Thea Decosta, Meta Monsanto, and Mary Itallie were all too much of a risk for others to take, so they stayed with us, too.

In all we had eight people at the house who were going to be with us until the end of the war. *End of the war*—that's how we talked about the future. We never counted on anything less than an Allied victory and removal of the Germans from our country. Considering a future holding anything less than total victory offered us no hope and we needed all the hope we could get.

With eight extra people at the house, the secret room was packed when they all squeezed into it. I kept reminding them it was better than being caught by the Germans, to which they all agreed. We devised a plan to inform them by word of mouth when a threat appeared, but without a buzzer system it was cumbersome. Even so, we conducted regular drills and worked to get our disappearing time down to the three minutes Smitt had advised. We never made it that quickly but we improved with each drill.

Smitt's suggestion that we install a buzzer system was a good one, but I didn't know how to do it or even who to ask. Consequently, it didn't get done. At night, three of the extra residents slept in the secret room. The others all slept on the same floor but in a bed down the hall from Corrie. We relied on one of them to hear the soldiers below, alert the others, and get into the room quietly enough and quickly enough to avoid being discovered.

During the day, our word-of-mouth scheme relied on at least one of the permanent residents being on the second floor. That person would then ascend the stairs, informing the others as they made their way up to the top floor. It was not the best system but it was all we had until I could figure out what to do about a buzzer. As events would soon show, we were much closer to trouble than we realized.

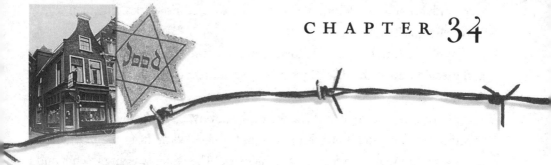

CHAPTER 34

NOT LONG AFTER the secret room was finished a truck stopped in front of the shop and four German SS soldiers climbed out. Meyer Mossel was on the second floor with me and as soon as we saw the truck, I sent him to warn the others. While he moved quickly up the steps toward the third floor, I remained on the second floor and stood near the kitchen doorway. From there I could listen to what was happening in the shop below and be ready to delay anyone who might try to search the upper floors of the house. Hopefully, that would give Meyer and everyone else plenty of time to hide.

As the soldiers entered the shop one of them took a position near the door from which he could see up the stairs and out the front window. Another stood near the bottom of the steps not far from Corrie's desk, and a third moved to a position farther inside, from which he could watch the back door. The fourth man, who seemed to be in charge, looked over at Papa. "We have heard rumors," he began, "of people coming and going from here at all hours of the day. Yet I do not see any watches on display in your cases."

"As to the people coming and going," Papa replied as he had many times before, "this is a shop. I hope for all our sakes people are coming and going. The more the better. And as to the lack of watches, I would be glad to order more if your superiors would assure that my deliveries would arrive from Switzerland."

"You make a valid point," the soldier said. "But just the same, we should have a look around your house to make sure everything is in order. Then perhaps we will see about those orders of new stock for your display case." He turned to the staircase and started up the steps, but I noticed the soldiers who were with him did not follow. If this was to be a serious search, one man would never attempt it alone.

When I heard him coming toward me, I moved to the head of the staircase and greeted him with a friendly smile. "Would you care for some tea?" I asked in my best German.

"Certainly," he replied. "Tea would be lovely." It was much too casual a comment for a soldier, but I didn't argue. I backed away from the hall, moved quickly to the stove, and reached for the kettle. The water was already hot and I poured it into the teapot. To my amazement, the soldier took a seat at the table and waited while I brought him a cup.

"Would you care for a slice of bread to go with it?" I was glad for the delay and certain the others were safely inside the secret room by now. "It came fresh from the baker this morning."

"Bread would be delicious," he answered, but while I sliced the loaf and took out the butter, he rose from his chair and stood beside me, close enough that his shoulder rubbed against mine. I was concerned about what might happen next—we'd heard numerous accounts of women being assaulted by soldiers in situations just like this—but I took a deep breath and forced myself to keep quiet. Then he leaned closer and in a whisper said, "My men and I are members of the SS. We were selected for our unit because we have displayed unwavering loyalty to the German nation. We are proud to serve our country and are honored to be assigned the most difficult tasks."

"I am certain for a German that must be a high honor," I said, not knowing exactly what to say but feeling compelled to say something.

"We are soldiers who must follow orders, but we do not like many of the things we have seen happening, especially to the Jews. Sometimes we find ways to avoid the worst of it, but other times that is not possible. We have done many terrible things. Now they have assigned us the worst task of all." The veins in my neck throbbed as my heart rate quickened. My palms were clammy and I was certain they meant to kill everyone in the house, but he kept talking. "There are Jewish babies in an orphanage in Hoofddorp. We have been ordered to travel there by truck, take the babies from the orphanage, and kill them. We don't want to do it. Can you help us?"

Waves of emotion swept over me—relief that he apparently meant us no harm, horror at the thought of what he'd been ordered to do, and fear again that this was all a trap.

"How much time do we have?" I sounded far too eager but it was the only thing I could think to say.

"We are on our way there now. Can you help us?"

German soldiers had proved themselves artfully deceptive. If they knew what we were doing to assist the Jews, a trap like this would be something they might try. But with the lives of children hanging in the balance, I felt compelled to act. I closed my eyes for a moment to pray, hoping for a Word about what I should do. In that instant, standing at the counter with a member of the German SS next to me, an image from that oft-repeated dream flashed through my mind—the large house with lush gardens all around and flowerbeds filled with tulips in full bloom. I took it as a sign from God and smiled at the soldier. "Yes. I can help you. Who could refuse an opportunity to help the children?"

"Good," the soldier nodded. "What shall we do?"

"Bring your men and come with me." He moved to the top of the staircase and called down for the others. They made their way quickly up the steps, then followed me into the parlor. "Stay here and wait," I said, pointing to the chairs. "I'll be back in a few minutes."

While they waited in the parlor, I ran downstairs and used the telephone to call Hendrik. Using our coded language I told him I had four deliveries, but they were going in different directions and all of them were for immediate delivery, which meant I needed four couriers right away. Twenty minutes later, Hendrik arrived at the house with three of our teenagers. I gathered them together near the back staircase and told them the soldier's story. "This is an incredible opportunity," I said when I was through. "We cannot ignore it."

Hendrik was suspicious. "I think it's a trap."

"Maybe so," I nodded, "but when I prayed about it I felt confirmed in my spirit that we should do this. These are children. The future of a generation. This is an opportunity we dare not avoid merely because we fear for our own safety."

Hendrik thought for a moment, then glanced around at the others. "You three should have a say in this, too. It's not just my decision to make."

"I'm in," the first one replied eagerly.

"Me too," the next added.

"Can't let them go without me," the third one shrugged nervously. "What do we do?"

"That is why I wanted four of you," I explained. "There are four of them. You will wear their uniforms, go to the orphanage, and get the babies."

Hendrik's eyes opened wide in disbelief. "That's it?"

"That's it," I said with a smile.

"That's the whole plan?" someone asked.

"The whole plan," I responded. "Anything more than that and it gets too complicated. Put on German uniforms, go to the orphanage, get the children."

Hendrik had a telling look. "If they find out what we're doing we'll be shot on the spot."

"Yes," I conceded. "But if you succeed, many will survive because of it and people will talk about you for centuries to come."

The others seemed to like that idea, and Hendrik asked, "What do we do with the babies after we get them from the orphanage?"

"Take them to Willem, leave them there, and come right back here. No stops along the way. No shooting or blowing things up. Just come right—"

"No shooting?" one of them interrupted. "We're taking guns?"

"You're taking their guns."

"No way," he said, shaking his head vigorously. "They'll have us in front of a firing squad by sundown."

"It's the only way," I insisted. "You won't look authentic without their weapons."

"When do we do this?" Hendrik asked, ignoring the obvious skepticism growing among the others.

"Now," I replied and without further discussion I led them upstairs. I placed Hendrik and the others in my room, then went down to the parlor.

"Okay," I said to the German soldiers as I entered the room, "take off your uniforms." They gave me an amused grin but without a word of protest or a hint of hesitation. I waited in the hall while they tossed out their clothes, then carried the uniforms up to my bedroom where I repeated the same process with Hendrik. While Hendrik and the others dressed as soldiers, I brought their civilian clothes down to the Germans and casually added, "I'll need your weapons, too."

The one who'd been doing the talking shook his head. "We can't give you our weapons."

"Why not?"

"Well, for one thing, it's against the law for Germans to arm anyone in the occupied territories. And besides that, no soldier would ever give up his weapon except as an act of surrender."

He was correct, of course, but I was certain this plan would fail unless our men were armed, so I looked him in the eye and quietly said, "Then you'll just have to trust me to give them back."

His forehead wrinkled in a puzzled look. "What will you do with them?"

"Give them to the men who are going in your places."

His eyes twinkled with amusement. "You want us to clothe a patrol of Dutch volunteers in German uniforms *and* arm them with German weapons?"

"It's the only way," I shrugged.

"There has to be another," he argued.

"Look," I was unwilling to let the opportunity slip away. "You trusted me enough to tell me about this, and I've trusted you not to shoot my family or take us all to jail. Now trust me for the solution. I have four men who will take your places for this assignment. But in order to be successful they must look like German SS soldiers. And as you so eloquently admitted, no German SS soldier would travel without his weapon." With a heavy sigh he handed me his rifle and nodded to the others. They gave me theirs, too, and I lugged them to my bedroom.

Ten minutes later, in what must have been the strangest sight of the occupation, Hendrik and three of our young men, wearing German army uniforms and carrying German army rifles, climbed into a German army truck and drove away on one of the most incredible missions of the war. I prayed that they would be successful.

◈ ◈ ◈

Late in the afternoon, Hendrik and the others returned with the truck. I heard a commotion downstairs as they arrived and went to the top of the steps to see. Hendrik and the three teenagers, still dressed as German SS soldiers, were inside the shop. A woman who'd come as a customer was frightened by their sudden appearance and rushed to get out of the way. Hendrik played the part to the hilt, angrily shouting in German for her to get out. When she was gone and the door was shut, Hendrik burst out laughing. I rushed downstairs to quiet him.

"No, no, no," I said angrily. "This is not a joking matter. You can't do this."

"We were only having fun," he chuckled.

"You were being reckless," I said, scolding them all. "Now get upstairs and get those uniforms off before someone reports you."

With their shoulders sagging, Hendrik and the others trudged up the steps. As they did, Hendrik tried to tell me about the venture but I cut him off. "Did you get the babies?"

"Yes."

"Did you take them to Willem?"

"Yes."

"And you left them there?"

"Yes, but—"

"Never mind about the rest right now," I said, cutting him off once more. "Get up to my room and get those uniforms off. I'll wait in the hall while you toss them out."

A few minutes later, I carried the uniforms back to the soldiers in the parlor and retrieved from them the clothes they'd been wearing, then took them back to Hendrik and the others. "Wait in here," I said as I tossed the clothes through the doorway. "I'll come get you once the soldiers are gone." Then I picked up the weapons and carried them back to the soldiers in the parlor.

By then, the Germans were dressed and anxious to leave. I gave them back their weapons, and as they turned to leave the leader asked finally, "Were your men successful?"

"Yes," I said proudly. "Very much so."

The soldiers appeared genuinely relieved. "Thank you for saving us from that mission."

"Thank you for giving it to us."

"You are very welcome, though I'm not sure how I will report this when we return."

"Tell them the mission was completed and the babies are gone," I suggested.

"All babies are gone," he grinned. "I'll put them off with that. All babies are gone." Then in a nervous gesture he took my hand, kissed it lightly, and stepped from the room.

❀ ❀ ❀

When the soldiers were gone, I went upstairs and rapped on the door to the secret room to let those inside know they could come out. "What happened?" Meyer gasped as he crawled through the tiny space. "Why were we in there so long?"

"I can't tell you," I replied, "other than to say that everything is okay now."

While they filed downstairs, I caught hold of Hendrik's arm and gestured for him to wait. "Sorry about what happened downstairs," he said sheepishly.

"That's okay. I was just worried that the soldiers would hear you and rush out to see what was happening. I didn't want the whole thing to unravel."

"I realize that," he nodded. "I should have paid more attention."

"You tried to tell me what happened at the orphanage. Did it go well?"

His face lit up with excitement. "There were almost a hundred babies."

My mouth fell open and my eyes were wide with amazement. "A hundred—"

Just then the telephone rang downstairs, and a moment later Corrie came upstairs. "That was Willem. He says the clock in the hall has stopped working. It's too large to transport and he needs it fixed immediately. I am going out to see what he wants."

A broad grin spread across my face. "I can tell you what he wants," I beamed.

"What?"

"Our fine young men rescued almost a hundred babies from the orphanage at Hoofddorp. They are now at Willem's."

Her eyes opened wide. "Then I must go at once!"

❖ ❖ ❖

Late that night, long after the curfew hour, Corrie returned to the Beje looking tired from pedaling the bicycle, but she came alive with excitement as she talked about what she'd seen. "Eighty-six babies," she said in a rush. "I don't know how they did it, but they rescued eighty-six babies!"

Hearing her talk made what we'd done sound even more incredible, but that was a lot to drop on someone unannounced, as we had deposited them on Willem. "How are Tine and Willem?"

"They're overwhelmed. Glad the children are safe, for now, but overwhelmed."

"We have to get those babies out of there."

"Yes," Corrie nodded. "We must. Besides being overwhelmed, Willem and Tine face a serious risk that someone will report them."

We talked about ways to place the babies with families, but after the response we'd received from Karel, neither of us saw that as a viable option. Corrie suggested Herman Slurring might help. "He has many more contacts than we do," she offered. "And his people are already familiar with our work." But I was suspicious of Slurring. In spite of having known him almost my entire life, and in spite of Papa's endorsement, I was suspicious of anyone who had fresh tea and real sugar during the occupation, and my mind could not stop imagining what he must have done to secure a ready supply, though I never turned down any that Corrie brought home, which is why I said nothing to her at the time.

As we talked, I remembered Johan Andriessen, the priest at Peter's church whom we had met that day he played "The Wilhelmus," and his comment to me as we were leaving that day. *"These are trying times. We must all find the courage of our convictions."* That stuck with me and I thought of it again while we struggled over what to do with the babies. Finally I brought it up. "I think Father Andriessen might help."

"Andriessen?" Corrie had a questioning look. "From Peter's church?"

"Yes."

"We've had no contact with him since that day we attended Peter's first service."

"But he has used his position in the church to visit Peter in prison," I countered, "which is something none of the rest of us have been able to do."

"I don't know," Corrie mused. "We need to get this resolved quickly. Herman Slurring's friends could solve this problem without delay. I'll go see Slurring in the morning."

"No," I said, taking advantage of my prerogative as the older sister. "I'll see Andriessen in the morning. You've done all the going. The trolley goes out to the church. I can at least do that much."

"I don't mind the bicycle. It's rather relaxing, actually."

"Let me see what Andriessen says. I don't think talking to him will do any harm, and if he can't help, then you can talk to Slurring."

CHAPTER 35

EARLY THE NEXT MORNING, I boarded the trolley and rode out to the church in Velsen. I found Father Andriessen in the sanctuary and we took a seat on the front pew. Glancing around at the room I said, "Do you remember the day my nephew Peter played "The Wilhelmus" here?"

"How could I ever forget?" he smiled. "That was one of the greatest moments in the life of our congregation. They haven't been the same since."

"My sister was so angry with him for doing that."

"It was risky, but it was so spontaneous and it gave everyone a moment to say they disagreed with the current situation, spiritually as well as personally."

I wanted to ask him just how spontaneous the music was and whether he knew in advance what Peter was going to do, but I refrained and instead asked, "Was everyone pleased with it?"

"Not all. We had a few who were disgruntled, but on the whole most people found the moment very invigorating."

"I noticed some who didn't look too happy while he was playing. Did anyone have any trouble from it, other than Peter?"

"Several were questioned but Peter was the only one arrested. Is something on your mind?"

I nodded. "I've been thinking about that day, when we were leaving. You spoke to me. Do you remember what you said?"

"I said we should all have the courage of our convictions."

"Did you mean that?"

"Yes. Of course. We should all have the courage to live by our convictions. I think that is one of the chief aims of Christianity. That we should have convictions and then live by them."

"You have convictions?"

"Of course, but what are you asking me? Convictions regarding what?"

"Regarding …" I wanted to move carefully toward my point, to make certain he was with us and at least not against us, but I was having trouble getting on with it. "Regarding our current situation," I said finally.

"Oh, well," he began with a note of disgust, "I find our current condition deplorable. The Germans are lost in a web of evil and have not a single clue how to get out. They're doing things they never would have done just fifty years ago, and *we* are paying the price for it."

"And what about the Jews?"

"Well, yes, they are paying the worst price of all."

"So you are with them?"

"If you mean am I sympathetic to their predicament, then yes. Of course." I could tell he was growing impatient. "What most people don't realize is that God has not forgotten His covenant with them. 'Vengeance is mine, I will repay, says the Lord.' If the Germans do not repent, He will bring judgment on them. I say that to you and to anyone who asks, though I would say it to them in private."

"Why not say it from the pulpit?"

"I have asked the Lord that many times and the response I get is that I must be here, looking after the flock. My people. Teaching, leading, protecting them as I can. If I spoke my heart on Sunday, I would be in custody before Monday morning." He gave me a curious look. "Is all this really why you came out here to see me? Just ask me." He gestured to our surroundings. "This is a sanctuary. I am a priest. You will not be reported."

I shook my head. "This isn't what I want to ask you, but I wanted to make sure our conversation was safe."

"Well, now you can be sure. As sure as our current circumstances will allow. So tell me, what is on your mind?"

"If …" Voices in my head were screaming at me to keep quiet, but my spirit said speak, so I took another breath and tried again. "If you had the opportunity...could you place small children with Dutch families?"

"Yes. I'm sure I could."

"What if those small children were Jewish?"

"Could I place them with Dutch families?"

"Yes. Could you?"

He took a deep breath. "How small?"

"Very small."

"Here, in local homes, or anywhere?"

"Anywhere."

"I think so." He nodded his head. "Yes. I think so. Jewish children would be more difficult, but it could be done."

"I need your help."

His face softened in a kindly smile. "If you're interested in helping children..."

"Infants," I noted.

"If you are interested in helping infants, I have someone you should meet. Do you have time to take a drive?"

A drive meant access to a car and the gas to operate it, and that raised questions on many levels. "A drive? As in a car?"

"Yes, come on. I'll show you."

Andriessen led the way through the building to a driveway out back where a shiny black automobile was parked. I was already suspicious just from the mention of it, but seeing the car made my heart skip a beat. Automobiles were rare since the occupation and gas even more so. But my spirit did not object so I pushed aside the worry and climbed into the car with him. He backed it from the parking space, drove up the street a ways, then turned and headed across town.

A few minutes later we entered what had obviously been an affluent neighborhood before the German invasion. Large houses, surrounded by expansive grounds, were set back from the street with lawns that once had been interspersed with gardens and shrubs. Now the shrubs were unkempt with branches sprawling in every direction. Weeds cluttered the gardens and flowerbeds, and ragged stumps were all that remained of the trees that once stood tall.

We passed half a dozen houses before Andriessen slowed the car and turned into a driveway that ran toward a huge three-story mansion. As we idled toward it, I could see the trim was crumbling and in need of a coat of paint. A downspout dangled precariously from one corner, and a long piece of gutter lay across a clump of bushes.

Andriessen brought the car to a stop near the garage and got out. "Come on. We can let ourselves in from here." Then he led the way to the back door and opened it without knocking.

Inside, the house was damp and cold. Hardwood floors that once had been polished and smooth were now scuffed and dusty. As we made our way down the main hall, our footsteps echoed through the house and I saw room after room empty of furniture. I imagined what it must have looked like just a few years before—filled with antique furniture, the walls covered with expensive paintings, and servants attending to every need. Now everything was gone.

At the end of the hall we came to a grand staircase that wound its way up to the second and third floors. He turned right and we stepped through a doorway into the front parlor where we found a man standing at the window gazing out to what was left of the lawn. He turned and smiled at us as we entered. "Father Andriessen. I thought that was you when you drove up." They shook hands and then Andriessen introduced me.

"Mr. Keesing owns a publishing business," Andriessen explained.

"I did once," Keesing corrected. "Now, it seems, I merely operate a printing press for the Nazis. I suppose I shouldn't complain. Someone has to print their propaganda pieces and it affords me a better living than most." He paused to gesture to our surroundings. "Though it's nothing like what it used to be."

Andriessen continued, "Mr. Keesing was instrumental in organizing the children's transport. Your brother helped with that effort. We managed to get all the Jewish children out of the refugee camp before the Germans invaded."

"And," Keesing said, picking up the topic, "after that we expanded the effort to include Jewish children from anywhere and with the help of others were able to rescue almost two thousand children." He had a wry smile. "The Germans still hate me for that. Only keep me around because they need my printing capacity and don't have anyone else to make the machines operate."

"Betsie," Andriessen urged, "ask Mr. Keesing what you asked me earlier."

I felt uncomfortable launching straight into what I wanted to ask. I hadn't even explained everything to Andriessen, so I began with a question. "If you had an opportunity to help eighty-six Jewish infants, would you do it?"

Keesing answered immediately, "Without a doubt." His words were clear and firm, and his eyes didn't dart away when he spoke to me.

"Right now?" I pressed.

"It would take a day or two to coordinate things, but yes. I'd be ready to assist you immediately. You have these babies now?"

"You would place them in homes where they would be safe?"

"Absolutely. Do you have the babies now?"

"Yes, sir," I said softly. "We have them."

"Good. Tell Willem to come see me at once. I know what to do."

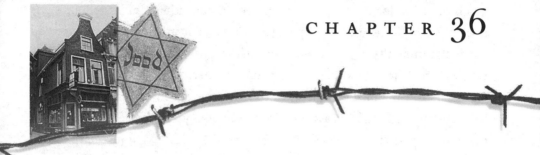

CHAPTER 36

WE NEVER KNEW where the babies went, but Kik, who was involved with Willem in placing them, assured us that most of them made it safely out of the country and those who stayed were hidden with good families. We never saw or heard from them again.

We didn't see the SS soldiers again, either, but the scare of having them show up unannounced at the shop turned our attention to installation of a buzzer system to warn of danger. Our guests were neither quick nor agile and needed as much time as possible in order to reach the secret room without being discovered. If the soldiers who came that day had been serious about searching the house, we would have been in trouble.

Leendert knew something about electricity and offered to install a simple system—a centrally located buzzer with small buttons mounted discreetly around the house. I agreed for him to do it, and the day after I visited with Father Andriessen we began assembling the pieces necessary to make it happen. We found wire and screws in the shop, which meant all we needed was the buzzer and a few button switches. I dispatched Hendrik to find them. Several hours later, he came back with half a dozen switches and a buzzer. No one asked where or how he procured them. By morning, Leendert had the system installed and working.

Over the next month we conducted drills for getting Meyer and the others out of sight and making the house appear as though only three people lived there. Perfecting that was difficult and took careful observation. During several of the early drills everyone made it into the secret room quickly enough, but Corrie and I failed to notice an extra plate at the table, a man's jacket much too large for Papa left lying on a chair, and other similar telltale signs that might indicate additional people were present in the house. Corrie had particular difficulty with the late-night drills. She was a heavy sleeper. When we awakened her from a deep sleep and peppered her with questions, she often said too much. Eventually we reduced our response time to less than four minutes, but that was still slower than many thought acceptable. One night at supper, after weeks of practice, I finally said, "We'll just have to rely on stalling them to build in some extra time."

After we rescued the babies from the orphanage, daily life at the Beje once again settled into a rhythm of eat, work, relax, sleep, and do it over again the next day, a cycle that was interrupted only by the occasional hiding drill and one or two panicked alerts. At night electrical blackouts became a regular occurrence with the power typically shut off around six in the evening. We burned candles for light and many times simply sat in the dark and talked until bedtime. Both Corrie and I played the piano well enough to do it without seeing the keys and we sometimes played from memory while everyone sang along.

People continued to arrive at our door after curfew and we continued to place them, but finding new locations was increasingly difficult. By then our network, already large and unwieldy, had become a sprawling collection of friends, couriers, and contacts that reached beyond the Netherlands' borders. It was exceedingly useful in providing people a safe place to live but much too large, I worried, to go unnoticed. And I was becoming concerned about the number of people living in the house with us—at mealtime we had twelve people wedged in place around the table. As those extra people grew accustomed to their surroundings they became more lax about noise and casual about being seen during the day. All of that caused me great concern. As events would prove, my anxiety was well founded.

During Christmas 1943, we celebrated Hanukkah for our Jewish guests by singing traditional Hebrew songs. One night the singing became particularly enthusiastic, and a neighbor appeared at our door to complain about the noise. "Tell your Jews to be quiet," she fussed. "We can hear them right through the wall." That's when I realized we were in trouble.

After she was gone I looked over at Corrie. "A policeman, a squad of German soldiers, Kik and his friends, the neighbors, and most of the Jews remaining in the city know what we are doing."

"Apparently," Corrie said with a sardonic smile, "our secret work is the worst-kept secret in the city."

"And I don't see any way to change things."

"We can't send our people away."

"No, we can't." We'd had other residents who were difficult to place, but after staying with us for an extended period we found people willing to take them. Most of them were eventually discovered, which led to imprisonment for them and for their hosts, as well. Sending Meyer or any of the others to live somewhere else, to us, would be the same as handing them over to the Germans. They'd gone undetected at Beje far longer than any of the others simply by staying elsewhere. "But we ought to try, at least, to limit our exposure."

Corrie had an amused look. "Do you really think that's possible?"

"No," I chuckled. "I think as soon as the doorbell rings we'll forget the risk and do all we can to help whoever asks."

"And I think that's the way it should be," she replied.

Corrie had come a long way from the simpering girl of fourteen who fell madly in love with everyone she met. We'd had our difficulties, even more so than most sisters I've known, but she was an unusually talented and energetic person. Once God got hold of her heart, that talent and energy became focused on singular purposes. In the process, she'd become a wonderfully balanced woman, grounded in a firm, genuine, personal faith in God. I loved her when she was a child, and I especially loved her as an adult.

As if there wasn't enough activity at the house already, Willem got the idea of conducting a Bible study structured around the scriptural notion of praying for the peace of Jerusalem. By extension, he suggested, David's call in the Psalms for prayers on behalf of the Holy City should be viewed in our contemporary context as a call for concerted prayer on behalf of the Jews living under German occupation. It was a renewal of sorts of our great-grandfather's commitment. We continued to pray for Jerusalem each morning after break-fast when Papa concluded reading the day's scripture lesson. Willem wanted to conduct a series of meetings that included Dutch believers beyond our household. We were all in favor of him doing it, and they began meeting in the parlor each Wednesday morning. Those gatherings were an instant success. Almost immediately attendance grew to include dozens. More people than ever were coming and going from our house.

◆ ◆ ◆

In January, Rolfe, the policeman from the station just up the street, came to the shop, supposedly to inquire about a problem with his watch. Another customer was present when he arrived and he loitered near the display case until she was gone. After she left, he asked about me, and Corrie brought me down from the second floor. We stood near the rear staircase and talked. He had a worried look. "The Jewish Council has been asked to provide another round of names of non-Jewish sympathizers."

"You know this for a fact?"

"Isaac Franken, one of the Council members from Amsterdam, was in the police station talking to the Germans."

"That can't be good," I sighed.

"Your neighbor from across the street was there, too."

"Cornelius Mussert was there with Isaac Franken?"

Rolfe nodded. "Yes, they were all in the meeting together. Talking with the Germans about people they suspect are involved in helping the Jews hide and escape."

Corrie came from the shop and joined us. "I knew Mussert was trouble."

"And that's not all," Rolfe continued. "The Germans, with at least some cooperation from the Council, have been sending out informants. Some of them are Jews. Others are Dutchmen posing as Jews or Jewish sympathizers. They claim to be in need and ask for help. Gain entry. Learn incriminating details. Relay that information back to the Germans. Their effort has already netted dozens of arrests, and even right now Gestapo agents are on their way to a house at Ede."

Corrie's eyes opened wide in a look of concern. "We must warn them. Who is it? We can call them."

For an instant I saw something in Rolfe's eyes that told me he hadn't previously known that our telephone was working. I wasn't sure I liked what I saw, but the moment passed as quickly as it came, and he said, "There's nothing we can do about it now. And even if you could, they would know the information came from me."

"They're doing this with help from the Council?" I asked, trying to move the conversation forward.

"Yes," he replied. "They have penetrated deeply into the Jewish and Christian communities. Almost every non-Jewish organization that's trying to help has been compromised."

Corrie shook her head in disgust. "Why would the Council cooperate like this?"

"Trying to stay alive," I replied.

"I think some of them have trouble believing the stories they hear about what the Germans are doing," Rolfe offered.

"People like Isaac Franken," I added, "think they can outlast the war."

Rolfe turned to leave, "Just be careful. If the Council's informants haven't already been here, they will be soon."

I walked with him to the door and said good-bye, then turned to Corrie. "We knew Isaac Franken was going to be trouble."

"He's giving up his own people just to outlast the war."

"Might make it, too," Papa said from his place behind the desk.

"Well," I sighed, "if they're making up lists of Dutch sympathizers, we're on it."

"And I am thankful to God to be counted among the faithful," Papa said with a smile. "Make sure you are, too."

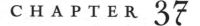

CHAPTER 37

THROUGHOUT THE OCCUPATION I struggled to maintain my daily dose of the liver extract first prescribed by Dr. Tromp and later modified by Dr. Van Veen. Along with it I also took daily vitamin supplements, which were administered in liquid form. Dr. Van Veen supplied enough of it for Corrie and Papa, too. As a result, the food shortages we encountered did not have the same deleterious effect on us as they had on others, and we suffered fewer illnesses than most of our neighbors. Nevertheless, in February 1944, an outbreak of influenza swept the country, and Corrie became ill. I sent her to bed, hoping that by confining her to her room others in the house might avoid getting sick. The last thing we needed was twelve people coughing in the night. With Corrie unable to work I spent my days helping Toos in the shop in addition to my regular duties upstairs.

Corrie had been in bed two days when Willem arrived for the Wednesday prayer meeting. That week's gathering was a special meeting that commemorated the day when our great-grandfather and his priest agreed to pray together regularly for the peace of Jerusalem. Nollie and Kik were with us, as were several dozen others. Papa came up from the shop, too.

As Willem was beginning, Louis appeared in the parlor doorway and gestured for me. I excused myself and went out to see what he wanted.

"There's a man downstairs to see you," he explained.

"Can't it wait? I asked. "We're just beginning."

"He said it was urgent."

Reluctantly I followed Louis downstairs to the shop, where I found the visitor waiting near the display case. "We need to talk," he said. "In private."

I didn't know him and didn't feel comfortable meeting with him alone. "This is as private as it gets around here. Everyone here pretty much knows everyone else's business. How may I help you?"

He introduced himself as Jan Vogel, a carpenter from Ermelo, a town situated about one hundred kilometers east of Amsterdam. He was a long way from home and I was immediately suspicious. "My wife and I have been helping Jews in our area," he explained. "Hiding some, finding places for others with families who think as we do."

Something in his voice didn't sound right—the words were correct but the way he said them made it all seem hollow and meaningless. I was still thinking about how far he'd traveled to get to us, so I said, "Ermelo is a long way from here. Why have you come to me?"

"Two days ago, my wife was arrested. The officer in charge of her case says he will release her if I pay him six hundred guilders. Otherwise, he will turn her over to the Germans and I will likely never see her again."

I studied his face as he spoke but saw no light in his eyes. No fire of passion when he mentioned his wife. His eyes never quite met mine and he still hadn't told me why he came to us for help. We were a long way from his home. "So you had to come all the way here to find someone who would give you the six hundred guilders?" I said it more as an observation rather than a question, but if he had no answer I intended to send him away.

"I asked and they said you were the person to see. That you had helped many and you never turned anyone away."

That was a key phrase. *Never turn anyone away.* Corrie and I had said that to each other many times. It was our method of operation, our ethos, or driving principle. Only someone who knew us would know that about us. I was both curious and scared by the remark. "Who told you that?"

"Many," he replied. "That is what they all say. Practically everyone I asked said you were someone who could help. And someone who would."

He was saying all the right words but never once made eye contact with me. And I could not escape the thought that if he had saved the train fare for a round trip from Ermelo to Haarlem and back, he would be well on his way to having enough for the bribe. "I don't know," I said with a slow shake of my head. "Bribing police officers is a risky business."

"I can take care of him myself," Vogel said. "I can deliver the money. I just don't have it to deliver."

"How much time do you have?"

"The policeman will be there tonight. If I bring him the money, he will let her go immediately. If I don't, she will be sent to prison in the morning."

It was a tough choice and for the first time that I could recall, the intuitive part of my mind was in conflict. A thousand bells were ringing in my head telling me to send him away. And a thousand more told me I should help. I needed help discerning the truth and there was only one person I trusted to give it to me, so I said, "Wait here." Then I turned toward the steps and started up the back staircase.

Corrie was asleep in bed when I reached her room but I shook her awake and told her about Vogel's request. She listened attentively and thought for a moment, then said, "Tell him to come back in the afternoon. We'll have the money by then. That will give us time to think it over. Saying we'll get the money isn't the same as actually giving it to him."

That made me feel better, but I was still anxious. She was right. Saying we would get the money wasn't the same thing as actually doing it. And if we were subject solely to local authorities I would have felt more confident. But we weren't. We were under the control of the Germans, who saw themselves as occupiers of a land filled with humans far inferior to themselves. They would think nothing of trampling Netherlands law. "Should we even do that?" I asked. "Is it safe to have any connection with him?"

"I don't know if it's safe or not. But we've never turned anyone away, and certainly not because we were afraid. Before we refuse we should take time to consider it thoughtfully."

"But Rolfe said to be careful. That people would approach us who were informants."

"I'm sure they will," Corrie smiled. "But that is their problem. Not ours."

"What do you mean?"

"Jesus said we should give to those who ask. If they want to use that against us, they have to answer to Him for it. Our job is to obey."

I was still troubled by Vogel's demeanor but I had no real argument against Corrie's suggestion. So I went downstairs and delivered the message. "Come back later this afternoon. We'll have the money then." He said he'd return at three.

Vogel left and we never saw him again, but not long after he was gone a squad of German soldiers arrived at the house. Unlike the SS who visited us earlier, these men were serious about searching the Beje. Nollie, who was still in the prayer meeting, was seated near the front window of the parlor and saw them coming. She pressed the button, and when the buzzer sounded, our guests moved quickly but quietly to the secret room. I took my often-practiced position near the top of the steps and prepared to delay the soldiers as long as possible.

Seconds after the warning, the door to the shop flew open and a squad of men rushed inside. One of them went immediately to the rear staircase, blocking the exit. The others took up positions inside the shop. When they were in place, two officers entered. One of them was Captain Bormann. The other identified himself as Lieutenant Krüger.

Bormann glanced at Papa and gestured toward the steps. "Upstairs," he ordered. Then he looked over at Louis and Toos and told them the same.

Papa rose from behind the desk and made his way to the stairs. Louis followed and, as we'd instructed many times before, they walked slowly toward me, taking as much time as possible but moving fast enough to avoid being abused by the soldiers.

I was waiting in the hall when they arrived on the second floor. "Captain Bormann," I said politely. "You are back again?" He pointed to the chairs around the kitchen table and said simply, "Sit." We did as he instructed and waited.

Krüger called down to the soldiers below and two of them came up to where we were sitting. He posted one of them at the parlor door and took the other to search the second floor. Bormann remained with us. He waited impatiently, glancing down the hall as if waiting for word from Krüger. We heard them opening drawers and smashing things on the floor. Tears filled my eyes. Papa seemed unaffected by it.

When the search of the second floor produced nothing, Krüger moved upstairs. Four more men arrived and Bormann dispatched them to assist in the search. Eventually they reached the top floor, rousted Corrie from her bed, and dragged her down to the kitchen. She joined us at the table and we watched while Bormann methodically questioned those who'd been gathered in the parlor for the prayer meeting. Working his way around the room, he seemed to know that Willem was our brother and Nollie our sister, though they had little to do with our affairs at the house. Kik sat quietly staring ahead, his eyes focused on nothing in particular. I'm sure he was worried. Of all of us, he knew the most about where the people we'd helped had actually been placed. And at that moment I realized we'd never given him a plausible story to cover his association with us.

One by one Bormann dismissed members of the prayer meeting who'd been uninvolved in our work. Only Toos, Louis, Willem, Nollie, and Kik remained. The others were allowed to leave. When he was finished with them, Bormann left the soldier at the parlor door in charge of us and ordered Corrie downstairs to the shop. I heard him shouting at her and once or twice I was sure I heard the sound of a slap.

While we waited, I caught the soldier's eye and said, "Would you care for tea?" The water in the kettle on the stove was already hot.

"It is unthinkable," he snarled, "for an officer in the German army to drink from a cup first offered to a Jew." Papa opened his mouth to say something, but the soldier growled at him, "Shut up, old man. I don't want to get rough with you."

A few minutes later, Bormann returned with Corrie. Her cheeks were red and her hair was a mess, which confirmed my earlier notion that he'd slapped her face. I expected to receive the same when he grabbed me by the arm, snatched me from the chair, and dragged me down the steps.

When we reached the shop, he jerked me around to face him and said in an angry voice, "We have reports of people entering this house and never leaving, yet I see no one except the group that was praying in the room upstairs." He pressed his face closer and snarled, "Even that is illegal, but what I want to know is, where are the Jews?"

"We have no Jews," I replied.

Quicker than I could see it coming, he struck me across the face with the back of his hand. "Do not lie to me!" he shouted. "We have that idiot Vogel. He has given you up. We know that you were planning to help him bribe a police official in order to gain the release of his Jew-loving wife. He gave us names and locations of many witnesses who will testify that you have been assisting Jews in their efforts to escape deportation. So, Miss Ten Boom, I'll ask you again. Where are the Jews you've been hiding?"

"There are no Jews," I said, this time more forcefully than before.

Bormann grabbed a handful of my hair and yanked it hard, pulling me toward him as he lowered his voice. "I have visited here before," he said calmly. My head was pressed against his chest so tightly that the buttons on his jacket dug into my flesh. "I know you are the reasonable one," he continued. "Can you not give me a straight answer and save yourself more misery?"

"Misery," I replied. "I have seen what you do to the Jews. Loading them on trucks and hauling them away. And I have heard reports of what happens to them at the camps. Worked all day and fed very little while they slowly starve to death. Others shot on sight. And I have heard you are now gassing them in mass killings. Do you not fear for the loss of your soul?"

He struck me again, and when I bent over in pain, clutching my cheek, he grabbed me by the hair once more and pulled me closer again. "Do not speak to me of my soul, or of God, or any other of your religious nonsense." His voice was cold but his eyes were ablaze. "Your God is the product of your imagination. Now I will ask you once more. Where are the Jews?"

"We have no Jews," I replied.

Frustrated he could not get a better answer, he shoved me toward the stairs and shouted, "Get up there with the rest of your vermin family!" I made my way up to the kitchen and found the table piled with silver and gold dinnerware plundered from the storage places throughout the house.

Bormann was sweating and he wiped his brow with the sleeve of his jacket. Then he looked over at Papa and said, "Old man, I would—"

Just then, the telephone in the shop rang. Bormann was startled by the sound. "How is it that your phone rings?" It rang again and he took me by the arm. "You will answer it. But you must not tell them I am here. If you do," he said, pointing to Papa and Corrie, "they will die." Then he shoved me toward the staircase and hustled me down to the shop.

When I picked up the receiver, the caller was talking excitedly, and I had to shout to get his attention. Bormann pulled the receiver away from my ear so he could hear. The caller asked about our shop hours, which was code for whether it was safe to come. I answered in an equally cryptic manner, telling him that we were open but parts were scarce and we could not guarantee timely repairs. That should have been sufficient to end the call right then, but he kept going, apparently either unfamiliar with what I saying or too excited to care. "You are in great danger," he blurted out all at once. "They have Slurring."

The bell for the shop door rang, diverting Bormann's attention. While he was distracted I hung up the phone. Krüger, who'd come downstairs after us, opened the door to find a middle-aged Jewish woman. "Is this Ten Boom's watch shop?" she asked.

"Yes," Krüger said with a grin. "Would you like to come inside?" He stepped back from the door and she entered the shop, all the while saying, "They came for my husband this morning. He sent me out the back door and I haven't been back—" She fell abruptly silent when she saw the soldiers in uniform. Krüger had a satisfied smile as he ordered her upstairs to join the others. I wondered why anyone would ring the bell when we were in obvious danger, then my gaze fell upon the *Alpina* sign still in the window, and my heart sank. With it in place, everyone would think the shop was safe. The soldiers could continue to wait, all the while netting unsuspecting visitors as they arrived to ask for help. And that is what they did, sending us back to the kitchen while Krüger manned the door.

Late that afternoon, after five more unsuspecting people had been nabbed in the shop, the telephone rang once more, and I was ordered downstairs to answer it. When I told the caller we were no longer accepting watches for face repair, he hung up. Bormann realized the word was out and that no one else would be coming. He stationed two of his men at the house—one at the front door, the other at the rear—then he turned to those of us who were his prisoners to get our coats. We all donned our coats and hats and followed Krüger up the street to the police station.

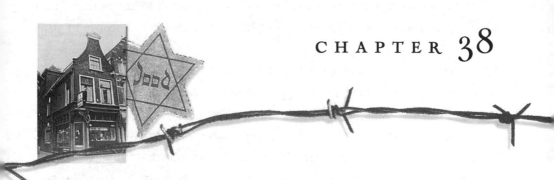

CHAPTER 38

AT THE POLICE STATION we were not enrolled on the record
or processed into official custody, as was the usual practice. Instead, we
were led to a large building one street over, which appeared to have once
been a gymnasium but had been converted to a holding room. Unlike the
typical police station, this site was heavily guarded by German soldiers.
Our normal Haarlem policemen were relegated to wandering among the
prisoners, functioning more like porters than patrolmen.

In the center of the room was a large table stacked high with files and
cluttered with papers. A German officer sat there, sorting through the fold-
ers. On the opposite side of the room prisoners stood in line, and I watched
as the officer at the table motioned to them. They dutifully crossed the floor
to stand before him. One by one he met with each of them, asking questions,
making notes, then sending them away.

Large mats were scattered across the floor, and one of the soldiers
ordered us to take a seat on one that lay to the left of the door. After helping
Papa to his place, I sat beside Corrie and rested her head in my lap. Already
sick with influenza, I was certain she was miserable.

Before long a soldier directed us to form a line along the wall. We rose
from our places and did as he said, then the officer at the table called us and
we stood before him. In a monotone voice, he asked for our name, address,

occupation, and marital status. It was all very perfunctory—neither the angry confrontation nor the formal judicial proceeding I expected.

When Papa reached the table, the officer looked at him a moment and said, "If you won't cause any more trouble, old man, I'll let you die in your own bed."

Papa squared his shoulders and said, "You might as well keep me. If you send me home today, I will help anyone who asks." The officer shook his head in disbelief and gestured for Papa to move along.

We returned to our place on the mat and took a seat with the others. A few minutes later, Lieven van Campen, a watchmaker from across town, came to where we were sitting and took a spot beside Papa. "Casper," he said in a friendly tone, "you are well, I hope?"

"Yes," Papa nodded. "I am fine. They arrested you, too?"

"These days, it seems everyone gets arrested," Van Campen quipped. "Have they told you the charges against you?"

"No. How about you?"

"One hears many things," Van Campen responded. "I suppose you will find out soon enough. Did they leave guards at your house?"

"Yes," Papa nodded once more. "Did they do that at yours?"

Van Campen ignored the question and continued, "The people left behind are the ones I think about. The ones left in the hiding places, afraid to come out for fear of capture. Waiting for someone to knock on the door and tell them it's okay." He cut his eyes at Papa. "You left them food, I'm sure, but only enough for a day or two."

While they talked, Kik leaned next to me and whispered, "This guy is an informant."

"How do you know?"

"Have you heard what he's been saying? He asks questions, but he never answers. And his questions indicate what the Germans are thinking—that we have a secret room and that others are hiding there right now. They just can't find it and they sent this guy over here to try and get it out of Grand Papa."

It was like a blindfold had been removed from my eyes. At once I knew Kik was right. I'd heard what Van Campen was saying, and even as he talked,

his words did not have the ring of truth, but there in the gymnasium, surrounded by friends and family members, all of us facing an uncertain future,
I'd ignored what I sensed inside myself and let them talk. Now I could see
the truth and I wanted to warn Papa to keep quiet, but there was nothing I
could do or say to tip him off to the danger Van Campen posed. Papa loved
people and he loved to talk, two traits not particularly helpful in the situation we faced. I was sure he would answer Van Campen's questions, launch
into a long and rambling discourse, and disclose things that would imperil
us all, but I needn't have worried.

Papa stared at him a moment, as if studying his face, then said quietly,
"I don't see you much anymore, Lieven. What happened?"

"Ah," he shrugged. "You know. Work keeps me busy."

"You sold well this year?" Papa asked.

"Best year we ever had," Lieven said proudly. "These Germans are a pain
but they buy our goods."

"Tell me something. How did you do it?"

"Do what?"

"How did you get watches to sell in your shop?"

Van Campen looked perplexed. "What do you mean?"

"I mean," Papa repeated, "how did you get watches? I only ask because
everyone else I know is unable to get them. They place orders, but the
watches never arrive. Yet you seem to have no trouble."

"That's what I do." Van Campen looked around nervously, as if searching for somewhere else to go. "I place orders. They arrive at my shop."

"And who do you have to bribe to get them?"

Van Campen's eyes narrowed. "You are accusing me of bribery?"

"What did you have to give them, Lieven? Did you give them your soul?"

Van Campen jumped to his feet and in a loud voice said, "I don't have
to take this from a Jew-lover!" and stormed off in a huff.

After an hour or so it appeared the officer seated at the table had inter-
viewed everyone in the room. He closed his files, stacked them neatly in
place, and departed from the room. When he was gone, Corrie started talking. "We should agree on what to say, get everything worked out between us.
If we all say the same thing, we can be sure—"

"Wait," I said, cutting her off. I stood and gestured with a nod of my head for her to follow. We walked a few steps away from the others and I whispered, "There are informants among us."

"Who?" she asked, glancing around.

"Van Campen, for one."

"I heard what Kik said, but Van Campen is gone."

"There are likely others. So we should keep quiet while we are in here."

"But what if our stories don't match?"

"The only way they could not be the same is if we do not tell the truth."

"If we tell the truth, we'll be in prison for life. Or worse."

"I think we're going to be in here a long time either way. Don't you?"

Corrie's shoulders slumped and tears formed in her eyes. "I am scared."

"I know." I put my arm around her. "But we are not going to react from fear."

"How can we react any other way?"

"We will remember what the angel said to the shepherds, *Fear not. For behold I bring good news of great joy.*" She rested her head on my shoulder and I led her back to where the others were seated.

In a little while, Rolfe entered the room with a group of policemen and announced that they would provide an escort to take us to the toilet. A number of people availed themselves of the opportunity. As we made our way in that direction he came alongside us and quietly said, "You will be alone at the toilet. You can flush any papers there."

That evening we were served hot rolls and water, both of which tasted very good, and the next morning we had rolls again. There was not much to do except lie on the mats and rest, which is what most of us did.

Around noon of the day after we were arrested, additional German soldiers entered the room and took positions on every side. When they were in place, a young lieutenant strutted to the center and announced that we should prepare to exit the building. A few minutes later, the soldiers began herding us toward the door.

A large crowd was gathered outside and as we left the building I scanned the faces, looking for someone familiar. Buses were parked nearby and the soldiers nudged us in that direction. Corrie and I took Papa by the arms and steadied him as we walked. And then I saw Tine's face and her hand waving to us. I called to Corrie and pointed her out. We were all crying by then but at least we had the assurance that someone knew where we were.

Onboard the bus, Corrie and I took a seat with Papa between us. Willem, Nollie, and Kik were in the next row. It was a beautiful Haarlem day with the sun shining brightly, though the air was bitterly cold. Once we were settled in place, I stared blankly out the window at the glare reflecting off the windows of the buildings around us.

Then a rear door to the police station opened and two soldiers appeared, dragging a man between them. His clothes were tattered and dirty and his head was bloodied. I was about to say what an awful sight he was when Corrie exclaimed, "That's Herman Slurring!"

A soldier stepped through the open door of the bus and with a stern look on his face barked, "Silence! There will be silence in here!"

We paid him no attention and watched out the window as they dragged Slurring to the bus beside us, lifted him up the steps, and dropped him onto a seat inside. Corrie was beside herself with anger. "Look what they did to him," she fumed. "Who would do such a thing?"

At the sight of him, waves of sadness swept over me, and for the first time I felt for myself what Papa had tried to explain to me many times before. The Germans were in a perilous position, worse even than our own. "Yes," I said softly. "It's so sad."

"Sad?" Corrie jerked her head around to face me. "It's infuriating. How can they treat someone like that?"

"They can't even see what they have done. They're trapped in a web of evil. Think of how sad it is that they feel compelled to do such things."

Papa nodded and added, "They will rue the day they raised their hand against God's chosen people."

While we talked, the sadness inside me gave way to the utter and complete realization of the hopelessness that enshrouded the Germans. As if staring into the abyss myself, I sensed how completely impossible it was for them to see what they had become—hopeless and impossible except for God. So I closed my eyes and, right there on that bus, I prayed for them.

❖ ❖ ❖

Though my stomach ached from hunger and my back ached from sleeping on the mat the night before, the bus ride from Haarlem was not unpleasant. We meandered through the city before turning toward the coast, then drove south along a coastal road. The Dutch countryside was beautiful and I was struck by how much of it remained untouched by the war. From the way we'd stripped the trees from Haarlem for fuel, I was sure the countryside must be bare, as well, but it was not and I found it refreshing.

Two hours later we arrived at a government building in The Hague. Someone said it was Gestapo headquarters for the Netherlands, but a sign out front noted it was home of the Ministry of Justice's administrative division. With the bus at a stop, the driver switched off the engine and we were ordered out. We assembled in the cold and were directed through a side door of the building.

Inside, a wide hall led to a large meeting room with a table atop a raised dais at the far end. Seated there was a man dressed in a business suit. A clerk sat at a second table an arm's reach away. Someone in line with us said the man on the dais was Rudolph Schakel, a civil magistrate. A group of prisoners that apparently arrived ahead of us was just leaving the room and while we waited for them, Captain Bormann and Lieutenant Krüger appeared at Schakel's side.

Slowly and methodically, each person in turn stepped forward to the table. The clerk handed Schakel a file and he paused a moment to scan the documents inside. Once or twice he returned the file to the clerk, said something to the person standing before him, and then they were led out a door near the corner. Most, however, were shuffled to the opposite side of the room, where they formed a line and waited some more.

When I appeared at the table, Schakel asked the same perfunctory questions as the army officer back in Haarlem, inquiring about my name, age, marital status, and number of children. He seemed tired and distracted. I was tired, too, and I had given the same information several times already. When he asked me, I said, "I gave that already." He looked up at me and said calmly, "To whom did you give it?"

"To the army officer in Haarlem when they brought us to the police station."

"That was for the army," he sighed. "This is for the court. Did anyone tell you the charges against you?"

"No."

He looked at the papers in my file and said, "Sedition. That's all it says. Sedition." He glanced over at Captain Bormann. "You have to specify what they did. You can't summarily charge them. And there is no complaining witness. How was this charge brought?"

Bormann stepped to Schakel's side, rested one hand on the desktop, and leaned closer. "This one is one of the ringleaders in Haarlem." He pointed to the file. "That is the complaining witness."

Schakel looked again. "Vogel?"

My heart sank. If I had only listened to the voice inside, none of this would have happened.

"Yes," Bormann answered. "They were hiding Jews and helping them escape." He pointed to Corrie. "That one is her sister. They were in it together."

Schakel looked at me and glanced over at Corrie. He was serious about what he was doing, processing prisoners through his court in a way that at least gave a nod to the Netherlands' tradition of justice, but I noticed also in his eyes a warm kindness, and a hint that he'd rather be anywhere else than where he was.

After several hours in the judicial building we were bused to the penitentiary at Scheveningen. It was after midnight when we arrived. We'd had nothing to eat since the hot rolls Rolfe gave us that morning.

German soldiers led us from the bus into a large building where for the first time we were met by uniformed prison guards, both male and female. By their uniforms and personal demeanor I knew that they were civil employees of the Dutch government—fellow Netherlanders. From that point forward we were under their immediate control, but German soldiers manned the doorways to the prison and they were stationed strategically throughout the building. We might have been in Dutch custody, but no one could doubt we were prisoners of the German army.

In the corridor, the guards divided the men from the women. Men on one side, women on the other. I was apprehensive about this and realized that Corrie, Nollie, and I were about to be separated from Papa, Willem, Kik, and the other men in our group. From the look in her eyes, I knew Corrie realized it, too. A few minutes later, the guards ordered the women down the corridor. I glanced back at Papa one last time, and he gave me a wave to say good-bye.

Farther on we came to a corner and turned onto a narrower hallway lined with steel doors on either side. Ten doors down we stopped, and a guard called my name. As I stepped forward, they opened one of the doors to let me into a cell. I glanced back at Corrie and Nollie and mouthed the words *I love you*. Then the door slammed shut behind me.

◆ ◆ ◆

Three women were in the cell already, two of them seated in opposite corners at the far end of the room. A single cot occupied the center and on it lay a third woman. She was curled in a fetal position, her body covered by a thin woolen blanket. Her body shook as she trembled with fever.

Sleeping mats not much thicker than the blanket lay on the floor, one near each of the two women in the corner and a third one by the door. A row of pegs ran along the wall, apparently put there for us to hang our coats, but they were empty, as the building was cold and everyone wore all the clothes they owned. I supposed the mat near the door was mine and I sat down beside it with my coat pulled tightly around my waist.

The woman in the far corner, older and somewhat larger, said in a gravelly voice, "Good, you're finally here. Now they can turn out the lights and we can all get to sleep."

A young girl sat in the corner to my right. She smiled at me and said, "My name is Nel. Nel van Houten from Halfweg. Ever hear of it?"

My mind was reeling from the shock of first being arrested, then taken to jail, and now to prison. I was separated from Corrie, Nollie, Willem, Kik, and Papa. In one fell swoop the Germans had shattered our family and all because we helped others escape the tyranny of the German death camps. I wanted to scream and cry. I wanted to hit someone and pound on them until they came to their senses and released us. I wanted...many things, but the last thing I wanted was to engage my cell mates in meaningless conversation. Yet when I looked down the wall to Nel and opened my mouth to say all of that, I heard myself say instead, "Halfweg. Of course. Halfway between Haarlem and Amsterdam. But I've never known anyone from there who was named Van Houten."

"How about you?" she asked. "What's your name?"

"I'm Betsie," I replied, sensing no harm in telling her that much.

"Where are you from?"

I didn't really want to say, but she seemed nice and I had no way of knowing how long I would be in that room with them. Better to be there with friends than enemies. "Haarlem," I answered.

The older woman looked over at me. "So, what'd you do to wind up in here? You don't exactly look like the law-breaking type."

"They have accused me of hiding Jews." It felt like a betrayal to answer so indirectly, but I was unsure of myself and apprehensive about admitting to anything.

"Accused you of it? Is it true?"

"Is what true?"

"The charge." Her tone was becoming more strident. "Were you hiding them?"

I still didn't want to answer, but she was sitting only a few feet away, which made it difficult to avoid the question and I was already feeling angry with myself for the manner in which I had replied at first. Finally I said, "I would never turn my back on God's people."

"Hah!" she scoffed. "They're no more God's people than we are."

At that point I decided that she was as open to questioning as I was, so I returned the favor and asked, "What's your name?"

"Helen."

She didn't give me her last name, so I asked, "Helen what?"

"Bruna." Her eyes darted away and her voice changed. "Helen Bruna."

"Where did you live?"

"Amsterdam," she grumbled. "As if it's any of your business."

I ignored her attitude and glanced over at the woman lying on the cot. "Who is she?"

"Nobody knows her name," Helen replied. Her eyes darted away once more and she pulled the sleeping mat closer to her side. "They put her in here yesterday. Haven't heard a word out of her since."

"The guards gave her the cot," Nel explained. "They said we had to give it to whichever one is weakest. The rest of us sleep on the floor." She pointed to the mat lying nearest me. "That one's yours."

The mat was dusty and trampled with footprints. The thought of lying on it to sleep was repulsive. Instinctively, I stood to shake it out. As I did, a cloud of dust arose and the others complained. It really was dirty. The lights were still on so I rolled it up and stood it in the corner by the door, then took a seat in front of it and leaned back with the rolled mat as a cushion against the wall. Nel rolled hers, too, placed it next to mine, and sat down beside me.

From down the hall I heard the sound of the metal doors banging closed, then a *click, click, click* echoed toward us. "What's that sound?" I asked.

Nel listened for a moment and said, "That's the guards walking the halls. They patrol up and down. Night and day. Always there, watching and listening."

"Yeah," Helen spoke up. "They're always listening. Maybe you two should remember that and stop talking so much." Her eyes met mine. "In here, you never know who you're talking to or who's listening."

Nel nodded her head in agreement but spent the next ten minutes telling me about herself. I learned she'd been arrested for prostitution, a life she detested but one she felt was forced upon her by her circumstances. Both parents were killed during the invasion and she was left on her own. With no skills or training, all she had was a youthful body, which she rented out to anyone willing to pay. "It's not much of a living, but it's the only way I had to survive."

"Weren't you worried about what might happen?"

"You mean like...catching a disease?"

"Or getting pregnant."

A cloud came over her face. "I've never had a disease, but I was pregnant. Twice. I had an abortion both times." Her eyes went hollow. "After the first one, I cried almost every day. But with the second, I hardly felt any emotion at all. I wanted to quit being a prostitute, but everything seemed hopeless without something to eat, so I kept doing it."

In a quick jolt of emotion, anger shot thorough me as she spoke. *I had longed to be with a man in genuine intimacy, and here she was selling it as a cheap imitation. I wanted children but had denied them to myself out of a sense of moral responsibility.* Yet here she was telling me she'd killed two before they left her womb. My heart ached, my neck throbbed, and inside I was screaming at her, "How could you do that?" Then just as quickly, I thought of Jesus and how frustrated He must have been. I took a deep breath and did my best to let the emotion pass, then I heard the Holy Spirit say to me, *I want to give it to her.* The anger subsided and in its place I found compassion and kindness. She was a gentle person—I could tell that much from our brief conversation—but with life forced upon her she'd had to make some bitterly harsh choices. I reached over and took her hand. "Life is never hopeless with God."

"Yeah, well tell Him to hurry up and get here," Helen growled. "It looks pretty hopeless now."

Nel looked at me. "Is that how you stay calm?"

If she had known the torment I felt inside she would not have asked that question. but I chose not to tell her that and instead said, "I'm not always calm, but whatever confidence I have comes from knowing that no matter what happens to me, God is always with me and everything will work out in the end." Those were words I spoke to myself as much as to her and as I said them I sensed my spiritual equilibrium return.

Nel seemed intrigued by my answer. "Do you think God would give me that kind of confidence?"

"Of course."

"But how?"

"Just ask."

"You mean pray?"

"Yes," I nodded, and then I led her through a simple prayer of repentance, one I'd heard Papa pray many times. He would have been proud to hear us, and thinking of him brought tears to my eyes but I made it through without sobbing.

As we finished and I opened my eyes, I saw Helen staring at us. "I was arrested for hiding people, too," she said without prompting. "Teenagers.

Soldiers in our area had been deporting kids to work in the factories near Berlin. Awful way to die, being worked to death. I hid three in my basement, but they couldn't keep quiet. Somebody heard them. Soldiers came and took them. Then they arrested me. I didn't do it because I love God. I didn't do it because they're Jews, which they weren't. Or even because they're teenagers needing a future." Her face turned up in a sneer. "I did it because I hate the Germans."

Before I could respond, the lights went out and the room was totally dark. I heard Helen slide her sleeping mat across the floor. It made a crinkling sound as she lay down on it. Nel unrolled her mat, too, and lay a short distance from me. For a moment I just sat there listening to the silence, broken only by the sound of the guard's footsteps in the hall, then I reached behind me for my own mat, spread it flat on the floor, and lay down.

A draft came from beneath the door, and when I looked in that direction I saw a streak of light from the hall seeping through the gap at the sill. In a few minutes my eyes adjusted to the darkness, and the light falling across my end of the room from that thin opening seemed as bright as one might ever need.

Stretched out on the mat, I thought of all that had happened in the last two days. Vogel visiting us at the house to ask for help, and the soldiers coming shortly after he left. I was certain he had betrayed us, but Captain Bormann made it seem as though they had arrested him, too. Yet I didn't see him at the police station or the holding room in Haarlem, and he wasn't with us when we reached The Hague. Anger rose inside me again and a sense of betrayal swept over me. I was certain he'd turned us in to the Germans. Then I thought of Nel and the prayer we'd just prayed and how I'd suggested to her that God could make a way of hope even in an environment as hopeless as our small cell. "Help me, Lord," I whispered. And then I heard myself saying, "I forgive Jan Vogel. And I forgive Captain Bormann. And Lieutenant Krüger." Moments later, the sense of peace I'd felt earlier returned. I closed my eyes and, in spite of the hardness of the floor, soon drifted off to sleep.

Sometime in the night, the familiar dream returned—with me soaring high above a lush green landscape, looking down on a large house surrounded by gardens and flowerbeds filled with tulips. Men and women worked the beds, and Corrie was with them. This time as they looked up at me I saw one of them was Captain Bormann and beside him was Lieutenant Krüger, only they weren't dressed as soldiers anymore but as gardeners, and they were laughing and smiling.

CHAPTER 39

THE NEXT MORNING, I was the first to awaken. As I did when I arrived the night before, I rolled up my sleeping mat, stood it in the corner, and sat in front of it, using it as a cushion to rest my back against the wall. A chill ran through my body and I pulled my coat tightly around me, then jammed my hands in the pockets, my mind lost in thoughts of how cold it was and how awful it was to be there.

From somewhere in my mind I remembered a morning when I was a child and I complained of the cold at breakfast. Papa said, "Cold winters make the fruit trees more bountiful in the summer. Aren't you thankful for fresh fruit?" I was, of course, and he said, "Then you should be thankful for the cold that makes it possible." With the room quiet, I whispered a prayer of thanks for the solitude the cell afforded, for the three new friends I'd made the night before, and for the change of direction in my life. Then I recited scripture from memory and prayed, following the pattern we'd used every morning at home. I had to force myself to do it, but as I did, I found myself no longer bound by circumstance. My spirit came alive and my mind soon followed.

An hour later, a slot in the door opened and a dirty metal tray appeared. On it were four bowls of gray porridge. Helen and Nel were awake by then and they both hungrily grabbed for the tray. I took one of the bowls and set it on the floor beside me, then Helen took two and carried them to her corner. When she sat down to eat, I said, "Isn't one of those for the lady on the cot?"

"Look at her," Helen replied with a nod toward the cot. "Does she look hungry to you? She's not going to eat."

"She might if we help her," I suggested.

"I'm not helping her do anything," Helen scowled.

I took a sip from my bowl, then crawled over to Helen and retrieved the extra bowl from beside her.

"Hey!" she protested. "What do you think you're doing?"

"If you won't help her, I will." Then I stood beside the cot and gently nudged the woman awake. She was groggy and obviously ill, but I coaxed her into eating, and she sipped almost half the contents of the bowl.

When we were finished eating, I noticed a bucket in the corner opposite where I'd been sleeping the night before. It was black with a wire handle and a smooth round piece of wood for a lid. I pointed to it and said, "What's that?"

"The crapper," Helen chuckled. Then her face turned serious and she looked me in the eye. "When the time comes, you'll be glad to have it." I didn't want to think about that, so I returned to my place in the corner.

In a little while, the door to our cell opened and two guards appeared. One of them picked up the tray with the four bowls. The other handed us each two squares of tissue, and I realized it was our daily ration for the sanitary bucket. Prison life was more real than anything I'd ever imagined, reducing the day to the simplest bodily functions—eat, sleep, defecate—and all of it in an environment devoid of privacy.

Before the guards left our cell, they also collected Nel and took her with them. She protested, and I joined her in asking for an explanation, but they ignored our pleas. When she was gone, Helen lay down on her mat and closed her eyes. I assumed she was asleep, but watching her led my eye to the woman lying on the cot and suddenly I had the strong urge to pray for her. So I rose from my place in the corner, knelt by the cot, and placed my hand gently on the woman's arm. Then I began to pray. It was a short prayer but to the point, asking that she would be healed. When I finished, I stepped back to the corner and took a seat.

"You think that stuff works?" Helen asked abruptly.

"Prayer?"

"Yeah. You think people actually get healed from it?"

"They get healed from God," I explained. "Prayer is just asking Him to act."

"So," she continued, "if you ask, He'll come at your beck and call and do whatever it is you want?"

"Not exactly," I replied with a smile.

"Right," she said with a snide tone. "That's what you people always say. God will act, but then He doesn't and you cover it by saying He isn't your own private genie."

"He's not. And I'm not covering for Him. I'm covering for my lack of understanding."

Her eyes were open by then and she was looking straight at me. "What does that mean?"

"The powerful prayers are the ones we say when we ask God to do what He already wants to do. Specifically. Not just general prayers for the world, or a shopping list of things we want, but when we hear Him tell us what He wants to do, and we ask Him to do it, those are the prayers that have the most effect."

"So you think He wants to heal her?"

"Yes," I nodded. "That's what I think I heard."

"Well," she sighed and closed her eyes. "I reckon we'll find out if it works."

"No," I corrected, "we'll find out if I heard rightly."

In a little while the door opened and Nel returned. Her cheeks were bruised and red, her lip cut and swollen, and she had a scrape along her forehead, but she was smiling triumphantly as they shoved her into the cell.

I stood and slipped my arm around her shoulder. "What happened?"

"They offered to let me go free if I became a prostitute to their officers."

"And you refused?"

"Yes," she nodded. "I refused. I told them I was a Christian now and that I don't live that life anymore." Her face was radiant as I helped her to the corner. "Last night, while we were praying, Jesus saved me." She eased down to a sitting position. I rolled up her mat and stuffed it behind her, then she leaned against it and looked up at me. "They tried to make me deny it, but I stood up to them. I didn't get angry. I didn't scream and curse. I remembered something they told us at church when I was younger, about Jesus being crucified between two thieves and how He said, 'Forgive them, for they don't know what they're doing.' So I kept telling myself that." I sat down beside her and she looked over at me. The tone of her voice turned serious and she said, "The guards are so blind to evil, they can't even see it has them in its grip." I chuckled to myself. It had taken me a lifetime to learn that simple lesson, and here she'd learned it in only a single day.

"Hush," Helen snapped, interrupting us with a glare. "They're standing right outside the door. They'll hear every word you say."

"I don't care if they hear me," Nel replied, lifting her chin up to strike a defiant pose. "They need to hear me."

"Well, I care," Helen insisted. "If you get in trouble, we'll all get in trouble." She shook her head in disbelief, and her voice took a mocking tone. "I can't believe you'd be so stupid as to take a beating like that over a prayer you prayed with her." She gestured toward me.

"It wasn't just a prayer," Nel argued. "Jesus has really made a difference in me."

"Are you crazy?" Helen lifted both hands in a gesture to our surroundings. "Look around you. Has anything changed?"

"I've changed."

"Well, all I want to know," Helen continued, "is whether they need any more prostitutes. I'll go right now. Anything to get out of this cell and away from you two."

I looked over at Nel and our eyes met. An irrepressible grin spread over our faces and we said together playfully, "Forgive her. She doesn't know what she's saying."

CHAPTER 40

IN SPITE OF EVERYTHING I did to keep my mind active, boredom overtook me. I counted and re-counted the cracks in the wall, the imperfections in the squares of toilet tissue they gave us each morning, and racked my brain for a way to make use of the sanitary bucket more private.

At the same time, hunger pangs in the pit of my stomach sent a dull ache through my body, and without the daily liver extract treatments I became noticeably tired. Afternoon naps, something I'd not needed after I returned from treatment under Dr. Tromp in Amsterdam, now became a regular part of my day. All of which narrowed my worldview to the rhythm of the day—food call in the morning, sanitary bucket call, dish pickup, afternoon nap, food in the evening, lights out at night.

On the morning of the fourth day, when the slot in the door opened and the tray appeared, I lunged for it as Helen had on my first day. I scooped up one of the bowls of porridge and retreated to my corner, slurping it without regard for how it sounded, greedily eyeing the fourth bowl and thinking, *Helen is right. The woman on the cot doesn't need it. She spends her days sleeping and when she's awake she only stares at us and never says a word.* And then guilt descended on me like a heavy weight. How could I think such thoughts? How could I entertain the notion of depriving someone of such a basic need as food? I was—mentally, at least—consigning her to death for a bowl of something that could never satisfy me. So I pushed aside those thoughts, took the fourth bowl from the tray, and coaxed the woman on the cot to eat.

When we were finished with breakfast, I redoubled my effort to pray and recite scripture from memory and resolved to make it a habit after each food call. If food was crowding out all my priorities, I would push back with scripture. And I resolved to never let a mealtime pass without rousing the woman on the cot and helping her to eat.

In between the highlights of our day that attended our bodily needs, we still faced long periods with nothing to do. To fill that time, I recited scripture out loud from memory. At first I repeated random verses as they came to mind, but after a while I started over, beginning in Genesis and working systematically through each of the books in order, challenging myself to remember as much as possible from each book. When I could not recall any more, I told myself the stories from each section—Adam and Eve, the tower of Babel, Noah and the flood. I tried to do it quietly, but as I was telling myself about Noah releasing doves from the ark, Helen heard me and of course had something to say.

"I suppose you think that works, too," she chortled.

"You mean the Scripture?"

"You chant it like it's some kind of magic. Just like your prayers."

"There are no magical answers," I replied. "Only mystery."

"Whatever," Helen shrugged.

Then in a moment of inspiration, I suggested we play a game. "I'll say a verse and you see if you can repeat it word for word exactly as I say it." It was silly but we needed something to do.

"And what do we get if we're right?" Helen asked.

That was prison life, summed up in one simple question: What do I get? Everything about our circumstances—lack of food, lack of privacy, lack of productive activity—invited each of us into a world where we were the sole focus of attention. Every woman for herself. An invitation to complete alienation.

I had nothing to offer her, so I said, "We'll keep score. One point if you're correct. But you'll lose two points if you're wrong."

Nel seemed interested, so I began. "Now the Lord said to Abram, 'Go from your country and your kindred and your father's house to the land that

I will show you. And I will make of you a great nation, and I will bless you, and make your name great, so that you will be a blessing.'"

Nel and Helen looked at each other as if waiting to see who would go first, when suddenly the woman on the cot spoke up. "'I will bless those who bless you, and him who curses you I will curse; and by you all the families of the earth shall bless themselves.'"

My mouth fell open at the sound of her voice, and I laughed. "That's exactly right!"

"No it's not," Helen protested. "That's not what you said at all."

"But it's what comes next," I replied with a grin. Then I scooted over to the cot and brushed back the hair from her face. "You're awake."

She smiled weakly. "Yes, I think so."

"Good. Then you can tell us your name."

"Christina. Christiana Bruna." She turned her head to look over at Helen and pointed. "She's my sister."

My mouth fell open once more and I turned to Helen. "She's your sister?"

Helen shrugged. "What can I say?"

She'd shown no regard at all for Christina, and while that had been troubling before, now that I knew they were sisters, her attitude was all but incomprehensible. Helen had taken food meant for her. She'd sat in the corner and ignored her. She'd left her to languish near the point of death, and apparently only for her own comfort. Didn't she know what a gift they were to each other? Was there no love at all between them? And if not, was there not even a sense of familial obligation?

"Why weren't you helping her?" I demanded.

"She's mad at me," Christina said flatly.

"About what?"

"She was arrested because of me," Christina continued.

"What were you doing?"

"Hiding Jews."

"No," Helen chimed in, "she was helping them escape…from the camp at Westerbork."

"I was helping them get away," Christina argued. "They got themselves out of the camp. I just picked them up and gave them a ride."

"That's a long way from Amsterdam," I observed. "How did you make the trip?"

"She drove herself up there," Helen offered.

I looked back at Christina. "You have a car?"

"Our father is a businessman. He owns several stores. At least, he did before all of this."

I turned back to Helen with a puzzled look. "I thought you said you were hiding teenagers?"

Before Helen could answer, Christina spoke up. "She was. But that's not why she got arrested. She was arrested because they found me in the car with three Jews from the camp. Then they searched the house and found the two boys hiding in the basement. Never would have found them if they hadn't found me first."

I looked over at Helen. "You can't ignore your sister just because you're angry."

"She ignored *me*," Helen protested. "I told her not to go up there anymore. She'd been there four or five times already. I told her she'd get caught. But she didn't listen to me and now we're in here." Helen folded her arms across her chest defiantly and slumped against the wall.

Christina smiled. "That's the way she is when she gets mad. Folds her arms like that and pouts. Tells people she doesn't know me. She's been like that since we were little girls." There was a twinkle in her eye. "But I know her secret." Her voice was soft and kind. "She loves me anyway."

Slowly, Helen turned toward Christina until their eyes met, then she started to cry. Seconds later, she came from the corner to the cot, wrapped her arms around Christina's shoulders, and lifted her from the bed in an embrace. I was envious of them for all of it—their fights, the anger, the frustration, and the love that could not be quenched by even the deepest heartache. Right then I longed to see Corrie and Nollie more than ever.

❖ ❖ ❖

As spring approached, the cell grew warmer during the day. After morning food call we took off our coats. At first we folded them neatly and laid them atop our mats, which we all now rolled and stood against the wall, but that proved messy and gave the room an unkempt look. So I hung mine on the pegs that lined the wall to the right of the door. The others did the same.

Christina continued to improve. Each day the reconciliation between her and Helen that had begun with tears grew deeper and deeper until all animosity between them was replaced by the joy and pleasure of each other's company. When Christina was strong enough, she moved to a mat on the floor and we took turns night to night sleeping on the cot. It wasn't much more comfortable than the floor but it was a treat and we all enjoyed our turn.

We'd come a long way in how we viewed one another, our cell, and the restrictions of our confinement. Our relationship to one another grew deeper with each passing day, and our minds remained alert and active. But the one thing we could not change was the dull, aching pain of hunger that permeated our bodies.

The night of April 14 was my night to sleep on the cot. Corrie's birthday was the next day, and as I lay there in the dark, I said a special prayer for her. It had been months since I'd seen her and although I'd thought of her often, I did not dwell on her. Those times that I did linger over her in my mind proved painful and all I could see was the look on her face as they led me into the cell. Such sadness. Such longing. It was more than I wanted to bear so I relegated myself to remembering her in bits and pieces of thought examined but for a moment then pushed quickly aside.

That night, however, I allowed my mind to remember her and to dwell on each one. I thought of the times as a child when I read to her and the day we first planted tulips in the window boxes at the Beje. We'd both known they would not bloom, but I insisted on planting them anyway. The memory of her giggle as we slipped the bulbs beneath the soil brought tears to my eyes, and in my mind I saw the flowers blooming in those boxes—bright, beautiful, and lovely. Tulips, I told myself, were a sign from God, even though they only existed in my mind. So I clung to the thought of them as encouragement, a sign from God that this was not the end and that one day I would see Corrie again.

After food call the next morning the cell door opened and we were ordered out. We were apprehensive about what might happen next, but no one spoke a word. The guards led us down the corridor and around the corner to a large open room, which I realized was a shower. It had been months since I'd washed myself.

A guard watched us while we undressed and laid our clothes on the benches that lined the room, then she retreated as we stepped beneath the shower heads. I'd expected cold water, but it was tepid and as pleasurable as a hot soaking bath. Small trays attached to the wall held soap and we each took a bar, then lathered our skin and hair. Afterward, we stood with the water running over our heads and watched it trickling between our toes. No one wanted to leave.

Finally the guard returned and ordered us out. Towels were stacked on the benches where we'd left our clothes and we dried off. We only had the same dirty clothes to put on, but after a shower they didn't seem so bad.

On the way back to the cell, I saw Toos being led up the hall with a guard on either side. Our eyes met and she mouthed to me that she was going home. I was delighted that she was released and thought of it as another present from God for Corrie's birthday. But that also made me think there was more to our imprisonment than I'd yet realized. A present for Corrie could have just as easily been her own release and the fact that it was not told me God had something more for us to do right where we were.

Five days later was April 20, Hitler's birthday. We'd heard the guards talking about it among themselves when they came to the cell during our daily routine. Something about a party with cake and ice cream. At first we thought they meant for us, and our spirits soared. I'd gone two months without the liver extract or vitamin supplement, and even with afternoon naps fatigue was a problem. Although it was a celebration for Hitler, the prospect of cake and ice cream was a treasure trove of calories too great to avoid. Then we realized the party was only for the guards, and our spirits plummeted.

On the day of the party the hall fell strangely silent as the guards left us to enjoy their celebration. About the time I noticed the silence and began to consider what that might mean, someone down the way shouted in a loud voice, "Is anyone from Bennebroek?"

For a moment there was only deafening silence as we all waited for a guard to shout and curse for quiet, but when none came, someone called out, "I'm from Heemstede," which was a town not far from Bennebroek.

And then a chorus of voices rose from the cells as women up and down the corridor shouted out their names, asking about loved ones and acquaintances. I opened the slot in the door and shouted out for Corrie, but every time I did, someone in the cell beside me drowned out my voice. Frustration grew but I shouted all the more, and then someone up the hall said, "Corrie is looking for Betsie."

Tears came to my eyes and a lump formed in my throat. Corrie was alive and asking for me, but I could not speak. Helen was kneeling beside me and gave me a nudge. "Isn't that you? Isn't that your sister asking for you?" I could only nod my head in response, so Helen shouted through the slot, "Betsie is in cell 272!"

"What about Nollie?" I whispered through sobs.

"Betsie wants to know about Nollie!" Helen shouted. And a few moments later came the reply. "Nollie was in cell 318, but she was released last week."

Relief overwhelmed me. I turned my back to the door, sank slowly to the floor, and wept for joy. Corrie and I were still in prison, but Toos and Nollie were safely home.

LATER THAT MONTH the door to our cell opened and two guards led me out to the corridor. Flanking me on either side, they escorted me to the corner where we'd turned to go to the showers, only this time we turned in the opposite direction. Down the corridor I saw a door with a window in it. Sunlight streamed through the window and I stared at it, drinking in the wonder and beauty of the bright natural light. I hadn't seen the sun in months and expected I would not for a long time to come, so I made the most of it, knowing that at any moment we would turn to one side or the other into yet another long, dark hallway. Instead, we continued straight toward the door. As we reached it, one of the guards pushed it open and to my amazement we stepped outside to a courtyard in the center of the prison.

In the middle of the yard were three cottages standing side by side. The two on either side were faded and drab but the one in the middle had been freshly covered with paint. Well-kept flowerbeds lay along the foundation and in them were robust, thriving tulips. It was early spring and the mornings were still cool, but already the flowers were on the verge of blooming. My heart skipped a beat at the sight of them, and hope welled within me as the guards led me toward it. I was certain God was sending me a message, but I had no idea what He might be saying.

When we reached the cottage, one of the guards rapped on the door with her knuckles, then pushed it open without waiting and led me inside. A desk stood to the right of the door and seated behind it was Rudolph Schakel, the magistrate I'd seen when I first arrived at The Hague. At the opposite end of the room was a fireplace with a low fire burning. Lamps on either side of the desk cast a warm yellow glow that, with the fire in the fireplace, made the room seem cozy.

Schakel stood as we entered and gestured to a chair across from the desk. "Have a seat," he said to me, then dismissed the guards with a nod and returned to his seat. By then I was tired from the walk and breathing heavily, so I collapsed on the chair he offered and waited while the guards left the room.

His gesture of standing when I entered told me he was more than polite and suggested he thought of me as something more than a prisoner, which was more decency than anyone had shown since my arrival. When we were alone and the door was closed, I felt the freedom to make a comment, so I said, "You have beautiful tulips outside."

A smile came to Schakel's face, and for the next few minutes he told me about his father, who was a gardener, and about the flowers they grew on their small farm when he was a boy. I remembered my great-grandfather growing vegetables and fruits in the winter and recounted the story for him. He seemed kind, considerate, and actually listened while I spoke.

As we continued to talk, Schakel turned to a table behind him where a pitcher of water sat with several glasses. He took a glass and filled it with water. I watched as the water splashed against the bottom, swirled around with a gurgling noise, and slowly rose toward the top. My lips were dry and parched and I wondered how anyone could be so blind as not to see what a cruel gesture it was drinking water in front of prisoners, especially the way the prisoners were being treated.

Then Schakel reached across the desk and set the glass in front of me. "I'm sure you are thirsty," he said, gesturing toward the glass. "Please. Drink up."

As if in a dream, I picked up the glass and drank it in one long gulp. He chuckled as he refilled it, then reached back to the table where the pitcher sat and brought out a plate of bread with a small pat of butter. He set that before me, too, and said, "I thought you might be hungry," then he refilled the empty glass a third time.

While I ate the bread and drank the water, Schakel opened a file, and his face became serious and brooding. "They know that you and your sister developed a network of operatives who gave assistance to the Jews." His eyes were focused on the papers before him and he spoke as if summarizing what he saw on the pages. "The soldiers who were assigned to kill the babies at the orphanage have been executed." He glanced up to see my reaction, which I did my best to suppress, then he kept talking. "But they have reason to believe your sister, not you, was actually in charge. And they have information from your physician about your medical condition, which is an extenuating circumstance." He looked me in the eye. "If you give a statement outlining how the network operated, naming names, and implicating your sister, they will agree to let you go home."

So this is the way it works. Give me bread and water, treat me like a decent human being, and then suggest I can go free if I betray my sister. I leaned back in the chair and rested my hands in my lap, thinking of what to say next. Part of me wanted to lash out, the other part thought better of it, and as I sat there I became convinced that Schakel was merely offering me what the Germans told him to suggest. If he knew me and my family as well as it seemed he did, then he knew I would never agree to such a deal. So I decided to take the conversation in a different direction. "Do you know who my sister is?"

"Yes," he nodded.

"How is she?"

"Doing well enough, for being in here." Schakel looked again at the file. "Your nephew was released from prison. As was your brother, Willem. They were sent home a few weeks ago, along with your friend Herman Slurring. Only you and your sister remain."

He seemed not to press the issue of a statement, so I continued. "What about my father? Can you tell me about him?"

Schakel glanced away with a somber look and stroked his chin with his finger. "I am sorry to say, he is dead."

Tears came to my eyes and a thousand memories flooded my mind, but I had to focus on the moment, so I allowed myself only one question. "What happened to him?"

"I don't know the details." Schakel turned to look at me. "All I know is that he died not long after he was transferred here."

"He died in his cell?"

"No." Schakel glanced down at the file. "I think he died in the hospital." He paused for a moment to let me catch my breath, then leaned forward and said in a hushed but serious tone, "As difficult as it may be to imagine, you have bigger problems than your father's death." He took papers from the file. "The police searched your house and found these documents." He laid them on the desk for me to see. "This does not look good for you or your family," Schakel sighed.

Suddenly my mind was no longer on Papa but on the documents that lay before me. As I glanced at the pages, I saw lists of names and contact information, locations of drop sites, and the identity of safe houses. I knew immediately where they had come from. We devised our placement method in a way that limited the knowledge of where any one person was hiding to only the family with whom they hid and the last courier who accompanied them. In helping people to hide, we'd been forced on occasion to divide some families. Several of our couriers were concerned about how those people would find each other after the war ended—assuming it ended in an Allied victory—and they approached me about keeping records so they could offer people a means of getting back together. I shared their concern but warned against putting anything in writing for this very reason.

Now, confronted with the reality of what I'd contemplated then, fear rose inside me and I thought of all the things that one could do with that information. A German soldier bent on rooting out every single Jew in the Netherlands could take those lists and find more than half the people we helped, plus the people who helped them.

Then I remembered how Schakel had stood when I entered the room and how well our conversation had gone thus far. If they had wanted to use this list, they would not have left it in the file, and if they had already used it they would not need my help now in disclosing what it meant. I studied the lists a little longer and a sense of calm returned. Words from scripture came to me and I repeated them in my mind. *We have not been given a spirit of fear, but of power, love, and self-control.*

There was nothing I could do or say that would make those documents go away, so once again I decided to take the conversation in a different direction.

"You seem like a kind and considerate person. Are you a Christian?"

Schakel's forehead wrinkled in a frown. "Miss Ten Boom, that is dangerous talk for the times in which we live." He sat up straight and began shuffling papers on his desk. "I may be sympathetic to your situation, but I am still a magistrate and sworn to uphold the law, even if I disagree with it."

I smiled at him. "It has always been dangerous to talk of obedience to God that transcends mere compliance with the law. No one wants to hear the truth."

"I must remind you, it is now illegal to promote any form of religion, and I insist that you—"

"I'm not really trying to promote religion," I said, interrupting him. "But I am compelled to obey God first. You know I can't give them the statement you suggested, and I'm certainly not going to implicate my sister to save myself."

"Well, you needn't worry about my soul." Schakel picked up the papers he'd shown me—the lists the soldiers found at the house—then he pushed back his chair and stood. "I am in good hands for eternity," he continued as he came around the end of the desk, "even if I can't quite articulate it the way you would. But you should be careful about your own life. The Germans who came to your house want to kill you." Papers in hand, he moved past me to the fireplace, took a poker from a hook near the mantel, and stoked the fire until it burned brightly. "Our friend Rolfe told me about what you have been doing." With the flames leaping higher up the chimney, Schakel tossed the papers into the firebox and watched while they disappeared in the fire. Then he looked back at me with a smile and said, "I will do as much for you as I can, but the final decision about your release is not mine to make. I am only a magistrate. I make recommendations, not decisions."

"Thank you," I said meekly. I wanted to hug his neck and kiss his cheeks but it didn't seem appropriate.

"I only wish I could do more," he said as he returned to his seat at the desk. With the file still open on the desk, he flipped through several pages, then said, "Tell me about your medical condition."

"I have pernicious anemia."

"Pernicious?"

"Deadly."

"But you are alive."

"Yes," I nodded. "It's treatable, but it requires daily doses of vitamins and liver extract."

"I assume you have not received any of this since you arrived here."

From the way he asked the question I was certain my condition had become obvious. Before I left for Amsterdam to see Dr. Tromp, I'd noticed dark circles beneath my eyes. Mama told me they were hereditary from her side of the family, but after I began taking the liver extract the circles went away. I could have told Schakel all of that but decided not to and instead, when he assumed I'd not had the treatments since coming there, I simply nodded and said, "That is correct."

"I will see what I can do." He closed the file, checked his watch once more, then stood. "Well," he sighed, "I think that's about it."

As I rose from my chair, I said, "You've done so much for me I almost hate to ask, but do you think it would be possible for me to see my sister?"

"I will try to arrange something, but don't get your hopes up. I have little influence over how they treat prisoners here. The staff may be Dutch but the Germans control everything. If I say too much, they will become suspicious of me, but I will see what I can do." He pressed a button attached to his phone and in a moment the door opened. Two guards appeared and gestured for me to come. I rose from my chair and glanced in Schakel's direction. Our eyes met and I gave him a smile as a way of saying thank you once more, then followed the guards outside.

On the way back to the cell, I wondered what it all meant—a magistrate with compassion and an apparent respect for the law. Tulips growing by his cottage. Water with fresh bread and butter. And most of all, the documents he destroyed in the fire. God was at work in my life, I was sure of that, and the light had not gone out completely in the Netherlands. But where the future would take me I had no idea.

◈ ◈ ◈

A few days later, after food call and tray pickup, and for no obvious reason, the door to our cell opened. At first I thought nothing of it and didn't even look, expecting to hear it slam shut when the guard realized they'd come to the wrong place, but when it didn't close immediately, I turned to look. As I did, my heart leapt against my chest as I saw Corrie walk by. She looked thinner, and from the dark circles beneath her eyes I was sure she was still as sick as the day we arrived, but she was strong enough to move on her own, and from her gait I knew they had not broken her spirit.

Schakel was right. It hadn't been much. Only a few seconds passed as she walked by and disappeared from sight. But I had seen her and I knew that she was alive. As the guard pushed the door to our cell closed, I sank to the floor to give thanks.

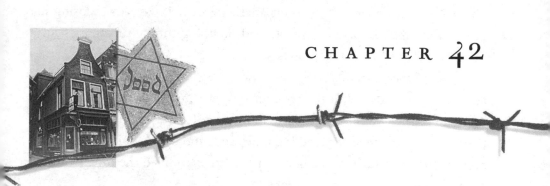

CHAPTER 42

LATE IN JUNE, the guards once again took me from the cell and led me down the corridor and across the courtyard to the cottage where I'd met with Rudolph Schakel. As we walked in that direction I wondered what would happen next and what lay ahead for me. Since our first meeting I'd heard nothing further about my case and there'd been no indication my status had changed.

Schakel had told me before that the people who arrested us had wanted me killed. I assumed he was talking about Captain Bormann and Lieutenant Krüger, but as we made our way through the prison that day, I remembered that Schakel had mentioned Rolfe during our previous meeting. Apparently they knew each other and that brought to mind my last conversation with Rolfe when he told us that Isaac Franken and Cornelius Mussert were at the police station giving the Germans a list of Dutch citizens who were assisting the Jews in their attempts to evade selection and deportation. If the Jewish Council was pushing my case, I might have little hope. They were in a much more advantageous position than I. But why would they pursue me? If their plan had been to avoid trouble for themselves by identifying us to the Germans, then they already achieved what they'd expected to gain. Continuing to suggest I should be prosecuted would only happen if they knew my case was yet unresolved, which seemed unlikely.

When we reached the cottage, I saw the tulips in the flowerbeds were still alive and thriving. The blooms had faded and only the lush green stems with their long, slender leaves remained. No blooms, but the plants were doing well. I wondered if it meant anything or if I was slowly losing my mind, searching for signs in plants and combing through memories for a hint of what the future might hold.

One of the guards pushed open the cottage door and the other held it as I stepped inside. With the weather now warm, the fire in the fireplace was out. Shades on the windows were lowered halfway, which enshrouded the room in dark shadows, making it pleasant and cool. A lamp on the desk and another on a table by a chair near the fireplace filled the room with the familiar soft glow I'd enjoyed before.

Schakel was seated at his desk when I arrived and stood as we entered. When the guards were gone and we were alone, he gestured to a table near his desk. On it was the water pitcher with drinking glasses and a small tray of pastries. "I took the liberty of preparing some refreshments for you and your family."

The comment caught me off guard. "My family?"

"Yes." A nervous smile turned up the corners of his mouth. "They'll be joining us soon. I had them bring you here for a formal reading of your father's will."

A frown creased my forehead. "Reading his will?" I'd never heard of such a thing.

"It's required by law."

"I wasn't aware we had to do that."

"Oh yes," he said insistently. "It must be done. With all the family present."

All the family. And then it hit me. I was about to see my family. I wanted to cry and laugh and jump up and down all at the same time. Instead, I forced myself to remain calm and took a seat near the desk to wait. He poured a glass of water and handed it to me, then we sat quietly while I sipped it. The moment was surreal and awkward and I didn't want to say anything that would jeopardize the meeting, but I was curious about Schakel's insistence that the will must be read, *with all the family present.* Something about the look in his eye made me wonder if it wasn't all just a ruse on his part.

A few minutes later the door opened and Nollie entered, followed by Willem, Tine, Flip, and Alphons van Gilse, a notary from Haarlem. I set the glass aside and reached for Nollie, wrapping her in my arms and squeezing her close. Willem just stood there, watching for a moment until I reached for him and pulled him to us, then Tine and Flip joined us, and the crying started as we all sobbed.

Finally Willem pulled away and wiped his eyes. As I untangled my arms from Nollie's neck, I noticed Willem was jaundiced. I asked about his health and he said he'd picked up something while he was in prison. The doctors weren't sure what it was but they hoped to run a few tests. I could tell by the way he spoke that he didn't hold out much hope for a successful medical treatment. I opened my mouth to ask about Kik when the door opened again and Corrie entered. Before she was two steps inside the doorway, we fell upon her as one, and the crying started all over again.

Meanwhile, Van Gilse seemed a little befuddled by the necessity of his presence and the requirement of a formal reading of the will. While Corrie, Nollie, Willem, and I visited, he kept saying, "I'm not sure why you need me for this." But each time he said it Schakel reminded him that it had to be done. With Schakel a magistrate, Van Gilse had little choice but to acquiesce, though he did so with a wary eye. I think he was worried they might keep him at the prison if he didn't cooperate.

After a few minutes, Schakel reminded us of the water and pastries, then excused himself for a moment and asked Van Gilse to join him outside for a word. When the door closed behind them and we were alone, Corrie and I grabbed a pastry and hungrily devoured it. Then I remembered Kik again and asked about him. "He is missing," Willem replied. "The Germans captured him a few weeks ago while he was helping a downed Allied pilot reach the North Sea. We aren't sure where he is."

"You know for a fact he was captured?"

"The American Red Cross sent us a message."

"The Americans?"

"Yes. Apparently the man he was helping was one of their pilots."

"They got the pilot, too?"

"No. From what I understand, the pilot made it off safely and was picked up by a boat. Kik was returning from the coast when the Germans nabbed him."

"Then he might have been picked up for one of their work conscriptions." I wanted to give him something, and hope was all I had. Consignment to a work detail in Germany was much better than confinement in a concentration camp.

"Perhaps," Willem said. "But the Americans seemed to think he was sent to a prisoner of war camp in Germany."

There was nothing more I could offer by way of consoling him except to give him a hug, which I did. Then we moved on to discuss the reason we were there and I asked about details surrounding Papa's death. Willem took a seat in a chair by the desk, and Nollie answered my question.

"He became sick in his cell just a few days after we arrived here," she explained. "They took him to a hospital at The Hague, but there was no bed available so they left him on a cot in the corridor. The hospital was overrun with sick and wounded. Somewhere in the confusion, he was separated from his medical records. No one was even aware he was there until an orderly found him the next morning, but by then he was dead. He died lying on a cot in the hallway."

The grief that I'd suppressed when Schakel told me of Papa's death earlier now overwhelmed me. Unlike before, this time I had no desire to block the memories that filled my mind. In quick succession I saw him seated at his desk, loupe on one eye, his head bent over a watch. He told me once when I asked about a bill he forgot to send, "Working on a watch is a pleasure and a joy mere money could never equal."

He was not given to obvious displays of emotion but he communicated his love and affection in unmistakable ways—riding with me on the train to Amsterdam when I moved there for Dr. Tromp's treatment, waving goodbye when he left to return home until the trolley turned the corner and he disappeared from sight, and the time he spent with Corrie after the awful way Karel treated her.

All of those memories rushed in and I did nothing to stop them or the tears they sent down my cheeks. Nollie put her arms around me and held me while I wept. Papa was a wonderful man, the center of our lives, the center of *my* life, and the thought of living without him filled me with sadness.

After a moment she reached into her pocket and took out a small Bible. "Here," she said. "I brought this for you." I stepped back from her embrace and wiped my eyes with my fingers. Willem handed me a tissue and I dabbed my eyes with it. Then I noticed the Bible had a cord attached. "So you can carry it around your neck," Nollie continued. "Beneath your dress." I was glad to have the Scriptures and opened it immediately to read a few sentences, then my stomach rumbled and I remembered the pastries. I looked up at her. "Do you want something to eat?"

She shook her head. "No, you eat it. I'm sure you don't get enough in here and we can all eat later." I took a pastry from the plate and handed it to Corrie, then took another for myself and devoured it as quickly as we'd eaten the first.

"Toos has the shop open," Flip offered. "Louis is working with her. Business is slow, but they're open and paying the electricity bill."

"Good," I nodded between bites. "Who's living in the house?"

"No one," Tine replied.

The pastry made my throat dry, so I filled a glass with water and said quietly, "Has anyone seen Vincent?"

"He's still in the food office," Nollie answered.

"So, he didn't have any trouble from what happened to us?"

"Apparently no one is the wiser." Nollie's eyes opened wide in a look of realization and she reached into her purse. "I brought this for you," she said as she drew out a small vial. I recognized it immediately as the liver compound Dr. Van Veen prescribed for me. I slipped the cord from the Bible over my neck and tucked it beneath my dress, then took the vial from her. My hands shook as I opened it, dribbled a few drops into the water glass, and gulped it down. Then I added more water and drank again to make sure I got it all. When the last drops of water were gone I put the glass aside, returned the cap to the vial, and placed it in my pocket. Just having it with me made me feel better already.

While I did that, Nollie reached inside her purse once more and took out a bottle of liquid vitamins. The cap was an eyedropper and I used it to place two drops on my tongue. I'd had neither vitamins nor the extract since the day we were arrested. Both tasted terrible but I knew they would prolong my life, and I didn't complain.

After a while the door opened and Schakel entered with Van Gilse coming in behind him. We turned to face them, and Schakel said quietly, "I suppose we should get on with reading the will."

Van Gilse reached inside the pocket of his jacket and took out the document. We all stood silently as he read. I already knew what was to happen. The watchmaking business and all its equipment went to Corrie. She and I were to have the privilege of living in the house as long as we wanted. After we were both dead, it was to be sold and the money divided between Nollie and Willem or their children. Papa's meager savings was to be split four ways. Reading the document took less than ten minutes.

When we were finished, Willem prayed, giving thanks for Papa and asking that Corrie and I be swiftly released, then we said good-bye and they departed. After they were gone, Corrie and I ate one more pastry together while we waited for the guards. We'd just finished a roll and were drinking another glass of water when they came for us. I hugged Corrie and kissed her on the cheek, then the guards led her away.

The guards who came for me insisted we wait in the cottage while Corrie crossed the courtyard. We stood near the desk, trying not to stare at each other as time slowly passed. In the awkwardness of that moment I gave Schakel a smile to say thank you once again. He'd insisted he was only doing what the law required, but I knew better. He had concocted the reading as a pretense to give our family a few minutes together, for which I was grateful throughout the remainder of my life.

CHAPTER 43

WITH DAILY DOSES of the liver extract and vitamins my body began to strengthen, and by the end of June I was almost as strong and healthy as the day I arrived at the prison. Near the end of July, however, the cell door opened and a guard told us to prepare to leave. We rolled up our sleeping mats and took a seat on the floor, expecting to leave immediately. As the morning hours passed, we talked among ourselves, speculating about where we might be going.

Noon came and went with us still in the cell, and as the afternoon wore on, Nel and Helen became irritable. To get their minds on something else I challenged them to a round of our scripture memory game.

In midafternoon, the guards opened the cell door again and ordered us out to the corridor. We grabbed our coats and stepped through the doorway to find long rows of our fellow prisoners already formed and waiting. One of the guards directed us to our place in line, and soon we shuffled along with the others toward the corner by the shower room and the hall that led to the courtyard, then past it to another door that led outside. For Christina, Helen, and Nel, it was their first time outdoors since arriving at the prison.

We came from the building to a paved area just off a drive in the service section of the prison. Buses were parked there and we were directed toward them. Prisoners ahead of us stepped aboard. As one bus was loaded, it pulled away and another took its place. I glanced around for Corrie but didn't see her. When it was my turn, I dutifully stepped aboard the next bus and took a seat. Nel sat beside me, but in spite of her company loneliness swept over me as I thought of what might lie ahead for us and whether anyone would ever find me again.

I was lost in thought when the bus lurched forward and we began to move. As we left the prison yard, I folded the coat in my lap and ran my hand over the pocket to make sure the bottles were still inside. That's when I noticed the prison guards were gone and in their place were German soldiers. Any pretense of who'd been in control before was now gone for good.

Thirty minutes later we arrived at a railroad freight yard. Railcars lined the tracks and in the distance I saw smoke and steam rising from a locomotive. The bus came to a stop near the tracks and we were ordered out. Coat in hand, I followed the others from the bus. Nel was with me, and I did my best to stay with her.

Outside the bus armed soldiers were formed in rows that lined our path. They urged us along, and if someone didn't move fast enough they nudged them with the butt of their rifles. As I stumbled toward the railcars someone grabbed my right hand. When I looked, I saw Corrie standing beside me. My heart leapt with excitement. I wanted to hug her and kiss her cheeks, but we dared not stop just then for fear of the soldiers.

As we drew closer to the railcars, chaos swirled around us with soldiers shouting and pushing us forward. Others were yelling and hitting prisoners who resisted their orders or didn't move quickly enough. Many were knocked to the ground, and the soldiers descended upon them, kicking them and striking them with their rifles, all the while yelling, "Get up! Get up!"

Ahead of us was a loading ramp of a kind that seemed suited for cattle. As people reached the incline, their forward progress slowed. With everyone pushing and shoving, I worried I'd lose contact with Corrie. She must have been worried, too, because she squeezed my hand so tightly it hurt. The soldiers continued to scream at us in an attempt to keep us moving, never once noticing the jam that held us back. This went on for what seemed like a long time until finally a group of soldiers gathered behind us and began pushing the crowd forward. Some caught unaware stumbled and fell to the ground, but still the soldiers kept driving forward, forcing us to trample the fallen beneath our feet.

When we reached the ramp, the size of the crowd narrowed to three or four people wide. Soldiers stood near the railcar doors, watching as prisoners stepped aboard. From the bottom of the ramp it seemed as though they were counting, but as I came nearer I saw that they were merely making certain we were packed as tightly as possible.

Just then, one of the soldiers reached over from the side and snatched the coat from my hands. "How stupid of you to carry a coat in summer!" he shouted. I tried to hold on to it, and he slapped me across the face. Another came to his side and shoved me up the ramp. Corrie turned to defend me, but I grabbed her arm. "Come on!" I shouted. "Let them have it."

"But the—"

"Never mind," I retorted and dragged her with me toward the railcar. Having found her, I didn't want to be without her again.

Clinging to each other, we trudged into the railcar and as we passed through the doorway I glanced over my shoulder. The trampled bodies of our fellow prisoners littered the path between the buses and the tracks. All of them were bleeding but only a few showed signs of life. Near the end of the ramp I saw my coat lying with them. One of the vials protruded from an open pocket. My heart sank at the thought of leaving it behind, but there was no way to retrieve it then. If I'd stepped from the car to get it, a soldier would have shot me on the spot. Seconds later, two soldiers appeared and slid the door to our car closed. I heard them latch it in place, and any hope of ever seeing the coat again was gone.

The railcar in which we stood was suitable for hauling cattle, and from the smell of manure that filled it I was certain that was the cargo it last held. Cattle were allowed enough space to stand without touching each other and enough circulation to keep them from overheating. We were squeezed shoulder to shoulder, and the air quickly became hot. Some among us fainted but never fell, as there was no space between us for them to slide to the floor. There also were no sanitary facilities, and soon the odor of manure was overcome by the stench of our own urine and feces. After a while, someone near the wall to the left broke loose a wall plank to let in more air. Then someone on the right side did the same and we at least had meager cross ventilation.

In a little while, the car jerked forward and we began to roll along the tracks. For no apparent reason other than my own internal sense of direction, it seemed as though we were moving south. I twisted my head to one side to glance out through the opening in the wallboard on our side of the car and saw we were passing a town. "Utrecht, I think."

"Then you were right," Corrie commented. "We're traveling south."

Just after sunset, the train came to a stop. Outside the railcar, soldiers were shouting and the sound of their voices grew louder and louder as they made their way down the line of cars toward us. Then the door of our car slid open and a soldier leaned in, his face snarled with anger, and he shouted, "Out! Out! You must get out of the car!" There was no ramp to step down on, and the floor of the car was almost two meters above the ground. Women near the door hesitated to jump, and when they didn't move at the soldier's command, he reached into the car and dragged the nearest out by force. Seeing that, the rest of us surged forward and forced those ahead of us to jump, then we did the same.

By then it was fully night. We stumbled in the dark over the uneven ground and the bodies of fallen prisoners as the soldiers herded us like animals from the tracks to a narrow dirt road. Someone said we were near the town of Vught, which was in the southern portion of the country. Based on the glimpses of countryside I saw from the railcar, I felt that was correct, and what I learned later proved it was right.

Down the road, we came to a prison camp that reminded me of the refugee camp near Westerbork where I'd gone with Willem what seemed like a hundred lifetimes ago. Like Westerbork, this camp had a wire fence almost four meters high with strands of barbed wire at the top and guard towers at the corners. Armed soldiers manned the towers and squads of soldiers on foot patrolled the perimeter.

Beyond the main gate was an area filled with large canvas tents that lay between the outer fence and an inner one that separated us from the wooden barracks of the permanent camp. The tents were made of heavy material, but they had no sides. There were no cots or mats for sleeping, either, only straw that had been scattered on the ground. We were hungry, dirty, and exhausted, and as we arrived beneath the tents, we flopped to rest. Others ventured out in search of a toilet, and finding none, they used a grassy area beyond the tents. I thought they would feed us, as we'd only had one meal that day, but as time went by I realized we were expected to endure the night without so much as a slice of bread.

With nothing else to do, I stretched out on the bare ground beside Corrie and went to sleep. A few hours later I was awakened by the sound of thunder, then it began to rain. Before long it was coming in torrents. Water washed over the ground we'd used as a latrine. Feces floated past where we slept, and even those near the center of the tent were soaked. Some cried, their anguished sobs rising above the patter of the raindrops. Others cursed the downpour and the soldiers who put us there. I was used to sleeping on a hard surface, but the rain made me cold and I slept in fitful episodes.

Somewhere in the night the dream returned and in it I soared above a large house surrounded by gardens with flowerbeds filled with tulips. Men and women tended the gardens and Corrie was with them, only now in addition to Captain Bormann I saw the faces of several guards we'd known at the prison and a soldier we'd seen when they loaded us into the railcar.

At sunup I awakened chilled to the bone and with a nagging cough. Corrie was worried about my health and wanted to take me to the camp hospital. I didn't think they had one, and besides, I was much more interested in telling her about the dream. "We have to figure out what it means," I insisted.

"It doesn't matter what it means if you aren't alive to live it." Corrie continued to nag me about seeking help, and finally I gave in and agreed, but when we approached the soldiers, they just laughed and said, "There is no medical support for prisoners." We limped back to the tent where we'd been sitting only to find that others had taken our place and now we were relegated to a spot on the outer edge.

Most of us thought we'd be moved into the main part of the camp right away, but the first day turned into the second and we remained on the ground under the tents in the space between the fence and the barracks, exposed to the weather that alternated between heavy rains and suffocating heat. Perhaps it was the extreme conditions or that I'd been weakened before and not fully recovered, but in a matter of days I felt the effects of not having the medicine. I was able to function, but fatigue was an issue and I spent most of the time dozing on the ground.

Nel was nowhere to be found, but Christina and Helen occupied a place not far from us. I watched as they cared for each other in much the same way Corrie and I did. Christina was well and healthy, but in a strange twist Helen was now ill and lay with her head in Christina's lap. As the rains continued, coughing became the sound we heard most each day. Nights were restless and each morning we awoke to find that someone else had died.

After Corrie and I spent the first two days arguing over whether to take me to seek medical help, we spent the next two dealing with the soldiers' response. On the fifth day I remembered the Bible hanging from the cord beneath my dress. We received a bowl of porridge that morning and after we'd eaten, Corrie read from the Scriptures. Afterward we prayed quietly together, asking God to heal those who were sick, provide food for us to eat, and a dry place to sleep.

Not long after that the rains ceased, but food continued to be scarce and what they gave us had little nutritional value. Hunger pangs in my stomach continued to send a dull ache through my body. I was sure my body was consuming its own tissue for energy. Some around us complained, but instead of joining them, Corrie suggested we talk about my recurring dream. "I've been thinking about it," she said, "and I think this is to be our work."

"Helping those injured by the war."

"Yes. This war has inflicted many casualties on our people. Netherlanders haven't really been in the fighting much but they've been wounded just the same. Sometimes it's the emotional and spiritual wounds that can be the most troublesome, and when this war is over there'll be plenty of our fellow countrymen who'll need a hand recovering. I don't think it will last forever, do you?"

"I think Papa was right. The Germans have raised their hand against the Jews, and God will not allow it to continue. This will come to an end and the Germans will be left with nothing. But I don't think it's our countrymen so much at the center of that dream."

"Why not?"

"Think of the people I see. Captain Bormann and the lieutenant who came with him when they arrested us. Now some of the guards from the prison and soldiers at the train."

"What about them?"

"They aren't Dutch. They're German. I think this is to be our task," I continued before she could say more. "Helping the guards and the soldiers. From either side."

She shot a look in my direction, and I could see the fire in her eyes. "Helping the Germans?"

"Yes," I nodded. "Helping them find their way to redemption."

Corrie was interested in helping the Jews and our fellow Netherlanders, but she was not excited at all about the prospect of helping those who'd fought against us, and particularly not the German soldiers. "I would like to help them find their way to eternity right now," she grumbled.

"Shh," I said. "Harboring anger against them will only lead to bitterness."

CHAPTER 44

WE'D BEEN AT VUGHT about two weeks when a large number of soldiers appeared at our tents shortly after the evening meal. Armed with rifles, which they held at the ready, they appeared serious, intent, and determined. Moments later, one of them began to shout, "Get out! Get out!" And they drove us from our places beneath the tents. When we were all standing in the open, they ordered us to form two lines and then marched us through a gate in the interior fence and into the main camp.

Rows of wooden barracks were separated by a narrow lane, and at every third building there was a tree. I had expected harsh surroundings, but what I saw was actually pleasant by comparison, though it struck me as odd that someone thought to plant trees in a place like that. Trees take a long time to mature. Whoever planted them must have thought the camp would endure an equal amount of time. I hoped with all my heart that they were wrong.

The barracks were unpainted and worn, but after two weeks on the wet ground beneath the tents, they looked like palaces to us. Each was constructed in an identical fashion, with wooden steps that led up to an open doorway. Through one of them I saw bunk beds three levels high. Images of a mattress with sheets and a pillow filled my mind.

At the third building we came to a stop and were formed into ranks five rows deep. An officer appeared and looked us over as if on inspection. He wore a dress uniform with shiny black boots and leather gloves. From what I could make of his insignia he was a captain.

With his hands behind his back, he reminded me of a peacock I saw once with its tail feathers spread wide in an attempt to impress us. He paced back and forth in a tight pattern and to look at us he had to turn his head to one side or the other. "This is your formation for roll call," he shouted with his head turned toward us, "which will be held at the beginning and end of each day. All names will be called in alphabetical order and you will answer to your name. Anyone present and not answering to their name will be shot."

A young girl three ranks ahead of us snickered at the comment, and the captain was immediately enraged. "Who did that?" he demanded. When no one answered, he stepped to a woman at the end of the row nearest his position and drew a pistol from a holster on his belt, then he placed the muzzle against her head and pulled the trigger. The sound of the gunshot made me jump, and a collective gasp went up from our ranks, but the captain seemed unfazed. "We have one rule in this camp!" he shouted. "Do as you are told or you will die!"

Two soldiers appeared with a detail of three male prisoners. The prisoners picked up the body of the dead girl, carrying her by the arms and legs, and hurried down the street with her dangling between them. Even from a distance I could see blood dripping from the hole in her head.

As they disappeared from sight, another officer stepped forward with a clipboard in hand. "Listen up for roll call!" he shouted, then began calling out names. One by one he read down the roll, with prisoners shouting in response as their name was called. Ten minutes later he reached the end of the list and we were ordered into the barracks building that stood behind us.

Corrie led the way up the steps and I followed close behind, clutching her dress in my hand as we jostled past the doorway. Nothing was going to separate me from her now. Beyond the door a central aisle divided the room in half. On either side were bunk beds like the ones I'd seen from the street, but they were nothing like what I'd imagined. Stacked three levels high, they were jammed together side by side in rows four beds deep. They had no mattress, no sheets, and no pillows, only a bare wooden platform on which to lie.

Other women were living there when we arrived, which meant all the spaces near the aisle were filled. Only those near the wall remained. To get to them, however, we had to crawl over everyone else in the row. We staked our claim to two spaces near the back wall, not far from the window. It wasn't much more comfortable than the ground beneath the tents or the mat on the floor at Scheveningen prison, but I was beside Corrie and that was all that mattered.

Not long after we climbed in bed, I folded my arms for a pillow, rested my head on top, and fell fast asleep. While I slept, the same recurring dream returned: the house and the gardens with tulips. Before the images faded from my mind, I was awakened by the shrill sound of a whistle. The sun was not up and the building was dark, yet a voice shouted from the doorway, "Fall out! Get moving! Fall out!"

Those around us who'd been at the camp longer seemed to know what it meant. They dutifully crawled from the bunks and started toward the door. Corrie and I glanced at each other and she said, "This must be how the day begins." She climbed down from the bed and turned to leave, but when I tried to follow I could hardly move my legs.

"They won't work." My eyes were wide with fear. "Can you help me?"

Corrie slipped her hands beneath my arms and eased me over the side of the bunk. When my feet touched the floor, I found that I could stand but only by leaning against her. "What is wrong with me?" I lamented.

"Nothing that the medicine from Dr. Van Veen wouldn't cure," she replied. "Come on. We're falling behind." Then she placed her arm around my waist to steady me and I hobbled toward the door. By the time we were outside, the others were formed in ranks. Corrie and I took a place beside each other near the center of the back row. I did my best to seem invisible.

Moments later, a soldier appeared at the front of our group. He was not the same officer we'd seen the evening before but conducted himself in much the same manner, pacing back and forth with his hands folded behind his back. Unlike the evening before, however, this one didn't shout at us and no one got shot. Instead, he nodded to a soldier who stood nearby, and that man stepped forward with a clipboard to call the roll.

Afterward, a woman appeared with several sheets of paper in her hand. She was dressed in civilian clothes and from all I could tell was neither a guard nor a regular soldier. Reading from the pages, in a tentative, halting voice, she called out a list of names, directing them to form a separate line beside her in the street. We listened as she read through the pages and part-way down the list she called our names. My legs were stronger then and I was able to walk on my own. Corrie and I hurried to join the line.

When everyone from the list was gathered, a soldier marched us down the lane to a large brick building that appeared to be some sort of manufacturing facility. It was located inside the camp, but it was clean and well maintained. Neatly trimmed shrubs grew around it and the cornice was freshly painted. Concrete steps led up to the door, and when we arrived there the soldier took a post near the bottom while we followed the woman inside.

Beyond the entrance was a broad corridor. As we walked along, I saw doorways to the left and right that led into large workrooms. The woman with the list directed Corrie and me to the third room on the right. We were met there by a short, thin man with gray hair and kind eyes. He wore woolen slacks that were pressed smooth with a crease down the front of each leg. His white shirt had a stiff collar that fit perfectly in the front, overlapping only the edges of the knot in his tie. I liked him immediately.

Worktables, each about three meters in length, were arranged in rows that lined the room from end to end. Women sat at each table assembling electrical parts from bins that sat atop the tables. No one looked up as we entered.

The man who met us at the door led us to a row on the far side of the room where he placed me at the first empty station. Corrie took a spot three stations away. The women seated beside me were already busy, so I watched to see what they were doing. After a moment I picked up a piece from the bin to the left and tried to follow along. My legs ached and I was more tired than I'd been in a long time. I had a persistent cough and I was sure I looked ill, but I was determined to do the same work as the others. The job seemed much better than any of the alternatives I could imagine and at least it was inside, away from the hot summer weather.

The first few parts fit together nicely and I was making progress until I noticed a label on one of them indicated it came from Philips Electronics, a Dutch company. Then I realized we were assembling radios. Anger flared inside me at the thought that a Dutch company would be helping the Germans and doing so with forced labor from a prison camp.

I'd been at my place less than ten minutes when a man wearing a white lab coat appeared. He came straight to my table and greeted me with a smile, then showed me how to assemble the parts and gave me a quota for the day. With his help I made the parts fit together quickly and even found a shortcut. He watched a moment, then nodded and smiled and left. I filled my quota by noon.

At noon the man with the white coat entered the room. Everyone around me stopped what they were doing and scooted back from their workstations. I did the same and wondered what would happen next. Without a word of direction they all stood and stretched. I did, as well, and found the morning at the table had helped me rest. I could move my legs much better than before. After a minute or two, and again without direction or instructions, everyone returned to their seats. Corrie and I exchanged glances and a smile but kept quiet.

After we were seated, the door opened again and carts appeared, bringing bread and water to our workstations. Everyone took a portion of their own choosing, no one fought or grabbed for the bread in someone else's hand, and we ate and drank in silence. Ten minutes later, again without an order or direction from anyone, the carts were wheeled from the room and everyone returned to work. For the first time since we left Haarlem, my stomach no longer growled and for that brief noontime moment it seemed as though heaven had opened and manna fell from the sky.

The woman seated to my left worked much slower than the others, and from the parts remaining in the bins on her table I could see she was in danger of missing her daily quota. With nothing to do, and not wanting to appear idle, I nudged her with my elbow and gestured for her to give me some of her parts. She looked skeptical but I urged her and she handed me the parts. When I assembled them and placed them in the bin with the rest of her finished pieces, she handed me more parts. While we worked, I whispered to her, "My name is Betsie. What's yours?"

"Maria," she answered. "Maria Deen."

Her name suggested she was Jewish but I knew better than to ask. Instead I said, "I can't believe Philips is using prisoner labor. And making radios for the Germans."

Maria looked startled. "We are blessed to have this job."

"What do you mean?"

She gestured to the others in the room. "Most of us are here because Philips has continued to run the company. They saved us. We're alive because of them."

"Who saved you?"

"The Germans wanted to send us to the camps in the east, but Anton Philips himself intervened and told them we were indispensable."

"But you're a prisoner in a prison camp."

"We're alive! And we don't live in the prison."

I arched an eyebrow. "Where do you live?"

"In a building near town." The look on her face turned serious. "But you live here?"

"Yes."

"It must be terrible."

"It isn't good."

She glanced at me again and shook her head. "You don't look well."

"I'm supposed to take medicine for anemia, but I don't have it."

Just then, the door opened and the man with the white coat entered. Maria lowered her voice even lower than the whisper we'd been using and said, "I will help you."

●　●　●

The next day when we reported for work, Maria was already seated at her station. I took my seat beside her and as I reached for a part from the first bin, I saw a small bottle of liquid vitamins sitting among my parts. I glanced at her and she gave me a smile. "My brother was a doctor. He told me what you need."

"He's here with you?"

"In another room."

I squeezed her arm. "Thank you."

With no place in the barracks to keep it, I hid the bottle among the clutter at my station and took a few drops at the break.

That night, lying on the bed with the others, I heard women around me coughing and wheezing. I thought of the vitamins back at my workstation and an argument began inside me. I told myself that I needed the vitamins because of my medical condition. But my conscience argued, "Others have medical conditions, too." The vitamins saved my life. "They might prolong it, but they can't save it." Fear returned and all I could think of was how short my life would be if I had to continue without treatment. Those drops would change my circumstances. Any vitamins I might give the women in the barracks would be merely a drop in the vast sea of need, but it would have no real effect on their circumstances.

In the midst of that internal debate, a verse came to mind. *"Trust in the Lord with all your heart, and lean not on your own understanding."*

"That's from Proverbs," I whispered.

Corrie lay on her side, but at the sound of my voice she glanced over her shoulder at me. "What are you saying? Is something wrong?"

"Go back to sleep," I whispered. "Everything is fine."

After work the next day, I brought the bottle of vitamins to the barracks. That night, when we were in the bunk, I gave two drops to the woman next to me. She had a terrible cough. The person beside her saw us and asked for drops, too. Corrie didn't like it.

"Put that away," she said. "You need those drops to live."

"I will trust God for that. And besides, vitamins alone can't help me. Dr. Tromp said I need the liver extract to be able to absorb it."

"We'll find the extract."

"Not in here." Our eyes met and we both knew what the result of my condition would be, but I didn't dwell on it. "These women need hope," I continued, "and I can give it to them with just a few drops from this bottle."

CHAPTER 45

A FEW MONTHS LATER we were awakened by the whistle for morning roll call. Corrie and I climbed from the bunk and filed out into the cool morning air. Summer had ended and autumn was rapidly approaching. We formed into ranks and stood quietly, most of us expecting to march down the street to the Philips facility.

In spite of my worry about sharing the vitamins, the bottle had not run out. I carried it every day in my pocket and when someone asked for some I gave them two drops on their tongue. It seemed impossible that it would last this long, yet every day at noon there were still two drops for me. I felt better by taking them but I knew vitamins alone could never solve my medical problems. That morning my legs felt heavy and my joints ached. I wondered if I had the energy to make it to the factory at the end of the street.

Our regular officer appeared and scanned the ranks as he'd done every morning since we arrived. Then he nodded to the man beside him and roll call began. When that was finished, we were ordered to face left, which was odd because we normally went to the right. Then rank by rank they directed us down the street toward the camp entrance.

Flanked by soldiers on either side, we continued past the gate on the dirt road we'd walked when we first arrived. As we started down the hill away from the camp I could see that we were all in a single line that stretched to the bottom and up the other side. No one said a word.

In a little while we came to the railroad tracks at the same place we'd arrived months before. A line of cattle cars awaited and as we drew near, the soldiers divided us between them, forming groups in front of each car. There still was no loading ramp, so we were ordered to climb inside. The floor of the car was about shoulder height, which meant we had no leverage to hoist ourselves up. Those who tried fell to the ground. Frustrated by our failure to comply with their order, the soldiers surged toward us. Confusion followed, with the soldiers shouting for us to move and prisoners screaming and crying. Then the beating started.

A soldier struck one of the women to our right with the butt of his rifle, and blood spattered across Corrie's cheek. Alarmed by it, she glanced back at me and barked, "Stay with me," then she elbowed her way to the front of our group with me holding tightly to her dress. When we reached the car she grabbed me by the shoulders and lifted me up until I was able to place my hands against the floor of the car and swing a knee over. Then she gave me a shove and I tumbled inside. Standing above her, I reached down to help her up, then we gave a hand to others and helped them up. Slowly the railcar filled and as it did, the beating and shouting subsided. When the last person climbed aboard, the soldiers slid the door closed and latched it in place.

The morning was cool and pleasant. We'd made the walk from the camp to the train without getting hot, but as the day wore on the temperature rose. By noon the heat was stifling inside the railcar. And, as before, there was no sanitary facility. Before long the place reeked.

In a while, the railcar gave a jarring jolt, then started forward, rolling slowly at first before steadily picking up speed. We'd been standing for more than six hours, and although there was no room to sit as individuals, we figured out a way to sit at once. When we were settled in place, the rhythmic motion of the car rocked most people to sleep. I was drowsy, too, and rested my head on Corrie's shoulder. "Are you still angry with me?" I asked quietly.

"Angry with you?" Her voice sounded alert. "What about?"

"Sharing the vitamin bottle."

"No," she sighed. "I'm not angry about that…never was. I just wanted you to have what you need."

"You know, if I had kept the bottle hidden at my workstation, hoarding it only for myself, it would still be there. But by surrendering it to the Lord and His will, and bringing it to the barracks to share, I have it with us now."

She nodded in agreement. "You were right. God always knows best."

Three hours later, the train came to a stop and the doors opened. A breeze swept through the car and I thought we were at our destination, then two soldiers appeared in the doorway and passed a bucket of water inside. They quickly shoved the door closed and in a few minutes the train started forward again. Those seated nearest the door took a drink from the bucket then passed it overhead to those behind. Between the sloshing and gulping, the water was consumed before the bucket reached us.

After a while someone sitting near the far side of the car looked out between the wooden slats that formed the wall. "I think we're in Germany," she said. Others turned to see and a discussion began about where we were. The discussion soon became an argument and for a moment I thought a fight would break out, but before long the heat and hunger overtook passion, and everyone fell silent.

By the middle of the afternoon, two women had died. One at the end of the car, where the heat was particularly bad, and the other just a few meters in front of us. Both died quietly. We had no way to inform anyone and were forced to sit with the bodies as the train continued through the night and into the following day.

Finally at noon of the second day we came to a stop again. This time when the door opened we looked out to see a freight depot with ramps for loading and unloading cargo. Armed soldiers lined the tracks and stood watch around the depot. Trucks were parked nearby and I thought they were going to use them to transport us wherever it was we were going, but then I saw machine guns mounted in back and wondered if we'd survive to reach the ground.

With the freight ramp at railcar height we had only to step from the train and walk to the ground. There was no shouting or yelling and no one was beaten. Just a simple order, "Out!" and everyone began to unload.

As Corrie and I came from the car, I noticed an acrid odor in the air that wrinkled my nose. "What's that?"

"Smells like something burning."

"Like a pot left on the stove too long," I added.

A smokestack stood in the distance and a thin, gray line of smoke rose above it, then spread out to form a cloud that filled a large swath of the sky. Sunlight filtering through it cast an eerie glow, as if the sun were in a perpetual eclipse.

From the railroad, we walked down a dirt road and up a low hill. When we reached the crest we saw a lake in the hollow below. As we continued in that direction, the sight of water was too much to resist and suddenly everyone broke into a run toward it, laughing and giggling as they went. I was fatigued beyond exhaustion and could hardly put one foot ahead of the other, so I urged Corrie to run on ahead—and she did. I watched with a smile as she dashed to the water's edge, knelt on both knees, and plunged her head beneath the surface. A few minutes later I caught up with her and did the same.

For almost half an hour the soldiers stood at a distance and watched as we drank and washed and played in the lake. The water was clear, bright, and cool and for those few minutes we almost forgot that we were prisoners and once again became young girls on a holiday. Then all too soon the soldiers ordered us out and we continued along the road. I was glad for the water but even more to see the smile on Corrie's face and to hear her laugh again.

In a little while we rounded a curve and the high brick walls of a prison came into view. Word passed through the group that we were at Ravensbrück, a women's prison on the east side of Germany. I had read an article about it in the newspaper when it opened in 1939, before the occupation, when we could still get reliable information from our local paper. We later heard about it in reports on the radio. Even then it had a notorious reputation.

As with Vught, the permanent part of the prison was surrounded by a wire fence about four meters high. Inside the fenced area were tents. The ground beneath them was covered with fresh hay. I remember the smell even now. As we came through the gates, soldiers guided us to the tents and we collapsed on the hay to rest. Just as quickly, though, we jumped to our feet, scratching and digging in our hair as tiny lice attacked us. For the rest of the day we complained and finally a female guard appeared with a pair of scissors. We passed it through the group and cut each other's hair in an effort to reduce the insect problems, but it afforded little relief.

Autumn had arrived in eastern Germany and the air was cool even in the middle of the day. At night it was uncomfortably chilly. Sleeping on the damp ground in cold temperatures had a devastating effect on my health. The cough I picked up at Vught worsened. And then the rains began again. In addition to all that, the food was awful and diarrhea became a serious problem. Our latrine was an open ditch not far from the tents and I made frequent trips to it. Every day I became thinner and weaker.

On the tenth night we were rousted from the tents after the evening meal and moved through the wall's main gate to a large building inside the permanent prison. I'm not sure what use it had been originally designed for, but for us it was the inmate processing center. I glanced around for a clue about what would happen next. A group of prisoners ahead of us were just visible up the hall. They were naked and I saw them enter a room to the right. From the look of it, they appeared to be headed to the showers. The thought of a chance to wash put a smile on my face and I hoped that was what awaited us, too.

Before we reached the far end of the hall we came to a clerk who demanded all of our possessions. I had only the bottle of vitamins and the Bible and wanted to give up neither. A guard saw the bottle in my pocket and took it, but before they discovered the Bible my stomach cramps returned and Corrie asked if I could go to the restroom. One of the guards told us to use the shower and relieve myself over the drain. With Corrie's help, I hurried in that direction.

The group that was ahead of us had just left the showers. Water still dripped from the shower head as I squatted over the drain. Corrie held me by the arm to steady me while I relieved myself. We'd known each other through many circumstances, yet right then I found it deeply embarrassing to be there with her like that, but I had little choice. I was so weak I could not stand on my own. When I was finished Corrie said, "Give me the Bible."

"What are you going to do with it?"

"Hide it."

"Where?"

She pointed to a stack of wooden benches along the wall. "There."

"Do you think it's safe?"

"I think it's our only chance," she replied. She was right. Vitamins were no threat to Nazi ideology. In fact, it was perfectly consistent with all that they espoused—the love of human achievement, power, and vigor, and the drive to attain it—but the Bible was another matter. If they found it, they would not only destroy it but punish us, as well. Perhaps even the entire group. Once again I saw a principle at work. The only way to save it was to lose it. Jesus talked about that often. So I took the Bible from around my neck and handed it to Corrie, then she tucked it out of sight among the benches.

We came from the shower room and joined the others who'd formed a line in the hall. Moments later we were forced to strip naked and hand over our clothes. Male soldiers stood nearby and I was humiliated to be seen by them, but I was too sick to complain. When all our clothes had been collected, someone ordered us into the showers and we dutifully filed inside.

The water sprayed from the shower heads as we moved beneath them. It was tepid but not cold and felt good. I let it wash over my head and did my best to rid my scalp of the lice. In a few minutes the water switched off and we were directed to the next room. Towels were stacked there and we dried off. I noticed then that the skin of my arms hung loosely. All the fat was gone and only the muscle remained, but even that was less than before.

Somewhere in the shuffle of leaving the shower room and picking up a towel, Corrie retrieved the Bible. A cart near the wall to the right was piled with thin cotton prison dresses. Another next to it held poorly made shoes that required no laces. We sorted through them to find ones that fit and put them on. Through all of that, Corrie concealed the Bible from view until we were dressed, then she placed the cord around her neck and tucked it out of sight beneath her dress.

In the next room we came to a table where several men were seated. As I stepped to the table one of the men checked my records and assigned me a number. Another picked up a tattoo stamp and configured it to form the assigned number. Before I realized what was to happen, a female guard came behind me and slid the top of my dress off the left shoulder, then grabbed my arms and held them tightly to my side. Thus restrained, a man at the table stood, dipped the tattoo stamp in ink, and slammed it against my chest. He smiled as he struck me and watched while the ink mixed with blood from the needle pricks trickled down my exposed breast. I was prisoner 66729.

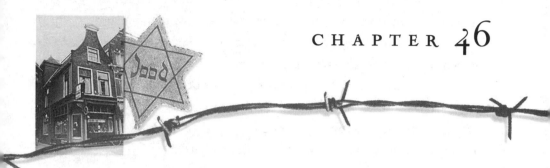

CHAPTER 46

MOST OF THE PEOPLE from our group were assigned to barracks number twenty-eight, a short walk from the processing center. We arrived there shortly before midnight. I had expected the guards would put us in formation and call the roll before sending us inside, but instead they simply ordered us up the steps into the building. The soldiers we'd seen at the train station and while we were in the tents were gone now, leaving us in the custody of female guards.

Unlike the barracks building at Vught, this one was divided into two parts. The first part was a large room that opened from the entry. In it were several tables around which were chairs and a couple of stools. The tables were piled high with knitting yarn. I asked a woman at the door about it and she said it was for women who could not perform manual labor. "They knit socks for the soldiers," she giggled.

I enjoyed knitting and wondered why she reacted that way, so I asked, "What's so funny about that?"

"They do it in a way that makes the toes and heels thin. That way, when the soldiers use the socks, their feet get blisters."

Through an open doorway was a dorm filled with bunk beds three beds high and five beds deep. Each bed was wide enough to accommodate two people but the ones I saw held four and five. A guard stood at the doorway watching as we made our way past while an inmate standing next to her

369

handed out small, thin blankets, one to each of us. "Find an open bunk," she said. "Five in a bed."

I took hold of Corrie's elbow and followed her down the aisle between the bunks, determined that we should stay together. We found a spot on top in the corner and Corrie boosted me up. I was too sick and weak to do it myself. A dozen women lay between us and the unoccupied place on the last wooden platform. We had to crawl over them to get to our spot. They all made sure we knew how little they appreciated the disruption. As we finally wedged our way into the bunk something bit me on the leg, then the arm, then behind my ear. Corrie felt it too and said loudly, "What is that?"

"Fleas," a voice answered from across the way.

"I hate these insects," Corrie complained. "Lice in the tents. Now fleas in here."

"Shh," I said. "Complaining isn't going to make it better."

"It makes me feel better," she grumbled.

"Scripture says to give thanks in all things. We should try it."

"All things?"

"Yes. For being tired. For being crammed together."

"But not the fleas," she retorted. "Don't give thanks for the fleas."

"Yes," I chuckled. "We must give thanks for the fleas, too."

"That makes absolutely no sense."

"Maybe. But we can't think only of ourselves or dwell on our own misery. We need to give thanks in all things."

A loud voice called out, "Shut up!"

"But why give thanks for the fleas?' Corrie whispered.

"I don't know. I just think we need to give thanks for them." I wrapped myself in the blanket and leaned my head against Corrie's back. For the next five minutes I whispered a prayer of thanks to God for keeping us together, for giving us a place to sleep that protected us from the rain, and for as many other things as I could remember. As I was about to drift off to sleep I heard Corrie add, "And I give thanks for you."

❀ ❀ ❀

The next morning we were awakened before sunrise by a shrill noise from a loudspeaker mounted on a pole near the corner of the building. At the same time, two guards appeared in the doorway. "Get up," they shouted. "Get up!" I thought it was curious that they came no closer than the door.

Groggy and tired, Corrie and I crawled from the bunk and followed the others out to formation. From our previous experience, I had expected to hear our names called and to receive a work assignment promptly. Instead we stood in ranks until sunrise. The weather had turned cold in the night and there was a wintry chill in the air. Most people from the dorm welcomed the change but I was already sick and had a low-grade fever. In the morning cold, my body shivered.

When the sun was fully up a guard appeared with a clipboard and called roll. Afterward a second woman stepped forward with two pages in her hand. As with the camp at Vught, she was dressed in civilian clothes, but from the tone of her voice I decided this one was not nearly as nice. She called out a list of names from the pages and when she said ours we joined the others who'd gathered around her, then walked with her up the street.

A hundred meters beyond our dorm, we passed a large rectangular building made of brick. The smokestack I'd seen from the train rose above it and a thin line of smoke drifted in the air at the top, creating a cloud that spread out over all the camp. Tiny flecks of ash fell from the cloud like snow covering the ground with a white dusty film. Some of it landed on our shoulders. But the thing I noticed most was the heat that radiated from the site all the way out in the street where we walked. It felt good and for a moment my body stopped shaking. I wanted to stay right there and go no farther. While Corrie walked on ahead, I slowed my pace, allowing others to pass while I fell to the back until the woman with the list noticed and I caught up with the others.

A hundred meters farther on, we came to a large factory building. Almost a carbon copy of the one at Vught, this one was used by Siemens, a German company. Apparently doing business with the Germans was particularly lucrative when prison labor was involved. We followed the woman with the list up the steps at the front entrance, through heavy double doors, and went inside.

A broad corridor led through the center of the building. It was spotlessly clean, and armed German soldiers were posted every ten meters. All of them seemed to stare at me as I walked by. I didn't like it, but the woman with the list paid them no attention and took us to a room on the left that was filled with workstations. As before, we were placed in open seats not far from each other. I'd seen this at Vught and knew right away we were assembling parts for an electrical device.

As I settled into my seat, a man entered the room and came to my station. He was of medium height but slender and his skin was remarkably white. With nimble fingers, he showed me how to fit the pieces together, then he looked at me with concern and said, "Will you be able to do this?"

I nodded my head. "Of course." I knew by then I wouldn't survive long in an outside job.

He hesitated a moment as if considering my answer, then gave me the daily quota and turned to leave. A few paces away he stopped and came back, then leaned close and whispered, "Are you sure you can make the quota?"

"Yes."

"If you can't do the work, tell me now," he insisted. "Otherwise, it will be bad for you *and* me if you fail."

"I can make it," I assured him. "I'll be fine." He stared at me a moment longer, then turned away and left the room.

Fitting the parts together was easy for me. I was seated. The work wasn't complicated. It took no great effort to do the job. But when I glanced to my right I saw the woman seated next to me was assembling the device incorrectly. I leaned near her and said, "That's not the way it goes together."

"I know," she replied.

I was astonished by her response and said, "Then why are you doing it that way?"

"These are bomb triggers," she explained. "We don't want any of them to work, but that would cause trouble for everyone. We only have to meet minimum quality standards to keep everyone out of trouble. And that's what they get. They'll get no more from me than that, and I do it only so the others can avoid punishment."

For the remainder of the day I wrestled with what she said. Bomb triggers were certainly more lethal than the radios we made at the previous location. No one wanted to contribute to the German effort of killing. But I'd been

reared with the notion that doing my best was a moral obligation, a requirement from God. The final result was His responsibility. Now, with the suggestion that I purposefully assemble a device that would not work, I faced a
new dilemma, much like Corrie had faced when she turned in only one of our
radios. The answer was not easy to find.

We worked until sunset without food or water, then were marched back
to the barracks. On the way we again passed the rectangular brick building
with the tall smokestack. In between working and wrestling with whether to
make faulty products, I'd been thinking of the building all day and how good
the radiant heat that came from it felt to my aching body. Even before we were
alongside it again I could sense the warmth as we made our way down the
street toward the barracks. As we came closer and the heat grew more intense,
the feel of it made me smile.

At the corner of the building a door was open and I glanced inside. My
mouth fell open and my heart sank at the ghastly sight of naked human corpses
stacked on the floor like firewood. Workers picked them up one at a time and
piled them on metal racks. Beyond them the furnace doors were open and I
saw the flames dancing inside. With workmanlike effort, the men shoved the
loaded racks into the furnace. The hair on the heads of the corpses burst into
flames as the men shut the heavy iron doors that sealed them inside.

"It's a crematorium," I gasped.

A woman beside me jerked her head in my direction. "What did you
think it was?"

"Quiet!" a guard shouted. "No talking!"

My stomach muscles contracted in a visceral reaction and I doubled over
with dry heaves.

❦ ❦ ❦

At the barracks, we formed into ranks for evening roll call, then moved
inside for supper—a piece of bread and a bowl of lukewarm porridge. I was
already too sick to eat, and after what I had seen at the crematorium wasn't
interested in food. Corrie forced me to eat the bread and traded the porridge
to someone for half their bread. She handed it to me. "Eat this." Reluctantly, I

took a bite and then the stomach cramps started again. I waited until I could wait no more, then nudged Corrie and said, "I need your help." She took my arm with one hand and used the other to push our way through the crowd, clearing a path for us as we hurried toward the toilet.

The bathroom was located at the far end of the building, but calling it by that name was an exaggeration. Placed in a separate room, which at least gave a nod to personal privacy, it had no running water. Toilet tissue was limited and some days nonexistent.

A plywood box that stood about knee high ran the length of the back wall with holes cut every two meters. Beneath each hole was a vat made from a steel drum. The room was filthy with feces, and urine tracked across the floor. Only the seats were dry and I sat on the first one past the door. Corrie refused to leave me in there alone and stood nearby ready to grab me if I fell over, which happened more than once.

When the cramps eased enough to talk, I said, "I had no idea that building was a crematorium."

"I thought of that when we passed it this morning," Corrie said. "But the heat felt good."

"Too good," I quipped.

"One day we'll be in there," she added with a wry smile.

"I would never want that job."

"I didn't mean we'd be working there," Corrie responded.

"Stop," I chuckled. Sometimes she had a warped sense of humor. "We're not going to die in here."

"They will work us to death, and when we are dead they will burn our bodies in the furnaces."

"Well, maybe so," I conceded, "but nothing that happens to us will happen that isn't from God. And if they send us to the crematorium, it will not matter. We will be with Him long before the flames reach our hair."

When I finished, we returned to the aisle beside our bunk. Corrie handed me the Bible and I leaned against the wall near the window to read from the glow of a light at the corner of the building. I read the scripture aloud, though quietly, and Corrie stood behind me listening. Then we prayed.

As we finished, I closed the Bible and turned to hand it back to Corrie.

With my head tilted at an angle I caught a glimpse of my face reflected in the windowpane. My cheeks were hollow and pale, my eyes dark and deep in their sockets. All the extra flesh was gone from my skull, and the skin hung over it like a thin film. I realized then why people at the Siemens building were staring at me earlier.

◆ ◆ ◆

Sometime late that night I was awakened by screams and loud shrieks coming from outside. Corrie, who was lying beside me, shifted positions in the bunk. Hoping she was awake, I whispered, "What was that noise?"

She didn't respond, but a voice from several bunks away said, "It's coming from the punishment barracks next door."

"Punishment barracks? What's that?"

"Where they take people who break the rules."

"Nobody told me about rules. What rules?"

"Whatever they tell you to do—that's a rule. Now be quiet or we'll both get sent over there."

"But what are they doing?"

"You don't want to know. Go back to sleep."

A third person spoke up. "Shut up, both of you."

The next morning as we stood in ranks, a truck rolled to a stop in front of the barracks next to ours. Two men came from the cab and went inside. A few minutes later they emerged, dragging a body by the arms. They pulled it around to the back of the truck, then one man held the arms and the other grabbed the feet. They swung the body back and forth between them twice to gain momentum, then flung it onto the bed of the truck. Before roll call was finished they brought out two more.

During the walk to the factory building that morning my body began to shake. From the way it felt I was sure I had a fever, but I said nothing. When Corrie asked, I told her only that I was cold. As with the day before, we passed the crematorium, but now that I knew what really went on there I no longer took pleasure in the warmth that came from it. The truck we'd seen at the barracks during formation was parked there. It was empty but the two men who'd loaded the bodies were standing at the door near the corner of the building—the door I'd looked through the day before. They were laughing and talking and smoking cigarettes as if what they were doing was only part of a job. As we walked by I turned my head in the opposite direction so as not to see the ovens, but my body responded to the warmth it gave and I felt ashamed.

By the time we reached the steps to go inside the factory, I was chilled to the bone and so exhausted I could barely move. Corrie helped me inside and I leaned against the wall in the corridor while the others passed. The temperature was warmer there and I needed a moment to rest. Corrie stayed with me but then a soldier posted a few meters away noticed me. I avoided eye contact with him and said to Corrie, "You better go. He's getting suspicious." She hesitated but I urged her all the more, and finally she started after the others. That seemed to satisfy the soldier and he relaxed, so I stood there a moment longer trying to get control of my trembling body.

As our group turned aside to enter the workroom, I started up the corridor and came in after them. My workstation was located near the back of the room. I found it without obvious trouble and made myself busy assembling parts that were already there.

From my seat I glanced around and noticed soldiers posted in each corner. Armed with rifles and dressed in fatigues, they were both imposing and menacingly intimidating. They'd never been there before, and I wondered why they were there now. Others most have wondered, too, but everyone was busy with their heads down. No one was looking around.

We'd been there only a few minutes when the door opened and the woman with the list who'd given us our assignment the day before entered the room. A few meters inside she stopped and caught the eye of a soldier, then gave him a nod. Without a word, the soldier stepped to the nearest workstation and grabbed the woman who was seated there by the arm. "Come," he ordered and tugged at her to move her from her chair.

"Why?" she protested. "What have I done?" She drew back from his grasp and wrapped both arms around the leg of her workstation. "I haven't done anything," she argued.

The guard, unmoved by her attempt to resist, simply lifted his rifle with both hands and struck her between the eyes with the butt. Her hands slipped from the leg of the workstation and she tumbled unconscious to the floor. Then he shifted the rifle to one hand, grabbed her by the arm with the other, and dragged her out the door.

Two more soldiers did the same thing, and when the three workers had been removed from the room the woman with the list looked at us and said, "Switches from this room failed at a rate too high to be acceptable. Some think it was deliberate. If it happens again, you'll all go to the punishment barracks." She turned to leave but then she focused on me, and I saw her face brighten. With quick, long strides she crossed the room and stood before me. I heard the rustling of pages as she checked her lists, but I kept my head down and continued to work, placing the parts together as quickly as my fingers would move. She stood there staring down at me for what seemed like a long time, but I kept working and those seated around me did, too. Then she pulled the collar of my dress down to reveal my prisoner number, made a note of it on her list, and stalked away. As she left, the remaining soldiers followed her out. When they were gone the woman beside me whispered, "We'll have to build better switches for a while."

◆ ◆ ◆

That night after supper Corrie and I stood by the window to read the Bible and pray together. Before we started I brought up the incident from that morning at the factory building. She didn't really want to talk about it. "But it's like Kan and the Germans all over again," I insisted. "When they threw him out of his shop and we did nothing. We agreed to never let that happen again. But this morning we just sat there and watched while they took those people out. We can't do that."

"We can't get in a fight with them, either," she argued. "You saw what happened when they tried to resist."

"Yes, but what if we'd joined her?"

"They were German soldiers, Betsie. We'd never stand a chance."

"They were four or five at most and we were twenty or thirty. And you saw how the woman with the list focused on me. I might be next."

She tried to sound unconcerned. "Don't worry about it. You make your quota, they'll leave you alone."

"I didn't like her writing down my number like that."

"I'm sure it was nothing. They're Germans. They keep records of everything." She took the Bible from beneath her dress and handed it to me. "Let's read."

I opened to the place where we'd left off the night before, in Paul's letter to the Romans, and began to read. Papa always read a chapter each time, but our attention span wasn't that long right then, so Corrie and I only read a paragraph. As I closed the book to pray, someone behind us said, "You two were over here last night. What are you doing?"

My heart skipped a beat as I glanced over my shoulder to find a woman from the dorm standing in the aisle with us. She slept two rows over from us and I'd seen her that morning in the group that worked at Siemens. I was apprehensive about answering her question. As I'd said earlier, there were no stated rules but everyone knew prisoners were not allowed to own Bibles. Turning us in to the guards might be worth a lot to an inmate—extra food for a month or an additional blanket, maybe first choice at a better place to sleep. But I didn't want to lie, either. Then she noticed the book in my hand. Her eye opened wide and she whispered, "You're reading the Bible?"

"Yes," I replied.

"I haven't been to Mass in over a year. Read it to me."

I glanced at Corrie and she nodded, so I reread the passage from Romans. When I concluded I said, "We are going to pray now. Care to join us?"

"Yes," she replied. "I do." Then she made the sign of the cross on her chest.

From the way she acted and talked, I assumed she was Catholic, so I led us in praying the Lord's Prayer. Tears filled her eyes as we said the words, and I knew right then we had found a friend. Her name was Marjolein Blokland.

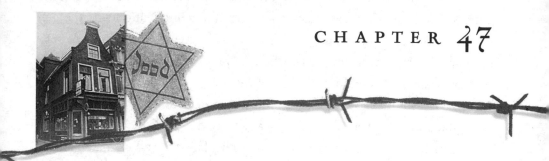

AS THE DAYS PASSED the weather turned colder, yet we still only had the single small blanket at night. Even sleeping as we did, crammed together side by side with no room to roll over, I was cold all the time. Sleep came in fits and starts as my body shivered. Corrie swapped places with me so I could be on the inside, and most nights she slept with one arm around me to give me as much of her body heat as possible, but I could not stop shaking.

Diarrhea, at first only a nuisance, was now a serious threat. Every time I ate I had to run to the toilet, and with no extra water to drink I was seriously dehydrated. My weight continued to drop and my skin took on a translucent appearance. When I looked at my arms it seemed as though I could look past the skin and see the tendons moving with the muscles. All of my subcutaneous fat was gone.

And each morning when I awakened, the cough was worse. I thought of Mama and how tuberculosis had taken such a toll on her. We had lived through it with her, and even though during her worst episodes she confined herself to the bedroom, I wondered if I hadn't contracted the disease, too.

Others noticed my condition, but now instead of staring at me when I approached, they turned away. No one wanted to be near me. Even the guards looked away when we assembled for morning roll call. But at the Siemens building things were different. The soldiers who stood watch in the hall followed me with their eyes as I made my way down the corridor, and in the workroom the woman with the list hovered near me constantly.

In mid-November the snow began to fall. At home it would have been beautiful with the streets and rooftops covered in white, but outside the barracks it was most unwelcome. Morning roll call, already a miserable experience, quickly became torture as we stood for hours in the snow and ice. By the time we were dismissed for work, all of my energy was gone. Corrie did her best to cover for me, and most days I made it to my workstation only because she walked with her arm around my waist to hold me up.

Then one morning the woman with the list failed to call my name for the Siemens assignment. Corrie was forced to leave me behind. We were still in ranks and I stood there watching as she and the others trudged up the street. A thousand memories flooded my mind and I felt again the sadness of being separated from her when we were in the prison at Scheveningen.

A second group was selected that morning to work outside, but again I was left behind. Finally only a few of us remained, and I realized we were the weakest and the sickest. A guard ordered us back inside the barracks building, where we were directed to the knitting tables.

From my seat at the table I could see through the doorway into the dorm. Two women were lying in their bunks, apparently too ill even to report for roll call. I would have preferred to remain in my bunk that morning, too, but I was afraid it would only bring trouble if I asked.

Guards who watched us stood in the doorway between the two rooms and when it was time to check on those in their bunks, they sent a prisoner in to do it. As I thought about it I remembered several times when the guards came only as far as the doorway. They stopped there in the morning when they rousted us for roll call. When food was distributed, they did it in the knitting room. And if someone was ill, they had others bring her out so they could see. I wondered about it, so I asked the woman seated next to me at the knitting table.

"That's right," she nodded, thinking that I was merely deriding the guards for their behavior. "They think they're so tough," she continued with a smirk. "They can beat us to the point of death but they won't even walk two feet beyond the doorway."

"But why not?" I asked again. "I don't understand. Why won't they go into the dorm?"

"They hate the fleas," another offered.

"Think of it," a woman to the left giggled. "They push us around like we're nothing, but then they get pushed around by a flea that *is* nothing." Everyone at the table laughed until the guard caught our eye with a mean look, and we fell silent.

That evening after supper, Corrie and I gathered by the window to read and pray. Marjolein joined us. We continued reading from Romans, then prayed. This time, however, we did more than recite the Lord's Prayer but prayed for the specific needs of our fellow prisoners. I added a prayer for the guards and soldiers, which Corrie reluctantly supported. And then, instead of simply ending with an Amen, I began to recount the things for which I was thankful and encouraged Corrie and Marjolein to do the same.

Afterward, I told them what I'd learned about why the guards wouldn't enter the dorm because of the fleas. I looked over at Corrie. "And that's why we gave thanks for them when we first arrived here."

Marjolein looked surprised. "You gave thanks for the fleas?"

"She did," Corrie said, pointing to me.

"Paul said to give thanks in all things," I shrugged, "so I was giving thanks."

Marjolein nodded her head. "Interesting."

"Don't say that," Corrie quipped. "You'll only encourage her."

But it was too late. I was already encouraged by the Holy Spirit. For the next hour Marjolein and I talked about how God takes the things that seem to be nothing and makes them important, and the things that seem important He turns into nothing. "Those fleas," I grinned, "are a gift from God."

❖ ❖ ❖

A few days later, coats were issued at morning roll call. Mine was much too large but I was thankful to have it. When I sat at the knitting table, I wrapped the coat around me in a bundle that extended almost to my ankles. There was no heat in the building, but the extra fabric in the coat helped keep me warmer than I was before.

Two days after we received the coats, Corrie was taken off the job with Siemens and sent with the crews that worked outside. Her group maintained the dirt streets that crisscrossed the prison grounds. They spent long days leveling and packing the surface, performing some of the hardest physical labor assigned to prisoners. Each evening she returned to the barracks exhausted and dirty.

From one day to the next my body grew weaker. I could feel the energy leaving me, and even my fingers, which had always been fast with a knitting needle, failed me. I tried to keep up with the others at our table but I was soon unable to meet my daily quota. My mind still remembered how to do the work and what my fingers were supposed to do. I just couldn't make them do it well or quickly anymore. Those who were seated with me were forced to pick up my work so that none of us had any trouble.

Early one morning in the first week of December, I awoke and was unable to move my legs. This had happened before but never quite like this. Corrie urged me to stay in the bunk, but I was worried the guards would not like it and would take their frustration out on the others in the barracks. We argued but finally I convinced Corrie to help me and she pulled me over to the edge of the bunk, then carried me to the door. With her help I made it down the steps and we took our place on the back row of formation.

The wind that morning was bitterly cold and the snow that had accumulated on the ground was frozen solid. Every bone in my body ached and I was shaking from a fever. My breathing was labored, coming in short gasps, and I was able to stand only by concentrating all my remaining energy on the effort to hold my knees in place.

As was their practice, the guards withheld the roll call until sunrise, which was at least two hours away. Less than half an hour into the wait, a woman three rows ahead of us collapsed. Guards who'd been lurking around the edges of our formation dragged her to the punishment barracks, laughing and joking as they went.

From the moment we were arrested I had determined that the Germans would never change me. That I would not allow my circumstances to determine my attitude and would always keep my mind and heart on God and His purpose in my life. I'd been vigilant in that effort even when it would have been easier to give in to bitterness and hatred. Moments like we were experiencing tested my resolve, yet God always strengthened me and allowed me to use whatever happened like wind beneath my wings to lift me above the trouble. That morning I felt Him near, and in my mind and spirit I spread my wings to let Him once again lift me above the misery my body was experiencing. My feet were numb with cold and my body trembled with fever, but inside I was at peace.

Ten minutes after the first person collapsed, a woman just down from us fell over. Two of her friends, who were standing beside her, caught her before she hit the ground and propped her up, hoping the guards wouldn't notice. The guards did, however, and all three were sent to the punishment barracks. The guards who took them shouted and berated them, saying, "You cost me money. I bet no one would fall that soon after the first." Others who stood around watching us joined in the laughter and compared the times they'd selected in the betting pool for wagers on who would fall next. Sadness swept over me at the sound of their voices.

At first I had not seen what Papa saw—that the Germans were trapped by the evil to which they yielded themselves and in danger of losing their souls forever. Even after I came to understand what he meant, it took a while for me to actually sense the presence of the personal evil that the Germans embraced. That morning, as they laughed and joked and made bets over who would collapse next, I sensed the presence of evil among us like I had never felt it before, but it wasn't searching for me. It was searching for Corrie.

When we were younger, I was the bossy older sister. She was the impetuous youngest child, always given to impulse, reacting without thought for the consequences. That attitude and disposition caused her some problems as a young woman, but those troubles were nothing compared to the stakes she was about to face.

I had reached my end. The strength in my body was gone and there was no way to restore it. My body had been damaged beyond repair. Whatever we were to accomplish by our time in prison, or afterward as a result of our experiences, she would have to see it to the end. I was not going there with this body. But to get there, she had to get past the morning. So I leaned my head in her direction and said quietly, "They are most to be pitied."

My voice was hoarse and weak and I could barely hear the words, but Corrie's eyes brightened at the sound of them, and she said, "What are you talking about?"

"They make jokes and bets about us," I said as strongly as I could, "but they are making a much bigger bet with the Enemy. A bet that God will not hold them accountable."

"They don't care—"

"The Enemy wants you, Corrie."

"I don't—"

"Whatever happens," I continued, cutting her off, "you must promise me that you will not give in to the evil that they embrace."

Ignoring the guards and what they might do, Corrie turned to face me. "Don't talk like that."

That was the Corrie I'd known all my life. Never a regard for the consequences. "Promise me that you will not let the Enemy have your soul," I pleaded.

"I've never—"

"Promise me," I insisted with all my remaining energy.

"I promise."

Then my legs buckled and I fell to the ground.

Sometime later I became aware that I was lying on the ice. A guard stood over me yelling at me to "Get up! Get up!" When I didn't move, I felt the toe of her boot strike me in the abdomen and I heard Corrie shout, "Stop! She's sick!"

One of the guards who'd been with us in the knitting room appeared, and I heard people talking. The one who'd kicked me snarled, "I got a prison full of sick women. Some of them are sick, and some of them are fakes." The guard from the knitting room said something in response, and the one who kicked me turned away in disgust.

Corrie bent over me and slipped one arm beneath my back and the other under my legs, then she lifted me from the ground, and I felt the jarring motion of her heavy steps. Seconds later Marjolein appeared at her side. She ran her fingers over my forehead and winced. "We need to take her to the infirmary."

Someone shouted after us, "If she's pretending, you'll all be in the punishment barracks tonight."

With Marjolein leading the way, Corrie carried me up the street. I knew when we reached the crematorium because I felt the warmth of the furnaces. Two buildings later we arrived at the infirmary. By then I was alert enough to know that a long line of people stretched ahead of us, waiting to be seen by a doctor.

For two hours we waited in the snow just to get inside the building, but we weren't the last in line. As we finally passed through the door, I glanced back to see as many more behind us as were there when we arrived.

A nurse placed a thermometer in my mouth, and in a few minutes she came back to read it. "One hundred two," she said, shaking her head. "Not enough."

"Not enough," Corrie cried. "What do you mean not enough? Not enough for what?"

"We can't keep anyone in here with a temperature that low. Take her back to the barracks."

Corrie and Marjolein helped me back to the barracks and placed me on the bunk, then the guards sent them to catch up with the work crew. All day long I lay there bundled in the coat and wrapped in the blanket, shivering with a fever. When Corrie returned that evening she took one look at me and called Marjolein to our bunk. "We have to get her back to the hospital." Marjolein agreed and the two of them carried me to the guard. To her credit, the guard never said a word but just pointed toward the door.

At the hospital there was once again a long line of people waiting to be seen. Snow was falling and it covered the ice already on the streets, which made standing outside even more treacherous than before, but I insisted Corrie set me down. I was trembling from the fever so violently that I couldn't talk but I managed to stand for all of ten minutes, then I sagged against her shoulder. At that, Corrie scooped me up in her arms and carried me past the line. The others protested loudly but she ignored them and took me up to the front door. Marjolein came with us and held the door open while Corrie took me inside.

This time when the nurse checked my temperature it read one hundred four, and they found a bed for me. It wasn't really a bed, just a cot with a cotton tick but it was softer than the wooden bunks we slept on and it had a real bottom sheet. There was only one blanket, but when the nurse saw how much I shivered, she gave me a second and let me keep my coat.

When I was settled on the cot, Marjolein retreated to the door. Corrie lingered at my side. "Do you want the Bible?" she whispered. I could only shake my head in response. "Okay," she said. "I'll check on you tomorrow and we can talk then."

A nurse took her by the arm and nudged her toward the door, but Corrie resisted. She didn't want to leave me there alone any more than I wanted to be there without her. "I'll be back tomorrow," she said, but I knew what she really meant was *Please don't die.*

CHAPTER 48

CONDITIONS AT THE PRISON hospital weren't like any hospital I had ever seen. Certainly not at all like the hospital in Amsterdam where I'd been treated by Dr. Tromp. Except for the cot and cotton tick, it was more like the dorm with heat—very little heat.

The bathroom had sinks with running water and toilets that flushed, but all the fixtures regularly overflowed, leaving urine and feces on the floor and a foul stench in the air. Smelling it reminded me of the odor from the railcar on the train that brought us there. To make matters worse, the bathroom doubled as a temporary morgue for the corpses of dead patients, which the nurses piled against the wall at the far end of the room. It made an awful slapping sound when they stacked them too high and the bodies fell to the floor.

Food was the best part of their care for us. They served no porridge, only bread and water, but the bread was baked fresh every morning and the water was clean and drinkable. At first I thought they were being kind to us because we were sick. Then I learned the nurses insisted on it because the porridge and dirty water created a big mess when patients defecated in bed.

Bread was much easier on my stomach and the clean water gave my digestive system time to recover. I was still too weak to move on my own and had to be assisted to the toilet twice each day, but the cramps in my stomach subsided and I was able to rest easier. People were dying all around me, most from inattention, but I slept better on the cotton tick and had the luxury of dozing as much as I wanted.

When I slept, the dream returned and I once again soared above the house with the gardens and the tulips in the flowerbeds. Below me, Captain Bormann worked alongside Lieutenant Krüger. The woman with the list from the Siemens factory building stood next to a guard from the prison at Scheveningen, and this time Rudolph Schakel was there, as well. All of them tended the gardens under Corrie's watchful eye.

When I awakened I thought of it and smiled to myself. *This is what we must do. After the war, we will get a big house, with plenty of garden space where prisoners, guards, and soldiers can find redemption.*

As I continued to think about the dream, I realized one person was missing from it—me. I was above the scene, looking down, but never in the images on the ground. Tears came to my eyes at the thought of it. I moved my hand from beneath the blanket and held it up so I could see. The sight of it made me wince. My arm was even skinnier than before when I'd seen my image in the window at the barracks. Skin hung loosely over bone. Almost all the muscle was gone and even lifting it from beneath the cover made my arm shake with fatigue. "I'm not going to recover," I whispered. And in the next instant I thought of Corrie. She wanted me well and wanted us to be together. She expected it and refused to consider any other possibility. How would I tell her what I now knew the dream meant? I wasn't sure I'd have the opportunity to see her again, much less talk to her, but if I did, would I be able to tell her? "Lord," I prayed, "give me the opportunity and the strength to speak."

❖ ❖ ❖

Sometime later I heard a noise coming from the bathroom. The nurses had been in and out of there all day, so I thought the sound I'd heard was them delivering another corpse. I closed my eyes and immediately images of the crematorium appeared with the furnace doors open and the flames dancing inside. Then just as quickly I saw the corpses on the rack as the workmen shoved them into place. Fire licked around the dead bodies, steam rose from their chests and stomachs, then the hair atop their heads burst into flames.

The image was so real I jumped at seeing it, and my eyes popped open to find Marjolein standing over me.

She smiled. "Hello, how are you feeling?"

My eyes darted from side to side, searching. "Where's Corrie?"

"She didn't come," Marjolein replied. "You look better."

"My stomach is a little better," I sighed. I had wanted to see Corrie and found it difficult to hide.

"You actually have some color in your cheeks," she replied.

It was a kind remark but I knew better. "How did you get in here? They let you in?"

"No," she said with a mischievous look. "I climbed through the window."

It sounded odd and I wondered if I were dreaming. "The window?"

"In the bathroom," she explained.

"It's a mess."

"I know. But I wanted to see you."

"Why didn't Corrie come?" I had things to tell her that only she would understand.

Marjolein's countenance dropped. "She wouldn't come."

"Why not?"

"She...doesn't like seeing you this way. It's so far from what she remembers as a child. And...I think she's afraid of what she might find."

A puzzled frown wrinkled my forehead. "What she might find?"

"Yes," Marjolein nodded with a knowing look. "You know ..."

Then I realized what she meant. "She thinks I'll be dead when she gets here?"

"Yes."

I should have known Corrie would react that way, but I had things to tell her. Things that she needed to hear. "Tell her how I look," I gasped, "and ask her to come see me." Marjolein said something in reply but I wasn't sure what. Talking even for that brief period sapped all my strength and left me short of breath. I closed my eyes and tried to relax in an effort to slow my heart. When I opened them again, Marjolein was gone.

❖ ❖ ❖

After Marjolein came to see me—I'm not certain just how long—I drifted in and out of consciousness and in and out of sleep. The sounds around me melded into the world inside my head and the dreams that came to me in my sleep, forming a single conversation in which I was both listener and participant, but I was keenly aware that time was passing and my physical condition was deteriorating.

At intermittent moments, a hand touched my shoulder or my arm and I opened my eyes to see a nurse standing over me. At first they took my temperature and checked my pulse. Later they only checked my pulse. Once or twice I ate a few bites of bread, and the lady on the cot beside me helped me take a sip of water. She had kind eyes and a lovely smile and the touch of her hand on mine gave me a sense of peace.

As I drifted between lucid intervals and dreamy sleep, my orientation to a visual world evaporated. Sound became my primary source of information. A familiar rhythm emerged from the dissonance that first surrounded me, and I came to recognize people not so much by their appearance as by their footsteps. The nurse who walked quickly everywhere she went and whom all the others seemed to like. The one with a slow, lumbering pace who was liked by no one. Another who walked with a heavy thud at each step and couldn't care less what anyone thought of her.

And then one day there was the sound of a different footstep—one that was both familiar and unexpected but which nevertheless took me back to the Beje and memories of a time I'd forgotten I could remember. I opened my eyes at the sound of it and saw Corrie standing beside my cot, gazing down at me with a worried look.

Her eyes told me she was on the verge of tears, so I worked my hand free of the blanket and she took it in hers. This was the moment I'd been praying for, so I avoided the temptation to indulge my emotions and went right to the point. "I've been having that dream," I said, struggling to form the words with my mouth. "Every time I have it…more people show up to tend the flowers with you." I labored to take a breath. "Bormann is there…and Krüger, but so is Schakel. You remember him?"

"Yes," Corrie nodded. "The magistrate who helped us when we were at Scheveningen."

I nodded. "He was in the dream."

"Am I still in it?" she asked as tears spilled from her eyes.

"You are always in my dreams." I paused then, unsure whether to say more, but she needed to know and I'd prayed for the chance to tell her, so I struggled for breath and kept going. "Corrie, there is one thing about the dream you must know." My voice was weak but I was determined to say what was on my heart.

"What?" she sniffed, wiping tears from her cheek with the back of her hand.

"You are in it...and the other people are in it...but I am not." Tears ran unrestrained down Corrie's cheeks, and I began to cry, too. "I think we both know what that means."

"No, we don't," she sobbed. "Don't talk like that."

"Corrie, this is not easy ..." I paused to take another breath, "...but we should face the fact that I am very sick." My mouth was dry and my voice was reduced to barely a whisper. "And there isn't much chance of me getting well."

"No," she said in protest. "You'll get better. You have to get better. We have to go home and plant flowers and—"

I shook my head to interrupt her. "When I'm gone, you can't give in to bitterness...or hatred. The Germans did, and that's why we're here like this."

"I don't think I can ever love them," she murmured.

"Maybe not...but God can."

"They make us hate them," she argued. Her face was twisted in a look of anguish, and I wanted to hold her close.

"No," I replied weakly. "Hate is a choice, just like love. If you give in to hatred, you will become like the Germans. You don't want that."

"I don't want you to die."

"I know," I nodded. "But that's not up to us."

"I don't know how to love them," she wailed, "or anybody else. You have to stay alive so you can show me."

"That's what the house is for. With the lawn and the gardens."

"And the tulips?" she said with a lonely smile.

"Yes," I nodded. "Lots of tulips...planted where they have plenty of sunlight...to grow and bloom."

"I don't think I'll ever look at a tulip again without crying."

Whatever energy I'd had when she arrived was gone. My chest heaved in an effort to fill my lungs with air, but even so I was on the verge of losing consciousness. Still I forced myself to speak. "Tending those gardens…is how… they will find a way out. And…it's how…you will, too."

"Then you will have to help me do it."

"I'm not going to be there. But you will."

"I don't know how."

I nodded. "Yes, you do."

Corrie knelt in anguish on the floor and draped her body over me. "You're the only thing of beauty in my life," she sobbed. I rested my hand on her shoulder and listened to her cry. There was much more I wanted to say, to remind her of all the things we'd done and tell her how those things were preparation for what lay ahead. To remind her that the mission we'd been given was one that started a hundred years ago with our grandparents and had been passed from generation to generation until it came to us, but I no longer had the strength or breath for it. So I just lay there and enjoyed the pleasure of her company for what I was sure would be our last time together.

While Corrie cried herself out, a nurse appeared and tapped her on the shoulder. "You're not supposed to be in here," she scolded. "You must leave." Corrie hesitated and the nurse said louder, "Now!" At that, she stood and looked down at me one last time, then leaned over and kissed me on the forehead. I smiled up at her until she moved away, then closed my eyes and listened to the sound of her footsteps as she crossed the room to the hallway.

As Corrie's footsteps faded into the sounds around me, I took a deep breath and relaxed, confident that everything would turn out right and that whatever happened to me next would come from God.

BETSIE TEN BOOM was born in Amsterdam, Netherlands, on August 19, 1885. When she was still a young girl, her family moved to Haarlem, where her father took over the family watchmaking business. Betsie was diagnosed at an early age with pernicious anemia, a condition caused by her body's inability to produce proteins necessary for the absorption of vitamins. Easily treatable now, the condition was often deadly back then. She survived to adulthood on a regimen of vitamin therapy and a sedentary lifestyle. Because that condition made childbearing impossible, Betsie never married.

Long before she was born, her grandfather and his priest decided to take seriously the psalmist's challenge to "pray for the peace of Jerusalem," offering daily prayers for Jerusalem and for blessing on the Jews. That prayer commitment was passed down to Betsie's father and taken up by his children. From 1844 until the Nazis raided their home in 1944, the Ten Booms offered daily prayers for the Jews. Their compassion, however, was not limited to prayer alone. They also acted.

In 1940, the German army invaded the Netherlands. Shortly thereafter, they imposed rigid restrictions on the daily life of Dutch Jews. Eventually, a program of systematic deportation was developed by which most of the Jewish population was removed. Incensed by the Nazis' anti-Semitic policy, the Ten Booms, along with a network of supporters, sought places of refuge for Jews seeking to escape what was by then almost certain death. That effort saved more than eight hundred lives.

However, in February 1944, acting on a tip from an informant, the Germans raided the Ten Boom home, seizing a group of approximately thirty people, many of whom were attending a prayer meeting conducted by Betsie's brother. The group included Betsie, her sisters Corrie and Nollie, their brother, Willem, their father, Casper, and a nephew named Christiaan. After a brief detention in Haarlem, they were transferred to the Dutch prison at Scheveningen. Ten days later, Casper died. He was eighty-four. Christaan, who had worked with the Dutch underground, was sent to the German camp at Bergen Belsen and never returned.

Nollie and Willem were released at Scheveningen, but Corrie and Betsie were sent to a work camp operated by the Germans at Vught in southern Netherlands. Later they were transferred to the women's prison at Ravensbrück, Germany, where, on December 16, 1944, Betsie died. Corrie survived the war and went on to write about her family's experiences. You can read about them in her book *The Hiding Place* and in the many other books she wrote, and in the movie, "The Hiding Place," produced by Dr. Billy Graham.

In 1986, I and a dedicated group of friends purchased the ten Boom home and clock shop in Haarlem, Holland. It was completely restored and is open to the public as a museum. A virtual tour is available online at www. tenboom.org.

In 2008 Betsie was honored posthumously by the State of Israel as one of the *Righteous Among the Nations*. I had the privilege of delivering an address at her induction ceremony.

This novel is loosely based on a compilation of events from Betsie's life and information drawn from accounts of the Dutch underground, develop-ment of the Nazi Final Solution, and other historic resources. I have attempted to portray these events as realistically as possible, but with an eye toward creating an entertaining and engaging story. Characters, events, and locations in this book are the work of fiction. The hope is that in reading this book you will be inspired to learn more about the Holocaust, the need for justice in the world today, and the healing that can only come through forgiveness.

ACKNOWLEDGEMENTS

My deepest gratitude and sincere thanks to my writing partner, Joe Hilley, and to my executive assistant, Lanelle Shaw-Young, both of whom work diligently to turn my story ideas into great books. And to Arlen Young, Peter Glöege, and Janna Nysewander for making the finished product look and read its best. And always, to my wife, Carolyn, whose presence makes everything better.

BOOKS BY: MIKE EVANS

Israel: America's Key to Survival

Save Jerusalem

The Return

Jerusalem D.C.

Purity and Peace of Mind

Who Cries for the Hurting?

Living Fear Free

I Shall Not Want

Let My People Go

Jerusalem Betrayed

Seven Years of Shaking: A Vision

The Nuclear Bomb of Islam

Jerusalem Prophecies

Pray For Peace of Jerusalem

America's War: The Beginning of the End

The Jerusalem Scroll

The Prayer of David

The Unanswered Prayers of Jesus

God Wrestling

Why Christians Should Support Israel

The American Prophecies

Beyond Iraq: The Next Move

The Final Move beyond Iraq

Showdown with Nuclear Iran

Jimmy Carter: The Liberal Left and World Chaos

Atomic Iran

Cursed

Betrayed

The Light

Corrie's Reflections & Meditations (booklet)

GAMECHANGER SERIES:
  GameChanger
  Samson Option
  The Four Horsemen

THE PROTOCOLS SERIES:
  The Protocols
  The Candidate

The Revolution

The Final Generation

Seven Days

The Locket

Living in the F.O.G.

Persia: The Final Jihad

Jerusalem

The History of Christian Zionism

Countdown

Ten Boom: Betsie, Promise of God

COMING IN 2013:

1948: Israel's Rebirth

Commanded Blessing

Presidents in Prophecy

TO PURCHASE, CONTACT: orders@timeworthybooks.com
P. O. BOX 30000, PHOENIX, AZ 85046